BESTSELLING AUSTRALIAN AUTHORS

BARBARA HANNAY

AMY ANDREWS & LEAH MARTYN

AN
Outback
AFFAIR

MILLS & BOON

Published by
Mills & Boon
An imprint of Harlequin Enterprises (Australia) Pty Limited (ABN 47 001 180 918), a subsidiary of HarperCollins Publishers Australia Pty Limited (ABN 36 009 913 517) Level 19, 201 Elizabeth Street
SYDNEY NSW 2000
AUSTRALIA

MIX
Paper | Supporting
responsible forestry
FSC® C001695

Printed and bound in Australia by McPherson's Printing Group

CONTENTS

CONTENTS

Princess In The Outback

Barbara Hannay

Reading and writing have always been a big part of **Barbara Hannay's** life. She wrote her first short story at the age of eight for the Brownies' writer's badge. It was about a girl who was devastated when her family had to move from the city to the Australian Outback.

Since then, a love of both city and country lifestyles has been a continuing theme in Barbara's books and in her life. Although she has mostly lived in cities, now that her family has grown up and she's a full-time writer she's enjoying a country lifestyle.

Barbara and her husband live on a misty hillside in Far North Queensland's Atherton Tableland. When she's not lost in the world of her stories, she's enjoying farmers' markets, gardening clubs and writing groups, or preparing for visits from family and friends.

Barbara records her country life in her blog, *Barbwired,* and her website is www.barbarahannay.com.

For the Gladstone Street girls—
princesses, all three.

CHAPTER ONE

THE FIRST PALE fingers of wintry dawn crept through the hospital as Isabella left the ward. Time to get home to a long, hot bath and a steaming cup of ginger tea. Then sleep.

Cheered by thoughts of comfort and warmth, she pulled her thick woollen cape over her shoulders, wrapped a long red scarf about her head, and prepared to face the icy blast outside.

'Your Highness?'

She turned, surprised to see her personal physician, Dr Christos Tenni, hurrying towards her down the chilly corridor.

'You look very tired,' he said when he reached her. 'You're working too hard.'

'Nonsense, Christos. You know I thrive on this work.

It makes up for all the razzmatazz.'

But, despite her blithe response, Isabella felt a stab of alarm. Her good friend looked worried, almost frightened. It was rather unnerving to see one of Amoria's most level-headed and respected physicians throwing hasty glances over his shoulder, as if he needed to ensure that he wasn't overheard.

'You've been here all night,' he insisted. 'You must be exhausted. Please have something to eat and drink now, before you leave.'

'All right. Coffee would be lovely,' she said, lowering her voice to match his furtive manner.

He escorted her across the highly waxed corridor into his office and closed the door. She frowned when he pulled a bolt across, and her frown deepened when she saw that his desk had been set with a silver coffee pot, two fine gilt-edged porcelain cups and saucers and a platter covered by an engraved silver dome. It was most unusual for the hospital staff to worry about royal protocol at such an early hour.

Trying to stay calm, she unwound her scarf and massaged the stiffness in her neck, a legacy from the night she'd spent on a hard hospital chair while she held the hand of a lonely dying man.

The doctor poured her coffee, and as he handed her the cup he glanced again towards the door.

'Christos, what's the matter? You seem very on edge.' He didn't answer until he'd walked around to the other side of the desk and was seated. Then he seemed to take great care to compose his features into a calm and benign mask, and Isabella couldn't help fearing that this was how he looked when he was about to tell his patients bad news.

'My dear Princess Isabella,' he said slowly, leaning towards her with his strong, neat hands clasped on the desk in front of him, his voice barely above a whisper. 'You are in grave danger.'

Her hands shook and her coffee cup rattled against its saucer as she set it back on his desk. 'What—what kind of danger?'

He took a long, deep breath, and the pained expression on his face suggested he was hating this moment. 'I'm very sorry to be the bearer of this news, but it has come to my notice that your fiancé, the Count of Montez, means to harm you.'

'For heaven's sake!' Isabella gaped at him. 'You must be wrong. How could Radik want to hurt me? It's ridiculous. He—he loves me.'

Dr. Tenni cleared his throat. 'Isabella—your Highness—'

'Please, Christos, forget the formalities. We're friends.'

'Isabella, you've known me all your life.'

'Yes, but I can't believe this.'

'If I told you something about your health—even that you had a life-threatening illness—you would trust me, wouldn't you? You'd believe me?'

'Yes…'

'Then please believe me when I tell you that you're fit and in wonderful health, but you won't live your life to its full span if you marry Count Radik.'

'*No!*'

'I'm afraid it's the truth.'

'But why? What on earth has happened?'

The doctor rose and came around his desk to stand beside Isabella's chair. He rested his hand gently on her shoulder. 'When I was in Geneva last week I overheard a conversation between the Count of Montez and a woman.'

She couldn't suppress an involuntary shudder. 'Marina Prideaux?'

'You know about her?'

Oh, God. This was awful. Just last week she'd walked into Radik's rooms and quite inadvertently seen a letter he'd been writing to a woman he'd called *My Darling Poodle*. When she'd mentioned it Radik had been furious, unjustifiably so.

She was quite sure he'd been writing to Marina Prideaux… *Darling Poodle.*

'I don't know much, except that she was Radik's girlfriend some time ago, but I must admit—' She drew a sharp breath. 'So he's still seeing her?'

'Yes, but I'm afraid that's not all.'

A cold wave of nausea rose from her stomach to her throat. 'Just tell me the worst, Christos. You're—you're frightening me terribly.'

He squeezed her hand. 'I'm so sorry, Isabella. The Count of

Montez seems to view your wedding as a merger rather than a true marriage.'

'A merger?'

'I know he wouldn't be the first man to marry into royalty to gain access to money and wealthy estates, but this time there is more at stake. I heard him reassuring the Prideaux woman that he still loves *her* and that she just has to be patient. Within six weeks of your marriage he plans for you to have an unfortunate accident—most probably a car crash, because everyone knows how treacherous the Alpine roads in Amoria can be.'

'Oh, God!'

Had Christos gone mad? How could Radik want to kill her?

'He knows that after your—ah—demise he will still be able to retain his entitlement to a handsome percentage of your worldly goods,' Christos added.

'It can't be true,' she whispered. But even as the denial left her lips she felt a ghastly suspicion that Christos Tenni was correct. She stared back into the doctor's worried face and her stomach took a sickening plunge. His preposterous claims had touched a raw nerve, exposing things about her fiancé she'd been working hard to overlook.

Radik, the Count of Montez, was as handsome and glamorous a suitor as any European princess could hope for. He'd waltzed into her life eight months ago and she'd been swept away by his dashing charm.

Oh, he'd flirted prettily with her, flattered her and brought her little presents. He'd escorted her to glittering social occasions—kissed her.

She knew that under her father's strict governance she'd been overly protected. Compared with most young women she was naïve about the ways of men and romance, but, on the whole, the experience of being engaged had been very pleasant.

Until recently…

Apart from the incident with the letter, lately she'd sensed the cold flicker of something like menace in her fiancé's handsome dark eyes. It lurked behind his smooth smile and caused her sleepless nights.

And there was his mounting obsession with money... She drew in a sharp breath. If she was completely honest with herself, she had to admit that there had been rather too many disappointments. Radik had shown little interest in her charity work. She'd tried to suppress her growing feeling that something wasn't quite right about the royal engagement. There'd never been talk of love. God knew, she'd tried to ignore her qualms. The very thought of speaking to her father about breaking off a royal engagement filled her with dread. It was like trying to hold back a tidal wave single-handed.

But if it was a choice between that and her death?

She jumped out of the chair. 'What can I do? The wedding's next week. The newspapers are full of it.'

Every detail had been followed closely by the Amorian public: the wedding gown made by a Parisian couturier; the wedding cakes baked in San Sebastia'n from a traditional royal recipe and transported to Madrid to be iced; the presents that had been flooding in from all over the world.

Gifts of jewellery, clocks, decanters, candlesticks, pieces of silver, antique furniture and tapestries had all been placed on display in the Valdenza Palace in aid of charity.

A magazine had even leaked details of the wardrobe Radik insisted she needed for their glamorous honeymoon—three morning ensembles, five afternoon dresses, six evening gowns, two coats.

'I *can't* ask my father to call off the wedding at this late stage.'

'I'm afraid you must,' Christos said gravely.

'But Father will have apoplexy. He urged me to marry Radik. His advisers all supported it. They think he's wonderful. Perfect.'

'I'll admit it won't be easy. His Majesty's friends have always been strong supporters of the Montez family and they'll be loath to admit a mistake now.' Christos's eyes gleamed damply as he looked at Isabella. 'But think of what's at stake, my dear.'

She felt a surge of panic, as if she were running through a maze, turning corner after corner only to find her way blocked at every turn. 'I'm not even sure that Father would listen to me. He'll probably think I'm just having pre-wedding nerves.'

Oh, mercy! Isabella pressed a hand to her hammering heart.

She began to pace the office, folding her arms across her stomach. She bowed her head as she tried to think through the horrified tumble of her thoughts.

'Christos, what should I do?'

'If your mother was still alive—' the doctor began, and then paused and cleared his throat. 'You've always had unerring instincts. It's what makes you so wonderfully sensitive with the patients here. You should trust those inner promptings now.'

Yes, she should. The more she thought, the more she was sure of that. 'Whatever happens, I mustn't marry him,' she said, and with the announcement she felt a flood of relief. Despite the shock of learning that her life was in danger, she was suddenly free of a shadowy but worrying burden.

At least she could be grateful that she'd never given in to Radik's attempts to seduce her. How awful to have discovered too late that she'd squandered her love on an A-grade cad.

But deciding to call the wedding off was one thing. Finding the courage to do so, marshalling the nerve to speak to her father, would be a very different matter.

'Christos, will you come with me when I speak to my father?'

'Of course.'

'I'm afraid he won't be back from New York for another two days.'

'That's a pity.' He sighed and looked thoughtful. 'I don't think it would be wise to discuss this over the telephone.'

'No, but I'll make sure we can see him the very minute he returns.'

'Very well. That will have to do.' Christos hugged her. 'In the meantime, be very careful, my dear. I don't wish to alarm you any more than I have, but I think I'm being watched.'

CHAPTER TWO

A THUNDEROUS RACKET woke Jack.

It penetrated his dreams and sent his heart racing. Adrenalin did the rest, priming his body into action before he was properly awake. In one seamless motion he yanked his sleeping bag aside and leapt from the bed.

Rain as hard as bullets pelted against the hut's corrugated iron roof, and over its drumming he heard a thumping and crashing sound—something or some*body* trying to break his door down.

With no moonlight or starlight to guide him, he stumbled towards the door and stubbed his toe on the metalframed bed. He let fly with a loud curse and was still cursing as he wrenched the door open.

Sharp, stinging rain needled his face, and a second later a very wet body pitched past him into the hut.

'What the—?'

He couldn't see a darned thing, but someone was shivering and gasping in the dark beside him.

'What do you want?' he shouted as he stepped back and

dragged the door shut against the driving rain. 'What are you doing out here?'

The only answer was his intruder's breathless panting. What the blazes was going on? His instructions had been clear. He'd insisted on no interruptions. This week was his time off. A week of solitude and sanctuary in the remote bush at Pelican's End. Away from the office, the phone, the fax and e-mail. Out of contact in the Outback.

Apparently not.

'Sit there. I'll find a light.' Reaching out into the darkness, he shoved the shivering figure down onto the bed then groped his way towards the rough-timbered kitchen bench. After a few blind miss-tries, his fingers closed over a box of matches. He struck a light, lifted the lantern glass and held the match to the wick.

Soft light leapt around the small interior of the tiny one-roomed hut, bringing to life the ripple iron walls, the simple rustic furnishings and the crude stone floor. Holding the lantern at head height, Jack turned to inspect the intruder. And was met by an ear-splitting scream.

Bloody hell! A woman. He nearly dropped the lamp. Dumping the lantern back on the bench, he snatched his jeans from the floor and rammed the zip into place so fast he almost did himself serious injury. 'Stop screaming! I'm not going to hurt you.'

She stopped the noise but remained huddled on his bed, wet and whimpering, looking up at him with dark, frightened eyes, huge in her pale, oval face.

What the heck was a woman doing out here, roaming around this isolated neck of the Outback in the middle of a stormy night?

She was young, at a guess in her mid-twenties. And very wet. Drowned-rat wet. Her black hair fell to her shoulders in a wild and sodden tangle and the rain had made her white shirt transparent. Her drenched denim skirt clung to her slim, pale thighs, revealing slender mud-splattered legs and a grazed knee. Her trainers were soaked and covered with slippery mud.

Shakily she rose to her feet, looked down at the bedding and muttered something in a foreign language that he couldn't make out.

'My French is rusty,' he said. 'Can you speak English?'

She frowned and pressed her fingers to her right temple, but this time when she spoke the words sounded like Spanish.

Terrific. Not only did he have a hysterical stranger invading his precious retreat and ruining his sleep, but he had communication problems as well. 'English,' he demanded. 'Hello? Goodnight? How are you? Can you speak English?'

'Yes,' she said at last. 'Yes, of course I can speak English.'

Jack's eyebrows lifted. She spoke English all right with a cultured intonation hinting of Oxbridge.

'Good. Now, listen, I'm not going to hurt you.'

She nodded. 'Thank you.' Then she looked around her. 'Do you have a telephone?'

'Telephone? You've got to be joking. I don't even have electricity out here.'

'I see.' She looked down at the bed and pointed to the damp patch she'd made. 'I'm being a nuisance. Look, I've made your bed wet.'

'I'll get you a towel,' he said, dredging up a reluctant gallantry.

There were a couple of thick towels in his pack on the floor and he dragged one out. As he offered it to her he realised she was still shivering. 'You're soaked through.'

With two fingers she pulled the sodden sleeve of her shirt away from her arm. Rivulets of muddy water ran down her elbow and dripped onto the floor. She stared at the puddle that had formed at her feet.

'What happened?' he asked.

'I must have taken a wrong turn off the highway and I think I crashed my car into a river.'

'You *think* you crashed it?'

She looked up at him and her dark eyes clouded with bewilderment. 'I—I don't really know for sure—the water was coming up so fast. One moment I was on a track and next—I—there was water everywhere.'

With a surge of dismay he saw the colour leaching from her face. Then her hand wavered up to cover her mouth as a soft moan escaped. She swayed and her eyelids drooped closed.

'Hey, steady, there.' Taking her by the shoulders, he lowered her back to the bed. 'Don't start fainting on me.' He rolled his swag and bedding out of the way, exposing the bare mattress. 'Get your head down. A little damp won't hurt this old mattress.'

Gingerly, she stretched out on the bare ticking mattress, and he frowned as he saw how very pale her cheeks and lips remained. 'Are you hurt?'

'I think I must have banged my head.'

Bringing the lantern closer, he set it on a stool beside the bed. Then he gently patted her hair with the towel, searching as he did so for signs of injury. Once or twice she winced, but there was no blood and he couldn't find a wound.

'Was there anyone else with you?'

'No.'

That was a relief. At least he didn't have to go charging off into the stormy darkness to test his heroism in a flooded creek.

She lay very quietly with her eyes closed as he lifted the heavy dark hair from her shoulders and wound the towel around it, squeezing out the moisture. He tried not to look at her wet blouse, but he could see straight through it to her white lacy bra and the rise and fall of her breasts, exaggerated by her frightened breathing.

'What's your name?' he asked.

Her eyes flashed wide open and he saw how very dark her irises were—really, really dark, almost black—and fringed with thick black lashes. She stared at him without speaking, and after a prolonged moment of silence she opened her mouth to say something, but then she turned away and closed her eyes again.

Jack frowned and abandoned the questions. There wasn't

much point in grilling her anyhow. She was a foreign tourist stuck in this isolated drover's shack in the middle of the Outback at the start of the wet season and her car was lying in the bottom of a flooded creek. Where she came from wasn't half as relevant as how she was going to get out again, and the prospects weren't too good.

But, for now, she needed to get out of these wet clothes.

'We'll have to get you dry.' He turned and dragged a long-sleeved shirt from his pack. It was a heavy denim number, and should be enough to keep her warm. 'You can put this on.'

She didn't answer.

Turning back to her, he frowned. 'Can you manage by yourself?'

She was very still as she lay on the bed with her eyes closed. Her cheeks were too pale. Had she fainted?

'Hello?' he said, tapping her shoulder.

She moaned softly, in what sounded like Spanish, but he could hardly hear her above the thunder of the rain on the roof.

'Hey, Carmen,' he called, grabbing for the first Spanish name that jumped into his head. 'Don't go to sleep till you've got dry clothes on.'

Still she didn't answer.

Hell, she was out to it. Could she have concussion? Jack knew it was selfish, but he felt a stirring of resentment. A mercy dash to a hospital would completely wreck his plans. Besides, it could be impossible. From what she'd told him they were probably cut off by the creek.

One thing was certain: he couldn't leave her lying in those wet things. He wiped a hand over his brow. It wasn't as if he'd never removed a woman's clothing before, but in the past he'd had the advantage of the other party's consent and open-hearted co-operation.

Taking a deep breath, he gingerly unbuttoned her blouse and peeled the wet cotton away from her, lifting her shoulders as he slipped her arms out of the sleeves. It was impossible not to notice how neat and pretty she was. Her skin had the kind of soft, white flawless perfection that was impossible for a sun-drenched Australian girl. Her collarbones were exquisitely symmetrical, her shoulders smooth and round. His hands shook slightly as he unsnapped her wet bra and removed it to reveal her pale breasts, small and round and tipped with delicate rosy peaks. Oh, God. Swiftly he covered her with the towel and began to rub her arms vigorously. The rough movements seemed to rouse her. Her eyes opened and she cried out in alarm when she saw him bending over her.

'*Au secours!* Don't touch me!'

He dropped the towel to cover her. 'Calm down. I was trying to get you dry. You passed out.'

Obviously she didn't believe him. She jerked quickly into a sitting position and the towel slipped. Her eyes were huge and terrified as she glared at him.

Jack grabbed the towel from her lap and shoved it at her. 'You have to get dry,' he growled. 'Do it yourself. Just get the rest of those wet things off and put this shirt on.' He scowled at her. 'And stop looking at me like I'm going to eat you. I've had my dinner.'

'Would you please turn away?' she asked, clutching the towel to her chest.

'Naturally,' he drawled, sending her a gritted-teeth smile. 'And I'll boil the billy for some tea.'

'Boil the billy?'

'Boil water *in* a billy and make a cup of tea.' He spoke with exaggerated patience, then very deliberately turned his back on her and made a business of fiddling with a small gas ring. 'You let me know when you're done.'

As he filled the kettle with water from the tank in the corner, and rummaged for an extra mug, the downpour on the roof continued. If it kept raining at this rate the creek would flood its banks. He wished he'd paid more attention to the weather forecasts, but he'd been too keen to grab the chance to get away. He would have come to the hut whatever the predictions had been.

Of course if he'd been here on his own he wouldn't have cared two hoots about the rain. The hut was on high ground, and if the creeks cut him off all the better. No one could get near him. He'd be assured of the solitude he craved.

But with this woman here now he needed the rain to stop. He needed to get her out.

He was aware of her hesitant movements behind him as she removed her shoes and the rest of her clothing. And he was annoyed when his mind kept straying to thoughts of how the bottom half of this stranger would be as lovely as her top half.

'You'll have to have your tea black. There's no milk,' he called over his shoulder. 'Do you take sugar?'

'A teaspoon of sugar, thank you.'

As he stirred the sugar and broke open a packet of oatmeal biscuits a flapping movement in his peripheral vision caught his attention. He saw that she'd finished the drying process and had put his shirt on. It was huge on her, hanging down to her knees, with the sleeves extending way beyond her hands. She was rolling them back with small neat movements.

'It's just your size,' he said. 'A perfect fit.'

In the lamplight he saw her mouth twitch into a tiny *almost* smile. 'It's very good of you to lend me your shirt.'

'Do you think you'll be warm enough?'

'Yes. I am very comfortable now.'

He walked closer, caught her chin between a forefinger and thumb and peered into her eyes. Both pupils seemed evenly dilated. 'How many fingers?' he asked, holding two in front of her.

'Two.'

'Terrific.' He handed her a mug and pointed to the three-legged stool beside the bed. 'Take a seat and drink this.'

'Thank you.' As she took the mug she said, 'You are very kind.'

Jack didn't agree. He wasn't being kind. He'd had no choice.

'I could hardly have left you out in the storm.' Using an up-turned fuel drum for a seat, he sat, and they sipped their tea in the gentle lamplight while thunder rolled and rain crashed on the roof and against the walls.

'How are you feeling now?' he asked. 'You had me worried when you blacked out before.'

'My head hurts a little, but I feel much better, thank you.' She touched the side of her head and lifted her damp wild hair back from her face. He couldn't help noting that the bone structure of her face and hands was exquisite. Was there such a thing as a high-class gypsy? That was how she looked to him. Carmen with class.

'Do you realise how lucky you were to find this place in the dark?'

She shivered. 'The lightning showed me the way. I was so scared, but it lit up the bush and I could see the track because it was shiny with wet mud. So I followed it up from the creek and—and I bumped into your hut.' He had to admit she'd been rather brave to set off through the bush in the storm. 'What are you doing way out here anyway?' he asked. 'Where were you heading?'

She looked worried again, as if she needed to consider the best way to answer his simple question.

For a nanosecond Jack wondered if she was on the run, then dismissed the notion as fanciful in the extreme. Just the same, he knew in his bones that she had a secret or two. But, hell, didn't everyone?

'I was driving down from Darwin. I'm on my way to visit friends,' she said, and suddenly she sat a little straighter and leaned forward, extending her hand towards him. 'My name is Isabella Martineau.' She sounded very formal, even a little haughty.

'Isabella,' he repeated, returning her handshake. 'Hi.' He guessed a fancy name like Isabella suited her, but for some odd reason he preferred to think of her as Carmen. 'I'm Jack,' he said quickly. 'Jack...' He paused, suddenly unwilling to give his family name. His parents were so well known that even foreigners seemed to have heard of them. If he couldn't have solitude, at least he could have anonymity. 'So, what are you doing in the Northern Territory?' he asked to cover his evasion.

'Are you a backpacker?'

'No.' Her reply was abrupt, as if she was as reluctant to disclose personal details as he was. She took another deep gulp of tea, looked down at something on her leg and screamed again.

'What is it this time? What's the matter?'

Her mouth trembled as she pointed. 'Are th-they l-leeches?'

He studied her leg. Sure enough, two slick black leeches were clinging to her ankle. One of them had grown quite shiny and swollen with her blood. 'Yeah, they're leeches all right.'

'Oh, God.'

'You must have picked them up down near the creek. Nasty little bloodsuckers, aren't they?'

She shuddered and looked ill. 'Please, can you pull them off?'

'I can, but it'll make you bleed too much. Hang on, I've got a better way.'

Grabbing the box of matches from the bench, he returned quickly to crouch beside her, but she jerked her legs away from him. The dark wariness in her eyes told him she still didn't trust him.

'Don't panic. I'm not into torturing women for kicks, but some carefully applied heat will make these little mongrels let go.'

She drew a deep, shuddering breath, as if gathering strength for an ordeal. 'Thank you,' she whispered, and gingerly moved her leg closer to him once more.

With one knee bent, Jack lifted her foot and rested it on his thigh, then lit a match. She leaned forward, her dark head close to his, her eyes fearful as he slipped one hand behind her shapely calf and took hold of her, keeping her leg steady as he lowered the match. 'Hold still now,' he murmured. 'I just want to get a little heat close to him.'

He could feel tension vibrating through her as he guided the small flame closer. Hell, there was tension in him, too, but it wasn't fear. It was too long since he'd been this close to a beautiful woman.

The instant the leeches sensed the heat they released their grip and it was a simple matter to remove them. They left pinpricks of bright blood on her skin.

'Thank you,' she murmured fervently as he blew out the match. Her dark eyes were very close to his and he realised he was still holding her leg.

'Let's check your other leg and make sure you don't have any more,' he said abruptly as he took his hand away.

She lowered one foot and lifted the other. Her foot fitted neatly against the curve of his thigh. Too neatly. He quickly scanned her leg. No sign of leeches, but her skin was smooth, her ankle trim, her foot daintily arched. Yeah, the bottom half of her seemed to be every bit as pleasing to the eye as the top half.

Annoyed to catch himself thinking like that, he lifted her leg and swung his thigh well clear of her, then jumped to his feet. 'I think we've got rid of the lot. Would you like some more tea?'

She shook her head and winced, as if the movement hurt her.

'You need to rest. There's nothing more we can do tonight.'

Scanning the room, her dark eyes grew wide and worried again. 'There's only one little bed.'

He considered teasing her, suggesting that they would have to share it, but figured she'd had enough nasty surprises for one night. 'I know this isn't a palace, but there's a fold-out stretcher over in the corner.' He risked a grin. 'There's plenty of room for the two of us.'

The savoury aroma of frying sausages woke Isabella. Her first feeling was surprise that she'd slept so well. The constant drumming of rain on the roof must have worked on her like a non-stop lullaby.

But then came an onslaught of memories, slamming into her

like physical blows, bringing again the ghastly shock of Christos Tenni's death. The poor man had been killed by a hit-and-run driver as he was crossing the road in front of the hospital.

She'd flown into a horrified panic. Her father was still away and she'd felt so suddenly ill and alone and vulnerable that her only thought had been to escape from Radik—from Amoria.

But when she'd reached the other side of the world she'd driven headlong from one danger straight into the jaws of another—the terrifying flood of creek water, the struggle to escape through the current. And now she'd lost everything—her passport, clothes and all her money.

And where on earth was she?

Her eyes adjusted to the gloomy interior of Jack's hut, and she tried to calm herself by taking in details of her surroundings.

It was still raining outside. There was only one small square of foggy window pane, which let in a faint stream of murky light to reveal a very humble hut. Above her a rusty iron roof sagged and the rain dripped through a hole in the corner into a blue plastic bucket. Nails had been driven into the walls to hang old horseshoes, a battered hat, rolls of wire and ancient cooking utensils. She thought of her bedroom in the palace, where her maid Toinette tiptoed across thick carpet to draw back whisper-quiet velvet drapes from floor-to-ceiling double-glazed windows.

Here the floor was made of stone and needed a good sweeping and—oh, no—in the corner there were huge, thick spider webs! *Help!* Had spiders crawled over her during the night? Had their ghastly hairy legs touched her? Could they bite?

She sat bolt upright and spun around, looking for Jack.

He was over by the kitchen bench, standing with his back to her, slowly turning sausages in a pan on a gas ring.

He didn't seem too bothered about spiders.

Her fear subsided as she watched him. This morning he was dressed, thank heavens. He was wearing faded jeans and an ancient smoky blue T-shirt, but his simple clothes only served to enhance his rather magnificent broad shoulders, his narrow hips and his long legs.

He was something of a puzzle.

His hut was poor, but he didn't exactly look like a wild man. His clothes were shabby, but his hair seemed to be expertly barbered. It was nice hair, mid-brown in colour, short and thick with a tendency to curl. She suspected that in sunlight the tips would be light, almost blond.

And somehow, despite the very domesticated task of cooking, he managed to look incredibly rugged and masculine.

He turned and saw she was awake. Against the gloomy interior of the hut his eyes were an amazing blue, the colour of an Alpine lake in high summer.

'Good afternoon,' he said. 'Afternoon? What time is it?'

He smiled. 'Only teasing. It's a bit after eight. So you slept OK?'

'Very well, thank you. Your bed is surprisingly comfortable.'

She swung her legs over the edge of the bed and stood carefully. Her head hurt only slightly, and her back was a little stiff, but otherwise she didn't feel too bad.

She sent a swift, anxious glance around the hut. 'May I use your bathroom?'

His eyebrows lifted. 'Sure.'

'Where is it?'

'Outside.' He cocked his head towards the rainsplashed window.

'Out in the rain?'

''Fraid so. This isn't exactly the Ritz, you know.'

She wanted to groan in protest, but just in time she remembered her manners and, clutching his huge shirt around her bare legs, took a tentative step towards the door.

'It's primitive,' he warned, 'like everything out here.'

'*How* primitive is it?'

'It's not too bad. Just like this hut, but much smaller. No flushing system, of course.' He unhooked an oilskin coat from a nail on the wall and held it out to her. 'Here, put this on or you'll get my only spare shirt soaked.'

As she took the coat she had to ask, 'Will—will there be spiders out there?'

One corner of his mouth lifted. 'Sure. You should always check under the seat for redbacks.'

'Red—redbacks?'

'Little black beggars with a red stripe on their rump. They're deadly.'

Deadly! She couldn't bear this. 'What—what do I do if I see one?'

'Kill it. Take a shoe with you and hit it hard.'

He must have seen the sheer dread in her face, because he added, 'But you can yell for help if you really have to.'

'Th-thanks.'

'Keep an eye out for centipedes, too. This wet weather will bring all sorts of creepy-crawlies looking for shelter.'

'Oh, mercy.' Isabella shrank away from him. Could she do this? Could she really go out there? Her knees were shaking so badly she could hardly walk.

Jack stared at her and his eyes narrowed. 'Are you frightened of spiders?'

'I—I'm not used to them.'

'Where do you come from?'

'Amoria. Have you heard of it?'

'Yes,' he said. 'It's that pint-sized country tucked away in the mountains somewhere between France and Spain, isn't it?'

She nodded.

'Surely you have spiders?'

'Our creepy-crawlies are very well behaved. They stay in the forests.' *Or the servants deal with them.*

At the thought of servants, Isabella squared her shoulders. She'd spent a lifetime protected by maids and footmen, but if the recent turmoil in her life had taught her anything, she'd learned that it was time to grow up. To take care of herself.

'If I can get myself out of a flooded car in a creek, I imagine I can look a redback spider in the eye.'

'That's the spirit, Carmen.' Jack continued to stare at her and she couldn't be sure if his eyes were laughing at her. 'You'll be fine,' he said, more gently.

'Yes, I will. I'll be perfectly fine.' Grabbing the coat, she hauled it on and dashed out into the rain before she lost her nerve.

CHAPTER THREE

ISABELLA WAS HUNGRY.

Jack noted with surprise that she wolfed down three sausages, two eggs, plus toast. At this rate he'd be out of food in no time.

'That was wonderful,' she enthused as she took her plate to the sink, and then she turned and beamed at him as if she'd been struck by a brilliant idea. 'Can I do the washing up for you?'

'Sure,' he said. 'I've heated some water and the detergent's in that squeeze bottle.' He glanced towards the tangle of sheets where she'd slept. 'Were you thinking of making your bed?'

'Oh.' She looked shame-faced. 'Yes, of course. I forgot.'

'And I guess you forgot about all your wet clothes, too.' He let his eyes drift to the sodden heap that she'd left lying on the floor at the foot of her bed. 'I know this hut's not the Taj Mahal, but there's no need to turn it into a pigsty.'

'I'm sorry,' she said, looking stricken. 'What should I do with the clothes?'

He blinked. 'What do you normally do with wet clothes?'

She blushed. 'I—' With a shrug, she said, 'I wash them, of

course. But you don't have a washing machine, do you? Or a dryer?'

Jack snorted. Trust him to be saddled with an airhead. 'I've got a bucket, water and soap,' he told her. 'And I can string a fishing line in the corner of the hut for a clothes line.'

Half an hour later he stood at the window, staring grimly out at the grey wall of driving water. 'This rain looks really set in, like proper wet season rain. It could go on for days.'

Behind him, Isabella finished hanging her washed clothes over the fishing line and came to stand beside him. Her hands, damp and pink from washing, rested on her hips. He had to admit that once she turned her mind to domestic tasks she did a pretty good job.

She was still wearing his shirt, and her uncombed hair lay about her shoulders in a black, glossy, just-got-outof-bed tumble. It should have looked messy, not sexy, but to his dismay looking at Isabella was fast becoming a guilty pleasure, almost an addiction.

'Surely the rain will have to stop soon?' she asked, and scowled at the sheets of water. 'Isn't the Australian Outback supposed to be hot, dry and dusty?'

'Not in the middle of the monsoon season. You didn't do much research before you set off on your travels, did you?'

Her jaw jutted stubbornly. 'If it rained like this in Amoria the entire country would wash down the mountains into Spain.'

'Yeah? Well, sometimes it only takes one night of heavy rain to cause flooding in these parts. If the catchment areas have had a lot of rain, the creeks around here fill up quickly and then no vehicles can get through.' An inexplicable tightness dammed his throat as he added, 'We could be cut off for some time.'

'But I can't stay here.' Her cheeks flushed faintly. 'I can't impose on you. Isn't there some way I can get out?'

'If the weather gets too bad the police will send out a helicopter to check if anyone's in trouble.' He shrugged, making the movement carefully casual. 'Don't worry, as soon as there's a break in the rain I can mark out rocks on the ground to catch their attention and let them know you need airlifting out.'

'By the police?'

An unmistakable flash of fear flickered in her big dark eyes. Jack frowned. Why should the mention of police make her look suddenly scared? 'Don't tell me you're on the run from the law?'

She didn't answer, but stood looking down at her hands while she massaged the cuticles of her left hand with her right thumb.

'For Pete's sake, I'm not harbouring a criminal, am I?'

'Of course not,' she cried, slapping her hands to her sides and looking him straight in the eye. 'No, Jack. I promise you. I swear I'm not a criminal.'

'Well, come on,' he said, his impatience rising. 'You can't leave it at that. If you're not on the run, why are you so uptight at the thought of the police finding you?'

She drew in a sharp breath. 'If you don't mind too much, I'd rather not say.'

'If I don't mind?' he repeated, his voice scathing. 'Cut the hoity-toity politeness, thank you. Of course I mind.

I mind very much. If I'm stuck with you here, I'd like to know who you are.'

But it was clear her mind was working on a different wavelength. 'While I'm here, no one will be able to find me, will they?'

'No,' he agreed, frowning at her. *She really was hiding from someone. Hell!* 'That's beside the point,' he growled. '*I* know you're here. You're sleeping in my bed, eating my food. I have a right to know who you are.'

She sighed heavily. 'I admit that you do have a right to know about me,' she said. 'But I'm sorry, I have to protect my rights, too. I have to think about my safety.'

His arms flung wide to proclaim his innocence. 'Isn't it perfectly obvious you're safe with me?'

'It's not especially obvious. I don't know anything about you,' she said, just as sharply.

He made a startled grunt of protest, but she ignored him and continued.

'You've been very good to me, and I'm extremely grateful, Jack, but I don't know how far I can trust you. I don't even know your full name.'

What a cheek! Why should he tell a woman on the run from the law who he was? Heaven knew what stunt a beautiful felon might pull if she discovered his identity. 'You're right,' he growled, annoyed to find himself trapped by her logic. 'I'm no more prepared to trust you than you are to trust me.' He sighed impatiently. 'I guess that means we have a stalemate.'

She nodded, but she looked as unhappy as he felt, and she went back to the bench and began to tidy the cooking utensils with nervous, quick movements. Jack stared out into the rain, seething.

First and foremost he was angry with this stranger's secrecy. It was bad enough having her here—but if she was in trouble he deserved to know. He watched the raindrops hitting the muddy ground outside with sharp, bouncy splashes like hundreds, thousands—billions of tiny water bombs. He wondered how high the creek was now. How long would they be stuck here?

Perhaps it was better not to know who this woman was. That way he wouldn't have to deal with the consequences.

Problem was, it wasn't only her secrecy that bothered him. He was angered by her air of vulnerability. And her haunting European beauty. He didn't want her around. She stirred his blood and he didn't want to be stirred. He didn't want to be locked away in a hut in the rain with a beautiful woman.

Not now. Not *this* of all weeks. This week was for Geri.

He spun on his heel, strode over to his pack and pulled out two thick paperback novels. 'We should make the most of the bad weather. Our conversation doesn't seem to be going anywhere.'

She murmured thanks as she picked up the book he tossed onto the bed, then turned it over and studied the plot summary on the back cover.

'It might not be to your taste,' he admitted. 'It's very much a bloke's book, but that's all I've got.'

'No, it's fine,' she said. 'I like reading all kinds of books.'

To his surprise, she glanced away quickly and gave an abrupt little laugh, as if she'd suddenly thought of something that tickled her funny bone.

'What's the joke?'

'Oh, n-nothing,' she said, growing pink.

His simmering temper peaked. Did this girl have to keep everything a secret? 'Come on,' he urged. 'I've put a roof over your head. You can at least share one joke with me.'

'You won't think this one is funny.'

'Try me. I have an excellent sense of humour.'

Her expressive eyes signalled her big doubts about that possibility, then she blushed again. 'It's just that this whole situation feels so corny.'

'Corny?'

'Like a Hollywood movie—except that if it was a movie...' Jack waited.

'This is embarrassingly silly, but it—it occurred to me that if this was a Hollywood movie the stranded couple wouldn't be reading books, they'd be too busy falling in love.' Then her face glowed brighter than a red sunset. 'I can't believe I actually said that.'

'I can't believe I forced you to,' Jack muttered. A wave of unexpected heat arced between them and he drew in a sharp, angry breath.

'I'm so sorry. It's just that—'

'It's just that this isn't Hollywood,' he finished through gritted teeth. 'We're in *my* hut and *I* get to write our script.' His voice was as heavy and black as his anger. 'Happy reading.'

Then he veered quickly away to the far side of the room,

slumped down onto the fold-out stretcher and prayed that his book would be good enough to help him forget about her for an hour or two.

Isabella read as if her life depended on it. She lay stiffly on the bed and stared grimly at the pages, turning them at regular intervals. She was quite used to reading in English, but for ages nothing on the page made sense. All she could think about was her stupid gaffe.

How on earth had she said something like that to Jack? She'd been trained to speak carefully and behave appropriately in all kinds of social situations, to be discreet and tactful, diplomatic, caring, polite...*modest*.

She turned another page, dimly aware that the story was some kind of action adventure with lots of male characters. Jack was right about it being a bloke's book. She preferred stories with at least one or two females to provide a woman's perspective and perhaps a love interest. Oh, no...there she went again. Her mind had become a one-way track.

With a deep sigh, she put the book down.

The really silly thing was that she actually cared what Jack thought of her. Why? They were mere strangers whose lives were touching briefly. As soon as she could she would leave him in peace.

She shivered and felt a stirring of panic as she turned her thoughts away from Jack to what might be happening back at home. How much time did she have? How long would it be before her fiancé found her?

She could imagine the widespread panic when they discovered she had vanished. Her father would be worried, but Radik would be beyond furious. He would have summoned the Director of Amoria's Bureau of Investigations. Interpol would be involved.

But how long would it take for them to track her down? She let her gaze wander over her surroundings. Would it occur to

Amorians that their princess might escape from marriage to the Count of Montez by fleeing to a shabby hut cut off by floods in the Australian Outback?

It was unlikely.

She should be safe here. Yesterday she'd driven deeper and deeper into the Outback, and the sense of physical isolation had been overwhelming. But as the plains had stretched behind her, and the distant mountains and scrub had closed in, she'd felt a sense of sanctuary too—the same sense of safety she'd felt as a child when she crawled beneath her blankets to hide from bedroom monsters.

In reality, the hut's isolation was a blessing. This location was in one of the most sparsely populated places in the world. It was about as safe as she could possibly be.

If she didn't dwell on thoughts of snakes and spiders, scorpions and leeches…and if she stopped saying stupid things to Jack…she could be very safe, even happy here. For a day or so…

Jack stared at his book without seeing a word. He was thinking about Geri. This week marked the third anniversary of her death. That was why he'd come here to Pelican's End—not to dwell on the fact that she'd died, but to remember her life, her passion, her intelligence and her intensity for living.

For the past three years he'd worked hard, harder than was sensible, trying to keep his grief at bay. Finally, when he'd been on the brink, his doctor had insisted that he take a break. Time out.

Time to remember.

So he'd come here, to the place they'd both loved so much. And now this stranger had intruded on his peace, which meant that memories of his wife were more important than ever.

He'd met Geri at university. She'd been writing her honours thesis in Zoology and he'd been completing a Masters in Agricultural Science. Her flaming red hair had caught his attention first, and then he'd discovered that she had a passionate, fiery spirit to match and they'd become lovers almost immediately.

Once they'd completed their university studies their independent career ambitions had caused friction. Geri had been a fighter. Oh, yeah. But eventually they'd reached a compromise, adapting their need to be together to the demands of their jobs.

They'd married and set up a home base in Perth, and had returned there as often as their work allowed. But although Geri had been away for long stretches of time, pursuing her passion for her research and her growing interest in wildlife photography, she'd changed once she fell pregnant.

She'd planned to be an at-home mother when their baby arrived.

Thinking about that was the worst. His throat grew raw and knotted as he remembered how thrilled Geri had been when her petite figure had become increasingly distended with advanced pregnancy. And she'd been ecstatic when she'd developed nesting instincts.

'I'm just like a mother bird,' she'd chirped as they'd painted and decorated the nursery together.

Damn. Tears threatened. He mustn't break down. Not with this other woman lying a few metres away. Doubledamn. Even way out here at Pelican's End he couldn't find the space he needed to remember and to think.

Wiping his sleeve over his face, he forced his attention back to the words on the page in front of him, but he was distracted again as Isabella jumped from the bed and ran to the window.

'It's stopped raining!' she cried.

He lowered his book, boosted off his bed and came to join her. 'About time.'

'There's even a little break in the clouds.' She turned to him, her face bright with excitement. 'Can we go outside?'

He nodded. 'Sure. Let's get out before cabin fever sets in.'

The ground outside was squelchy beneath their feet, and water continued to drip and plop from the hut's roof and from nearby trees. The humid air pressed close, smelling of dank earth and vegetation.

'This is lovely,' said Isabella.

She'd had no idea what to expect, and was surprised to discover that Jack's hut was built on top of a high, gently sloping bank overlooking a little lake. The lake's grey surface reflected the sullen rain clouds that still blanketed the sky, but its moody, smoky waters seemed to be home to hundreds of waterbirds—herons, pelicans, wild ducks and geese. On the far side, pale cliffs rose majestically from a base of soft, hazy blue-green bush. Yesterday, when she'd driven down the highway from Darwin, she hadn't been very enchanted by the harsh, almost frightening Australian landscape. But the bush that circled this little lake was different—nothing like the pine-clad mountains surrounding the lakes at home, of course, but it was clean and fresh from the rain, with its own brand of unique, if untidy beauty.

'I thought the Outback was all barren and harsh, but this is truly beautiful.'

'We call it Pelican's End.'

'I can see why. There are so many birds. It's amazing.'

He nodded. 'I came here for the birdlife. I wanted to photograph them.' He squinted at the sky. 'But we should make the most of this break in the weather to check out the creek first. We can see how your car has fared. I might be able to tow it out with my ute.'

'Ute? What's that?'

'A utility truck. It's parked round the back, behind the hut.'

Without waiting to see her reaction he set off through the rain-sodden scrub. 'Be careful,' he called over his shoulder. 'The track's very slippery.'

The narrow, winding track was indeed slippery, and there were several times when Isabella had to grab at the branches of saplings to retain her balance. She was surprised to discover how far she'd come on her own through the bush last night. It was a miracle she hadn't lost her way. From ahead of them came the roar of rushing water.

Jack came to an abrupt halt and turned back to her, his eyes wide with shock. She hurried to join him and her jaw dropped when she saw the track disappearing into a wide, swirling brown mass of water. There was no sign of her car.

He released a low whistle. 'That's a creek with attitude. How the hell did you escape? I've never seen it this high.'

'It wasn't this high last night,' she murmured. There was no way she could have fought her way out of that maelstrom. 'I must have a guardian angel.'

'And a good deal of courage,' he added.

'I don't think I was very brave. I was panicking and screaming for help.' Isabella shivered as she watched the brown tide hurtle past, and felt ill at the thought that her body could be lying trapped beneath all that ghastly whirling water.

'We won't be able to salvage any of your things.'

'No.'

'And even if there's no more rain it'll be several days before any kind of vehicle will be able to cross here.'

'So I'm stuck here?'

He didn't reply, but his jaw squared with displeasure. 'I really am sorry to be imposing on you like this, Jack. If I had a choice—'

'You'll be able to get out when the police chopper turns up.'

'Well, yes...' she said softly.

There was a lengthy silence while they both stood there, caught up in their thoughts as they stared at the floodwaters. Isabella's thoughts were mostly concentrated on praying that the helicopter stayed away. Police would feel compelled to report her whereabouts to Amorian authorities.

Jack released a long, deep sigh. 'Let's go back and have some lunch. There's no point in hanging around looking at this depressing sight.'

They ate bread and cheese, sitting on a towel spread on a log outside the hut and watching the birdlife on the water. At first Isabella tried to insist that she wasn't hungry. This morning she'd realised that the hut wasn't Jack's permanent home, and that he'd only brought enough food for himself for a short stay, but when she tried to refuse lunch he was adamant that he wouldn't allow her to go hungry.

'I can always catch fish if we run out of food,' he said, and he sounded so certain she believed him.

The rain held off, although the sky remained leaden and heavy with grey clouds.

'This is such a pretty lake,' she said again.

Jack squinted at the clouds. 'Actually, this soft light is rather interesting. I might grab my camera and try for a few shots now, before it decides to rain again.'

He disappeared back into the hut and emerged quite soon with a small backpack and a camera.

'You have a Hasselblad?'

'Yeah.' He slipped its strap around his neck. 'You know about cameras, then?'

'A little. Are you a professional photographer?'

'No way. Photography's just a hobby. This used to belong to—to—' Pain passed over his face like a shadow. 'Someone left it to me.'

Good manners prevented her from prying. She sensed a barrier around Jack, a silent wall of private sadness, and she could tell he wanted it that way.

'You go and take your photos,' she said, not wanting to encroach on his life more than necessary. 'I'll be happy pottering around the lake, and I can always read some more of my book.'

He stared out across the stretch of grey water. 'I'd like to take the canoe. It's better to photograph waterbirds from a boat, because I can keep a lower profile and I'm less likely to scare them away.' He shot a sharp glance her way. 'You'll be OK here, won't you?'

'Yes—sure.' She tried to sound nonchalant. She told herself that Jack wouldn't be gone for long and she was perfectly safe, but unexpectedly she felt a stab of panic at the thought of being left alone in this strange wild place. With a shock she realised

that her sense of security in the Outback was disturbingly fragile. It depended on how close she was to this man.

Her attempt to hide her concern must have failed, because
his eyes narrowed and he frowned at her. 'You can come with
me if you want to,' he said.

It wasn't so much an offer as a statement of fact, but she didn't
need a second invitation. 'I'd really like that.' Relief and excitement skittered through her as she helped him to haul a water-
logged tarpaulin off the canoe and to slide it down the bank to
the water's edge. Jack held it steady while Isabella stepped in
and took the seat in the bow, then he handed her a paddle before he took the rear seat and pushed off from the bank. 'Do
you know what to do?' he called.

She'd actually done quite a bit of canoeing on the lakes at
home. 'Like this?' she asked, sweeping her blade smoothly
through the water.

'That's it. Terrific!'

She felt a little spurt of pride as they glided out across the
silky surface of the lake, and that feeling was quickly followed
by a surge of elation, a wonderful sense of freedom.

Her recent ordeals, the escape from Amoria, the long plane
flight and the equally long drive from Darwin had been bad
enough, but after last night's accident and the cramped conditions in the hut, to be surrounded by fresh air and space and to
be out on the water felt as if she'd been given a reprieve from a
harsh jail sentence.

No doubt she was very foolish to feel so happy. But the
thought of her pursuers hot on her trail couldn't suppress her
sense of enjoyment. All her life she'd been crowded—by her
family, servants, bodyguards, the public. Now, to be completely
alone in an isolated world with just one other human being was
like a gift from a good fairy.

She would worry about Amoria when the creek went down.
Or when the police helicopter came…

'Stop paddling,' Jack called softly, and she quickly pulled her oar out of the water and rested it on the canoe's rim.

A patch of sunlight had broken through the storm clouds and lit a path across the water, picking out the snowy white back of a tall waterbird in the shallows. It was standing very still, its elongated neck poised as it stared down into the water with its head angled to one side.

She held her breath, aware of Jack behind her hurriedly getting his camera ready. As they watched the great white bird speared its head beneath the surface in a lightning stroke that didn't make so much as a ripple. She heard a soft cry of delight from Jack and the click of his camera.

When it raised its head once more there was complete silence, except for the distant quacking of ducks in the reeds near the shore. Then, at the very instant she heard another quiet click of the camera shutter, the bird flapped its great wings and took off.

'Did you catch him?' she asked, turning back.

'I'm not sure,' he said, and he grinned ruefully. 'It doesn't matter. Photographing birds is mostly a matter of near-misses. You end up with the subject too small, or too dark, or out of focus, or with bits of foliage in the way.'

'But every so often you get a perfect shot?'

'Yeah.'

Isabella smiled and Jack smiled back. Their gazes held and she was helplessly trapped by the magnetic blue of his eyes. Against the backdrop of colourless water and subdued bush he looked heart-stoppingly alive. Brutally handsome. Suntanned, rugged, and beautiful in an essentially masculine way.

She felt her heart lift and thud. A pulse in her neck began to beat fast, and then faster still, mimicking the swift beat of the bird's wings when it had lifted away from the water.

Heavenly stars, she was so overcome she couldn't breathe. She'd never felt this way before, not even when Radik had been at his most debonair and charming. It was silly. Jack had made it clear that he tolerated her presence with great reluctance, and yet she wanted him to like her. Very much.

He was the first to break the gaze that bound them. He dropped his chin and his mouth turned grim as he picked up his paddle and gave a curt nod to their right. 'Let's go over closer to the cliffs.'

'Sure.' Isabella kept her eyes firmly in front as she dipped her paddle once more. And as they continued around the lake she made sure she didn't look at Jack again. Heaven knew, there was absolutely no point in getting caught up in girlish romantic fantasies about an anti-social loner who would no doubt be horrified if he knew her real identity.

She focused her attention on the scenery and her paddling. And her problems. She had to work out how she could continue on to her destination without transport or money.

CHAPTER FOUR

THAT EVENING THE ground and kindling were still too wet for a fire, so Jack carried the gas ring outside and they toasted their bread on the end of long forks he'd fashioned from pieces of wire.

'This is so much fun,' Isabella said as she held her toast to the flame.

Her eyes glowed with transparent delight and she looked as excited as she had when they were out on the water. Jack snatched his gaze away. She looked as happy as a child at a fairground. Since when had making *toast* become one of life's big thrills?

He stared out to the sky above the lagoon, where the evening star was making a brave effort to shine through the lingering layers of cloud, and he tried to remember if Geri had been as excited about the meals they'd shared when he'd brought her out here. But her focus had always been on the birds and capturing the perfect photograph.

If Geri had been here now she would have abandoned the toasting fork for her camera. She'd be stalking the ducks and geese that were darting back and forth across the water in frantic search of last-minute snacks before retiring to their roosts.

'Hey, Jack, eat up. This tastes so-o-o good.'

Isabella had piled heated-up tinned curry onto their toast. As he turned to her she tipped her head back to wipe spilled food from her chin, and the movement made her dark hair fall silkily down her back, exposing the pale curve of her throat. He picked up his plate and began to eat quickly.

'I've always wondered what it would be like to live on simple food,' she said between mouthfuls.

He frowned at her strange comment. 'I take it you only get to eat fancy stuff?'

Colour flashed along her cheekbones and she dropped her gaze. 'I—I guess I dine out a lot.'

'Well, if you're looking for a change you're in luck. You'll only get simple fare here.' He finished his curry and toast and picked up a tin of pears. 'These do for dessert?'

'Absolutely.'

He attacked them with a can opener. 'I think I was right when I christened you Carmen.'

She looked up again, her expression puzzled. 'I don't understand that. Why *do* you call me Carmen?'

'Well…you turned up here, coming in from the storm, with long dark hair and big dark eyes, fainting at my feet and mumbling gibberish, and you made me think of a gypsy. Carmen was the first name that popped into my head. And here you are now, enjoying the outdoors and a makeshift campfire. Are you sure you're not some kind of gypsy?'

She flushed quickly and flicked her gaze abruptly away from him to stare up at the starry sky.

'Have I said something wrong?'

'No,' she said, turning his way once more. 'You just made me remember something I'd almost forgotten.' She sighed deeply. 'I'm not a gypsy, but I rather fancy the idea of being a girl called Carmen. Actually, I love it.' As if to prove the point, she speared her fork into the can of pears Jack offered her, tossed her hair again and tipped her head back as she lowered the juicy fruit into her open mouth. A trickle of pear juice ran down her chin and she laughed as she used a finger to catch it.

Jack watched the performance, and he also watched the movements of her creamy throat as she swallowed and felt the unwelcome throb of desire.

She speared another piece of pear, but before she ate it she said, 'I'm sure Carmens have more fun.'

'I thought it was blondes who were supposed to have more fun.'

'Well, yes, I've heard that too.' She gave him the full benefit of her warmest smile. 'Perhaps it's blondes *and* Carmens. Between them they grab all the fun.'

'And what happens to Isabellas?'

'Isabellas…' Her smile faded and she turned away from him and stared out into the gathering darkness. 'Isabellas have to be careful. Too careful for fun.'

'You reckon?' Jack couldn't resist teasing her. 'So there's no fun for a girl who wears Yves Saint Laurent lingerie?'

The startled and prudish look on her face surprised him.

'You left your underwear hanging all over the place,' he hastened to explain. 'Wasn't hard to miss.'

Neither of them mentioned the fact that he'd removed some of that underwear last night, but the knowledge hovered between them.

Annoyed with himself for broaching such a volatile subject, Jack quickly grabbed another topic. 'So, tell me why being an Isabella isn't much fun.'

She shrugged.

'What kind of work do you do?'

'I—I work in hospitals.'

'As a nurse?'

'No, I'm not a nurse, exactly. My work is mostly to do with charity.'

'Fundraising? Sponsorship?'

'Yes—among other things. What about you, Jack?' she asked, quickly deflecting his curiosity. 'What do you do?'

He almost fabricated an answer—*any* answer—but he was getting a little annoyed by the way they both kept tiptoeing around the truth. 'I'm head of a cattle company.'

'Head? Goodness, that sounds important.' He nodded. 'Whereabouts?'

'All over. My company has holdings spread across the country, but I have an office and a house in Perth, in Western Australia. I get back there fairly often.'

'So are you with one of those huge companies that produce millions of cattle?'

'Not millions,' he replied guardedly. 'Although we're building all the time.'

'I don't understand why your holdings are spread out? Wouldn't it be better to consolidate in one place?'

'Not really—not if you want to diversify and stay competitive.'

'So you have more than one breed of cattle?'

'Yes—and one part of the country is more suitable for breeding Brahmans, for example, and another area suits Santa Gertrudis. Then once the calves are weaned we send them on to fattening properties in other areas. And if the seasons are bad in one part of the country we can shift the cattle around.'

'It sounds like big business.'

'It is.'

'So is your pastoral company like the Kingsley-Lairds'?'

He felt a slam of shock and frowned. 'You know them?'

'Yes.'

'Honestly?'

'I first met John and Elizabeth Kingsley-Laird in England, and then they visited Amoria last year,' she said, but she looked suddenly worried, as if she was anxious to drop this subject. That suited Jack. Their conversation was getting a little too close to the bone. Any way he looked at it, talking to Isabella was damned difficult. It was like trying to dodge landmines.

She slapped at a mosquito on her arm and he jumped to his feet. 'We'd better go back inside for coffee. Once night starts to fall the insects bombard anyone outside.' Together they gathered up their things. 'The lantern should be good enough to read by,' he said. 'How's your book going?'

'It's excellent,' she answered hastily, but he suspected she was lying.

'I'm just getting to the big climax in mine.' He was definitely lying, but he was pretty damn sure that reading until he fell asleep was the safest thing he could do tonight.

Before breakfast next morning, Isabella felt brave enough to set off around the lake to find a secluded cove where she could bathe. The day was already warm, but the water was cool and surprisingly clear, and she let herself float, staring up at the sky.

A flight of herons winged overhead, their long necks stretching forward like miniature jets, and a mere handful of fluffy flat-bottomed clouds sat low on the horizon like floating islands. The rest of the pale blue heavens were as clear and clean as a freshly laundered tablecloth. She laughed aloud. What would Toinette, her maid, think if she could see her princess bathing in the outdoors, protected by nothing but a fringe of reeds and a stern-eyed pelican?

She would probably be even more shocked if she could see her living alone with a man. A tall, lean, gorgeous man. Not a hermit, but a successful king of the Outback.

She hadn't been too surprised to learn that Jack was the CEO of a huge cattle company. He was the kind of man people noticed and obeyed. But she wished she'd asked him what he was doing here at Pelican's End. Was he hiding too? It was strange that, despite the mystery that surrounded him, she felt she could trust him. She was safe with him.

After she was dry, and had changed back into her own clothes, she felt deliciously clean and invigorated and ready to face the day ahead. There were all sorts of things she should be worrying about, but it was hard to focus on anything beyond the beauty of the morning and the simple pleasure of drying her hair in the sun.

The world was so quiet and peaceful here. Her fears about the past and the future faded as she drank in the innocent beauty of now. Here, by the lake, it was easy to imagine that her problems could be put on hold indefinitely.

They breakfasted on fried tomatoes and the last of Jack's sausages, followed by tea, toast and ginger marmalade. While they ate they watched squadron after squadron of black shags fly in over the lake, skimming so close to the water their wings almost touched its surface.

Isabella was so absorbed in watching the birds that at first she took no notice of the pulsing throb-throb throbbing sound in the distance.

But Jack looked towards the horizon and frowned. 'Sounds like the police chopper's on its way,' he said.

Her toast fell to the dirt.

So soon?

Her heart began a fearful knocking and her stomach clenched as she scanned the sky. A tiny speck hovered in the distance. 'Are you sure it's the police?'

'There's a very good chance.' Without another word Jack set down his mug and jumped to his feet.

The black dot moved relentlessly towards them, and Isabella felt so panicky she wanted to dash inside the hut and hide. But it was more important to stop Jack from attracting the police.

'I'm going to signal them down,' he shouted, and rushed towards the lake. 'Quick—come and give me a hand.'

'No,' she cried, hurrying after him. 'Jack, please don't wave at them.'

'Don't be ridiculous,' he yelled over his shoulder. 'You can't hide here for ever.'

'You don't understand.'

'You're dead right,' he yelled. He swung back and glared at her. 'I've Buckley's chance of understanding you because you won't tell me a damned thing.'

She tried to grab his elbow, but he yanked it free. 'You can't turn me over to the police.'

His blue eyes burned. 'Why the hell not?'

'It's dangerous for me.' She heard the panic in her voice and knew that he must have noticed it too. 'Please believe me.'

For a moment he hesitated, and in the sudden stillness the sound of the approaching aircraft loomed. His gaze flickered to the sky, then back to her. 'Sorry, sweetheart. You've had plenty of time to explain your problem, but now you've lost your chance.'

He raised his hands above his head.

Isabella screamed, 'If you send me back to Amoria I'll die!'

'For God's sake!' Jack leapt at her and grabbed her shoulders so hard his fingers dug into her flesh. He glared at her as if he wanted to shake her. 'You've got one last chance, Carmen. Tell me exactly who you are, and why you're here, or I stand here waving and jumping up and down till they see us.'

She threw a frantic glance to the sky. The helicopter was a big black blot against the sun, growing bigger every moment. 'Come inside the hut quickly and I'll tell you.'

'No! Tell me here. Now. Hurry.'

'They'll see us! Please, come!'

'Tell me, Isabella!'

Panic flared. Already there wasn't time to reach the hut.

'Do you promise to believe me?'

'Yes. Of course. Stop wasting time.'

'I'm a princess.'

Jack's head jerked forward as he gaped at her. 'You're a *what*?'

'Princess Isabella of Amoria.'

'Like hell you are.'

But Isabella wasn't waiting another second. 'Let's go,' she

shouted, and she turned and dashed into the nearby trees, her heart thumping so hard it seemed to hit her throat.

Once she reached cover she turned to see Jack standing, staring after her, still frozen with shock. 'Jack!' she screamed. 'Come on. Please, hide!'

She hurried deeper into the bush, and at last, behind her, she heard the crashing and thumping that told her that he was following. Ducking low, she crouched beneath a dense shrub with silvery leaves.

Above them the loud clatter of the helicopter thundered.

'Down here,' she called to Jack, and the next minute he was beside her.

In the crowded space beneath the leaves Jack's hard, muscular arm and thigh crammed against hers. Their hiding place smelled of damp earth and crushed eucalypt leaves. And Jack. He shouldn't have smelled good. She shouldn't have been noticing how Jack smelled.

Sharp branches were poking into her hair and back, and her heart was pounding so fiercely it might well have been competing with the overhead throb of the helicopter. And yet she was noticing that Jack smelled of shaving soap and manly perspiration.

'Did I hear you right?' he shouted close to her ear. 'Did you say you were a princess?'

'Yes.'

'A proper blue-blood member of a royal family?'

'Yes,' she repeated, and was surprised to hear the note of apology in her voice. 'My father is King Albert of Amoria.'

Above them the helicopter's roar lessened as it arced away to circle the lake.

'And you're running for your life?'

'I'm afraid so.' She peered through the overhead tangle of leaves and branches, trying to see the chopper, but she could only catch frustrating tiny glimpses of sky. 'Why are they staying here so long?' she asked as the engine's roar continued on the far side of the lake. 'Do you think they saw us?'

'They wouldn't know I'm out here. They're just checking to see if anyone's in trouble.' He frowned at her. 'Could they be looking for you? Do they know you're here?'

'I don't know,' she said. 'I don't think so. I hope not.'

'But you really believe you're in danger?'

'Yes. And if I went to your police there would be pressure for them to hand me back. It's best that no one knows where I am.'

Jack let out his breath with a whoosh. 'I can't believe this. A runaway princess. It's so crazy. It's surreal.'

She craned her neck, trying to see where the helicopter was now. 'What if they saw the canoe?'

'It shouldn't matter if they're just doing their normal check. Unless they're specifically looking for you they probably won't land, because we haven't signalled that we're in trouble.'

She flashed an anxious glance back to him. 'You're sure?'

'That's how it's always worked in the past.'

Up this close, his eyes were such an indelible blue they made her head spin. 'So if the helicopter moves away, can we assume they don't know about me?'

'I'd say it's a safe bet.' He cleared his throat and cast a hasty glance around them. 'I'm sorry about these cramped conditions.'

He was *sorry*? There was no way she could be sorry to be shoulder-to-shoulder with him, to have the solid length of his thigh pressed so closely against hers. She was tingling all over. 'I don't mind,' she said quickly, and then wondered if that had sounded too much as if she was enjoying herself. 'You don't need to apologise. You're not responsible for the undergrowth.'

After that, neither spoke as they crouched together, waiting for the chopper to move away. When at last it did, Jack crawled forward on his hands and knees and then turned and held out his hand to help her.

She was surprised when he helped to brush the leaves and twigs from her hair and clothes, and although it was nice that he cared, she felt a spurt of irritation. First he'd been apologising; now he felt compelled to assist her. Already his behaviour was changing. He was reacting to the news that she was a princess.

All her life her royal title had shaped the way people treated her, and she couldn't help regretting that she'd had such a brief time to enjoy being plain Isabella. It had been fun.

'OK,' Jack said, once he was satisfied that she was comfortable. 'Let's go back to the hut and you can explain exactly what you're doing here.'

A princess! Jack grappled to wrap his head around the notion. As they walked his gaze kept sliding sideways, as if he needed to check that Isabella still looked the same. It was so hard to believe that this slip of a girl, in wrinkled, unironed clothes, with her untidy hair tied back loosely by a piece of string, was a true-blue Amorian princess.

Who would have thought?

And he'd suggested she might be a gypsy.

Nevertheless, in a roundabout way her claim seemed to make sense. He was surprised by how ready he was to believe her. There was an air of gentility and dignity about her—an other-worldliness—and clues like her luxurious underwear and her fascination with simple food.

Hell...

He felt a flush of heat redden the back of his neck when he thought about the offhand way he'd treated her—chipping her for not making her bed or washing her clothes, sending her off to the outhouse to kill her own spiders, making fun of her underwear...

When they reached the hut he said, 'I need a drink, but all I've got here is tea.'

'Let me make it,' she said quickly.

He fended her off with outstretched palms. 'It's OK. You take a seat.'

Her eyes sent him a dark warning. 'Jack, you don't have to

treat me any differently because you know who I am. I don't expect you to start waiting on me.'

He frowned, and turned with a shrug to light the burner. 'I don't mind.'

'I've had a lifetime of being treated like a princess.

I've been enjoying the change.'

His eyes made a cursory sweep of the interior of the hut. 'Like the prince and the pauper?'

'I suppose so.' She propped her hip against the bench, crossed her arms over her chest and eyed him levelly. 'Can you promise me one thing?'

'What's that?'

'Whatever you do, don't start calling me Your Highness. I'm still Isabella.'

He laughed. 'No fear on that count. I'm an Australian. We're not big on titles anyway. So, what are your other names? Are you like British royalty—with a string of them?'

Her eyes flashed and her chin lifted to a haughty, very princess-like angle. 'I'm Isabella Mary Damaris Alice Martineau—second in line to the throne of Amoria, behind my brother, the Crown Prince Danior.'

He couldn't help grinning. *She was the genuine article!* 'Isabella-Mary-Something-Alice. All those fancy names and still no Carmen.'

'I don't mind if you want to call me Carmen.'

The vulnerability in her eyes and her timid smile made his chest tighten and his grin fade. Isabella gave a little sigh and moved away.

'Perhaps you'd better tell me your story,' he suggested, and his voice sounded unnecessarily serious. He didn't want her to think he was flirting.

She shook her head. 'You don't want to be burdened with my problems.'

'That's for me to decide. There's no burden in listening.' He set the billy full of water to boil. 'I'm not promising I can help.'

He stood facing her, his hands resting lightly on his hips, his mood intent and expectant, and he could sense the instant that she decided to tell him. One moment she was shaking her head and looking away, her white teeth biting her lower lip, the next her pretty dark eyes had found his and he could see a brief internal struggle and then release.

Almost without emotion, she said, 'My fiancé' plans to kill me.'

'Bloody hell.' The exclamation slipped out, but before Jack could apologise Isabella rushed to explain.

'I know it sounds crazy. I had trouble believing it at first.'

'Are you sure he means to harm you?'

'Yes.'

'Why?'

'He views our marriage as a merger. A business venture. All he wants is access to my money and my estates.'

'How did you find this out?'

With quick nervous movements she began to rearrange the tins of food on the bench in front of her. 'A very good friend of mine, Dr Christos Tenni, was at a conference in Geneva and he overheard Radik, the Count of Montez—that's my fiancé'—discussing his plans with his lover.'

'The mongrel!'

Isabella swallowed and her hands shook.

Jack stepped towards her, took the tin she was holding and set it aside on the bench, then he captured both her hands in his. He stroked her fingers lightly with his thumb.

For several seconds she looked at her hands in his, and then she glanced up at him from beneath trembling lashes.

'Apparently Radik—that's my fiancé'—favours a car crash on a mountain for my demise.'

It seemed so unreal to hear her talking about her own death this way. 'You're not joking, are you?'

'Believe me, I wish I was.'

'I assume this informant, this Dr Tenni, is completely trust-worthy?'

Her eyes filled with tears. 'He was my own doctor—but I also worked in his hospital, so I knew him professionally as well. I would never doubt Christos's word. He was a very good friend.'

'You said he *was*—has something happened to him?' This time the bright tears overflowed and spilled down her cheeks. 'The day after he warned me of my danger—' She pulled a hand from his grasp and pressed it over her mouth as she struggled to hold back sobs. 'Oh, God, Jack.'

His arm slipped around her shoulders, holding her closer. 'What happened?'

Sobbing, she shook her head against him. It took some time and several deep breaths before she could go on.

'It happened the very next day. A hit-and-run accident right in front of the hospital.'

'He was killed?'

'Yes.'

Jack swore under his breath.

'I panicked,' she said in a very small voice. 'My father was away and I lost the nerve to wait. I grabbed my passport and a wig and sunglasses and headed straight for the airport.'

Her words caused an ache in his solar plexus. Damn.

Despite his best intentions, he was feeling involved.

As if she'd sensed the sudden tension in him, Isabella pulled out of his arms. 'Look... I'm really sorry to be burdening you with this,' she said.

'What puzzles me is why you wanted to marry this fellow in the first place. You weren't being forced to, were you?'

'In a way I was...'

'I thought arranged marriages were a thing of the past?'

She shrugged. 'At first I thought I really was in love with Radik. He's very handsome and charming.'

'Bully for him.' Jack crossed his arms over his chest. 'But

once you found out how utterly lacking in charm he was, couldn't you have called off the wedding?'

'It's hard to explain. You've no idea what happens to a princess as soon as her engagement is announced. I lost all control of my life. A royal wedding is a *huge* deal. In Amoria it felt as if the entire country had an emotional stake in *my* marriage.'

Remembering the ruckus his own wedding had caused, Jack nodded.

Her mouth pulled into a shame-faced grimace. 'I know I'm a coward for running away, but I was so scared. I wasn't sure I could convince my father to call off the wedding. Our relationship is somewhat…strained.' She looked embarrassed. 'I suppose you find that difficult to understand?'

'Not at all.' *I understand more than you could possibly guess.*

She sighed. 'Father and his advisers think the world of my fiancé. And Radik has a smooth tongue. He would have found a way to convince them I'd been misinformed—deluded.'

'And there was no one else you could talk to? No other family or friends?'

Slowly she shook her head. 'Not really. My mother died when I was young. My brother's too absorbed with his studies in England and the stream of hot and cold running blondes flowing to his door. As for my friends—' She shrugged. 'When your father's a king, there's only so much girlfriends can do.'

'So you came down here to escape?'

'Australia is so far away. It seemed the best plan.'

Jack grimaced as he looked around the hut, trying to imagine what it looked like through her eyes. 'You must be finding this accommodation just a little different from home.'

'I'm getting used to it.' She shot a glance towards the cobwebs in the corner. 'Except for the spiders.'

With an uncomfortable throat-clearing growl, he turned to the bench.

'Jack, please understand that just because I've told you all this it doesn't mean I expect you to help me.'

He handed her a chipped enamel mug of tea and she sat on the stool while he used the upturned petrol drum again. He leaned forward, staring thoughtfully into his mug, and shrugged.

'So when's this wedding supposed to take place?'

'On Saturday.'

'Saturday?' He almost dropped his tea. 'Not this Saturday coming?'

'Yes. That's why I freaked. The Amorian papers are full of nothing but the wedding. Half of Europe knows every detail.'

He released a low whistle.

'Trying to stop all that single-handed seemed—'

'Like trying to stop the Olympic Games when the athletes are in the starting blocks?'

'Exactly.'

Jack stared at the floor, with his elbows resting on his knees and his mug of cooling tea cradled in his hands. 'So this Count of Montez will be looking for you, won't he? I imagine he'll be desperate to get you back and get you safely to the altar.'

'I suppose so. I'm trying not to think about that.'

Jack drew in a long, deep breath, then let it out again slowly. 'It's all happening now for you, isn't it?' he said. 'First you get lost. Then you narrowly escape drowning in the flooded creek. You struggle through the bush in the middle of a storm and end up here half dead.' His grin was shaky. 'Isabella, there's more of Carmen in you than you realise.'

She knew this was his way of paying her a compliment, and she felt absurdly pleased.

'But where were you heading when you crashed?' he asked.

'To John and Elizabeth's.'

'The Kingsley-Lairds? You weren't heading for Killymoon, were you?'

Her eyes widened with surprise. 'As a matter of fact, yes, I was. When they left Amoria last year they extended a very kind invitation. And Killymoon is so far away from Amoria, and so isolated, it seemed perfect. Do you know them?' She half expected him to say that he did know the family well.

He didn't meet her gaze, and he seemed to choose his words carefully before he replied. 'There's no doubt the Killymoon homestead would suit your purposes.' He sent another quick, sardonic glance around the hut. 'And it would be a darn sight more comfortable than here.'

She sighed, disappointed by his evasive reply. 'I'd be there now if I hadn't taken that wrong turn in the dark and ended up in the creek.'

'Why didn't you phone the Kingsley-Lairds from Darwin? They would have arranged for a plane to fly you in.'

'Would they?'

'Sure.'

'Do you know them well?'

A shutter seemed to fall over his eyes, shielding his thoughts. 'Well enough.'

'I was so anxious to keep moving and not attract attention that as soon as I got to Darwin I hired a car and hit the highway. I don't know how I'm going to get to Killymoon now.'

'You're already on the property.'

'Really?' She frowned. 'I thought I was still about a hundred kilometres away.'

His mouth tilted in a faint ironic smile. 'You *are* still a hundred kilometres away from the homestead, but Killymoon is a big property. One of the biggest in the world.'

'Good heavens.' She shook her head in amazement. 'It must be bigger than Amoria.'

Jack drained his mug and rose to his feet. Isabella told herself she shouldn't be admiring the way he moved, but although she knew it was totally inappropriate, she found everything about him undeniably impressive. His controlled casualness fascinated her.

'I could take you to Killymoon homestead,' he said, not quite looking at her.

'But how? If the creek is cut we're stuck here, aren't we?'

'We don't have to take the roads. In fact, we're probably better off keeping away from the highway. You never know, your Count might already have people out there, trying to find you.'

'But how else could we get to Killymoon? I don't think I could walk one hundred kilometres in this heat.' He looked out through the doorway of the hut, and she followed his gaze and saw the canoe pulled up on the lake's shore. 'I wasn't thinking about walking.' Jumping to her feet, she hurried to stand beside him.

'Are you saying we could take the canoe?'

'That's exactly what I'm thinking. The creek's flowing fast, but not as fast as yesterday, and it's not rising any more. It runs into the Pinnaroo River, which can take us all the way down to Killymoon homestead. With a bit of luck we could be there in two days, three at the outside.'

'But what about your own plans? A trip like that would take up a lot of your time.'

Did she imagine the flickering shadow that seemed to darken his face momentarily?

He shrugged. 'My plans are flexible.'

She might have pursued the question further, but something in his face, his air of calm authority, cautioned her not to push. If Jack didn't want to help her he wouldn't have offered.

He looked at her thoughtfully, as if he were taking her measure. 'Do you think you're up to it?'

'Up to it?'

'How do you feel about canoeing that far?'

'I'd love it,' she said, without hesitating.

'We'd have to camp out overnight. It would mean sleeping in the open.'

She blanched as she tried to squash visions of being eaten by wild animals.

'We'll be OK. I've got mosquito nets,' he said, noting her hesitation.

'I wasn't thinking of mosquitoes. Um—I know you don't have lions and tigers in Australia, but...'

The skin around his eyes creased. 'But?'

'But what about all the snakes and the crocodiles? You have them, don't you?'

'There are freshwater crocodiles around here, but they only eat fish. As for snakes—yeah, we have them, and they'll be hanging around at the moment because of all the rain, but they usually only bother you if you bother them.'

His gaze was unexpectedly gentle, and he touched a finger to her cheek and let it trail down to her chin. 'I wouldn't take you down the river if I thought it was too dangerous. The point of this exercise is to keep you safe.'

Keep you safe.

Those three words, in company with the gentleness of his touch, the kindness in his voice and the steadfast look in his eyes, made her feel so protected she could have cried.

The past few days had been a nightmare, and Jack was fast becoming the hero who'd figured in all her girlhood dreams. Like a storybook knight in shining armour. 'You'll be my hero, Jack,' she said, sending him a smile that was a mixture of coyness and teasing. And she couldn't resist adding, 'Will you be the princess's champion? Can I trust you to take me unharmed through the Valley of the Dragons?'

He looked shocked. 'Don't get carried away. There's nothing romantic about this. I'll take you down the flooded creek to Killymoon, but that doesn't make me Sir Lancelot escorting Guinevere to Camelot.'

Isabella wasn't so sure.

CHAPTER FIVE

THEY ATE ONE last meal on the banks of the lake, looking out over the stretch of water and watching cheeky black shags try to steal fish straight from a pelican's bill. Isabella felt a guilty pang at the thought that she was dragging Jack away from this lovely setting, but if he resented leaving he showed no sign.

They set off straight after lunch, first carrying their gear along the track to the creek and leaving it on the high bank while they went back for the canoe, which also had to be carried.

'Make sure you cover that Alpine complexion of yours with plenty of this,' Jack said, handing her a bottle of sunscreen.

She slathered it on while he stowed everything very carefully in plastic drums in the bottom of the canoe.

'You'd better have this, too,' he said, and he dropped his wide-brimmed akubra hat onto her head.

'But it's yours.'

'My nose isn't as delicate as yours.'

'Well, thanks, but I'm afraid this hat's too big for me.' To her surprise, he picked up a handful of her dark curls. 'What if we tuck your hair up under it? That should help to keep it on, shouldn't it?'

'Perhaps.'

'Hold still, then.'

It was such a simple thing for Jack to wind her heavy hair into a loose knot and tuck it up inside the hat, yet Isabella hardly knew how to deal with the blaze of warmth that flashed through her. She couldn't remember any time in her life when a man, apart from her hairdresser, had handled her hair in such an intimate way. She was sure her neck must be bright red.

'Shake your head,' Jack instructed, ducking to smile at her beneath the wide brim.

She shook her head carefully, and then a little more vigorously. The hat stayed in place.

'That should do the trick,' he said. 'OK, let's get going.'

Although the creek's current wasn't quite as fierce as it had been, it was still very swift, and Isabella quickly discovered that they had to paddle even faster than the water's flow to maintain control over the canoe.

A rush of adrenalin, more excitement than fear, sent her heart racing, and she had to concentrate on deliberately steadying her breathing and willing her shoulders to relax, so that she could match her strokes to Jack's strong, even paddling rhythm.

Fleeting impressions of the scenery flashed by—thicktrunked trees with peeling white papery bark—thin tapering leaves and branches hanging low over the water like Outback versions of weeping willows. Out of the corner of her eye she caught sight of a red kangaroo, its long tail bouncing behind it as it bobbed through the scrub.

'The current will be slower when we reach the main river,' shouted Jack.

'Don't worry. I'm fine,' she called back over her shoulder. And she meant it. She knew the muscles in her arms and shoulders would be aching by the end of the day, but despite her slender frame she was strong and fit. At home she skied in winter and canoed in summer, and she was savouring every moment now.

But her stomach dropped when they rounded a bend and she saw menacing dark rocks looming out of foaming white water.

'Rapids!' she yelled.

'Pull your paddle in and hang on to your hat,' Jack called back. 'I'll steer us through here.'

For a split second she sensed a prickle of hurt pride. Why couldn't she help? But as the current picked them up and hurled them towards the rocks common sense prevailed. Jack was in the canoe's stern, the best position for driving and steering, and a wrong move from her might capsize them or send them slamming into the basalt. Quickly she pulled her paddle out of the water and held her breath as their light craft catapulted forward.

The angry water tossed them about like a leaf in an autumn wind gust, and she knew that it took all of Jack's stronger muscles and superior skill to keep the canoe clear of the black boulders.

She didn't dare turn back to watch him, but sat very still, holding onto his hat and crouching low so he could see over her. She held her breath as the canoe skipped and skimmed at a reckless pace, dodging danger by mere inches.

And then suddenly they were shooting out into a wider expanse of calmer water.

'This is the junction where the creek joins the Pinnaroo River,' Jack explained. 'How are you holding out?'

She turned back to look over her shoulder and saw the breathtaking blue sparkle of his eyes. He was grinning and she smiled back at him. 'That was very impressive canoeing. I'm having the time of my life, thanks.'

And how true that was. This was like living her personal fantasy—stepping out of the royal spotlight and having her own private adventure. And even though this interlude in the Outback with Jack would only be for a few days, she knew it would leave a lasting legacy. It would be an exciting memory to hold in her heart. At points in the future, when the tedium of life in the public eye got her down, she would be able to remember this.

She had to forget about the threat of Radik and live in *this* moment. Absorb everything.

Now, to the right and left of her stretched a magnificent wide river with tall limestone cliffs on the far side and a huge blue dome of bright sky overhead.

'Now we just keep heading downstream,' Jack said, and his big shoulders rolled smoothly as he lifted his paddle and dug it into the water once more. 'And the further we go down the Pinnaroo, the clearer it will get. All the feeder streams from now on come out of limestone country and are spring fed.'

They settled into an easy paddling pace and the canoe slid happily forward. There was so much to see. Like the lake, the river teemed with birds. Pleased that already she'd learned to identify many of them, she watched with delight as black ducks, pelicans, divers and cormorants swam, dived, frolicked or sat in the sun and spread their wings to dry their feathers.

Each bend in the river brought an exciting new vista.

On the tops of the high banks beautiful gum trees with huge towering white trunks and buttresses of dark brown bark stood sentry. Mobs of silvery-white cattle with big faces, floppy ears and camel-like humps stood in the shade of these trees and seemed to watch the canoe's progress.

The only frustration was that she couldn't see Jack without turning back, so she contented herself with imagining his rippling muscles and the powerful strength in his tanned arms as he paddled. It was fun to pretend they were intrepid explorers, and that the Pinnaroo River was the Amazon or the Nile.

She and Jack were alone in a hot, steamy wilderness. Tarzan and Jane…

At the next bend the limestone cliffs closed in on both sides, the river narrowed and they shot into a race of fast water that spun them out into a surprisingly clear pool with a sandy bottom and a fringe of shady trees and fan-like palms.

'Are you hot?' Jack called. 'I am. I need a swim.'

She was terribly hot. Beneath the hat, her hair felt damp and itchy, and her shirt stuck to her in wet, sweaty patches. The water looked clean and very cool and inviting. But...

'I don't have a swimming costume.'

She heard Jack's chuckle as he steered for the shore. Once they were both standing on the bank, he said, 'Pardon me, Princess, but when you're out in the bush you don't stand on ceremony.'

With that he kicked off his shoes, stripped off his shirt, undid his jeans and stepped out of them, letting his discarded clothes fall in a careless tangle on the bank behind him.

Heavenly stars, he was wearing nothing but a brief pair of underpants. But she wasn't so shocked that she didn't appreciate his superbly sculptured, almost naked masculine physique.

Seeing Jack now was a different experience from the night she'd arrived, when she'd caught a terrified glimpse of him in the lamplight. Now, in broad daylight, his big shoulders, smooth brown back, lean hips and long, strong legs sent sexy quivers rippling under her skin.

He shot a winking smile her way. 'Are you going to join me?'

Her hand touched the top button of her blouse. 'I—I don't think so.'

He nodded, as if he understood that there were limits to a European princess's sense of adventure, then strode to the water's edge and dived in—arching, sleek and pure in mid-air, before disappearing head-first beneath the water.

Isabella watched his powerful strokes as he progressed across the pool. Did she dare to follow? The afternoon was so hot, a swim would be perfect. But how could she undress here? Even though Jack had seen her body when he'd removed her wet clothes on that first night, to strip down to her underwear now was a step that seemed too huge to take.

He was already halfway to the far side. Perhaps he was giving her space and relative privacy?

If I'm having an adventure, I should do this. If this were a Hollywood movie...

Why did she keep thinking of Hollywood? Was it because her life was becoming increasingly less real?

She looked out again to where Jack was floating on his back, kicking in a leisurely style and staring up at the sky...not interested in her...not looking her way...

Jack heard the splash and glanced back towards the bank to see rippling circles and then Isabella's dark head emerging above the water.

'Well, I'll be...' he said softly, and he smiled, treading water as he watched her swim towards him with sharpelbowed, inexpert strokes.

His own breaststrokes were lazy as he swam to meet her halfway. 'What do you think?' he asked when he drew near to her. Her curly hair had been straightened by the weight of the water and fell in dark satiny curtains on either side of her face.

'This pool is beautiful,' she said, laughing. 'I feel so free.' She flicked water into the air and watched the droplets catch the sunlight before falling around her like sparkling diamonds.

'We *are* free here,' he said. 'That's why I love to come out here. We're free as the birds.'

A sudden piping call high above them caught his attention and he looked up to see a pair of grey falcons tumbling and swooping in the air. It was rare to see grey falcons in these parts. They were desert birds. Floating on his back, he squinted to bring them into sharper focus and continued to watch them as they flew to the top a dead gum tree on the far ridge.

'Jack! Help! *Help!*'

Isabella's scream and sudden thrashing sent a bolt of fear ripping through him. In a split second he was at her side. 'What is it? What's the matter?'

She flung her arms around his neck and clung to him, shivering with terror. 'Something touched me,' she cried, and he could feel her heart pounding against his chest. 'Could it be a crocodile?'

'I shouldn't think so.' He couldn't help grinning. 'It's not funny. Oh, God! I have to get out of here.'

She began to pull out of his arms, but as soon as he released her she was seized by panic, thrashed wildly and went under again.

Ducking beneath the water, he caught her around the waist and hauled her high. 'No need to panic,' he told her as she gasped and spluttered. 'I'm here. I've got you. Try to relax and I'll take you to the shore.'

Holding her against his chest, he swam using sidestroke and brought her back to the bank.

'Oh, Jack—oh, dear God,' she sobbed, still clinging to him in the shallows. 'Thank you.'

She huddled there gasping, struggling to steady her breathing. Without speaking Jack held her with her head tucked against his shoulder, and did his best to ignore how perfectly her slim, soft smoothness fitted against him.

After some time she said, 'I'm sorry I panicked, but that was so bad. I hate it when things touch me in the water.'

'Don't apologise,' he said, lifting a strand of wet hair from her cheek. 'I should have warned you. There are all sorts of things in the river—fish, eels, turtles—but nothing really dangerous.'

She lifted her beautiful dark eyes and looked up at him from beneath long lashes glistening with starry water drops.

'It touched my leg,' she said. 'And I've heard so many stories of people being eaten by crocodiles in Australia.'

'The only crocs that eat folk are the salties.'

'Salties?'

'Saltwater crocodiles. Any crocodiles up here would be the freshwater ones.'

'Are you sure?'

'Absolutely. The Pinnaroo Falls are just a few kilometres downstream from Killymoon homestead. No crocs can get past them.' He grinned. 'They can't climb cliffs and they can't swim up waterfalls. Relax. I'm looking after you. I wouldn't be swimming with saltwater crocs.'

He eased his body gently away from hers and hoped she hadn't noticed the embarrassing effect of having her dainty curves so near him. Serve him right for stripping down to next to nothing.

'I've spoiled your swim,' she said.

'Doesn't matter. I've cooled off.' What a joke! He turned away from her, strode towards his jeans and hauled them on over his wet jocks.

Glancing back to Isabella, he saw the way she looked down at herself and her cheeks grew pink, as if she'd just realised how transparent her wet undies were. Turning her back to him, she grabbed up her own clothes.

'I guess we'll dry off quickly once we start paddling again,' she said, looking back at him over her shoulder, while holding her clothes in front of her like a shield.

She'd hooked her long hair over one shoulder, inadvertently exposing her slim, pale back, and Jack found himself noting the perfect line of her backbone, her neat shoulderblades, the delightful roundness of her buttocks. He turned abruptly and strode away along the riverbank while she dressed. Hell, he needed to think about Geri. He summoned a mental picture of his wife and found himself struggling to remember the exact shape of her back, her shoulderblades, her buttocks.

With a groan he covered his face with his hands and concentrated hard, willing himself to forget this girl and to remember every detail of how his wife had looked, how she'd felt in his arms.

But he couldn't find Geri. Panic threatened, and for frantic seconds he couldn't breathe. Just when he began to see Geri the image would dissolve. He tried again, and she wouldn't come. A cry of rage erupted from his throat, and he knew if he didn't snap out of it he would give way to tears.

Dragging in a noisy deep breath, he willed himself to get a grip.

When he returned to Isabella she stood stiffly, watching him, her face troubled. 'Jack, I feel so silly now. I hope you don't think I'll need rescuing every time I get a fright on this trip.'

'Of course not,' he said gruffly.

Her cheeks grew pink again. 'I'm sorry I threw myself all over you.'

'Don't give it a second thought. I won't.'

Yeah, right, he thought, making sure his eyes didn't meet hers. With more haste than necessary he moved towards the canoe and pushed it back down the bank to the river.

They kept going until the sun slipped towards the western rim and long shadows stretched across the water.

When at last Isabella stepped onto the shore, at the spot Jack had chosen for their campsite, her arms, shoulders and back were painfully stiff, but as she watched Jack haul the canoe high and dry he showed no signs of discomfort.

She hadn't meant to stare, but she couldn't help herself. There was something about the confident, casual way he did things that kept drawing her attention. While she gathered dry wood for their fire, she kept sneaking peeks at him. He was tying a piece of rope between two trees and stretching a mosquito net across it, and a green lightweight nylon tarpaulin over that.

'It shouldn't rain, but this will keep away stray showers,' he said, squinting quickly up at the cloudless sky. Then he knelt and scraped two body-sized dents in the sandy loam to take their sleeping swags.

She gulped when she saw the two canvas swags, lying so close, side by side. Tonight she would be lying there beside Jack. The thought brought a warm and tightening sensation low inside her.

'Will this be enough timber for our fire?' she asked quickly, needing to switch her attention to safer matters. Jack shot a quick glance towards the pile of sticks she'd collected and flashed her a sardonic smile. 'That's not a bad start, but we'll need bigger logs to burn down into coals if we want to bake our fish.'

'Right,' she said, using a businesslike voice to cover how silly she felt. No doubt he'd guessed that she'd never collected firewood or baked a fish.

'I'll help you,' he offered.

'It's OK. I can manage,' she snapped crossly, and was instantly sorry for her rudeness. Jack was going out of his way to escort her safely to Killymoon and she had an obligation to be polite in return. 'I'm happy to look for bigger pieces of timber,' she said in a more conciliatory tone. 'You get on with your fishing.'

Once the fire was started, she sat on the sand beside it, with her arms wrapped around her bent knees while she watched Jack bait a hook with an earthworm and throw his line out into the river.

The setting was lovely. The last rays of the dying sun warmed her back and gilded Jack's bronzed, outflung arms, and coated the quiet water with liquid gold. A solitary white heron fished the far bank, moving through the sunlit shallows with slow, focused stealth.

The peaceful scene should have relaxed her and uplifted her spirits. But instead she felt horribly down. Perhaps it was simply her tiredness from the long canoe trip that made her feel so sad, but she had a sinking feeling that her low mood was linked to Jack.

She liked him too much. She enjoyed being with him too much and she cared far too much about what he thought of her. But such feelings were pointless. Apart from the fact that she belonged to another world and would have to return very soon, there was a remoteness about Jack, an inner sadness and a sense of loss that formed a barrier she could never hope to get past.

She knew nothing about his personal life and he had no wish to share any of it with her. Not even his family name.

She stared at her bare toes, half buried in sand. The problem was that although she accepted these realities with her head, her heart refused to be sensible. She really was becoming a hopeless romantic. Even now, as she watched him standing at the water's edge, alone and apparently unaware of her, she felt an intense yearning that was so painful she wanted to cry.

How crazy!

A loud splash sounded and Jack gave a sudden whoop of triumph as the fishing line strained in his hands.

'You little beauty!' he shouted as he hauled the line in and a large, glistening fish flapped onto the sand at his feet.

She hurried over to him. 'Can we eat it?'

'Too right. This is a golden perch. It'll be delicious.'

'But how can you cook it? We don't have a pan.' She cast a puzzled glance around her at the sandy beach and the simple fire. Jack had mentioned baking. She couldn't imaging baking a whole fish without a kitchen, or at the very least an oven.

Jack's grin was the kind that seemed to reach right inside her. 'I'm going to wrap it in paperbark and cook it bush tucker style. You won't complain when you taste it.'

Fascinated, she watched as he used his pocket knife to cut wide strips of white papery bark from a nearby tree and then fashioned an envelope to hold the fish and the dried onions and carrots that he'd brought from the hut. He bound the parcel with a yam vine he found in the scrub, then looked up at her. His blue eyes flashed as he smiled, and her silly heart did a little gavotte.

By the time he'd finished preparing their meal the coals in his fire had burned down, but he threw some sand onto them to reduce the heat further, then placed the paperbark parcel on top and covered that with another sheet of bark and more sand.

'There's your oven,' he said. 'Now I'll build another fire for warmth and light. The temperature will drop as soon as the sun sets.'

He did this very quickly and efficiently, and in no time they had a bright crackling fire, then he settled his long frame onto the sand beside her.

Having him so close upset the rhythm of Isabella's breathing. She concentrated on a spot on the horizon. The sun had disappeared now, but a fire-like red-gold glow lingered along the distant rim of the hills.

'It's going to be a hot day tomorrow,' Jack said as he watched the sunset. 'It's always like that in the wet season—bearable while it's raining and then hot and steamy afterwards. It gets hotter and hotter until there's another lot of rain.'

'It's very pleasant now,' Isabella suggested. When Jack didn't respond, she added, 'All we need is a predinner G&T or sherry while our dinner cooks.' She wasn't desperate for a drink, but she needed to say something light and frivolous to distract her thoughts from Jack and the astonishing realisation that she would really, really like him to kiss her.

His deep frowning reaction was a surprise. 'I didn't bring any grog on this trip,' he said.

'You don't approve of drinking alcohol?'

'It's not so much that I don't approve, but I tend to give it a miss these days, especially when I'm on my own.' His eyes narrowed as he stared off into the distance. 'I went through a rough patch a couple of years back. There was a time when I lost— someone. Drink and grief can be a bad mix.'

A rash of goosebumps prickled Isabella's arms. Sympathy and surprise formed a lump in her throat. Over the past twenty-four hours she'd become increasingly attuned to Jack's air of sadness. Who had died? Was it a woman he'd loved? A wife?

'I'm very sorry,' she said gently.

He nodded curtly without looking at her and sat very still beside her, staring out past the flickering flames to the river. She could see the tension in his jaw, in the set of his shoulders and the hand fisted on his knee.

Was he already regretting his confession? She switched her attention to the evening star, shimmering brightly against the plush mauve backdrop of the twilight sky. Perhaps he needed to talk…

'Whenever I'm outdoors in the early evening and I'm watching the stars come out I remember my mother,' she said, without looking at him. 'She loved the stars. She knew the names of all the constellations and she would tell me wonderful stories about how they were formed.'

Jack nodded, and his chest rose and fell as he drew in a breath and let it out slowly and deliberately, as if he was willing himself to relax. 'You'll be able to see the Southern Cross soon.'

'Please show it to me. I've always longed to see it.'

Although she wasn't looking at Jack, Isabella was aware that he'd turned to face her.

'You said your mother died, didn't you?'

'Yes,' she said carefully, wondering if he wanted to talk about grief. She kept her gaze ahead, looking out at the water. 'I was only ten, and I was so desperately sad I thought I might never recover.'

'But you did get over it?'

'Eventually, but I'll never stop missing her. She was the most important person in my life. And afterwards…my father didn't seem to know how to talk to me.' Leaning forward to hug her knees, she said, 'Actually, I feel as if I need Mother more than ever now. I have no doubt that she would have helped me stand up to my father against Radik.'

Jack shifted on the sand, moving much closer, and her heart began a hectic dance. His fingers touched her cheek. 'Poor Carmen,' he whispered.

His deep voice was as gentle as the whispering breeze on the water, so tender it stole her breath, so intimate it lit a golden flame low inside her.

'Don't encourage me to feel sorry for myself,' she said with forced brightness.

'How can I distract you?'

Oh, Jack, what a question. You could start by touching your lips to mine.

What was the matter with her? Had she lost all sense of right and wrong? How could she sit here with every cell in her body wanting this man to kiss her when she knew he was deeply troubled by grief?

'Do you want to talk about—your loss, Jack?'

'Not tonight.'

The sudden roughness in his voice made her turn. Shadows and firelight played on his face, showing her tantalising glimpses of the rugged lines of his forehead, nose and cheekbones, the strong beauty of his mouth. 'What do you want to talk about?'

His unsmiling eyes held hers. 'I'm open to suggestions.'

'Well…we'll have to find something to discuss. Otherwise…'

'Otherwise?'

She saw in the flickering light from the fire that he was looking at her with a strange dark hunger. It stirred the heat inside her till her skin felt too tight for her body. 'Otherwise I'll start wishing I really was a gypsy called Carmen.'

'If you were Carmen, what would you do?'

Now? Alone in the wilderness with you, Jack, you impossibly gorgeous man? She tried to laugh, but it came out like a shaky hiccup. 'What do you think Carmen would do?'

He didn't answer.

His gaze held hers and his silence seemed to fill the night. Isabella's heart thudded and the silent sky loomed over them like a purple diamond-studded cave. The scent of sandalwood smoke drifted from the fire, weaving around them like incense.

A burning log snapped and spurted a shower of sparks.

Jack leaned closer.

And Isabella's gasp of surprise was lost inside his kiss. In his wild and wonderful kiss. His mouth was so hot and demanding there was little she could do but cling to his shoulders as he hauled her closer. She couldn't think what was right or wrong; she could only feel herself melting with astonishing speed—surrendering to Jack with trembling willingness. Her lips softened and parted so he could kiss her more deeply, more passionately.

When he pulled back, she made a soft sound of protest.

Their gazes met and held. His intense blue eyes and her midnight-black—sharing amazement at what they'd just done and the surprised certainty that they must do it again.

'Sweet Carmen,' he whispered hoarsely, and he lifted his hand to smooth a strand of hair away from her brow with an exquisitely gentle touch. Her heart fluttered. Lightning flashed through her veins. In a cloud of heat she raised her mouth to meet his.

And this time their parted lips came together with less impatience and more exquisite focus. Jack's hands cradled her face, and gently, slowly, he sipped at her mouth. His hot, hard lips became warm, soft and tantalising, tasting her with deeply sensitive appreciation.

Kissing Jack was different from anything she'd ever known. In the past, the chaste Princess of Amoria had *allowed* herself to be kissed. Now Isabella wanted, no, *needed* to be a full participant.

She wound her arms around his neck, and each time Jack shifted the angle of his mouth to seduce her with the lush, warm slide of his lips and tongue she matched him move for sensual move.

And when he showered her neck and shoulders with a scattering of kisses she arched her head back, to give him access to her needy skin. His fingertips traced pleasure tracks up and down her arms. Each touch made her shivery-hot with desire. She wanted his touch *everywhere*.

She was lost in shocking sensation.

They sank back onto the sand and the full length of their bodies pressed close. Breast to breast, hip to hip, thigh to thigh. Isabella gasped at the force of her reaction.

'Oh, Jack,' she whispered. He felt so strong, so manly, so sexy. Fire and fierce longing spiralled through her.

But he was releasing her again, and this time he swung some distance apart from her. She felt the sudden coolness of the river breeze on her skin instead of his heat. They lay in stunned silence, staring up at the stars, their breathing equally fast and ragged.

'I'm sure I should apologise for that,' he said after some time.

'Please don't.'

She shot a quick glance his way. In the bright velvet moonlight his profile had become a stony mask. She couldn't bear it if he got tense or angry with her. She knew he hadn't planned to kiss her. It had happened spontaneously. Wasn't that the way the best kisses were supposed to happen?

'You wouldn't have apologised to Carmen.'

His smile was thoughtful, then without further comment he sprang to his feet and walked over to the cooking fire, crouched beside it and raked the coals aside with a stick. As he lifted a sheet of bark the delicious aroma of their meal seemed to fill the night air.

How could she think about anything as mundane as eating? It wasn't food she needed. She wanted Jack. She needed him to kiss her again, to hold her. Her body felt hot and hollow; she was burning with need for him.

But his attention was focused strictly on the food. 'That smells wonderful,' she said, forcing enthusiasm into her voice. 'I've just realised I'm starving.'

They ate in silence, balancing their baked fish and vegetables on rough plates fashioned from paperbark, and although she knew that they were both unnerved by the shattering intensity of their kiss, Jack behaved as if it hadn't happened.

'This is absolutely delicious,' she said, but he merely nodded.

After their meal, with the fire banked low and the moon climbing higher, she was surprised to find herself yawning. 'I guess all that paddling must have worn me out,' she said.

'We should get an early night.' His voice was clipped and careful.

Tension arced between them as they crawled into their makeshift tent and lay stiffly side by side in their sleeping bags. They exchanged brief goodnights without touching.

Isabella kept stealing glimpses at the silhouette of Jack's body so close and warm beside her. She knew that he was angry with himself for kissing her. But he *had* kissed her. Of his own accord, he'd kissed her with the kind of mindless passion she'd always dreamed of. Perhaps she was being foolish, but as she lay there, trying to calm down, trying not to think about snakes or other nasties that might crawl into their tent during the night, she allowed the memory of his hot kiss to settle inside her like a warm and happy promise.

For now it was enough.

Jack lay on his back with his hands stacked under his head, staring out at the triangle of starry sky showing in the inverted V of the tarpaulin.

What a mistake that kiss had been.

He groaned softly. He should have remembered that Isabella had wanted to see the Southern Cross. He should have spent time discussing astronomy instead of kissing the Princess of Amoria as if she was the last woman on earth.

What the hell had he been thinking? A kiss on the hand or the cheek might have been acceptable, but he'd kissed her with a passion that had shaken him to the depths of his being.

And the eagerness of her response had been electrifying— a dynamic blend of sweet, noble girl and sexy, earthy woman. Isabella and Carmen. Had he lost his head? He'd poured his heart and soul into a kiss that he had known was wrong from every perspective.

Apart from the obvious problem that Isabella was blue-blood European royalty and he was a rough-andready commoner— an alien from Down Under—he was supposed to be protecting the woman, not using her for his pleasure. And he'd broken a promise to himself too; he was supposed to be dedicating this week to the precious memory of his wife.

But, hell—there was another overriding factor he should have considered. Princess Isabella was young. She was an impressionable romantic and she was running from a rotten cad of a fiancé. The last thing she needed was another cad, a morose, mixed-up recluse, who dallied with her emotions and then abandoned her. And yet desertion was his only option. When they got to Killymoon he would have to set her ashore and then make himself scarce.

For certain there would be no welcome mat for him at Killymoon homestead.

CHAPTER SIX

A MIST HUNG over the river when they launched the canoe next morning. It hovered so low they could almost reach up and touch it. The summer morning was deathly still, and as their canoe slipped beneath the white veil there was hardly a sound, except the occasional hush of a rogue breeze stirring the mist-shrouded trees on the bank and the soft plash of their paddles dipping and lifting. Even the birds were quiet.

As the day warmed the mist parted like the curtains in a theatre, drawing open to a beautiful vista of high blue skies, wide brown river and a majestic wall of tall limestone cliffs.

Isabella felt the canoe slow suddenly, and sensed that Jack had braked with a powerful reverse action of his paddle.

'Stop paddling,' came his quiet but authoritative command.

She swung around to look at him, but her motion unsettled the canoe's balance and she heard him mutter harshly under his breath.

Why was he suddenly so tense?

He was staring at the high ridge that towered above the approaching bend in the river, and when she followed his gaze she saw them. Three dark figures on horseback. Standing perfectly still. Watching her and Jack. Fine hairs lifted on the back of her neck.

'Who are they?' she called over her shoulder. 'Is something wrong?'

'Be quiet. Just keep your voice down.'

Alarmed, and hurt by his abrupt tone, she sat very still while he manoeuvred the canoe into the shore, looped a tethering rope around a branch and stepped out onto the bank.

She started to follow him, but he reached out and gripped her roughly by both shoulders.

'Jack? For heaven's sake!'

Without answering he pushed her down so that she landed with an embarrassing jolt onto the seat. What was the matter with him? She'd been trying hard to cooperate. She didn't deserve this rough treatment. With a haughty toss of her head, she glared at him. 'I demand to—'

'This is no time for a royal tantrum,' he said softly through gritted teeth. 'I'll explain everything later, but this is one time you'll just have to take an order. Stay here. Don't on any account get out.'

She sat in stunned silence as Jack strode quickly up the bank. He looked back once, no doubt to check that she was obeying him, and then worked his way up the ridge towards the silent horsemen on the skyline. She could see that they were dark-skinned and dressed in bush shirts and jeans. Their wide-brimmed hats were much like the one Jack had lent her.

As Jack approached them two of the men handed their reins to the third rider, then dismounted and squatted on the ground. They were too far away for her to pick up their voices, but she noted that no one shook hands and that Jack joined them by squatting down on his haunches.

They seemed to be having a serious discussion. Was it her imagination, or was there a ceremonial atmosphere about the meeting?

Stirring uneasily in her seat, she glanced up and down the river, wondering if there were any other silent watchers in the bush. How very little she knew about this wild, remote country—or the man who held her fate in his hands.

The man who'd kissed her with such unexpected passion last night. Was she foolish to have placed so much trust in him?

The meeting didn't take long. Quite soon Jack stood up again and made his way back down the bank. Isabella's gaze lingered on him, watching his easy stride as he wound his way between the trees down the steep slope. Then she switched her attention back to the three mysterious riders.

They were gone.

She was startled. How had they disappeared so quickly? Obviously the men must have mounted their horses and ridden off, but she hadn't sensed any movement. It was hard to squash the feeling that they had simply vanished into the stillness of the bush.

When Jack returned she jumped up eagerly, anxious to join him on the bank.

'No, Isabella,' he said quickly. 'Stay in the canoe. I'll tell you what this is all about, but don't step onto the land.' At least his voice was softer, gentler, and she sensed an underlying plea for her to obey.

Puzzled, she sat quietly and waited as he squatted down, reached into the river with one hand and splashed water onto his face.

Then he spoke quietly. 'Those men are Wondarra, and this section of the river—the bend and the ridge—is sacred to them.'

'Are they Aborigines?'

'Yes.'

'I had no idea there were other people out here. I thought you said the Kingsley-Lairds owned this country?'

'They do, in legal terms, but the Wondarra people are the tra-ditional owners of this land. They've been here for many thousands of years and they have special right of access to sacred sites. We have to respect that.'

'I see, but why were you so tense?' *So rude to me,* she almost added, but thought better of it.

'I guess you're used to giving orders, Isabella, but so am I.' Jack sighed. 'In some ways I shouldn't be telling you this, but that ridge and the riverbank here are what they call men's business. As far as the Wondarra are concerned, it's no place for a woman. Even the sound of a woman's voice can be offensive. I had to go and pay my respects and quietly assure those men that there would be no problem with you.'

'Good heavens.' She digested the information. She didn't like it, but now didn't seem an appropriate moment to become a rampant feminist. And she couldn't help feeling grateful that Jack was her guide and understood the territory. If she'd stumbled on those men on her own she would have been terrified. 'So everything is OK now?'

'Sure—just keep quiet and do exactly what I say for the next twenty kilometres.'

'Twenty kilometres? You're joking, aren't you?'

He laughed. 'Of course. But it was worth a try, Your Highness.'

By the time they stopped for a swim Isabella was so hot and tired she didn't hesitate to join Jack in the water. And although there were slimy river weeds, that he knew must have touched her on the leg or wrapped around her ankle, she bravely refused to scream. In fact she didn't show any sign of fear.

After lunch they rested, sprawling on their backs in the shade of a wattle tree where the filtered sunlight played on their closed eyelids.

'Don't let me go to sleep,' Isabella said. 'I might never want to wake up.'

'You want to talk?' Jack asked lazily with his eyes still closed.

'If it will keep me awake.'

'Tell me a little more about this fiancé of yours.'

'What would you like to know?'

'You've told me he's dashing and charming. Does that mean you were ever in love with him?'

She didn't answer.

Jack opened his eyes and turned his head towards her. Dappled sunlight stencilled patterns on her face, but he could see the tension in the tightening of her mouth. 'Isabella?'

'Let me put it this way,' she said quietly, without looking at him. 'Radik—'

Jack rolled quickly onto his side to face her. She looked so suddenly distressed he had to butt in. 'He wasn't hurting you, was he?'

'He didn't hurt me physically, but he frightened me.' She swallowed, but kept her gaze strictly on the overhead tree branch. 'I'd been worried for some time about my chances for future happiness. We're nothing alike. Radik likes fast cars and all-night parties and champagne by the bucketload. Cannes is his favourite watering hole.'

'And what about you? What do you like?'

'I like simple things.' As she turned his way she smiled, and her right cheek dimpled.

'Define simple.'

'Oh, going for long walks in the countryside in the late afternoon, when there's a lovely soft glow over everything. Growing my own flowers and baking cakes.'

Jack laughed. 'You should have been a farmer's wife.'

Isabella's smile faded. 'Being born a princess is an accident. It's not necessarily a privilege.'

'Are you saying that you wish you hadn't been born into royalty?'

She frowned and sighed. 'Actually, I'd rather not talk about it. It'll spoil this lovely day.'

'But are you unhappy with your life?'

'Not unhappy, exactly…but… Oh, I don't know. Since my mother died my father's become more remote and pigheaded—'

She broke off and sent him a grimace, as if she felt guilty for betraying the King, but then she added, 'My father's main form of communication these days is to send me orders to attend a formal function or to receive certain guests.'

'Or to marry the Count of Montez?'

'It's very nearly as bad as that.'

'Well—I know all about pigheaded fathers.'

'Do you?' She sat up quickly. 'Will you tell me? Come on, it's only fair, when I've told you so much about me.'

It was damn tempting to tell her. After all, she was a stranger and she wouldn't be gossiping in his social set. But once started he might find himself telling her too much. Everything. 'Not now,' he said.

'Why are you so secretive?'

He sighed. 'There's no need to discuss my life. You have enough problems for both of us.'

Isabella's disappointment showed in her eyes and the drooping set of her mouth. But then she shrugged and looked off into the distance. 'You're right when you say I'd probably make a good farmer's wife. Sometimes I think I should have been born a peasant.'

'Or a gypsy?'

'Yes.' Her eyes met his again. She smiled and her eyes shone and the dimple returned. 'Or a gypsy.'

He felt a sudden catch in his breathing. It had been damn stupid of him to start mentioning gypsies after the trouble talk of Carmen had led to last night.

'Actually, I do have a link to gypsies,' Isabella said. 'In what way?' he asked cautiously. 'Well—according to my nanny, a gypsy woman came into the palace on the night I was born and announced a prophecy.'

'About you?'

'Yes. She said predictable stuff about the baby princess growing up to be beautiful—'

'Well, she got that wrong,' Jack interrupted.

Isabella poked her pink tongue at him and tossed a twig onto his face.

'That's not the interesting bit,' she retorted. 'She said that the princess would have the heart of a gypsy. And you know—I'd forgotten about that until you asked me the other night if I was a gypsy.'

Jack tried to ignore the jolt in his stomach as he stared at her. 'But you don't believe it, do you?'

'I don't know,' she murmured softly. 'I don't suppose so. But the other thing she said is kind of interesting too.'

'What's that?' He might as well ask. She would tell him anyway. But suddenly Jack wished they weren't having this conversation.

To his surprise Isabella looked embarrassed. She bit her lower lip, then sent him a guilty smile and shrugged. 'She said that I would only find lasting happiness in a distant land—a land where the cross hangs in the midnight sky.'

Another jolt flashed through Jack. He leapt to his feet. He'd heard *enough*. 'I suppose you believe messages in tealeaves in the bottom of a teacup, too?'

'You think it's nonsense?' She scrambled to her feet and stood looking at him with a complicated smile that managed to be both defensive and challenging at once. 'Yes, Isabella. I think it's a very pretty romantic story, but it's nonsense.' Without looking at her again, he strode back to the canoe. 'Let's get going.'

When they eventually pulled up at the end of the long day, they headed straight back into the water for another swim. Floating on their backs, they watched the clouds turn pink and gold as the cool water soothed their tired muscles.

And as their meal cooked they sprawled drowsily on the bank, keeping their hunger at bay by munching on dried apple rings.

Jack was determined not to make the same mistake as last night. One kiss was an error of judgement; a second would be

an idiotic disaster. He hunted for practical things to discuss—
something that had nothing to do with gypsies…

'Have you sent any messages back home since you left?' he
asked.

Isabella flopped onto her stomach so she could look at him
while she spoke. The casual movement was unexpectedly graceful. But then everything she did was graceful. All day he'd
been sitting behind her, watching her paddle the canoe, and the
smooth glide and lift of her shoulderblades and arms had been
damn captivating. 'I rang a girlfriend from Darwin airport,'
she told him.

'I didn't tell her where I was. I just asked her to let my father
know I'm safe and well.'

She frowned and threaded her last ring of dried apple onto
her little finger and stared at it. 'The first thing I should do when
we get to Killymoon homestead is make a phone call home. I
never meant to disappear quite so completely.'

'You'll have to be careful,' Jack said. 'Your fiance´ will probably have people waiting for your call so they can trace it.'

She sighed. 'Yes. I guess the palace will be overrun with de-
tectives by now. I'll have to think of someone outside the palace
to ring—perhaps one of the nurses at the hospital.'

Settling onto his side, he dug a bent elbow into the sand and
propped his head on one hand. 'Tell me some more about this
hospital work you do.'

Isabella's eyes signalled mild surprise and she shrugged. 'I
started it in my teens because I wanted to carry on where my
mother left off. Mother was greatly loved by our people. She
was deeply committed to her charity work—especially with the
homeless and the dying.' She smiled wistfully. 'For me, quiet be-
hind-thescenes work seems to make up for all the razzle-dazzle.'

'Of being a public figure?'

'Yes.'

'The dignity of service?'

She shot him a sharp look, as if she feared he might be making fun of her.

'It's deeply satisfying and a privilege to have the opportunity to serve people,' she said defensively. 'I find it incredibly rewarding.'

'What's the most rewarding thing you've done?'

She didn't hesitate. 'When I've spent time with people who are dying alone—people with no family around them. You'd be surprised—even in a tiny country like Amoria there are too many people brought in from off the streets. I like to be there for them, to show them that at least one person cares.'

Jack's jaw dropped as he stared at her. He was sideswiped by a mental picture of this vibrant, young and beautiful girl caring for a dying vagrant. 'That—that's quite something.'

'No matter who a person is, everyone deserves to depart this life supported by an atmosphere of serenity and respect. And love.'

Jack's thoughts flew to Geri, and a welling of pain dammed his throat and stabbed at the backs of his eyes. He swiped a hand over his face.

'I'm sorry, Jack,' Isabella said quickly, her eyes growing luminous with sudden sympathy. 'You probably don't want to talk about this.'

'No,' he insisted. 'It's—it's very interesting. How do you go about establishing this atmosphere of—of serenity?'

She sat up and leant forward, wrapping her arms around her knees. For a thoughtful moment she looked away, watching the flight of a black and white ibis, then she tipped her head to one side and looked back at him with such tender concern that his throat grew tight and painful.

'It depends on the circumstances,' she said. 'Many times it's simply a case of being there and being a calm presence. Holding a hand. Touch can be very reassuring. Some of these people have lived for years without any human contact.'

To his dismay, a strangled gasp broke from his throat. There'd been no comforting hand at the end for his wife. No gentle, peaceful release. Everything about her death had been so unfair.

'Jack?'

He heard Isabella's soft voice, but he couldn't see her.

His eyes were awash.

'Talking about this is upsetting you,' she said.

He closed his eyes and tried to blink them clear. Tried *not* to remember. But the memories forced themselves upon him.

He was back in that dreadful delivery room. Geri was pale and exhausted from her long and difficult labour. And a grim-faced doctor was telling them the harrowing news that their daughter had been stillborn.

Then, while their shock was still at its sharpest and most searing, he was listening in horror as the hospital staff became agitated again and began to talk about a dangerous haemorrhage. Next minute they were rushing Geri away from him to the operating theatre.

He'd hurried after her as they'd dashed her down the long hospital corridor. He'd never forget how alive her red hair had looked, like a startling bright flame against the white pillow. Poor Geri. She'd been so terrified. She'd reached her hand back to him.

He'd touched his hand to hers briefly and then she had gone, where he couldn't follow, disappearing through the swing doors of the operating theatre.

And, God help him, she'd never come back.

'I wasn't there for her,' he said, his voice cracking under the awful weight of his sadness. 'I wasn't there for Geri.'

'Geri?' Isabella whispered. 'My wife.'

'Oh, Jack, I'm so sorry.'

Swinging into a sitting position, he stared blindly at the ground between his feet. 'She died in childbirth. The baby died too.'

Isabella's cry sounded as filled with pain as the weight in his chest.

'I wasn't with her when she died. They took her away and they wouldn't let me go with her.' He was trembling now, shaking with the effort to hold back the force of his emotions. 'I didn't know she wouldn't come back. I refused to believe I might be saying goodbye. I—I didn't even tell her I loved her.'

Suddenly he couldn't help it. He was weeping. Weeping harder than he had in three years. The grief he'd fought so hard to bury claimed him now, and his tears came in painful chunks, like pieces of debris being chipped away from a fossil.

He had no idea when Isabella moved, but he could feel her behind him, her hands on his shaking shoulders and her cheek pressed against the back of his neck, her hands stroking up and down his arms.

'Jack, poor Jack,' she murmured softly, and she looped her arms around him and hugged him. With his back against her, she rocked him gently, silently. And he couldn't stop crying. There was nothing he could do but give in to the racking sobs.

For three years now he'd been carefully hoarding his grief, warding off sympathy, keeping well-meaning friends at a distance. Now he felt as if Isabella had cracked open the hard protective shell he'd drawn around himself.

And it felt perplexingly right to turn into her warm arms, for her to hold him with his head pressed against her shoulder. For her to thread her fingers into the hair at the back of his head and to rub his scalp with a slow, soothing touch.

When at last he managed to get his emotions under control and grow calmer again, he lifted his face and took a huge deep breath. Without a word, she released him from the hug.

She moved to sit beside him once more.

'You mustn't be too hard on yourself,' she said gently. 'It's terrible when there's a sudden emergency. There's so little you can do. You aren't given a chance to say goodbye.'

He wiped his face on his sleeve and looked out at the river, where the moonlit water raced and splashed over a rocky shelf of rock. Isabella remained silent, but her words kept echoing in his head.

You aren't given a chance to say goodbye.

That was the worst of it. He'd been so numb with shock that afterwards, when they'd taken him to see Geri, he'd just stood there in frozen disbelief.

He'd never said goodbye. Not then, nor in the years to follow.

For three years he'd resisted letting Geri go. First he'd drowned himself in drink, and then he'd buried himself in his work—and throughout it all he'd cut himself off from friends and family. He'd been so angry he'd locked himself away, but none of his defences had helped. For three years he'd been living in a half-dead limbo.

Even this week he'd planned at Pelican's End had been an escape from the reality that Geri was gone. He'd been planning to recreate the times they'd spent there together. But perhaps he should have been finding a way to say farewell.

Lost in these thoughts, he was dimly aware that beside him Isabella was standing and walking over to the fire.

'I think our dinner might be ready,' she said.

He sniffed the air and leapt to his feet. 'Struth, it's sure to be done.' He hurried to join her and raked back the coals. 'Just as well you spoke up, or we'd probably be going hungry tonight.'

As it was, their fish was cooked to perfection, but Jack was lost in his thoughts and Isabella was exhausted from her long day on the river. Her eyelids began to droop even before she'd finished her meal.

'I don't think I can stay awake a moment longer,' she said.

'Off to bed with you.' Jack chanced a light kiss on her cheek. 'Goodnight.' As she began to walk away he added, 'And thanks.'

He knew he didn't have to explain what he was thanking her for.

She smiled. 'Goodnight, Jack.' Somewhere in the distance dingoes howled, and she shot a nervous glance to their swags lying in the dark, out of range of the fire's light. 'I still don't enjoy being out in the bush at night. You won't be too far away, will you?'

'I'll be right here,' he told her.

I just need a little time...

Rolling a log over to the fire, he sat there, staring into the mesmerising flames. He needed time to sit and to think about Geri...

And to remember their tiny daughter, Annie—the poor little sweetheart with her cap of fine red hairwho'd never received the gift of life.

For ages he sat there, staring at the red and orange glow, replaying memories.

After Geri's death, despite his rebuffs, well-meaning folk had tried to explain the unexplainable in cliche's, and he'd dismissed their suggestions rudely. But tonight those few words of Isabella's had made sense... He didn't get to say goodbye...

Somehow tonight, out here beneath a million watching stars, the simple fact of Geri's death seemed so much more believable. It was as simple a truth as this river flowing beside him, always moving onwards towards the sea. Like the river, his own life was irreversible. He couldn't go back. He couldn't recapture his life with Geri.

He rose stiffly and dragged another thick piece of timber onto the fire. He watched the blue tongues of flame lick around it, growing bolder and redder. For three years he hadn't been living—he'd been merely surviving.

And yet surely if he'd learnt anything from this tragedy he had to recognise that life was a gift. What was he doing with his? Wasting it?

Throwing back his head, he let out a deep sigh as he stared up at the vast sky, resplendent with its lavish expanse of fiery stars. There was a lot to think about.

Isabella woke just before dawn.

The world was still shadowed and very quiet, although she could hear the sounds of the bush—a bird warbling, the soft ripple of the river running over rocks, the muffled lowing of cattle and the clomping of their hooves somewhere in the distance.

Overhead, a chink of sky between the treetops shimmered with the first pale glow of morning.

Soon it would be daylight.

And today they would reach Killymoon.

By Jack's calculations she'd be with the Kingsley-Lairds by lunchtime, which meant her time alone with him was almost over.

She turned her head so she could look at him as he lay beside her. The pearly pre-dawn light spilled through the treetops and slid under the tarpaulin to etch his profile with a watery sheen. On impulse, she propped herself up on one elbow to improve the angle of her view. Now she could see his rough curls and his strong brow, the thick stubby brushes of his eyelashes, the jut of his nose and the shadow in the little V-shaped valley that ran between his nose and his lips.

His lips!

Oh, mercy. A terrible thrill darted straight to her loins. The other night those lips had ravished hers. They'd swept her away to a sensuous world she'd only dared visit in her dreams. A world of reckless urgency. Delicate surrender.

She would have surrendered. If Jack hadn't stopped kissing her she probably would have gone the whole way with him— had *sex* with him. She, a king's daughter, had almost made love to a man who hadn't even told her his full name.

Even now, despite what he'd told her about his wife, the very thought of Jack making love to her made her burn. She couldn't get the thought out of her head.

No man had ever made her feel so restless and aroused. Never. Certainly not Radik—even though she'd thought she loved him enough to marry him. How strange that it should happen now.

Perhaps she was turning into Carmen. Out here in the Outback—where she had no possessions except one set of clothes, where she bathed in rock pools and used acacia seed pods for soap, where she let her hair go wild and her skin grow tanned—she felt as if she was throwing off a lifetime of restraints.

Losing sight of Princess Isabella?

Heavens, just thinking about how different she felt now made her want to reach out to touch Jack. Her fingers curled impatiently. She could imagine the sleepwarm heat of his skin, the alien roughness of his unshaved jaw, the supple strength of his arms, the springy hair on his bare chest... Oh, help! What about the rest of him? How would *that* feel?

A wave of longing rolled upwards through her, stealing her breath, making her shiver and tremble. Outside the mantle of darkness was fading. It would soon be morning. Jack would wake and jump out of bed. He'd spring into action, busying himself with the tasks of breaking camp.

But she wanted him to stay here beside her...

What would Carmen do if she wanted a man? Wanted him to hold her one more time?

Would she kiss him awake? Isabella leaned closer.

He looked almost boyish as he lay asleep. His lips were soft and relaxed now. The other night they'd been fierce and demanding. Could she make them come alive again? Oh, dear heaven, dared she?

Would he be angry with her?

A slight dip of her head was all it would take.

Her breathing grew fast and shallow and her heart raced as she leaned closer, then lowered her face...

Her hair brushed his cheek. His eyes snapped open.

'Isabella.' In a flash his arms gripped her shoulders, holding her in position, mere inches above him.

'Good morning,' she murmured.

'Morning.' His blue eyes were instantly alert and puzzled.

'I was just—um—checking to see if you were awake.'

He looked over her shoulder to the dawn shadows and lifted one eyebrow. 'So early?'

She gave a shy, twisted smile. 'I was feeling—restless.'

'Restless, Isabella?'

'Yes, very—restless.'

Jack shot another quick glance outside and Isabella felt a punch of dismay. Any second now he was going to become all sensible and businesslike. He would push her aside as easily as he would a sapling branch that blocked his path and jump up and start lighting the fire for breakfast.

She took a deep breath. 'I'm feeling a *Carmen* kind of restless.'

The puzzled wariness in Jack's eyes intensified.

For a long, long moment he held her inches from him. His Adam's apple worked in his throat as he stared hard, as if he needed to be very clear that he'd understood her message.

Then the steely coolness in his gaze melted. His mouth tilted. 'Are you coming on to me, Carmen?'

'Coming on?' She'd never heard the term before, but she was almost certain she knew what it meant.

A dark tinge crept up his neck and along his cheekbones. His eyes were glazed with heat. 'You know what will happen if we start kissing again?'

'Um.' She swallowed nervously. 'Yes. I think I do.'

'Shouldn't you be exercising some royal caution, Your Highness?'

'*No!* No, Jack.' Her impatience was *so* embarrassing. But she was trembling with the need to feel his kiss, his touch.

'No?'

She shook her head.

His eyes burned her as he watched the movement of her hair. He continued to hold her suspended above him while he let his smouldering gaze travel slowly, slowly downwards, to take in the rest of her. Touching her everywhere with his eyes.

Suddenly self-conscious, she remembered that she'd slept

in one of his old grey T-shirts. Perhaps he thought she looked a fright? Then she saw the scorching heat in his eyes. Perhaps not...

'Come here,' he whispered, pulling her down to him.

CHAPTER SEVEN

With excruciating slowness his hands caressed her skin. He kissed her lower lip, then drew it between his teeth and took a teasing, lazy nibble. The tug of his mouth and the silken touch of his fingers caused a sweet ache low inside her. She closed her eyes.

'You're a very interesting woman,' he murmured as he nuzzled her neck just below her ear. 'A man never knows what to expect.'

'And yet I know exactly what to expect from you.' She managed to sound a million times braver than she felt.

'Oh, yes? And what might that be?'

'Perfection.'

He chuckled lazily and tucked a strand of her hair behind her ear, then nipped her earlobe and traced the edge of her jaw with his tongue. Ripples of pleasure shivered over and under her skin.

'Talk about high expectations.' She knew he was secretly pleased.

His lips found her mouth again, and his kiss was hot and sleepy as his hands slid slowly down her arms, then found her hips and the hem of her T-shirt. His fingers toyed with the flimsy cotton, then ducked underneath to trace sensuous circles on her bare lower back and her buttocks.

Her mind almost melted. Already just having him touch her this way was driving her wild. How would she cope when he got to—to details?

She felt a brief moment of panic.

But then she told herself that this wasn't the moment to be afraid. This was what she'd been dreaming about ever since she'd met Jack. If he sensed her fear he might suspect her secret, and she couldn't bear for him to turn away from her now. She'd started this. She had to think and act like Carmen.

Hoping he couldn't see that her hands were shaking, she eased back from him and lifted the T-shirt.

'Oh, my...'

Jack's breath caught and he lost all hope of finding the words to remind Isabella again that this was dangerous. He couldn't even tell her how lovely she was.

The first light of morning crept through the bush, reaching into their tent to touch her skin with a creamy glow, and he wanted to tell her how perfect she was, how very sweet and lush her rosy-tipped breasts, how graceful the curve from her waist to her hip. But his throat constricted on an upsurge of need.

He could only hope that the touch of his hands and lips and body would speak for him.

But easy, man, he warned himself. Take it easy. Their makeshift tent became their world.

They were two warm bodies coming together in a sweet and tender pact. Their thighs entwined. His palms cupped her breasts and she was adrift on a sea of sensations.

She couldn't hold back her soft sighs of pleasure. Beneath the caressing pressure of his hands and his mouth her skin grew warmer and tighter, her limbs heavy with desire. He was so good to her, touching and kissing and tasting every part of her that longed for and needed his loving.

Why had it taken her twenty-five years to discover how impossibly beautiful lovemaking could be?

All sense of panic faded. Instead there was music building inside her. Grand music. Growing stronger, louder, more passionate, pulling her with it, tighter and higher.

From a long way off she thought she heard Jack's voice, whispering how desirable and sexy she was. But it was he who was sexy. He had made her this way. He'd turned her into this sensuous, exultant woman of fire.

And then, too soon, she was falling. But, oh, what a splendid, glorious, trembling fall it was.

'Jack. Oh, Jack.'

His heart drummed as she whispered his name over and over, as she clung to him and kissed him, trailed her soft lips over his jaw.

And he was rocketing out of control. This woman, who had been firing his blood for days now, had lured him to the point of no return. Hot need pulsed through him as he settled her slim hips beneath him.

She smiled up at him and her dark eyes reflected his heat. For a heartbeat he thought he also saw a flash of fear, but she was whispering his name again, wrapping her soft arms and silken legs around him, and he gave up the bitter battle with his conscience as she welcomed him into her sweet warmth.

Shortly before noon their canoe shot around a sharp bend in the river.

'There's Killymoon,' Jack said.

Isabella's stomach took an unexpected dive as she looked ahead at what might almost have been a mirage. A lush green sweep of carefully groomed lawn cut a wide swathe through the smoky grey-green tangle of bush. The lawn formed an emerald-green velvet curve from the riverbank to the top of a rise. On the crest of the slope a long, low house reclined with graceful ease beneath tall, spreading shade trees.

'There you have it—the complete pastoral symphony,' Jack commented dryly.

She squinted beneath her broad-brimmed hat, trying to make out details. The house looked rather grand for an Outback farmhouse. It seemed to be fronted by shaded verandahs with slender white columns. She thought she could make out panelled French doors with timber frames, deep blue storm shutters and large planter tubs spilling with a blaze of bright crimson and white flowers, possibly bougainvillaea.

After days of nothing but wilderness it was a shock to come across such classic signs of civilisation.

Here there would be hot baths and shampoo, comfy beds and clean sheets, milk and fresh fruit and brewed coffee.

'It looks lovely,' she said, turning back to Jack, but her heart stumbled when she saw the grim expression on his face.

All morning he'd been unnaturally quiet and withdrawn. Ever since...

What's the matter, Jack? She couldn't voice the question, but it echoed in her head. Was he thinking, as she was, that once they reached Killymoon there would be no more opportunities for stolen kisses—for making love?

'Let's pull over for a moment,' he said, and immediately matched his actions to his words by dipping his paddle deeply into the water and steering them towards the river's edge.

They slipped the canoe close to a shelf of sandy bank, hidden from the house by a pocket of thick scrub. Jack moored their craft by looping a hank of rope around a broken stump, then jumped ashore. He offered her his hand and the canoe rocked gently in the shallow water as she stepped out of it onto the bank.

She shivered and tried to shrug off a shadowy feeling of darkness, a kind of premonition of deep sadness. How could sadness follow so quickly on the heels of the intense happiness she'd experienced in Jack's arms?

He'd lit an astonishing fire in her. All she'd been able to think of since was how much she desired him. And it didn't feel wrong to want him so fiercely. Loving him had been like opening herself to goodness, embracing a perfect truth.

It didn't make sense that she should feel so low now.

Was her mood a reflection of the bleakness in his eyes?

'What is it, Jack? What's the matter?'

He stared at the ground between his feet. 'This is as far as I can take you. It's time to say goodbye.'

The sandy bank seemed to crumble beneath her. 'But you're coming up to the homestead with me, aren't you? Don't you want to speak to the Kingsley-Lairds?'

'No.'

No? How could he want to leave her so soon? 'Why why not?'

His jaw squared as he avoided her despairing eyes and looked out across the river. 'I have good reasons, but I don't want to expand on them now. Don't ask me to, Isabella.'

Oh, God. Why hadn't she thought this through? They'd never discussed it, but she'd assumed that Jack would stay with her. Somehow she'd kidded herself that her champion would stick by her side till the bitter end. How foolish. That only happened in Hollywood.

Wake up to the real world, Isabella.

'I've never pushed you to tell me anything about yourself, Jack. I guess it's too late now.'

'I guess it is.' He sighed loudly and finally brought his gaze back to meet hers. His eyes were hard, like blue marble. 'Just trust me when I say this is best,' he said. 'I'll hang around to make sure you're OK. If you don't come back in half an hour I'll assume everything is fine. Then I'll head back up the river.'

A shaft of pain strafed through her like a bullet. She wouldn't see Jack again.

It didn't seem possible that this was it. The end. 'It's such a long way for you to go, right back to Pelican's End on your own. You'll be working against the current.'

'Don't worry about me. I'll be all right.'

But I won't be all right, Jack. She couldn't pretend to be cool about his sudden desertion.

Reaching up, she removed his akubra hat from her head and set it carefully on top of the tree stump that moored the canoe. With the hat gone, her hair tumbled down past her shoulders and she saw him flinch. His eyes became dark, brooding storm clouds as he looked at her.

'I wasn't expecting to have to say goodbye so soon,' she said.

He shrugged. 'Sooner or later. It doesn't make a lot of difference.'

'I—I don't know how to begin to start saying thank you. And—and I have absolutely no idea how to say goodbye.'

He forced a weak grin. 'It's only a matter of one little word.'

'How can you be so flippant?'

'Because there's no point in being serious.' After a beat he added, 'Not about us.'

She felt so suddenly ill that she swayed and almost fell into the river. Jack's hand whipped out to steady her and she inhaled sharply when he touched her.

For breathless seconds they stood poised on the edge of the riverbank. His hand at her elbow.

'Isabella, why didn't you tell me?'

'Tell you? What are you talking about?'

'You know.'

Yes, she did. If possible, she felt even more wretched.

She opened her mouth, but she couldn't speak.

'I'm talking about this morning. Don't you think you should have told me you were a virgin?'

Her hand clutched her throat. He was angry with her. He'd been angry with her ever since… She shot him one distressed, desperate glance, then swung abruptly away. But Jack caught her arm again. 'It's a fair question,'

he said more gently. 'Why didn't you tell me?'

Because I wanted you, Jack. Because I think I love you and I don't think I'll ever get over you. I don't think I could ever feel the same about another man.

Her insides were collapsing.

She might have died on the spot from mortification if her years of palace discipline hadn't come to her aid. Gathering her dignity, she squared her shoulders and lifted her chin. 'I was afraid you would reject me if you knew.'

Jack sighed and rubbed a hand over his brow. 'Heck, Isabella, a princess's virginity isn't something to be taken lightly. You shouldn't have thrown it away on a chance stranger. A bloke you hardly know.'

Oh, Jack! She whipped her head to the side so he couldn't see the rush of tears. 'I didn't offer myself lightly,' she said in a small, choked voice.

He groaned. 'Maybe I phrased that badly.' He took a step towards her. 'I'm sorry, Isabella.'

'I'm not sorry, Jack.' This time when she turned back to him she did so without bothering to wipe her eyes. 'I'm twenty-five years old and I don't consider that I've squandered myself. I wanted you, Jack. I claimed the same right that every other woman has. I made a choice for myself.'

Suddenly he was reaching for her, pulling her against him, clasping her tightly to his heaving chest. He pressed his warm lips to her damp cheek, lifted her hair to kiss the curve of her neck.

'You are one very special woman,' he murmured huskily. 'I just need you to understand that what we shared can't lead anywhere. You do know that, don't you? We belong to different worlds.'

She couldn't help herself. His touch made her hollow and shivery. Aching with need for him. She wound her arms around his neck and pressed her body into his and kissed him full on the mouth. His answering kiss was as impassioned and urgent as hers. He tasted of sunshine and the salt of her tears.

He groaned softly, hauling her harder against him. His arms

imprisoned her in an embrace that stole her breath, but then, too soon, he tore his mouth from hers.

'Tell me you understand, Isabella.'

'I don't want to understand.'

'You must.'

With a miserable sigh, she loosened the circle of her arms. 'The only thing I understand for sure is that I've never felt about any other man the way I feel about you.'

'Oh, God. You'll get over this.' His voice was choked and hoarse. 'You'll go back to your world, where you belong, and you'll clear up this current problem and ditch your fiancé. And for sure there'll be some perfect prince waiting for you in the wings.'

She used the backs of her hands to wipe her eyes. 'That's a fairy tale, Jack.'

'No!' he cried, and he flung his arms wide to take in the river, the canoe, the bush. '*This* is the fairy tale. You'll see that when you get back home. To the *real* world.' He gave her shoulder an encouraging squeeze. 'The important thing is to keep your head. Be very careful. Make sure John Kingsley-Laird understands how serious your situation is and that you need to lie low until after Saturday.'

The conviction in his voice and the hard practicality of his advice sapped the last shreds of her hope. Jack really meant it. Their time together was over. In spite of her despair she felt a bleak resignation settle over her. This was it. She was on her own again.

Wiping her face on her sleeve, she drew in a deep, sad breath.

'Now go,' he said, giving her a gentle push. Looking over her shoulder to the right, she saw a narrow track winding through the tangle of scrub. Then she turned back to him and the ferocious blaze in his eyes almost broke her heart.

She tried to smile.

He nodded grimly. 'Good luck.'

Quite sure that her heart was breaking, she slowly began to
walk away from him.

CHAPTER EIGHT

A DOG CAME bounding towards Isabella as she emerged onto the lawn in front of Killymoon homestead. Tail wagging madly, the young golden Labrador sniffed at her legs and circled around her, leaping with doggy excitement.

'Hello, boy.' She gave him a tentative pat and he pranced beside her as she continued up the sloping lawn towards the homestead. As she neared it, a woman came out of the house and stood at the top of the wide stone steps. She shaded her eyes with a raised hand as she watched Isabella's approach.

Framed by her rambling, beautiful home, and dressed in pristine white trousers with a crisp blue and white striped cotton shirt, she looked the epitome of country charm. Her straight silver hair was held back from her classically handsome face by a black velvet band, and she carried a flat cane basket and secateurs as if she'd been planning a little light gardening.

'Buster, come here, boy,' she called to the dog as she watched Isabella's approach.

'Hello, Elizabeth,' Isabella said as she reached the bottom step.

Elizabeth Kingsley-Laird's mouth dropped open. 'It's notIt can't be—'

'I'm afraid it can be, and it is.'

'Princess Isabella?'

As she climbed the steps Isabella lifted the heavy tangle of curls away from her face. 'I'm not surprised that you had trouble recognising me. I'm sorry to arrive unannounced.'

'My dear, for heaven's sake, don't apologise,' Elizabeth cried. 'I'm just so surprised. Good heavens. You're getting married on Saturday. We're all packed to fly off to your wedding.' She flashed a worried glance towards the river. 'Where have you come from?'

Isabella told her briefly about driving her car into the flooded creek.

'Good heavens, dear. Pelican's End is so far away.

How on earth did you get here?'

'By canoe.'

'Canoe?' Elizabeth's jaw dropped. 'It's a long story.'

'I'm sure it must be.' Hastily setting the basket on the ground, she held out her arms to Isabella. 'You poor girl. I mustn't keep you standing out in the heat. Come inside. John's out with the vet today, making some last-minute checks on his prize bulls, but he'll be home later this evening. What a surprise he'll get.'

Walking into Killymoon's sitting room was like entering the private rooms in the Valdenza Palace. Walls in a soft shade of yellow, generous couches, vases of fresh flowers and floors covered by antique rugs created a feeling of refined elegance overlaid by a comfortable and welcoming warmth.

But as Isabella glanced around at the beautiful landscapes on the walls, the display cabinet of antique porcelain and the collection of silver-framed photographs on the table by the window, she felt strangely uneasy to be surrounded by creature comforts.

She glanced down at her broken fingernails, her scratched legs, muddy shoes and crumpled clothes, and grinned ruefully.

She felt as if she'd been living on the river and camping out in the wilderness for months rather than days.

'Let me guess,' said Elizabeth. 'A cup of tea or coffee first and then a long soak in a bubble bath?'

'That sounds like heaven.'

'And then you can tell me your story.'

Jack paddled like a man possessed, hoping against hope that the physical discomfort of pitting his muscles against a strong current might sidetrack him from thinking about Isabella.

It was a vain hope. While every dip of his paddle took him physically further from her, his thoughts held her plum at the centre of his focus.

He couldn't get rid of the memory of the tears in her beautiful dark eyes. They'd shimmered like brave stars when she'd said goodbye. He'd done that to her. She was already in trouble, running for her life from a cad of a fiancé, and he'd caused her more pain.

He cursed himself for his weakness. He should have resisted her. But three years of hard work and anger could only provide a man with limited immunity. He was bound to be susceptible to the appeal of a gutsy, beautiful woman.

But *this* woman? God help him, he'd deflowered a virgin princess! Surely that had to be a sin in any man's language.

Isabella had trusted him to be her knight in shining armour and he'd violated that trust. And the fact that she'd given herself so freely and tenderly didn't make him feel any better.

It was crazy. The last thing, the very *last thing* that should have happened this week was for him to make love to an exotic and attractive stranger. But she was so damn lovely, so warm and lush and willing, and just thinking about her brought a pain to his throat as if he'd swallowed broken glass.

It should have been a cinch to send her packing off to Killymoon, but as she'd walked away from him in her rumpled white shirt, with her dark hair falling past her shoulders, she'd looked so damn beautiful he'd almost called out. *Carmen*. Just in time he'd bitten back on the cry.

And the very minute she'd gone he'd started to worry. All the reasoning that had seemed like common sense before—the assumption that she would be perfectly safe—made no sense at all now.

She'd trusted *him* and she'd expected that he, Jack, would stick with her till all danger was past.

He'd damn well let her down. And he'd lost his peace of mind.

That was the dilemma, he realised grimly. Isabella had come to mean more to him than he cared to admit. When he'd watched her walk away from him into the bush he'd been hit by the thought that he might be losing his best chance of regaining his life.

But that was crazy.

How could he share his life with a European princess? Who was lost in a dumb fairy tale now?

Any way he looked at this it felt bad—a no-win situation. Which was why he kept paddling. And feeling bad.

It was mid-afternoon when Isabella saw the photograph. She and a shocked Elizabeth were in the sitting room, after an exhaustive discussion of her news about Radik, when her attention was caught by the collection of photographs on a nearby table.

'I must take a closer look at your family,' she said, conscious that she'd been talking about herself for too long.

'By all means,' Elizabeth agreed.

The silver-framed photos ranged from old sepia portraits of solemn-looking ancestors in the Victorian era to more recent wedding photos, holiday shots and chubby babies—and towards the back a tall, impossibly handsome young man with spectacular blue eyes.

Isabella's heart thumped sharply. She felt as if she'd stepped off a clifftop into thin air. There was no mistaking that face. Every feature was etched on her heart.

'Good heavens, it's Jack!'

Elizabeth's eyes widened. 'Do you know our son?' Her voice was strangely tight.

'Your *son*?'

'Yes,' Elizabeth said, rising to stand beside her. 'That's John Junior. We've always called him Jack.'

Fighting shock, Isabella darted her gaze to the window and its view of the river. What should she say? It was too late to pretend that she didn't know Jack, but why on earth hadn't he told her he was the Kingsley-Lairds'

son? 'I—I met him at Pelican's End. Jack was the man who helped me to canoe here.'

'Our Jack was *here*?' Elizabeth cried. To Isabella's dismayed surprise, she dashed to the door and peered down to the river. 'Is he still here?'

'I shouldn't think so. He said he would only wait for half an hour to make sure I was all right.'

Elizabeth looked as if she might cry. 'Why didn't you tell me? Half an hour! If I'd known I could have spoken to him. Oh, dear!' She compressed her lips, but a sob escaped.

'I'm so sorry, Elizabeth. I had no idea Jack was your son. He wouldn't tell me his last name.'

He said he wasn't welcome here.

Her hostess sank onto the nearest chair and covered her face with shaking hands. Isabella felt wretched. Taking a seat beside her, she said quietly, 'I probably owe Jack my life. I hate to think what would have happened if I hadn't found him.'

Elizabeth lowered her hands. Her eyes, as blue as Jack's, were now rimmed with red, and they looked unbearably empty and sad. 'How is my boy?'

'He's very fit and well,' Isabella assured her. And then, wanting to take some of the pain from Jack's mother's eyes, she added, 'He was very good to me.' Oh, heavens, given what had happened this morning, that sounded so coy. 'I—I mean he's a *good* man, Elizabeth.'

Speaking about Jack to his mother caused a sad ache to twist like a thorny vine around her heart.

'I suppose you must think we're a strange family,' Elizabeth said. 'And you'd be right. We have one son and we think the world of him. But we haven't spoken to him for five years.'

'What happened?' Too late, Isabella realised how nosy her question sounded. But she'd been so relieved that Elizabeth seemed unaware of her feelings for her son that she'd asked it without stopping to think.

But, unlike Jack, Elizabeth seemed quite willing to talk about their family's problems. 'Jack and his father had a terrible falling out,' she said. 'My husband has some very set, dare I say *antiquated* ideas about the role of wives, and he made some very cutting, thoughtless comments about Geraldine.'

'Is that Geri? Jack's wife?'

'Yes. John found her too unconventional. He wanted a corporate wife for Jack, someone who'd be happy to support him in his career. Someone like me, I suppose. You know—a girl who'd hostess important social occasions but stay in the background most of the time. Unfortunately he let Jack know how he felt— that he considered their marriage to be a poor match.' Elizabeth shot Isabella a sharp glance. 'Did Jack tell you about Geri?'

'He only told me that she died.'

'Yes, poor girl. And I'm afraid her death has made any chance of reconciliation less likely.' She released a long, shuddering sigh.

'I take it Jack resented his father's criticism?'

'Oh, absolutely. And I suspect Jack married Geri in response to his father's opposition rather than in spite of it. All the objections his father raised merely strengthened his determination to marry her.' After a pause she added, 'They're both such alpha males neither of them would back down. Jack refused to have anything to do with us while he was married, and then after Geri died he was so angry and hurt it was worse.'

Drawing a lace-edged handkerchief from her skirt pocket,

Elizabeth dabbed at her eyes. 'In the end Jack set up his own pastoral company, and for the past two and a half years he's been working in competition with his father.' She almost smiled. 'And doing very well, I might add.'

'I'm sure he misses you.'

Elizabeth looked wistful. 'I'm not surprised he came back to Pelican's End. It's always been a favourite spot, ever since he was a little boy.' Her eyes brightened and she sat straighter. 'I'll wait another day or two, until that creek goes down, and then I might drive up there to visit him.'

Around mid-morning the next day Jack heard the rattle of a low-flying helicopter tracking straight up the course of the river.

He stopped paddling and watched the chopper's approach through squinted eyes. The Killymoon brand was emblazoned on its side and it was dropping lower, as if the pilot planned to land on the bare patch of ground on the adjacent bank.

Jack's stomach took a dive. Almost certainly this meant trouble.

The chopper swooped closer and he recognised the man at the controls. His father. Hell! Definite trouble. Only something damn serious would bring John Kingsley-Laird looking for his son. Could the trouble involve Isabella?

At any other time Jack would have wrestled a maneating crocodile rather than face up to a reunion with the old man, but today he paddled madly for the shore and clambered up the bank, reaching the chopper as the rotorblades stopped turning. The door of the cockpit opened.

'What are you doing here?' he yelled.

His father didn't answer. Stepping down from the chopper with surprising ease for a man in his late sixties, he stood for a moment, holding his big body braced as if for battle, while his tanned, lined face remained expressionless. 'Good morning, Jack.'

Jack ignored the greeting. 'What are you doing here?' he shouted again. 'What's happened? How's Isabella?'

John Kingsley-Laird shrugged slowly. 'I heard you were on the property. Thought it was about time we spoke a civil word to each other.'

For half a second Jack almost believed him, but then he saw the wary flicker in his father's eyes, quick as a scorpion's tail. Civil? Yeah, right.

'Good morning, Father,' he said with exaggerated politeness. He waited a beat and then added, 'Now, tell me what's happened. Is Isabella OK?'

John's jaw hardened as he shoved his hands into his pockets and rocked back on his heels. 'I imagine she's fine.'

'You *imagine*?' Jack cried. 'What the hell's that supposed to mean?'

'I'm expecting to hear good news—'

'Cut the bull, Father. What the hell are you talking about?'

The older man shifted uncomfortably and crossed his arms over his chest as if to defend himself. 'Isabella was absolutely fine and perfectly happy last night. But when your mother and I woke this morning she wasn't in her room—or anywhere else around the homestead.'

'She's *gone*? Are you saying you've lost her?'

John cleared his throat. 'We heard a helicopter fly overhead earlier, before dawn, but we didn't take any notice. Thought it was probably a contract mustering team heading for White Gums station. But now—ahwe're wondering if perhaps it was people from Amoria.' Jack groaned and slammed his fist into the palm of his other hand. 'I warned Isabella to be careful. I thought she understood not to speak to *anyone* back at the palace—not until after the wedding day. But she must have told someone. How else could they know where she was?'

John's face took on a greenish cast.

Jack lunged aggressively towards his father. 'What is it? There's something you haven't told me.'

'I—I tried to telephone the King last night.'

'You *what*?' Jack spun away, his hands clenched. God help

him, he'd throttle the old guy if he wasn't careful. Just in time he bit back on an urge to curse or lash out. Losing his head wouldn't help anything.

'For God's sake, Jack, I had to try to speak to him. Your mother and I have been invited to the wedding. We were booked to fly out of Darwin today. I couldn't harbour King Albert's daughter under my roof and say nothing!'

'What did he have to say?' Jack asked quietly. 'That's the problem. I couldn't get through to him.

But as soon as I mentioned I was ringing about Isabella there was a flurry at the other end, and I was put through to some security fellow. He started to quiz me, but I took exception to his questions and hung up.'

'Didn't Isabella explain to you that her fiancé could have had the line tapped? Damn it, he'd probably already tracked her to Australia. All he needed was a precise location. And you gave it to him on a plate.'

John glared at him. 'Well, that may be so, but what's done is done.'

'I've been such a fool. I should have taken her fears more seriously.' Jack flashed a bitter glance towards his father. 'And I should have realised you'd want to do the macho thing and take over.'

Without meeting his son's gaze, John said grimly, 'I've come here because I guessed you'd want to help her, son.'

Son. That one word falling from his father's lips brought Jack up smartly, as if he'd been lassoed. Until now he'd been trying not to think about the huge effort it must have taken for his father to come after him.

Head down, hands in pockets, he kicked at a dried tuft of grass. 'Thanks—Dad.' He shot a sharp glance his father's way and realised with a shock that the old man was struggling to hide emotions as strong as his own.

'I thought you might want to hightail it over there,' John said grimly. 'You've always been a bit—'

'A bit headstrong? Like you?'

A tremor of a smile twitched John's mouth. 'I was going to say you've always had a strong sense of duty. You're quick to take on responsibilities.'

Mouth tight, jaw squared, Jack couldn't resist a challenge. 'What's this? A character reference after all these years?'

'Maybe. Take it as you like. But I know my son and I know you'll do the right thing, even if it means chasing this girl across the world.'

Jack let out his breath slowly. 'Yes, I'll have to go.'

'But you will be careful, won't you, Jack? Watch your step. You don't know what's behind all this.' John drew a white embossed envelope out of his pocket. 'This is the wedding invitation. It might come in handy—especially as we share the same name.'

'Yeah... Thanks.' Jack took the envelope in his left hand and extended his right hand to shake his father's. Over their gripped hands their eyes met, and Jack sensed the possibility that five years of animosity might crumble, given the force of the fierce emotion he felt for this old curmudgeon—the same emotion he saw mirrored in his father's eyes.

John blinked. 'You *will* be careful, won't you, son?'

'Don't worry. I'll be careful,' he said.

'It looks like you're dealing with dangerous people.'

Jack frowned. 'Is there something else you haven't told me?'

'I'm afraid we—er—your mother found a hypodermic syringe on the ground outside Isabella's bedroom.'

CHAPTER NINE

'GOOD MORNING, YOUR HIGHNESS. It's wonderful to see you looking so much better this morning.'

Isabella blinked as a maid swished open her curtains and morning sunlight flooded into her bedroom.

She blinked again...and looked around the room in bewilderment. Tendrils of fear snaked through her.

Nothing was the same as it had been when she went to bed last night. *How odd.* Everything was exactly as it was in her bedroom at home.

The alarm clock she'd had since her thirteenth birthday was sitting on the marble-topped bedside table. The bright silk cushions she'd collected from all over Europe were arranged along the window seat... The oriental carpet on the floor, the smoky-blue velvet curtains and the Tiffany lamp on the antique prayer table in the corner... She looked down at the long-sleeved silk nightgown she was wearing... *Her* nightgown. How was this possible?

How can these things be in Australia? And why is the maid speaking French?

'How did all these things get here?' she asked, pushing the bedclothes aside. 'These are all *my* things. What are they doing here?' She tried to sit up and was hit by a wave of nauseating dizziness that sent her sinking back to her pillow.

'What a strange question,' the maid said, shaking her head and staring at Isabella with a puzzled smile. 'Why wouldn't your things be here? This is your bedroom.'

'But I'm not in Amoria.' She shot a nervous glance towards the window and her heart lurched when she saw a pale European sky and—oh, help—snowflakes drifting against the angular lines of the Valdenza watchtower.

'Of course you're in Amoria, Your Highness.'

Isabella looked at the maid more carefully—at her icy grey eyes and sharp features—and she was quite sure she'd never seen the woman before. 'Who are you?'

'I'm your nurse.'

'My nurse? But I haven't been ill,' she cried. 'I'm as fit as a fiddle. I've been paddling a canoe. I've beenI'm in Australia—I—I don't understand.'

'Australia? Oh, dear, no. You've been ill in bed for days. Don't you remember anything? You've had a dreadful virus. We've all been out of our minds with worry.' The woman came beside the bed. 'Don't try to talk too much.'

'Where's my own maid, Toinette?'

'Toinette's been assigned to other duties.'

Isabella stared at the woman in horror. Toinette had looked after her all her life.

The nurse laid a cool hand on Isabella's brow. 'At least you don't have a fever any more,' she said. 'But you must rest today. You have to get all your strength back so you'll be strong enough for your wedding tomorrow.'

'*Tomorrow?*' Oh, God. Her heart vaulted. Beneath the sheets her legs began to tremble.

'The whole country has been praying for your recovery,' the nurse added with a smile.

'But I'm not getting married any more. I can't. I mustn't.' Isabella ignored the dizziness and forced herself into a sitting position. 'I want to speak to my father.'

'The King is busy at a very important meeting.'

'This early? Get my brother, then. Let me talk to Danior.' She shot an uneasy glance to her bedside table. 'Where's my telephone? What have you done with it?' A foxy caution flashed in the nurse's eyes. 'The Count of Montez suggested it would be best if it was removed while you were so ill. He didn't want its ringing to disturb you.'

'Did the Count hire you?' Isabella asked weakly. 'Of course. He's spared no expense. He's a wonderful, wonderful man. You're so lucky. His one desire is to see you well again.'

'I'm well now. I want my telephone back. I demand it. And I want Toinette.'

The woman's right eyebrow lifted. 'I'll have to consult the Count.'

Slumping back against the pillow, Isabella watched the nurse slip out of the room. But the minute she was gone she swung her legs over the side of the bed and, fighting panic and dizziness, forced herself upright.

Oh, Lord, she felt terrible. Dizzy and weak and swamped by fear. She certainly felt as if she'd been ill. Was it possible? Could everything that had happened in Australia been no more than a weird dream? Was Jack a hallucination?

The idea was unbearable.

She stood up gingerly, using the carved cedar post at the end of her bed for support, and once she was steady, she cautiously set out across the room towards the window. The view from the palace offered a stunning vista, clear across the rooftops of Valdenza to the tiered pine forests at the foothills of the Alps and then the towering mountain peaks.

But it wasn't what she wanted to see. Why wasn't she at Killymoon, looking out to the wide brown Pinnaroo River? She was supposed to be dodging the hot Australian sun by sheltering under a wide-brimmed hat. With Jack.

Oh, dear God, surely he wasn't a dream?

She dropped her anxious gaze to the palace courtyard below. There were people everywhere, scurrying through the snow like busy ants. Liveried footmen, warmly clad household servants, uniformed guards—a host of palace employees dashing in and out of the cloisters, the kitchens or the main entrance hall. And no doubt they all had one thing on their minds. The Royal Wedding.

Tomorrow? How could it be tomorrow? Where had the last two days gone?

A wave of nausea rose to her throat. Her legs trembled and she had to grab at the windowsill for support.

This couldn't be happening. She couldn't marry Radik. She mustn't. She wouldn't.

She turned to the long oval mirror in the corner of her room and shuddered at the sight of her reflection. What was the matter with her? Surely she didn't normally look this pale and fragile? And she'd never had those dark circles under her eyes before.

Was she ill?

Her hair was neatly braided into a French plait. Who had done that?

She felt so confused.

Behind her, the door swung open and the Count of Montez strode into her room with his arms outstretched. 'Darling!'

She shuddered.

Dressed in a dark Italian suit, with his black hair smoothly brushed back and an adoring smile pinned in place, Radik looked the perfect royal fiancé.

'It's so good to see you up and about,' he said warmly, taking her hand.

Isabella felt the room sway and he slipped a solicitous arm

around her shoulders. 'Take it easy, sweetheart. Here, let me help you back to bed.'

'I'm not ill.' She tried to shout, but her voice was as weak and shaky as her legs.

'That's so good to hear, darling heart.' He pressed dry lips to her brow and she automatically cringed away from his touch. 'Poor lamb, you've had a bad time. It's pre-wedding tension. There have been far too many official engagements.'

He patted her hand. 'But you've been a good girl, and now you're much improved. Nevertheless, you need to take the next twenty-four hours in easy stages.'

He steered her back across the room. Then, with unexpected gentleness, he slipped a hand beneath her knees and lifted her onto the bed. Sitting on the edge of the mattress, he assumed an expression of concerned interest.

'I want to speak to my father,' she said, pushing his hand away when he tried to stroke her.

Ignoring her attempts to brush him off, Radik picked up her hand. 'Of course. I've already sent someone to tell the King the good news of your recovery.'

Isabella looked with distaste as his slim pale fingers enfolded hers. Then she looked more closely at their clasped hands and frowned. Her heart gave a strange little jump when she saw the fingernails of her left hand. Two nails were broken and jagged.

I broke my nails on that first day on the river, when I helped Jack to carry the canoe.

Slipping her right hand under the sheet, she made a surreptitious exploration of her leg. Yes! There were scratch marks on her shins. She'd scratched her legs on lantana bushes when she'd been searching for firewood.

I *have* been in Australia.

The quick leap of excitement faded as she realised this meant she faced a new dilemma. How on earth had Radik transported her back to Amoria without her knowing anything about it?

Oh, dear heaven.

Had she been abducted from Killymoon and then flown back to Amoria? But why couldn't she remember? Had she been drugged?

Her heart thrashed against the wall of her chest like a frightened caged bird. That must be it. She'd been given something to make her forget. That was why she felt so disoriented.

The thought horrified her. 'Radik, please send for a doctor. I must see one. I insist.'

'Calm down, Isabella. You've been receiving the very best medical treatment.'

Was her fiance´ holding her prisoner in her own room? The urge to whip her hand away from his touch was strong. She wanted to leap away from him, to tell him she wouldn't marry him if he was the last man on earth.

But then she remembered poor Christos Tenni and the fate he'd met beneath the wheels of a car. Perhaps it was wise to hide that she was frightened and to play along with Radik. She let her hand lie limply inside his.

'I must say I *am* disappointed that my father hasn't come to see me yet,' she said more mildly.

'He was here yesterday.'

'But I don't remember. Why doesn't he come now, if he's been told I'm awake?'

'The King is extremely busy.'

She sighed. 'He always is.' But she suspected Radik had found a way to hold her father at bay.

'He's tied up with important discussions with the EU, but I'm keeping him well informed,' Radik said. 'He understands that you need plenty of rest and he sends you his love.'

'How—how thoughtful.'

'He's proud of you, my dear, and he's especially proud to be attending his only daughter's marriage tomorrow.'

With a supreme effort she fought back another urge to protest.

It was hard to think straight, but she was quickly understanding that she needed to stay as calm and clear-headed as possible.

If she made a fuss Radik might sedate her again. That mustn't happen. It was important to stay lucid. And docile. She mustn't arouse his suspicions.

No doubt he planned to keep her here until the wedding ceremony.

He leaned closer and studied her with narrow-eyed wariness. 'Your nurse mentioned that you've been having very strange dreams. She said you thought you'd been to Australia.'

A hectic pulse beat in her throat as his dark eyes pinned her with a piercing cold light. Her chest grew so tight she could hardly breathe.

'Australia?' She frowned. 'I—I was thinking about Australia when I first woke up this morning. But the nurse explained that I'd been ill and—and I realise now that she's right, of course. I know very well that I've never been there.'

Tension seemed to strain from every pore of his skin, drawing his mouth into a thin, downward curving crescent. 'Are you quite clear in your mind about that, Isabella?'

Now her heart hammered a wild tattoo. It thundered in her ears. How should she answer? Was he hoping that she'd forgotten about Australia? Or did he know that was impossible?

She clutched at the bedclothes for support. 'I—I'm so confused, Radik. This past week is a terrible blur. I'm not sure now if I've dreamt things or if they really happened. Can you tell me exactly what I've been doing? I couldn't have been all the way to Australia and back, could I?'

Radik took ages to answer her question. 'You've been behaving very strangely, but everything will be all right very soon,' he said finally.

His eyes glittered from beneath hooded eyes and his forefinger traced a line from her shoulder up her neck to her ear. The rasp of his fingernail felt as threatening as a knife blade. 'Don't be afraid, my sweet. You've no idea how much I'm looking forward to tomorrow.'

No! It can't happen. I can't marry you! I won't. I won't. I won't.

Her mind swam with fear. How on earth could she call off the wedding now? Why, oh, why hadn't she found a way to contact her father last week, when Christos had first warned her of this danger?

She struggled to force her thoughts into order. What could she do? She didn't know what lies her fiancé was feeding her father and brother, but one thing was clear: he planned to prevent her from gaining access to anyone who could call off the wedding. Which meant she was left with only one terrifying alternative.

I will have to let the wedding take place.

Her hand flew to her mouth to hold back a cry of fear. She would have to wait till tomorrow, till she was inside the cathedral. Only then, when she was standing beside her father and surrounded by the bishops and all the European dignitaries, would she be safe from the Count of Montez. He wouldn't be able to do a thing to hurt her.

She would have to speak up then. Oh, Lord. How would she find the strength to call a halt to a royal wedding? Would the people of Amoria ever forgive her? Would her father?

The very thought of having a showdown in public appalled her. It was utterly preposterous. But what was the alternative?

CHAPTER TEN

FOR THE FIRST time since he'd landed in Amoria, Jack was in luck.

He'd half expected to arrive at the cathedral where Isabella was to be married to find that the Cad of Montez had alerted police and the cathedral staff to send him packing. But when he flashed his parents' invitation beneath an usher's nose he was granted immediate access. Now he was surprised by how calm and quietly confident he felt as he joined the blue-bloods of Europe who were filing up the red carpet and through the huge cathedral doorway.

But there were too many interested glances from the surrounding women. Their heads swivelled so quickly they almost lost their tiaras. It was damn annoying. He was wearing the right clothes—white tie and tails—the same as the rest of the men. Obviously the gene pool for European royalty was so shallow that any new male caused a sensation.

Ignoring their frank, smiling appraisal, and the snooty scowls of the fellows who accompanied them, he followed the usher. His seat was in the middle of a pew, positioned well to the back of the central nave, but it offered a good view of the flower-strewn chancel steps where the ceremony would take place.

As he sat down he looked at the spot where Isabella would stand. And that was when the nerves kicked in.

Beneath his starched collar a film of sweat gathered.

His heart raced and his stomach bunched into knots.

He looked around him and his throat tightened as he studied the gothic splendour of the cathedral's magnificent interior. Soaring vaulted ceilings, huge stained glass windows above the altar, an enormous pipe organ.

He couldn't imagine a more imposing and dignified scene. Not a great setting for creating a scandal.

He prayed for some kind of divine inspiration. Or, better still, divine intervention.

Only a miracle could save Isabella now. A miracle...or *Jack*... But how could he, a mere commoner from Down Under, stop her wedding?

The worst of it was he had no idea of Isabella's condition. How was she feeling? What did she remember? If he could only take hold of her, look into her eyes.

There was so little he could do. And he was so afraid for her.

When the police in Darwin had tested the syringe his parents had found, they'd reported that it contained traces of hypnotic drugs, including scopolamine—a drug thieves used to rob unsuspecting tourists.

But the Amorian police hadn't believed Jack's claim that their princess had been abducted from Australia.

'That's impossible! Her Royal Highness hasn't been out of the country,' they'd insisted. 'In fact she's been ill and confined to the palace since last Friday.'

He had created a scene. Which hadn't helped matters. The police had decided he was a crazy ratbag from Down Under and had thrown him out with a warning. And there'd been no chance of support from the palace. Isabella's fiance´ seemed to have total control of the situation, and all Jack's efforts to make any kind of contact with the King or Prince Danior had been blocked.

Now he scanned the members of the congregation in the pews around him and tried to identify the people trained to intercept anyone approaching the Princess. Security would still be tight. There were sure to be operatives discreetly positioned amongst the wedding guests.

Normally a church could be relied on as a sanctuary, where weapons were not allowed, but there were so many Heads of State and VIPs present that Jack suspected that with one wrong move he could be shot.

Isabella was ready.

The princess bride—dressed in a breathtakingly beautiful gown of silver French brocade. Her dark hair was threaded with orange blossoms and she wore a medieval veil held in place by her mother's diamond tiara.

Diamonds sparkled at her ears, around her neck and on her breast. In her arms she carried a bouquet of white lilies of the valley, floral symbols of virtue and fertility. Every detail of her appearance spelled royal romance.

And, although she hadn't yet seen them, she knew that in the adjacent rooms her six bridesmaids were ready and waiting, dressed in white gowns of silk organza and carrying armfuls of snowy white roses.

In the palace ballrooms in the West Wing, the Master of the Household would be delivering a final briefing to the underbutler, the wine-butler, the pages and the footmen, to ensure that the wedding breakfast would be served with the precision of a military manoeuvre.

In front of the palace steps open carriages were lined up, waiting to take her and her attendants through the streets of Valdenza past cheering citizens. To the cathedral.

And all Isabella could think of was Jack.

She longed for him. Longed for him with an ache that brought a sharp pain to her chest and tears to her eyes. All night she'd tossed and turned, reliving every moment of their adventure on the river...remembering again the sexy warmth of his mouth... the heated mystery of his touch...the wonder of his hands gliding over her skin...the soul-shattering passion of their bodies joining in intimate communion.

She *loved* him.

Not merely because he'd rescued her and protected her. And made love to her. She loved the man. And she loved the person she became when she was with him.

Now, as she stood at the window in her wedding gown, taking one last look at her beloved city, the lilies in her arms trembled.

Jack heard the sound of deafening cheers outside the cathedral. It meant that Isabella had arrived. His heart pounded. Hot and cold chills chased up and down his spine. The cheering of the crowds swelled to a roar. His stomach clenched tighter and he reached into his trouser pocket for a handkerchief to mop his brow.

All too soon, another fanfare of trumpets announced the bride's arrival at the cathedral door. The congregation rose. A sea of heads turned towards the main entrance.

Organ music filled the cathedral and Jack's breath seemed to drain from his body as he turned and saw Isabella framed in the cathedral doorway. She looked so beautiful his mouth turned dry as dust. But she looked different—palely luminous, ethereal, other-worldly—as if she was walking in a dream.

His heart thumped like a locomotive piston. How had his week of solitude in the hut at Pelican's End brought him to *this*?

Isabella wished for numbness. She didn't want to feel anything. Not this awful fear. Not this ghastly sickness in her stomach. The trembling trepidation in her limbs, the dryness in her mouth and the shocking, panicky interruptions to her breathing.

Her attendants were making her even more anxious as they whispered and fussed nervously with her dress and train. She forced herself to drag in a long, deep breath and to let it out slowly. The deep breath helped a little, and she repeated the process.

Perhaps that was what she should do to keep her terror at bay. She should focus on her breathing. On that and nothing else.

That way she could close herself off from the hundreds of watching eyes. She would take two steps while she breathed in…another two as she breathed out.

Slow breathing and steady steps…they would propel her down the aisle.

'It's time to go, Your Highness.'

Oh, help! This was it. The moment she'd been dreading. Her father was waiting for her halfway down the aisle. In accordance with Amorian tradition, she had to make the first part of the journey by herself. She drew in a breath and forced a shaky foot forward. *Don't look to the left or right. Breathe in…* She stepped inside the cathedral. *Breathe out…*

It was happening. She was moving down the aisle towards her father. *Mustn't think. Just breathe. Don't think.*

Around and above her the loud organ music swelled to a crescendo. *Breathe, and then take a step.* The procession continued, and in what seemed like no time at all there were only two more steps till she reached her father. It seemed like years since she'd seen him. He held out a hand to her.

'Hello, my dear.' His voice was rich and low, softened by emotion.

Was he smiling? She couldn't tell. Her vision was blurred by the sudden rush of tears to her eyes.

Her father stepped closer, took her arm and slipped it through his, ready to progress with her to the very front of the cathedral. To Radik.

Isabella stood still.

'Let's go,' the King murmured.

Her heart seemed to stop, but then it picked up pace and began to thunder in her ears. 'No,' she whispered.

She felt rather than saw her father's frown. Then the pressure of his hand around her arm tightened and he tried to guide her forward. 'Come on, Isabella.'

'No.' Oh, God. Was she strong enough to stand up to this man? He'd dominated and ruled her life. 'I'm not going any further,' she said. 'I can't marry Radik.'

She felt the sudden tension in him. A terrible stillness. Felt fear as the grip on her arm turn to steel. 'Isabella, pull yourself together.' The King forced the command through gritted teeth.

'Father, please don't make me go any further.'

'What's come over you? This is nonsense.'

In spite of the loud organ music she heard a rustling of confused whispers spreading through the rows of people on either side of the aisle.

She looked down the nave and saw Radik at the front of the church. He was frowning, staring back at them with an intent, hard look.

'Are you still feeling ill?' the King asked, a little more kindly, almost hopefully. 'Lean on me.'

'I'm not ill, Father. I'm sorry to do this to you, but I have no choice. I refuse to be married today.'

Another frantic glance towards Radik showed her that his face had grown red. He looked as if he was about to charge down the aisle towards her. Did she have to shout her refusal? Could Radik and her father force this wedding?

There was a momentary pause in the music and she heard a different sound, a swelling of surprised, excited murmurs. And footsteps. Men's raised voices. A scuffle?

Then came the sound of another voice. A familiar voice calling, *'Carmen!'*

A tremor shook Isabella from head to toe. 'Jack?'

Was she dreaming? How could Jack be here? The last time she'd seen him he'd been about to paddle back to Pelican's End.

Swinging out of her father's grasp, she turned. *And saw him.* He was making his way down the aisle towards her, dragging two security guards as if they were nothing more than angry, snarling terrier pups attached to his clothing.

Jack. His blazing blue eyes were fixed on her. He looked fiercely determined. He looked wonderful. Surrounded by a scattering bevy of shocked, pale bridesmaids, he looked fabulously suntanned. Gloriously out of place.

Isabella was shaking—stunned—happy and scared at once.

'This is outrageous,' the King cried. 'Guards, arrest that man!'

'No!' shouted Isabella.

The aisle was filling with men in uniform. 'No!' she shouted again.

The organ music stopped abruptly on a discordant note. Heart racing, Isabella lifted her heavy skirt and began to hurry back down the aisle towards Jack. She was aware of a shocked collective gasp from the congregation. And the King hurrying after her.

Throwing a frantic glance back over her shoulder, she saw Radik storming after her father. And, behind him, a startled bishop.

The urge to hurl herself into Jack's arms was overwhelming. She wanted to fall against his shoulder and cling to him, to feel the lovely solid strength that she'd always found in his arms.

But he was in the fierce grip of security men and it was impossible. Their eyes met, and Isabella felt an exquisite thrill tremble through her.

'Who are you?' King Albert demanded, glowering at Jack.

Despite the strong hold of his captors, Jack squared his shoulders. He met the monarch's enraged glare with a level, cool gaze. 'Your Majesty, I'm Jack Kingsley-Laird,' he said, speaking in English.

'John and Elizabeth's son? From Australia?'

Her father's eyes narrowed as he darted a swift glance towards Isabella and then focused once more on Jack. 'And what is the meaning of this unforgivable disruption?'

'Your daughter needs my help, sir. And yours.'

'What absolute nonsense.'

'Please ask her,' Jack insisted.

'It's true, Father,' cried Isabella. 'I must talk to you.
I can't—'

'Don't listen to them.' Radik elbowed his way into the middle of the gathering. Beneath his slick black hair his face was as white and cold as a snow-covered mountain, and his entire frame quivered with anger as he pointed an accusing finger towards Jack. 'I demand that this criminal be thrown out of here and that the ceremony continues immediately.'

Isabella felt dizzy as she looked around at the circle of faces—at Jack's bristling determination, at her father's dismayed disbelief and the bishop's shock. At Radik's fury.

'It's too late, Radik,' she said quietly, but her heart was beating so wildly she feared she might faint. 'I'm not going to marry you.'

Horrified gasps seemed to echo in waves through the cathedral.

To the King, she said, 'Please, Father, you have to stop this wedding. I can't go ahead with it.'

'But, Isabella—'

'Please,' she insisted, more forcefully. She didn't dare look at Radik again.

'Are you sure?' the King whispered.

'I'm sorry, Father, but, yes, I'm very, very sure. I can explain.'

For an interminable stretch of time no one moved or spoke. But then the King nodded slowly. 'Very well,' he said, his gaze resting briefly on Isabella, then for a longer time on Jack. Finally he looked towards Radik. He frowned and shook his head. 'We had better discuss this in the vestry.'

To the bishop, he said, 'I'm sorry, your Grace, but you'll have to announce a short adjournment of these proceedings.'

By the time Isabella and Jack had told their story to King

Albert he looked like an old and defeated man—lost and bewildered.

'How could Radik have deceived me?' he murmured, shaking his head sadly. 'I had such high hopes for him. He had such interesting schemes for our estates.'

The King sat staring into space for several long minutes, but at last he snapped out of his gloom and became businesslike again. 'I can see I have no choice,' he said. 'The ceremony must be cancelled. The bishop will have to handle that.'

Isabella closed her eyes as relief washed through her. Her father rose stiffly to his feet. 'This has been a direct attack on the royal household. Radik must be brought in. I need to talk to my chief of police about poor Dr Tenni's death.' He crossed to the vestry door. 'And I'll need the palace secretary to handle the fall-out from this crisis.' He sighed deeply. 'What a mess. The guests will go into turmoil.'

'I'm sorry, Father. If I had been able to contact you straight away we could have called this off a week ago.'

His eyes regarded her sadly, but he didn't give her the absolution she longed for.

How silly of her to think that this morning's revelations might have softened her father's attitude. He hadn't changed. There was every chance he would never realise that this morning's fiasco mightn't have happened if he'd been more willing to talk to her—if he hadn't been such a difficult man to approach, even at the best of times.

He went to the door to speak to the guard posted outside and Isabella turned quickly to Jack. Throughout this session she had been greedily stealing chances to look at him—admiring the distinctive jut of his nose, the familiar, unsettling gleam in his blue eyes, the darkness of his skin, tanned by his life in the Outback, the grave, straight line of his mouth.

Having him here now made up for every horror she'd suffered. She longed to be alone with him, to feel his reassuring touch, to thank him for coming so bravely to her rescue. But he remained remote, sitting some distance away from her and paying her no more than polite attention. She felt the gap between them keenly.

'Isabella,' came her father's voice, snapping her out of her reverie. 'I think it's time you went back to the palace now. There are matters I need to discuss with Mr Kingsley-Laird.'

Matters to discuss? What matters? I need to talk to Jack, too. She was being dismissed like a child.

'Run along, my dear,' the King said.

Her nervous fingers pleated the stiff silver brocade of her skirt and she looked hopefully towards Jack. But he was watching her father with a disturbingly grave expression.

'Does this discussion involve me?' she asked, forcing her chin defiantly high.

The King's jaw dropped as if he couldn't believe that his normally submissive daughter had questioned him. 'It does,' he said.

Until that moment she had thought that the worst was over. She had been feeling almost normal again. But now she felt a fresh stab of dismay.

'Then I'd like to stay.'

On the other side of the room Jack made an uncomfortable throat-clearing sound, and when she darted another look his way he frowned at her and shook his head. He was dismissing her too!

This was too much! Why did she have to live her life surrounded by men with god-complexes? She wanted to stamp her foot, to throw a tantrum. 'Surely I'm entitled to know what you're going to discuss about me?'

The King sighed loudly. 'How can you be so obtuse, Isabella? From what I've heard of your time in Australia, and from what I've seen with my own eyes this morning, it's clear that I need to ask Mr Kingsley-Laird about his intentions.'

She gasped.

Jack flinched as if he'd been slapped in the face. The muscles in his throat worked. 'My intentions?' he repeated faintly.

'Exactly,' replied the King. 'You've come from the other side of the world to hijack my daughter's wedding.

I understand that your prime motive was Isabella's safety, but I can't believe you would have gone to such lengths if you didn't have strong feelings for her.'

A wave of embarrassing heat flooded Isabella and she closed her eyes. How could her father do this? He was putting Jack through hoops like a suitor caught in a compromising situation. She felt wretched—as if she'd unwittingly led her valiant rescuer into a trap.

The King hurried on. 'My daughter spent several days alone in your company. I'm sure there are things about this relationship that I should know.'

'Father!' she cried, so horrified and embarrassed she wanted to slide under the carpet. 'I think you're jumping to conclusions.'

'Am I?' the King demanded. His eyebrows rose as he shifted a shrewd glance from one to the other. 'Am I?' he repeated.

Jack cleared his throat. 'Your Majesty, Isabella and I haven't discussed—er—I mean—regarding my intentions, I haven't—' He broke off.

Isabella covered her face with her hands. She couldn't bear this. Jack had rushed over to this country to save her. But that didn't constitute *intentions*. Not the kind her father was suggesting. Not a marriage proposal.

Heaven knew, she'd been thrilled beyond belief to see him in the cathedral. Her first thought had been that he loved her as fiercely as she loved him, that he'd come all this way to do more than rescue her. To declare his feelings.

But now the granite-hard look on Jack's face told her that she'd been overly romantic to imagine he loved her.

He hadn't changed his mind since they'd parted at Killymoon.

She couldn't bear to listen while he told her father about his *lack* of intentions. It would be easier for everyone if she wasn't present.

'Perhaps I *should* leave,' she said in a small, tight voice.

The men eyed each other solemnly, then nodded. With a choked, angry cry, she rushed out of the room.

The King's lips pursed thoughtfully as he watched the door swing shut. His eyes met Jack's. 'I must ask you to put yourself in my position,' he said. 'I've had a shock this morning. I've learned that I've let down my only daughter rather badly. I didn't see what lay under my very nose. Isabella had to cross oceans to find safety and it took a total stranger to come to her rescue.'

'The circumstances—' Jack began, but the King cut him off with a flourish of his hand.

The royal complexion darkened. 'Since my wife died I haven't been a good father.'

Wisely, Jack didn't comment. He was thinking of the pain in Isabella's eyes when she'd left.

'Radik might have pulled the wool over my eyes, but I had both eyes wide open this morning,' King Albert continued. 'I saw you struggling with those guards in the cathedral, but I didn't sense threat or anger from you. All I saw was concern for Isabella. And desire. And there was the same response from my daughter.'

'Your daughter is a wonderful person, sir.'

'If I achieve nothing else,' her father said, 'I want to ensure her ongoing safety and happiness.'

'Yes.' Jack managed to squeeze the word past the tightness in his throat. 'That's very understandable.' Feeling like a guilty criminal, he dropped his gaze. He wanted to assure Isabella's father that his intentions were honourable, but right at this moment it was hard to get his thoughts past the fact that he'd stolen her virginity. And on that very same day he'd abandoned her.

Did he have the right to offer her ongoing safety and happiness? Was he any more worthy of her than the Cad of Montez?

'I'm an Australian, and a mere commoner,' he reminded the King.

'I'm aware of that, but it's most unlikely that Isabella will ever ascend to the throne. And you come from fine stock.' A flicker of a smile tweaked King Albert's mouth. 'Your family is about as high up the gum tree as Australian society tolerates, isn't it?'

Without waiting for an answer he stepped forward and slapped Jack on the shoulder. 'But perhaps I'm jumping the gun. You said that you and Isabella haven't discussed your plans. Well—go after her and talk to her. I'll give you till this evening.'

'This evening, sir?'

'You can come to the palace for dinner and I'll expect your answer then.' Turning abruptly, King Albert opened the door, and immediately the swarm of people waiting outside clamoured to speak to him. Over his shoulder he said to Jack, 'I dine at eight.'

CHAPTER ELEVEN

ISABELLA LAY IN a wretched huddle on top of her bedspread, dressed only in her petticoat and surrounded by a sea of sodden, crumpled tissues.

A maid tiptoed into the room. 'Your Highness,' she said softly, 'are you receiving visitors?'

Isabella moaned. 'No-o-o! I've told you, I can't possibly see anyone.'

She wanted to stay in this darkened bedroom for ever, away from prying eyes, wrapped in misery. Surely after everything she'd been through she deserved a good long cry? She was so angry with her father. The man had the sensitivity of a bulldozer. How could he have thrown those blunt questions at Jack? Couldn't he see that he was forcing the poor man into a corner?

And what on earth was he plotting? Why did she have to have a king for a father? Oh, God, already she was losing control of her life again.

The maid hovered uncertainly by the bed. 'Do you want me to deliver a message, Your Highness?'

Isabella groaned impatiently. Where was her *old* maid? Toinette would know what to do without asking these endless, tiresome questions.

'No, there's no message,' she cried, reefing another tissue from the box and blowing her nose loudly. 'Just offer my apology, say I'm indisposed and send any visitors away.'

Perched on the edge of an antique sofa in the Princess's sitting room, Jack eased his stiff collar away from his neck. He'd come straight from the cathedral to the palace without changing out of his formal clothes and his tie was strangling him. Nerves bunched in his stomach, and with a restless sigh he rose and crossed the Wedgwoodblue carpet to the window.

Outside snowflakes drifted down from a pale, chilly sky. He thrust his hands deep into his trouser pockets and flexed his shoulders as he watched the snow spread lacy shawls across the ancient cobbled courtyard. Beyond the palace gates the snow glittered over the winter-grey city, covering Valdenza's landscape with spotless beauty.

It was as pure and white as Isabella had been when she'd entered the cathedral this morning. His throat stung as he remembered how unbelievably beautiful she'd looked.

He'd been terrified as he watched her take those first steps down the aisle. Terrified that she was heading to her doom and that he would be powerless to help. But what had terrified him most was the discovery that Amoria's beloved Princess Isabella had broken through the careful wall he'd built around his heart. *He loved her*.

He'd been working hard to deny it—it was totally inappropriate—but he *loved* her. His lovely, courageous, gypsy princess had brought him back to life—brought him the happiness he'd considered forever lost.

He loved her in spite of his fears—in spite of the horror of losing Geri and his unwillingness to risk the pain of losing his heart to another woman.

No doubt it had happened long ago—long before that fateful

morning on the riverbank when they made love. Perhaps he'd fallen for her right back on that very first night in the hut...

All he knew now was that he was deeply, irreversibly in love. And she was safe. And her father had asked a question he hadn't been prepared to ask himself.

What *were* his intentions?

A soft groan broke from his lips and a horrible heaviness grew inside him as he stared at the snow-covered landscape. How could he ask Isabella to leave all this? Her homeland was like a grand old lady—dignified and genteel and steeped in tradition.

He couldn't imagine a scene more different from the hard red Outback of Northern Australia. By comparison the unkempt country where he spent most of his time was as rough and untamed as a badly brought up youth.

What could he offer her besides complications?

If he asked her to marry him he would have to ask her to divide her time between two countries...two worlds...two allegiances...

A sound behind him brought him whirling around, and his heart thudded as he turned to greet her. Would he find the right words to convince her?

To his surprise he saw that it was only the plain little servant who'd come through the doorway. She was looking very glum and shaking her head at him.

Isabella lifted her head from her damp pillow and tried to look grateful as the maid placed a cup and saucer carefully on the bedside table. 'Thank you.' She sniffed.

The girl stood by the bed, her hands plucking at her apron. 'I hope you don't mind, Your Highness, but there's a gentleman caller who won't take no for an answer.'

Isabella's head snapped up. 'Gentleman? What gentleman?'

'He said he was your doctor, and he insisted he *must* see you.'

'My doctor?' Isabella repeated, frowning at the girl. 'I don't understand.'

The maid's eyes grew round. 'I must say I thought it was strange for you to have a foreign doctor, ma'am.'

'A foreign—' An alarmed kind of excitement skittered through her. 'What—what kind of foreigner is he?'

'I'm not sure. He speaks English, but he doesn't sound English, if you know what I mean.'

'Oh, good heavens, it must be Jack!' Isabella leapt to her feet and grabbed the maid by the elbows. 'Are you telling me Jack's here? In the palace?'

The girl looked frightened. 'He called himself Dr Kingsley-Laird.'

'Oh, my God!' Isabella's heart crashed against her chest like a wave breaking on a sandbar. 'Where is he now?'

'I'm afraid he's right outside this door.'

She dashed towards the door, but halfway across the room she caught sight of herself in the mirror. Her nose and her eyes were red and swollen and her cheeks were streaked with mascara. 'Oh, no! I look like a scarecrow after a hailstorm.'

Spinning around, she headed instead for her bathroom.

'Tell him I'll be ready in five minutes.' Her mind was whirring so wildly she couldn't grasp at a single thought before it slipped away again.

Why had Jack come? What had he told her father? Oh, dear, her father hadn't forced him to come to her, had he?

Her hands shook as she cleaned the make-up from her face and tried not to think about the closed, wary look on Jack's face when her father had asked him his intentions.

She splashed her skin with cold water, desperate to flush away the evidence of her tears. With frantic, trembling fingers she tugged the orange blossoms from her hair, then dragged her brush through the tangles with savage thrusts, not caring how much it hurt.

What had Jack come to tell her? It couldn't possibly be good news, could it? She was sure her feelings for him would never be returned.

In her bedroom again, she threw open her wardrobe doors and began to hunt through the racks of expensive garments, searching for the right thing to wear. What would Jack like? Oh, dear heaven.

Behind her, the door opened.

'Your five minutes are up,' said a deeply masculine voice.

Her hands flew to her chest as she whirled around. Jack strode into the room, looking so tall and splendid she wanted to throw herself into his arms. *But she had no idea why he'd come.*

'I—I'm not quite ready,' she stammered, feeling foolish as she stood there with her arms crossed over the lace-trimmed neckline of her silk petticoat.

He flashed her a fleeting, crooked smile. 'A petticoat is an improvement on my old shirt.'

Her attempt to return his smile was even more shaky than his. 'It's very impertinent of you to barge into my bedroom under false pretences, *Doctor.*'

'I had to see you.'

'Your talk with my father—the discussion I wasn't allowed to hear. What did he say? Has he sent you here?'

'Well—sort of—I mean no, Isabella. The King did tell me to come to speak to you, but I—I wanted to come anyway.'

Did you, Jack? His words brought a momentary rush of relief, but her hope faded when she saw how strained and tense he still looked—as formidable and rock-like as the cliffs that stood sentry over the Pinnaroo River. It wasn't the look of a man who had come to her willingly or gladly.

It was how he'd looked when they'd parted at Killymoon.

Despite her scanty clothing, she tried to look dignified as she pointed to the sofa on the far wall. 'Please take a seat. Just push the cushions aside.'

She chose the small chair that stood in the corner and felt as tense and scared as Jack looked.

They stared at each other across the room. Isabella dampened her dry lips with her tongue. 'I haven't thanked you for what you did this morning. You can't imagine how relieved I was to hear you call out to me in the cathedral.'

He smiled again, but he didn't look any more relaxed. 'I had to come. I couldn't have sat there at Pelican's End once I'd learned that you'd been drugged and kidnapped.'

'How did you find out? Did your parents contact you?'

He nodded. 'Perhaps the one good thing that's come out of this is that my father and I are talking again.'

'I'm so pleased.' She took a deep breath. 'Is that the only good thing, Jack?'

'You're safe from Radik. That's the very best thing.'

'Yes.'

She rubbed her arms. Her room was heated but she felt suddenly cold. 'You must forgive my father's bossiness,' she said, anxious to fill any gaps in the conversation. 'He's so used to giving orders on a daily basis that he forgets he shouldn't boss people around in his personal life.'

'The poor man's had a major shock this morning. You can't blame him for quizzing me when I came charging after you from the other side of the world.'

'He didn't expect you to tell him—about—?'

His eyes seemed to pierce her. 'About personal details of our time together?'

She nodded, and hoped that the blush she was feeling didn't show.

'No, Isabella.'

'But he wants to know your intentions?' Her hands twisted nervously on her lap.

'Yes. And he's expecting my answer by dinner this evening.'

'This evening?' She knew she sounded frightened and she looked away from him, concentrating instead on a crushed orange blossom that had fallen to the floor. 'What—what have you told him so far?'

'I couldn't in all conscience discuss such a private matter with anyone else when I haven't discussed it with you.'

'But you have, haven't you?' Sudden tears stung her eyes and she blinked them away. This was awful.

Her heart raced, and although she didn't lift her gaze she sensed his escalating tension. He was sitting very stiffly on the edge of the sofa.

'I haven't—'

'It's OK, Jack,' she cut in, stopping his words with an out-stretched hand. 'I understand that you don't have *intentions*. Not the kind my father was hinting at. You came here to help me because you're a good man—a *gallant* man—but I know you have no plans for our future. You explained it all at Killymoon. So it's OK; you don't have to say it again. I'd rather you didn't. You can go. I'll tell my father that you came here, as he asked, and that you spoke to me and—and that everything's settled.'

Jack was on his feet, crossing the room. 'Isabella, stop babbling and give me a chance to speak.'

'No!' she cried. 'It's all right. You don't need to. It was only a matter of days ago when you stood on the riverbank and told me *exactly* why we have no future. You said we come from two different worlds. I understand that, and if you don't mind—I'd rather not hear it again.'

'Not if I've changed my mind?'

Her head shot up. 'What?' Jack's blue eyes were shimmering. He was looking at her with a strangely twisted, almost sad little smile.

'My dear girl, I came here to ask if you'd do me the great honour of marrying me.'

Oh, no, Jack, no. Not now. Not like this.

Suddenly ill, she dropped her face into her hands. *Now she knew why he'd looked so scared. This was terrible.*

'Isabella?'

It was wrong, so wrong. Her father had ordered Jack to propose. She hadn't even finished changing her clothes after one disastrous interrupted wedding, and already another poor man was being pressured into marrying her.

'I—I thought you cared for me,' he said, standing close beside her chair.

'I do, but—'

His hand reached down and he touched her cheek gently. 'You know I need you.'

Yes…she knew that from the way he'd made love to her. But he'd loved her with the unleashed passion of a man who'd been too long without a woman. That didn't mean…

'Carmen,' he whispered. 'Don't call me that.'

'I know it won't be easy for you to adjust to the kind of marriage I'm offering. We'd have to find a way to merge our two completely different lifestyles. But I think we could do it. I have a very comfortable house in Perth. I can appoint someone to take over many of my current responsibilities, and now that my parents and I are reconciled—'

'Don't, Jack, please.'

'Don't *what*?' he cried as his hands closed around her arms and he hauled her to her feet.

Their faces were inches apart and her heart rocked wildly. *Don't ask me to marry you because you think you must—to do the right thing.*

'Don't make an emotional commitment sound so business-like and so—so *logical.*'

She heard the impatient rasp of his sigh. He picked up a loose curl of her hair and rolled it between a finger and thumb. Her breathing seemed to stop as he stared at it. 'OK, let's drop the logic,' he murmured, threading his hand more deeply into her curls, taking a big handful of hair and drawing her head back so that her face was tilted to his.

How could she resist Jack? How could she hold back from the seduction of his warm, sexy lips—or the taste of him— that heady, familiar flavour that was purely Jack? Against her will she felt her body stirring—stomach tightening and limbs melting.

But, no. No! She was too easily seduced by this man. It would be bliss to give in to him. But she mustn't. She'd learned a hard lesson from her narrow escape with Radik. When she'd been engaged to him there'd been no talk of love, and now Jack hadn't mentioned it either.

Her heart felt as if it were breaking as she stiffened in his arms.

'Isabella, what's the matter?'

She longed to tell him. It would be so simple to say *I need you to say that you love me.* But if she had to ask…

Pride held her tongue. Pride and common sense. She might be able to induce Jack to say the words, but it would be as bad as her father persuading him to come to her.

Jack couldn't love her the way she needed him to. He'd told her how very deeply he'd loved Geri. If he felt that way now he would have said so, without having to be asked.

The knowledge was killing her. 'What is it, Isabella?'

'I'm sorry, Jack.'

'Sorry?' She felt him freeze with shock.

'I don't want you to kiss me. I want you to go away.'

'You don't mean that.'

'Yes, I do.'

'Are you sure?'

She opened her mouth to say yes, but the word wouldn't come out. Pressing her lips together, she nodded.

'Say it, Isabella.' His voice was rough, choked. Angry. 'Say the words. Tell me you won't marry me. Tell me to leave.'

The tears she'd been trying so hard to hold back forced their way into her eyes. 'Please,' she whispered.

'Say it.'

'Please…leave.'

'But you're crying. I don't understand.'

Go, Jack, go. Go now, before I break down and make an utter fool of myself.

She drew in a deep, shuddering breath, gathering just enough strength for this last ordeal. 'I'm very grateful for *all* your help.

I really am. But I'd like you to leave now.' Feeling ill and icy cold, she forced herself to cross the room to the door. 'I'll give Father your answer,' she said softly as she opened the door. 'I'll explain.'

Please, don't look so shocked.

He looked pale beneath his tan. 'Is this goodbye, Carmen?'

'Yes. Goodbye, Jack.'

Slowly, *too slowly*, he walked towards the door. She heard the tortured rasp of his indrawn breath as he passed her, and the sharp click as he closed the door behind him, and then her tears began to fall.

'More coffee, sir?' The airline flight attendant leaned over Jack, brandishing a coffee pot.

'Thanks,' he muttered, raising his cup to be refilled, although he doubted that an overdose of caffeine would give him the lift he needed.

He felt wretched. He'd totally stuffed everything. Everything about the meeting with Isabella had been a first-class fiasco. What a fool he'd been. Had there ever in the history of man been a more stupid, rushed, pathetic proposal?

He shouldn't have responded with such a knee-jerk reaction to the pressure from her father. He should have taken more time. Expressed his feelings better. Opened up to the woman he loved.

Problem was, he'd become socially incompetent since Geri's death. He'd spent too much time with his thoughts and emotions locked up—isolated himself as effectively as if he'd set up permanent camp in a remote gorge in the wilderness.

And he'd spent so much effort convincing Isabella that a relationship with him was hopeless that he couldn't reasonably expect her to accept a sudden change of attitude. It was impossible for her to understand the courage it had taken to risk his heart and propose to another woman.

But, damn it, getting onto this plane and taking off from Valdenza's airport, knowing that he was leaving her behind, was the hardest thing he'd ever done. The thought of returning to Australia without her, of never seeing her again, was unbearable.

He was drowning in memories, torturing himself by lingering over every disturbing detail of her lovelinessof how she'd looked in that silken petticoat, with her dark hair falling around her shoulders in a shining tumble. He could still see her faultless complexion, the dusky pink of her lips, the flecks of ebony in her beautiful dark eyes...

His body ached for her. His blood leapt with the memory of their time on the river—of her soft, warm lips locked with his, of her pliant, urgent body lifting beneath his.

But the worst memory was seeing her turning away from him...showing him the door...

And here he was, sipping coffee as his plane cruised somewhere over the Russian steppes on its way to Tokyo and then on to northern Australia.

Isabella and Amoria were far behind him. Gone. Out of his life. The tiny glimmer of hope that he might have a second chance at happiness had been snuffed out. And somehow he had to go on living—surviving—just as he had for the past three years.

Jack was back in hell.

CHAPTER TWELVE

'MR KINGSLEY-LAIRD, it's so good to see you.' The matron bustled forward as the sliding glass doors of the Royal Perth Hospital parted to admit Jack.

'I'm sorry I'm running late. My meeting ran over time.'

His excuse was greeted by a coy smile. 'I'm sure you're a very busy man. There's no need to apologise—besides, it's not every day we receive such a magnificent donation for women's and children's health services. Now, if you'll come this way, please, everyone is ready and waiting.'

Jack paid scant attention to his surroundings as the matron escorted him down endless corridors. Even though he'd visited several hospitals in the past few months, he still felt a need to avert his eyes from the sight of medical equipment and bedridden patients.

And he resisted thinking too hard about the reason behind his new interest in giving donations to hospitals, but he suspected that at some subconscious level he was trying to buy back happiness.

After too many lonely pre-dawn hours spent staring out at

the lightening sky, he could only hope that doing something good—giving away bucketloads of moneywould ease the new pain that had lain like a cold and empty hollow around his heart ever since he'd returned from Amoria.

'We're almost there,' the matron said, as if she sensed his growing tension.

He shook his head clear of the thoughts that shadowed him constantly these days and forced his attention to the bright murals on the walls of the ward they were passing. 'These look terrific,' he said, pointing to a colourful jungle scene.

'Yes,' the matron agreed. 'We have a wonderful new volunteer who's doing amazing things in the children's ward.'

As she spoke she nodded towards her right, and Jack followed the direction of her gaze. He caught a glimpse of a woman's dark hair. He looked again. She was sitting beside a bed on the far side of the ward, waggling a fluffy green puppet at a little girl who had both legs in plaster.

He stopped dead in his tracks. *'Isabella.'* The name burst from him like an arrow from a crossbow.

His companion looked understandably surprised. 'Do you know our delightful Isabella?' she asked.

'It can't be her,' he whispered, moving towards the ward doorway.

The child in the bed was grinning up at the woman.

It *was* Isabella. *His* Isabella. He could see her profile as she smiled at the child. Smiled that lovely, sparklingeyed, dimpling smile he knew so well.

How could this be? What was she doing here?

He'd kept abreast of events in Amoria. He knew that Radik was in prison. Isabella was supposed to be working in Amorian hospitals, seeking a life of privacy.

A horrible coldness swept through him. Why on earth had she come to Australia without contacting him? *He had to talk to her.*

There was so much he needed to tell her…so much to undo.

He wasn't sure how long he might have stood there staring

if the matron hadn't tapped him on the shoulder. 'Mr Kingsley-Laird, we're behind schedule,' she said. 'But I know that woman. I know Isabella. I have to talk to her.'

For the first time the matron's pleasant demeanour faltered. 'I'm afraid everyone's waiting, sir.' Years spent instilling the fear of God into young nurses had lent her voice a chilling edge. 'The Premier is already here—and the chairman of the board— all the press people. We're running *late.*'

'Yes, of course,' Jack muttered, quickly suppressing a sigh. 'Let's get on with the formalities.' *Then I'll find Isabella.*

In the reception room, beaming smiles and goodwill abounded.

Frustratingly long speeches were made, but at last Jack was able to hand a cheque to the hospital board's chairman. Cameras flashed, and there were more flashes as he shook hands with the Premier, board members, the doctors and the matron.

Journalists pushed forward, asking questions…

Jack turned to the nearest doctor. 'I'd like to make a quick getaway.'

'Of course.' With an imperious sweep of his arm the young paediatrician held the media pack at bay. 'Mr Kingsley-Laird has another important engagement,' he told them. 'But our publicity officer will be happy to answer your questions.' To Jack, he murmured, 'Follow me.'

Once clear of the reception room, Jack thanked the doctor and made his excuses. 'There's someone in the children's ward I need to see.'

'Oh? You have a special interest in that ward?' the doctor asked hopefully, as if he sensed another donation in the wind.

'Ah—not especially. I was impressed by—by theer—bright artwork.' With a brief saluting wave Jack turned quickly away.

His stomach was churning by the time he stepped through the doorway of the children's ward. He scanned the bright airy room, searching for Isabella, but all he could see were beds holding small children with an assortment of limbs in plaster.

Where in blue blazes was Isabella?

'Excuse me,' he called, hurrying towards a nurse. 'Can you tell me where I can find the volunteer who was working here in this ward an hour ago?'

'Do you mean Isabella?'

'Yes.'

'Oh, I'm afraid she's just left. I think she's gone home.'

Suppressing a curse, Jack resurrected his most charming smile. 'You don't happen to know where she lives, do you?'

The nurse's eyes narrowed as she studied him. 'We can't give out that kind of information.'

'No, I don't suppose you can,' he agreed, in his most concil-iatory tone. But his hopes rose when he noted a telling gleam of suspicion in the nurse's eyes. Chances were she knew Isabella quite well. He glanced at her name badge. 'This is an emergency, Nancy. I have to see Isabella.'

Nurse Nancy made a business of sorting the array of medi-cine bottles on the tray in front of her.

'When will she be working here again?' Jack persisted.

'I'm not sure,' she said, keeping her eyes downcast as she studied a medicine label with exaggerated care.

An impatient, despairing tremor vibrated through him. So near and yet so far! Shoving his hands deep in his pockets, he squared his shoulders and leaned closer. 'What if I was to ex-plain to you exactly *why* I must see this woman?'

Isabella was going to a party. Her first ordinary party as an ordinary girl. Like millions of single girls all over the world, she was getting ready to go out on a Saturday night.

It was just one of a host of new experiences she'd enjoyed re-cently. The first and most gratifying had been winning her fa-ther's approval to leave Amoria and come to Perth. But there'd been many more—finding her sweet little cottage, shopping for groceries in a supermarket, learning to cook, to grow pot-ted herbs, to keep house. It was all such fun.

Now, fresh from her bath and wrapped in a red silk kimono,

she smiled as she surveyed the things she'd bought for the party. In the little shop around the corner she'd found the perfect dress—soft and floaty, with copper-coloured flowers and shimmering mossy leaves on a black background.

And she'd found very sexy high-heeled, backless sandals—*kitten heels*, the girl in the shop had called themand new sexy black underwear, a cheeky little beaded handbag with a parrot on the clasp, and new make-upbrighter than what she'd worn back home.

Very soon she would be heading off to a suburban flat brimming with fun-loving nurses and spunky young doctors.

And any minute now she would start to feel excited. It was disappointing not to be excited yet, but she was blaming the weather. During the afternoon a storm had broken over Perth, and it had been raining heavily ever since. The darkness and dampness must have dulled her mood.

The sizzle in the stomach would come when she arrived at the party. Everything would be fine as long as she didn't think about Jack. Tonight she couldn't, wouldn't, *mustn't* think about him. This was the first night of her new, exciting, Post-Jack social life.

Parting the curtains on her bedroom window, she peered out at the rainy night and wondered for the hundredth time about the gypsy woman's prophecy. It was pathetically romantic of her to keep hoping that she might find lasting happiness in this country. She had to stop imagining that she might at any moment run into Jack.

But it was so hard—especially now that she'd seen the story on the early evening news. To think he'd been at the Royal Perth Hospital this morning.

This morning. If only she'd known she might have seen him. Spoken to him.

Stop it, she reprimanded herself. *Stop thinking about him. You'll ruin a perfectly good night. Jack's getting on with his life and you've got to try to get on with yours.*

She glanced back to the little travelling clock beside her bed and decided it was time to get dressed. Closing the curtain, she slipped out of her kimono and crossed to the bed. She'd put on her underwear first, then do her make-up before she put the dress on.

No doubt the sizzle would start once she was dressed and ready. She scooped up the black silk G-string panties, and at precisely the same moment her front doorbell rang.

Startled, she checked the time again. It had to be Nancy, calling to take her to the party, but she was terribly early. Heavens, now she would have to rush her preparations. And where should she ask Nancy to wait? Should she offer her a drink?

Feeling just a little fretful, Isabella reached for her kimono and tugged it around her again as she hurried in bare feet to answer the door.

There was a switch for the porch light in the hallway, and as she turned it on she saw the blurred outline of her caller and the black shape of an umbrella through the panel of amber glass in her door.

Unexpectedly, her stomach tightened.

Was this the beginning of the excitement she had hoped for?

'I'm afraid I'm not ready,' she called as she opened the door. And her heart stalled.

It wasn't Nancy.

Her knees gave way and she sagged against the doorjamb. *Jack!*

The porch light splashed over him, highlighting the gilded tips of his brown hair, the craggy planes of his forehead, nose and cheekbones—the intense blue light in his eyes.

He'd propped his dripping umbrella against the wall of her porch, and now he stood with one hand behind his back. Drops of rain glistened on the shoulders of his dark jacket and rain splashes darkened the bottoms of his stone-coloured trousers. Beneath his jacket he wore a blue shirt that matched his eyes. The top buttons of the shirt were open and she saw dark, curling hair.

Jack. In the flesh. 'Hello, Isabella.'

She hardly heard his greeting above the savage thundering of her heartbeats. When she tried to reply her voice wouldn't work.

So many times in her dreams she'd experienced a moment like this. Jack striding back into her life. But the dreams had always turned to nightmares. Whenever Jack had come close enough for her to touch him he'd fractured into a thousand pieces.

She half expected it to happen now. If she blinked he might dissolve into raindrops and form a puddle at her feet.

'What are you doing here?' she managed to ask at last.

'I heard you were in town,' he said easily, as if they were no more than casual schoolfriends catching up on gossip.

'But how did you know I was here?'

'I saw you at the hospital this morning.'

'Really?'

'Then you performed a vanishing act—so I made a few discreet enquiries.' His mouth tilted into a faint smile, but his blue eyes remained intense and watchful. 'How are you, Carmen?'

'I'm—I'm very well, thank you, Jack.'

A gust of wind sent the rain slanting onto the porch, adding to the splashes on his trousers. 'Are you going to invite me inside?' he asked.

'I'm—I'm expecting someone at any moment,' she said, gripping the doorknob for support. 'I'm getting ready to go out.' Nervously she slid her hand over her hip and down her thigh.

His eyes shimmered as he watched the path her hand took, and then he let his gaze travel slowly over her. She felt absurdly self-conscious and exposed as she stood there in her bare feet and silky kimono, but she resisted an urge to yank the garment more tightly closed over her chest.

Jack released a deep breath and took a step closer. 'I need to talk to you, Isabella.'

'Why?' she whispered, pressing herself away from him and against the door as pulsing, scary excitement flashed through her.

In the dark, rainy street behind him tyres swished and

splashed through a puddle. Car lights swept past, shining fuzzy and golden through the needles of rain. He glanced at the lights, then back to her. 'Do you remember a rainy night when you were beating at my door and I let you in?'

Oh, heavens! She'd been trying so hard not to think about that. Not the flooded creek, the storm, the dark bush. The lightning flashes. Not Jack in his hut...removing leeches, making her tea, giving up his bed for her. Or what had followed—on the river, in the tent...

'Isabella, would it help if I told you that your friend Nancy gave me her blessing to come here?'

Nancy? She felt dizzy and confused, as if she'd woken in the middle of a crazy, mixed-up dream. 'Perhaps Nancy knows something that I don't.'

From behind his back Jack produced a single longstemmed dark red rose. She pressed her hands against her thumping heart and stared at him, and then at the raindrops glistening on the velvety folds of the rose petals, at the ivory silk ribbons fluttering from its thorny stem.

'I almost brought you Australian wildflowers, but decided to stick with tradition,' he said. Casting another glance out to the rain, then back to her, he shrugged shyly. 'I've come to ask you for a second chance.'

Her heart felt as if it had taken off down a ski slope. 'I don't understand,' she whispered, but they both knew she was lying.

In an exaggerated gesture Jack held the rose against his heart. 'Isabella, unless you want the entire street to watch me propose to you I think you should invite me inside.'

Before she could answer, he was propelling her into the house and pulling the door shut behind them. Her legs were shaking so badly she had to lean against the wall. She was trembling from the riot of emotions that filled her. She couldn't take her eyes off Jack. He looked so gorgeous.

Without any hesitation he walked into her little sitting room.

In a daze, she followed, and wondered rather irrelevantly whether he liked the country farmhouse furniture she'd chosen.

'Please take a seat,' she said.

'I'd rather not.' He set the rose down on the coffee table, and when he straightened he stood very still, looking at her. His throat worked. 'I'm afraid I'm rather nervous.'

'That makes two of us,' she whispered. Outside in the dark, beyond her new floral curtains, the rain lashed against the windowpane. 'But if it helps I'd very much like to hear what you have to say, Jack.'

His mouth twitched as if he'd tried to smile but no smile had arrived. Then he plunged his hands deeply into his trouser pockets. The movement nudged his jacket wide open, and she couldn't help admiring the very masculine way his blue shirt tapered from his broad shoulders and chest to the trimness of his waist and hips.

'The thing is,' he said, 'I made a hopeless hash of asking you to marry me when I was in Amoria. You were in a state of shock and I went at things like a bull at a gate. I think I know why you rejected me, and I don't blame you, so I've come to ask if I can try again.' Tears filled her eyes and a tremor shook her smile. 'Why should people only have one chance?' *But, please, if you don't tell me you love me this time I think I might die.*

He smiled nervously and his eyes shimmered. 'I love you, Isabella.'

'Oh, Jack.' Her heart swelled with a painful, uplift of longing. 'Are you quite sure?'

He stared at her in amazement. 'I'm absolutely sure. I'm more than sure. I'm desperately, madly in love with you. You've got to believe me.'

'It's just that at Killymoon you were so certain we had no future. After your wife—'

He gave an impatient shake of his head. 'I was fooling myself. I had the cracked idea that I could avoid more pain by keeping you at bay. I was crazy, because it was already too late.' He stepped closer. 'Damn fool that I was, I didn't realise that I was already in love with you.' He reached for her hands, gripped them in his. 'These past months have been hell. I can only be happy with you. I want to devote the rest of my life to making you happy.'

Jack loved her. She could hear it in his words and in the choke in his voice, and she could see it in the sheen in his eyes, feel it in the tremble in his hands.

'I'm so sorry I sent you away,' she said. 'I've been desperately miserable too. But, you see, I thought you'd been forced into proposing by my father. You didn't say anything about loving me.'

'I know, I know. I can't believe I was so stupid.'

'And I needed you to love me as much as I love you.'

'Oh, Isabella.' With a tortured groan he hauled her into his arms. He held her against his thudding heart, embracing her fiercely, as if he feared she might vanish. He buried his face in her hair. 'I love you, my dear girl. I love you. I love you.' Tucking her head against his shoulder, he pressed his lips to her forehead. 'You *must* believe me.'

'I believe you.'

'I've even found out how to say I love you in French.'

'Tell me.'

Je t'aime.'

'Oh, darling Jack.' She was smiling and crying at once, laughing through her tears. *Je t'aime.*' She kissed the gorgeous underside of his jaw. *Je t'aime. Je t'adore.*'

Jack kissed her earlobe. 'And that's not all. I can also say it in Spanish.' He grinned and kissed her other ear. *Te amo.*'

Te amo,' she whispered happily, kissing his neck.

He kissed her eyelids. *Je t'aime.*' He kissed her throat. *Te amo.*' He kissed her chin. 'I'd better warn you, I'm going to learn how to say I love you in every language.'

'Don't make me cry,' she sobbed joyfully, turning her face to capture his next kiss. And at last he was kissing her mouth. She met him with eager, hungry, open lips. And he returned her kiss deeply. Taking her. Claiming her as she longed to be claimed. She was *his*.

Jack's woman.

His hands cradled her head and his kiss was hot and wonderfully fierce. Possessive. Hungry. Isabella clung to him, stunned by the jolt of violent happiness that surged through her. Jack, her gorgeous, gorgeous Jack, wanted her. Loved her. *Loved her!*

She let her head fall back so that their kiss could deepen. His hands travelled over her shoulders, moulding and exploring their shape, then slid down her arms. Up again, more slowly. Building her fever.

Oh, she loved his hands. Loved the way he touched her. She'd been too long apart from him. This was where she and Jack belonged—touching, loving. When his hand reached her breast a pleasure bomb seemed to explode inside her. She tugged impatiently at the ties of her kimono, letting it fall open, wanting no barrier between her skin and his touch.

Jack groaned, and she felt a tremor run through him as he touched her bare skin. 'Isabella…'

'I love you. *Je t'adore*.'

His hands spanned her ribs and he scattered a sweet, swift trail of kisses over her bare shoulder, then moved lower.

Oh, yes. Her breath escaped in a throaty moan. She needed his mouth on her skin more than her next heartbeat.

A loud ringing sounded on the front door.

Isabella froze, momentarily puzzled. And then remembered. 'Oh, goodness, will that be Nancy?' she whispered.

Holding her close, Jack half turned towards the hallway. 'No doubt she wants to make sure I haven't botched my second chance.'

'Oh, dear.'

'What do you mean by that—oh, dear?'

'Well…actually…you *have* botched it.' Jack blinked. 'Pardon?'

'As far as I know, you haven't actually asked me to marry you yet.'

'You will, though, won't you?'

'Sure thing, mate.'

He looked down at her with a quizzical smile.

The doorbell rang again, more insistently, but Isabella ignored it as she wound her arms around Jack's neck.

'That's Australian for, Yes, my darling Jack, there's nothing in this world I want more than to be your wife.' His blue eyes sparkled as he dropped another kiss on her shoulder. With an exaggerated sigh he pulled her clothing demurely into place and retied the belt. 'I guess we'd better go tell Nancy the good news.'

'Too bad I'll be missing that party.'

'But I'm planning one of our own.'

'Oh, yes. Let's hurry.'

EPILOGUE

IT WAS A perfect moonlit night. No clouds. Just the velvet-black sky stretched in a high arc to provide a stark backdrop for the silver half-moon and the brilliant sweep of stars.

Isabella and Jack spread a rug on the lake's shore and lay on their backs, gazing up at the heavens while close by in the hut their daughter Annie lay snugly asleep in her little cot.

'Do the individual stars of the Southern Cross have names?' Isabella asked.

'Sure.' Jack leaned on one elbow and raised his other arm to point. 'You start with Alpha, there, and then there's Beta, Gamma, Delta, and the tiny one in between them is Epsilon.'

'Mmmm… Alpha,' she repeated, and shot him a slow, cheeky smile. 'Perhaps we could call our next baby Alpha?'

'You're joking?'

She gave him a playful poke in the ribs. 'Don't you think Alpha has a certain panache? Annie and Alpha. Or perhaps you'd prefer Epsilon?'

Jack chuckled and reached under her T-shirt to caress the gentle bump of her stomach where their second child lay. He felt so much more relaxed this time round. When Annie had been born he'd been a bundle of nerves, terrified for Isabella and for the child. Terrified for himself—that he might lose them.

But Isabella, bless her, had been serene and calm. 'Everything will be fine,' she'd reassured him.

And it had been. They'd flown to Amoria for the confinement, and Isabella had chosen a water birth at an exclusive hospital in Valdenza. In a dark room lit only by candlelight their daughter had arrived with a minimum of fuss or distraction.

Such a sweet little dark-haired angel.

He'd been filled with awe when he held her for the first time. He'd cradled her sturdy, still damp little body, felt her tiny, vigorous movements, and had been completely disarmed when she'd opened her mouth and tried to nuzzle him.

'She's hungry already,' he'd whispered in amazement.

She'd been so healthy, so full of life.

And Isabella had been positively glowing with health and happiness.

'Would you like to call her Annie, after your first baby?' she'd asked.

And he'd wept. Tears of sorrow for his fragile, redhaired Annie, and joy for this beautiful, robust daughter with raven curls like her mother's. He hadn't been able to thank Isabella then, but he'd done so a hundred times since.

Now, as they watched the stars, Isabella snuggled closer against his shoulder and the night wrapped around them like a warm, silent cocoon. 'Aren't you glad I persuaded you to come here to Pelican's End for our wedding anniversary?' she asked.

'Very,' he murmured, kissing her. 'But, sweet girl, anywhere with you seems perfect.' He traced the soft curve of her cheek with his hand and watched the moonlight silver her lovely profile. 'Valdenza, Killymoon, Perth—as long as you're there, I'm a happy man.'

He hadn't known it was possible to find such peace in his life. The past three years had brought the private joy of his marriage, the happy merger of his company with his parents' business, and the success of Isabella's plan to use her royal allowance to launch the Christos Tenni Institute for Research.

'You know I love you to bits,' he said. 'Especially this bit.' He trailed his mouth over her lips, already parted in a warm, soft invitation.

'Nagligivaget,' he murmured, pulling her more closely against him.

'Naglig—what?'

'Nagligivaget.'

'What's that?'

'It's Inuit for I love you.'

'Oh, you darling man. How many languages are you up to now?'

'I've lost count.'

'You're so special, Jack,' she whispered, and, looking up at the Southern Cross again she smiled. *'Je t'aime.'*

He kissed her tenderly. *'Te amo,* Carmen.'

* * * * *

Nurse's Outback Temptation

Amy Andrews

Dear Reader,

It's been a while since I've written a Harlequin Medical Romance novel, but it's been extra special to come back to my roots, to where this whole roller-coaster author journey began.

Gotta admit, I was worried I'd forgotten how to do this, but then Chelsea and Aaron started whispering sweet nothings in my ear and it all came rushing back. The heart-pounding medical situations, the delicious pull of "will they, won't they," the incredible backdrop and drama of the Australian Outback. It was all just there waiting to get out of my head!

I hope you enjoy this fish out of water story featuring Chelsea, who is running away from a painful past and the strictures and restraints of her present life in the UK to finally be herself. And Aaron—tough and resilient. A man of the Outback who knows what he does and doesn't want. And he definitely doesn't want to fall for an outsider.

But sometimes life has other plans, and neither Chelsea nor Aaron are immune to the whims of fate! Cue evil author laughter.

Happy reading!

Love,

Amy xxx

Amy Andrews is a multi-award-winning, *USA TODAY* bestselling Australian author who has written over fifty contemporary romances in both the traditional and digital markets. She loves good books, fab food, great wine and frequent travel—preferably all four together. To keep up with her latest releases, news, competitions and giveaways, sign up for her newsletter—madmimi.com/signups/106526/join.

Books by Amy Andrews

Waking Up With Dr. Off-Limits
Sydney Harbor Hospital: Luca's Bad Girl
How to Mend a Broken Heart
Sydney Harbor Hospital: Evie's Bombshell
One Night She Would Never Forget
Gold Coast Angels: How to Resist Temptation
200 Harley Street: The Tortured Hero
It Happened One Night Shift
Swept Away by the Seductive Stranger
A Christmas Miracle

Visit the Author Profile page
at millsandboon.com.au for more titles.

I dedicate this book to Joanne Grant and Ally Blake.
I will be forever grateful for the hand-holding
and cheerleading.

**Praise for
Amy Andrews**

"Packed with humor, heart and pathos, *Swept Away
by the Seductive Stranger* is a stirring tale of second
chances, redemption and hope with a wonderfully
feisty and intelligent heroine you will adore and a
gorgeous hero whom you will love."

—*Goodreads*

CHAPTER ONE

CHELSEA TANNER WAS a puddle of sweat. Already. After three steps. The sun scorched like a blast furnace overhead and the heat danced in visible waves from the black tar of the runway. Of course, she knew that Australia was hot in November—Outback Australia even more so. And, yes, she'd checked the temperature this morning and knew it was going to be forty-one degrees when she landed in Balanora.

But knowing it and being plunged into the scalding reality of it were clearly two very different things. Because this was ridiculously hot.

Welcome to hell, hot.

Her pale skin already crackling beneath the UV, she scurried across to the modest terminal, a familiar mantra playing on repeat through her head. *It's for the best. It's for the best.* Because Christmas in England would be worse. Blessedly cool, sure, but ninth circle of hell worse, and Outback Australia was the furthest point she could travel—physically and metaphorically—from home.

So, there was no turning back and, as she stepped through

the sliding doors into the frigid blast of air-conditioning, she was grateful for the lifeline, no matter the temperature.

She just needed to…acclimatise.

Expecting to find as per the email, someone waiting for her after she'd grabbed her luggage from the carousel, Chelsea glanced around. People milled and greeted, hugging and laughing as pick-ups were made, but no one appeared to be there for her.

Maybe they were just running late.

She checked her phone—no messages. Finding a set of chairs nearby, she situated herself in view of the entrance to wait. No way in hell was she doing it *outside* the terminal. After fifteen minutes had passed, however, Chelsea grabbed her phone to call the number she'd been given.

'Good afternoon, Outback Aeromedical, this is Meg, how may I help you?'

Meg sounded as peppy in real life as she had in her emails. 'Hi, Meg, this is Chelsea Tanner. I'm terribly sorry to be a bother, but I'm at the Balanora airport and I thought someone was picking me up? I can get a taxi. I just don't want to jump in one and maybe miss my lift if they're just running late.'

'*What?* But…you're not supposed to be here until Thursday.'

Chelsea frowned. 'The plane ticket you sent was for Tuesday. So…here I am.'

'Oh dear, I have it marked on the calendar as Thursday.' There was the tapping of computer keys and a clicking of a mouse in Chelsea's ear. 'I am *so* terribly sorry. I must have got my "T" days mixed up when I was inputting it to the calendar. It's absolutely no excuse, but it can get super-busy here some days and I must have been distracted. Also that whole "pregnancy brain fog" thing turns out to be very real.'

The usual tangle of emotions around pregnancy rose up but Chelsea quashed them. She was thousands of miles away from the convoluted complications of her past and Meg had already moved on.

'Gosh, this is terribly unforgiveable of me, especially after all the flight hassles you've already been through.'

Hassles was an understatement. Between the UK snap freeze, mechanical issues forcing an unscheduled landing and then, of all things, a volcanic eruption in Asia, Chelsea could have been forgiven for thinking this venture was cursed before it had even begun. And, some time during her fortieth travel hour, spent *not* in the air but in a crowded airport terminal, she had pondered whether the universe was trying to tell her something.

'You must be exhausted.'

Actually she hadn't felt too bad when she'd landed in Brisbane thirty-six hours after she was supposed to, despite not having had much sleep. Two further nights of jet-lag-interrupted sleep later, however, had not been kind. And then, with her time in Brisbane cut short thanks to her travel debacle, she'd hopped her flight to Balanora, arriving into the oven of the Outback.

As if, by just mentioning the word exhausted, Meg had made it so, Chelsea's last spark of life leached away. She certainly felt every one of her thirty-two years. 'I could sleep for a week,' Chelsea admitted.

'I bet you could!' There was more key tapping. 'Okay, stay there. I'll be right out to pick you up. Unfortunately, there's a small issue with your house. Aaron is currently staying there due to the air con in his breaking down.'

That would be Dr Aaron Vincent, Chelsea presumed, one of the senior flight doctors on the staff.

'Which is fine, it'll be fixed tomorrow, but Aaron has gone camping with some mates and won't be back until this evening. And, as he's out of mobile range, I can't call him to come and get his stuff out of your house. I mean, it's not much, but still, we like to have our houses spic and span before we hand them over, so we'll put you up in the OA room at the pub. It's permanently reserved for us in case we ever need it for stranded staff or visiting head honchos.'

Chelsea was fading fast. She didn't mind where she slept. As long as there was air-conditioning. 'Oh, thank you. That sounds great.' Once again, not the most auspicious start to her new life, but she was far too tired to care right now.

'Well, it's not the Ritz, but it's clean, safe, friendly, the water pressure is great, they serve good, hearty meals and it's air-conditioned.'

Chelsea sighed. 'You just said the magic words.'

Meg laughed. 'Hold tight, I'll be ten minutes.'

Twenty-five minutes later, Chelsea was saying goodbye to Meg as she followed a guy called Ray, who'd been serving behind the bar at the Crown hotel, up the internal stairs to the first floor. He carried her bag to the door then handed over her key.

A proper, old-fashioned key. That *slid into* a lock.

'Thank you,' she said.

He nodded and Chelsea opened the door to the massive room. Not that she noticed any of the detail. All she noticed was the general stuffiness and the giant air-conditioning unit on the wall above the bed.

Leaving her bag at the door, she crossed to the remote sitting on top of one of the bedside tables. With desperate, shaking hands, she pointed it at the unit and pressed the button labelled 'on'. For a terrible few seconds, it stuttered, whined and didn't do anything, and Chelsea thought, *Dear God, what fresh hell is this?* Then it powered to life, delivering a wave of cool air across her shoulders.

She almost collapsed on the bed in joy and relief. But not yet. Chelsea knew if she got horizontal it'd be all over, and she needed a shower. A nice, cool shower. Then she could crawl onto the bed—no, she didn't care that it was only three in the afternoon—and sleep for the next twenty-four hours.

There was nowhere to be until this time tomorrow, when Meg was picking her up to take her to her new place, so *hibernating* until then seemed like a good plan.

Adjusting the temperature on the control to the lowest pos-

sible, Chelsea snapped the heavy curtains closed over a set
of French doors that opened out onto a veranda, immediately
plunging the room into semi-darkness. Dragging her suitcase
to the end of her bed, she grabbed clean underwear and a tank
top, along with some toiletries, and headed for the shower, lingering under the spray and hoping the room would be a thousand degrees cooler when she was done.

It was, and Chelsea almost cried as she lay on the crisp,
white sheet that smelled of sunshine. Her skin was cool from
the shower, her hair was damp and she knew it would be ten
kinds of fluff ball in the morning, but she didn't care. Right
now this bed felt better than any other surface she'd ever lain on
and she shut her eyes, falling head-first into the deep slumber
of a person who has finally found her way through the double
whammy of world time zones and militant body clocks to the
deep, dark relief of unconsciousness.

Aaron Vincent was getting way too old to be drinking several
nights in a row and roughing it in a swag on the hard tray of his
ute, even if he'd been in the company of guys he'd known since
he was a kid. Their annual camping trip out by the river that ran
through Curran Downs, his family's sheep station, had been a
tradition ever since they'd left school. It had survived, despite
three out of the six of them not living in the area any more, and
five out of the six of them being married with children.

He being the odd one out.

Luckily their wives, all women of the Outback, were understanding about this sacred time every year. Kath, Dammo's
wife, who was five-and-a-half months' pregnant with their third
child, called it their *knitting circle*, which they all delighted in
giving him shit about.

Aaron found her affectionate description hysterical. In an
area known for blokey blokes, all six of them easily fit the
mould, although him probably the least. Dammo and the others
were still working on the land in one form or another, whereas

he'd left over a decade ago to become a doctor before finally returning, three years ago, to work with the OA.

They loved taking the piss about *soft hands* and Aaron laughed along at the jokes, but he—and they—knew he could still shear a sheep, mend a fence and gets his hands dirty as well as he ever could. And did, whenever his sister, who had largely taken over the running of the property from their father now, needed some extra help.

But he'd be lying if he didn't admit to relief as he passed the *Welcome to Balanora* sign on the way back in to town. He was looking forward to an actual mattress to cushion the twinge in his lower back. Except he stopped into the pub on his way through for a bite to eat, because he couldn't be bothered to cook anything, and Tuesdays were always roast night.

Then he got talking to three women—nurses from Adelaide—who were passing through town on an Outback road trip. They were interested in the OA, and they chatted and laughed, and it felt good to feel thirty-five instead of the seventy-five his lumbar spine currently felt. Not a bad way to spend an evening. Better than five other blokes, who hadn't showered in three days, *and* Dammo's farting dog, Kenny.

Aaron left soon after the nurses departed, only to discover his ute had a flat tyre. Too tired to do something about it or even call a cab, he turned back to the pub to enquire if the OA room was empty. When Lyle, the publican, handed over the key, Aaron decided it was a definite sign from the universe to go to bed and fix the damn tyre in the morning.

Heading up the stairs, he let himself into number seven, the blessed cool of the room only registering at the same time he yanked his shirt over his head. Frowning, he flipped on the light switch to discover he was not alone. There was a barely covered woman he didn't know in the middle of the bed, staring at him wild-eyed.

And then she screamed.

Aaron winced as she sat bolt-upright, her sandy-blonde hair

in complete disarray, and dragged the sheet up to cover herself. '*Get out!* Get out *right now!*' she screeched, blinking against the flood of light. 'You come *any* closer and I will scream blue murder.'

If he hadn't been distracted by her cut-glass English accent, he'd be keen to know what colour it was she *had* screamed. 'I'm sorry, I'm sorry!' he apologised, holding out both of his hands, his T-shirt still clutched in his left hand as he backed up until his shoulder-blades hit the door.

'I didn't know anyone was in here,' he continued, keeping his voice even and low and, he hoped, reassuring. 'Lyle gave me the key. See?' He held it up. 'It's just been a terrible misunderstanding.'

She didn't say anything as she sucked in air noisily through her flared nostrils and glared. Someone pounded on the door behind him.

'What the hell is going on in there, doc? Open up or I'll kick the bloody thing in.'

Reaching behind him slowly so as not to panic the woman with any sudden moves, he turned the door handle, stepping aside to admit Lyle. Aaron greeted the publican with a *what the hell?* expression on his face. 'You said the room was empty.'

The older man scowled at him. 'What? There's nobody in the book.'

He glanced across the room at Exhibit A, who was on her feet now and watching them both warily, the sheet wrapped tight around her, one hand clutching it close to her breast.

'Oh.' Lyle stared at her as if she'd arrived from a spaceship…because how else would anyone have got past the hightech, triple-encrypted reservation system known as 'the book'.

Cursing under his breath, something about *bloody Ray and his testicles*, Lyle addressed her. 'I'm so sorry, m…miss.' He advanced into the room, his hands extended in some kind of apology, but her eyes grew bigger and she took a step back.

Lyle halted. 'I didn't know you were here.' He looked at Aaron. 'Somebody hasn't put her in the book.'

Aaron bugged his eyes. 'Clearly.'

Lyle returned his attention to the woman who somehow managed to look haughty despite her obvious discomfort and electric-socket hair. 'Ray shouldn't have rented out this room. It's for Outback Aeromedical use only.'

'I know.' She glared, taking the haughtiness up another notch. 'I'm starting there on Friday.'

'Oh.' Aaron smiled. Now it made sense. 'You're the new nurse? Chelsea Tanner?'

'Yes.'

The team had been looking forward to her arrival this past couple of months. Having someone permanent—even if just for the year of her contract—would give some certainty and stability to the team.

If this very English miss didn't baulk at the first spider and head for home, of course.

Aaron almost walked forward to introduce himself but quashed the impulse. *Not the right time, dude. Not the right place.* She looked as if she'd been roused from a very heavy sleep, and she was a lone female, in not many clothes, confronting two strange men.

'I'm Aaron,' he said, keeping his feet firmly planted on the floor and his eyes firmly trained on her face. 'Vincent. One of the flight doctors. We…ah…weren't expecting you until Thursday?'

She huffed out an impatient breath, neither acknowledging his introduction nor answering his query. 'Yes, I know, there was a mix up with Meg, but do you think we could possibly do this introduction at a later date? Perhaps when we're both more…' She glanced pointedly at the shirt in his hand. *'Clothed.'*

Damn it! He'd forgotten he'd taken it off. Hastily, Aaron threw it back over his head. 'Of course,' he said, emerging from the neck hole and pulling the hem down. 'We'll leave you to get back to sleep.' He started to back out, elbowing Lyle, who looked as if he was still trying to fathom how his system had failed. 'Apologies again.'

'Yes,' Lyle agreed, jumping in quickly, in response to the elbow. 'Huge apologies. I'll be talking to Ray in the morning.'

She just eyed them warily as they backed out, her hand still clutching the sheet tight to her front. Easing the door gently closed, Aaron glanced at Lyle.

'I'm going to kill Ray,' he said.

Aaron might just help. 'You got another room?'

'Nope.'

Aaron sighed. Of course not. Resigned, he went and changed his tyre.

After the night's interruption had dragged Chelsea out of the deepest darkest sleep of her life she feared she wouldn't be able to get back to that place again but her fears were unfounded. It took less than a minute to slide back into that cool oblivion, ably aided by the vision of a shirtless Aaron Vincent, all six-foot-odd of broad, smooth chest, solid abs and delightfully scruffy hair.

He'd oozed *male* right across the room at her but, despite the potential threat in the situation, she hadn't felt frightened. Sure, she'd been taken by surprise and had reacted as any woman would have at finding a shirtless stranger in her room in the middle of the night, but she hadn't felt he'd had any ill intent.

On the contrary, she'd felt…*attraction*.

Maybe it was just some weird jet-lag or body clock thing. Maybe her foggy brain had been in a highly suggestible state. But, for the first time since her husband's death three years ago, things actually *stirred*. She'd been aware of him as a *man*. Not an intruder, not a threat.

A man.

And that hadn't happened for the longest time.

To make things worse, he was also the first thing she thought about when she finally awoke at two in the afternoon, which

was exceedingly disconcerting. She hadn't come to Australia
to meet someone, to get involved or put her heart on the line
again. She'd come to start anew—*by herself.* To escape the cloy-
ing clutches of family.

Stand on her own two feet.

She'd been stuck in a rut, her wheels spinning, and it was
time—past time—to start moving forward again. But to do that
she'd had to leave London because to stay would have meant
continuing to live a lie. Minding her words and grinding her
teeth, holding back the torrent of fury that bubbled beneath
the surface, until her heart had become a locked box of resentment surrounded by the brittle shell of the woman everyone
wanted her to be.

The woman she used to be.

Okay, maybe flying to the other side of the world was extreme, but she knew if she was too close to call on she'd keep
being sucked back.

She needed to be out of reach.

She *needed* to be herself again, not just Dom's poor widow.
Poor Chelsea. And she wasn't going to achieve that by mooning over some other guy. No matter how good he looked with
his shirt off.

Rolling out of bed, she picked up her phone as she walked to
the doors and drew back the curtains, a blast of light assault-
ing her eyeballs. Turning back, she grabbed a pair of shorts to
go with her tank and stepped into them before scooping up her
phone and heading out the glass doors.

Heat enveloped her as she stepped out onto the decking, the
floorboards aged and worn beneath her feet. Placing her phone
on the small round table situated not far from the doors, she continued several more feet to the gorgeous wrought-iron lace work
of the railing, pleased at the full protection of the roof overhead.
Squinting against the sun reflecting off metallic awnings and
car roofs, she looked up and down the main street of Balanora.

It was wide, two lanes each side, with a generous section of
central parking between. The cars were mostly shaded by the

huge trees planted at regular intervals down the middle. Shops lined the street on both sides, cars pulling in regularly to angle-park at the kerbs. It seemed busy, with plenty of people coming and going, and more traffic than she'd imagined.

It didn't take long for the beat of the sun to drive her back and she sat at the table, the only occupant on the long veranda as she checked her texts and emails. There were several from friends, checking she'd arrived okay, and several more had come in overnight from her mother-in-law. Chelsea had texted Francesca when she'd landed in Brisbane to let her know she'd arrived safely but hadn't responded to any of the others.

The older woman hadn't wanted her to go, had fretted that she'd be too far away from the people who loved her, but she'd eventually understood Chelsea's need to get away. Still, she wasn't above turning the screws, as the video she'd sent two hours ago of three-year-old Alfie—Dom's son—testified.

Chelsea's finger hovered over the play button. That familiar chin cleft and expression was so like his father's. She wanted to listen to that sweet voice but was tired of the emotional wrench the mere existence of Alfie always caused. Through no fault of his own, Alfie was a living embodiment of her husband's infidelity, and she was tired of pretending she was okay.

Thankfully, a text popped up on the screen, putting off the dilemma.

Hi, Chelsea, it's Charmaine.

Charmaine White was the OA director. She had interviewed Chelsea via Zoom two months ago.

Sorry about the mix-up yesterday. Meg feels awful. I'll be in the bar in an hour if you're awake. If not just call on this number when you are and I can take you over to your new place.

New place. Sounded like heaven. Chelsea hit delete on the video and walked inside.

* * *

An hour later, Chelsea was ensconced in Charmaine's Outback Aeromedical badged SUV, driving around the airport perimeter. Charmaine had suggested a tour of the base first, to which Chelsea had enthusiastically agreed. Several aged hangar buildings, languishing in the sunlight, passed by. The largest of them loomed just ahead, gleaming white, with Outback Aeromedical painted on the side along with the logo of a red plane in the middle of a giant yellow sun.

Charmaine parked in a small car park and ushered Chelsea in the front door with a swipe card. Several offices and storage rooms occupied this area and Charmaine whisked Chelsea through, introducing her to anyone she came across, before opening a door that led out to the cavernous space of the hangar proper. Chelsea looked up. The exposed internal roof struts spanned the curve of the roof almost to the ground on both sides, giving the impression of ribs caging them inside the belly of a giant beast.

Two planes sat idle, one larger than the other, both somehow managing to look small in the great yawning space.

'That's the King Air,' Charmaine said, pointing to the smaller one. 'It's a twin turbo prop. We have two in our fleet here. This one did an immunisation clinic at one of the remote communities this morning.'

Chelsea knew from the interview with Charmaine that, as well as assistance in emergency situations, the OA also offered primary care in the form of remote clinics, dealing with things such as women's health, mental health and preventative medicine, as well as routine blood tests and screening.

'The other King Air is out on a job right now but should be touching down soon. They have a range of two thousand seven hundred kilometres. They take two stretchers and three seats.'

Charmaine walked towards the larger one and Chelsea followed. 'This is the Pilatus PC-24.' The door was closed but

Charmaine stroked its gleaming white flank as if it was a favoured pet. 'Isn't she beautiful?'

'She is.'

'It's only been with us for six months but already saved five lives in three separate road accidents. It can fly faster and longer, and can use a runway as short as eight hundred metres, which is a godsend out here. It takes three stretchered patients and up to two medical teams. It's like an intensive care in the air.'

Chelsea smiled at Charmaine still petting the plane. 'I imagine these are few and far between?'

'They are,' she confirmed. 'I had to lobby hard for it to be based here. But, because we're situated ideally as far as distance goes between Darwin, Adelaide and Brisbane, and we have a proportionally large amount of accidents, both car and farm, it was a no-brainer.' She sighed. 'Flies like a dream.'

'Well, in that case, I can't wait to go up in it.'

Just then an ambulance pulled into the area in front of the hangar which was now in shadow. Several people whom she'd met earlier came out from the door behind.

'ETA?' Charmaine asked a guy in maintenance overalls—Brett, maybe?—who was heading for a tractor parked just to the left on the inside wall of the hangar.

'Five.'

'C'mon, I'll introduce you to the ambos.'

Charmaine introduced her to Kaylee and Robbo, who were friendly and personable, as they discussed the details of the traumatic amputation of several fingers and partial degloving of the hand that was currently on board the King Air. The plane came into sight and a tiny trill of excitement rumbled through Chelsea's chest. Soon that would be her, flying all over the Outback, bringing help and hope to people who might otherwise find themselves in some dire situations where distance could make outcomes bleak.

This was what she'd come here for and she couldn't freaking wait.

Chelsea watched the plane grow larger and larger, the wheels unfolding from the undercarriage as it descended and landed smoothly on the shimmering tarmac with barely a screeching of the tyres.

'Perfect,' Charmaine murmured.

The plane taxied toward the hangar as Robbo got the stretcher out of the back of the ambulance. The moment the plane's props stopped spinning, the paramedics started towards it. 'C'mon,' Charmaine said with a grin. 'I'll introduce you to the crew.'

The heat was still intense but Chelsea followed her eagerly across the hot bitumen, squinting as the sun dazzled off the metallic fuselage of the plane. She made a note to hit the town tomorrow and buy the best damn pair of sunglasses Balanora had to offer.

It was that or end up with crow's feet ten-feet deep by the end of her year.

The door opened, lowering as they approached to form stairs. A woman, who looked about forty, in navy trousers and a navy polo shirt with the OA logo on the collar and *pilot* stamped in large red letters across the front, greeted them. 'Hey,' she said. 'Looks like we got us a welcoming party.'

'Hey, Hattie,' Charmaine greeted her. 'Textbook landing as per usual.'

'That's why you pay me the big bucks,' Hattie quipped as she descended the stairs and moved out of the way for the paramedics to move the stretcher in for the patient transfer.

'Hattie, meet Chelsea. She starts officially on Friday but I'm giving her the quickie tour today.'

The older woman held out her hand, saying, 'Pleased to meet you.'

Chelsea shook the offered hand and said, 'Likewise.'

'Ready to go?'

Glancing back to the plane at the familiar voice, Chelsea's

eyes met Aaron's. Standing on the top step, framed by the door of the plane behind, in navy trousers and shirt with *Flight Doctor* emblazoned on the front in block letters, a stethoscope slung casually around his neck, he looked calm and confident. His hair ruffled in the slight hot breeze as a surge of...*something* flooded her system.

Desire, she supposed. But there was something else too. A tug that didn't feel sexual, an attraction that *wasn't* sexual.

A feeling of...yearning?

'Ready when you are,' Kaylee said.

His eyes broke contact then and a pent-up breath escaped Chelsea's lungs in a rush, her body practically sagging. Holy *freaking* moly. She hoped this was just the jet-lag because this *whatever it was* was seriously inconvenient.

Maybe it was just that she went for a particular sort of man and Aaron had pinged her radar after three years of not noticing *any* man. Dom had been a combat medic, after all. Good-looking, though in a very different way from Aaron. More pretty-boy beautiful—high cheekbones, amazing eyebrows and long eyelashes that had been his mamma's pride and joy. He hadn't been as tall or as broad, and his hair had been jet-black and shiny, his skin bronzed, hinting at his Sicilian heritage.

Hattie excused herself, breaking into Chelsea's thoughts, and she forced herself to concentrate on the activity at the plane door as they unloaded the patient. It took a few minutes, the team all working as one, but the patient was soon out and on the stretcher.

He appeared to be in his fifties, one arm heavily bandaged and elevated in a sling hanging from a pole off the stretcher, the other arm sporting two IV sites. A bag of fluid was running through the cubital fossa site in the crook of his elbow and an infusion of what she assumed to be some kind of narcotic, given he didn't appear to be in any overt pain, was hooked up to the one in the back of his hand.

He was shirtless with three cardiac dots stuck to his chest

and his jeans and work boots were well-worn and dust-streaked with some darker patches of blood. A woman about the same age—his wife?—her face creased with worry, stood at the head of the stretcher, her clothes and sturdy work boots also streaked in caked-on dirt, dust and some blood.

Chelsea listened with half an ear as Aaron ran through the details for the paramedics, focused more on the deep resonance of his voice, his accent, than the content of the verbal hand over. Words such as 'mangled', 'traumatic amputation' and 'morphine' registered only on a superficial level until she heard, 'Two fingers on ice in the Esky.'

Esky? Glancing across, she saw a male flight nurse hand over a small Styrofoam container she assumed was a cool box.

The report ended and Kaylee and Robbo departed with the stretcher, the patient's wife following close behind. Aaron turned back for the plane and Chelsea wondered if he was avoiding her after what had happened last night.

'Chelsea,' Charmaine said. 'This is Trent Connor, he's one of our lifers.'

Dragging her attention off Aaron, Chelsea smiled at the statuesque indigenous man in the flight-nurse shirt. He had salt-and-pepper hair, salt-and-pepper whiskers and an easy grin. Trent's level of experience had been evident from his pertinent additions to the hand over process, his quick efficiency with the equipment and procedures and his rapport with the patient and his wife. Then there'd been the synergy between him, Aaron and the paramedics which spoke of a well-oiled team and mutual respect.

'Born and raised right here on Iningai country,' he said, offering his hand. 'Thirteen years with the service next month.'

'Hi, it's lovely to meet you.' They shook hands. 'I'll be counting on you to show me the ropes.'

'Most important thing to remember is not to eat anything in the fridge labelled "Brett" if you want to live.'

'I heard that.' A voice drifted round to them from the other side of the plane.

Trent grinned. 'He puts triple chilli on everything.'

'He does.' Charmaine shuddered. 'God alone knows what the inside of his gut must look like.'

'Still hearing you.'

Chelsea laughed. 'Duly noted.' Although she liked her food spicy too.

'When you get settled in, you should come round for dinner one night. The missus makes a deadly risotto.'

Chelsea assumed that *deadly* in this instance was a compliment and not meant in the literal sense. 'I'd love to.'

'How come I never get an invite to dinner?'

Every sense going on high alert, Chelsea glanced behind Trent to find Aaron striding across to their group, his mop of dark-brown hair blowing all around in the light breeze, the sun picking out bronzed highlights. His strong legs ate up the distance, his gait oozing self-possession.

'Because you flirt with my wife.'

'Ha,' Aaron said as he halted opposite Trent and next to Charmaine, his hand pushing his hair back off his forehead, where it had settled in haphazard disarray. 'Your wife flirts with me, buddy.'

Trent rolled his eyes. 'My wife is Irish. She flirts with *everyone.*'

Aaron laughed and Chelsea's insides gave a funny kind of clench at the deep, rich tone. 'True. Very true.'

'And of course,' Charmaine said as Trent excused himself and headed back to the plane, 'you've already met Aaron Vincent, one of our four flight doctors on staff.'

Steeling herself to address him directly, Chelsea schooled her features. 'Yeah, we did.'

He grimaced but a smile played on a mouth that dipped on the right. Up this close, and not in a fog of panic and jet-lag, she could see more detail than last night. Such as his eyes, that were a calm kind of grey but nevertheless seemed to penetrate right to her soul.

Thrusting his hand out, he said, 'Nice to meet you properly, Chelsea, and apologies again about last night.'

Keeping her smile fixed, Chelsea pushed the awkwardness from last night aside and took his hand. 'It's fine,' she said dismissively as a pulse of awareness flashed up her arm and their gazes locked. Those grey eyes were no longer laughing but intense, as if he could feel it too. 'These things happen.'

Aaron's features were more…spare than Dom's, she realised. Up this close, it was impossible not to compare him with the only other man who'd ever caused such a visceral reaction. Dom's face had been all smooth and perfectly proportioned, where Aaron's was kind of…battered. Like a thin piece of sheet metal that had been hammered over a mould, the indents still visible as it pleated sharply over the blade of his jaw and curved over the somewhat crooked line of his nose.

There was a slight asymmetry to his face too, the right cheekbone a little lower than the left, making his right eyebrow and eye slightly out of line with their left-sided counterparts, and causing a crookedness to the right side of his mouth, giving him that lopsided smile. A tiny white vertical scar bisected his chin at the jawline.

Once again, she was overwhelmed by the pure masculine aura of him. By a tug that was almost feral in its insistence that she move closer. Panicked that she might actually act on the impulse, she dropped her hand from his grasp, only just quelling the urge to wipe her palm on her shorts to rid it of the strange pulsing sensation.

'Will the patient be transferred to a primary healthcare facility soon?' Chelsea asked him, grabbing desperately for normality.

Just two professionals talking shop. *Nothing to see here.*

'Yeah,' Aaron confirmed. 'Balanora hospital isn't equipped for major micro-surgery but he'll get X-rays and have his condition assessed properly here first. Brisbane already knows about him. They'll be sending out a retrieval team, probably in the next couple of hours. His injury is stable but the viability of the fingers makes his transfer time critical.'

'He was lucky,' she said.

'Yep. There was a fencing accident out on one of the properties around here about five years ago that severed an arm and resulted in a fatality when the guy bled out.' He shook his head. 'It was awful. Trent was on the flight and it was an old friend of his. Rocked the community.'

'Does that happen often? Treating people you know?'

'Reasonably often, yes. Balanora might only have a population of three thousand but we're the major centre for the surrounding districts. People from all around shop here or see a doctor here or send their kids to school here. People with kidney disease come to the hospital for dialysis, babies are born here. There are a few restaurants and a couple of churches, and popular social events are run at the town hall every month. Not to mention the OA's regular district clinics. So, yeah, pretty much everyone knows everyone.'

Chelsea nodded slowly. Aaron's voice was rich with pride and empathy, as if he understood all too well the double-edged sword of living *in* and serving the health needs *of* a small community. That wasn't something Chelsea had ever had to worry about when she'd been flying all over the UK for the last decade on medical retrievals, mostly via chopper. The area was a similar size to the one she would be covering out here but the population differential had made the possibility of actually treating someone she knew remote.

Unlike Aaron, obviously. His steady grey gaze communicated both the privilege and the burden of such situations and, for a ridiculous second, Chelsea wanted to reach over, slide a hand onto his arm and give it a squeeze.

She didn't. But it was a close call.

After what felt like a very long pause, during which no one

said anything, Charmaine broke the silence. 'You ready to check out your new digs? Your boxes arrived this morning and are in the garage. Or do you want to explore some more around here?'

Chelsea jumped at the lifeline, finally breaking the sudden intensity between her and Aaron Vincent. She did *not* want to explore more—she didn't want to be anywhere near this man and his curious ability to stir her in ways she hadn't been prepared for. She was obviously going to have to deal with this soon, but for now she was happy to pretend it was a combination of jet-lag, unresolved emotional baggage and stepping outside her comfort zone. And would pray that it was a temporary aberration.

'New digs would be good. Might as well get a start on unpacking.'

'Right.' Charmaine nodded. 'Let's go.'

CHAPTER TWO

ALMOST THREE HOURS LATER, Chelsea had made some decent headway on the unpacking in her new house, situated in a modern development on the edge of town. The shady, tree-lined street with row after row of cookie-cutter houses drowsing in the Outback heat—low-set brick with neat lawns, concrete driveways and double garages—had made her smile and excitement stir in her belly as Charmaine had pulled into the drive.

It was as different from Dom's parents' detached Georgian behemoth in Hackney as was possible and she'd felt instantly lighter.

The fact she had subsidised accommodation *and* a car included in the contract—a standard OA offering to attract experienced medical professionals to the middle of nowhere—had sweetened the deal. Looking around her now, she realised the fully furnished house was a true godsend.

Chelsea hadn't packed much to bring with her—just a dozen boxes of her most precious things, a lot of them books. She'd down-sized significantly when she'd sold the martial home a few months after Dom had died. Moving in with his parents had seemed like the right thing at the time, united as they'd all been in their grief. And Francesca and Roberto had needed her in those months that had followed, clinging to her as their one last connection to their beloved son.

Hell, *she'd* needed *them*.

But it had grown increasingly hard since Alfie. Well, since before him, really, but that sweet little three-year-old had been the proverbial last straw.

Chelsea pushed the last of the six remaining boxes full of her books against the far wall in the living room. She was going to need to buy a couple of book cases because, although there were a couple of wall shelves affixed above the boxes, they weren't enough.

Francesca hadn't seen the point in Chelsea taking all her books to Australia when her contract was only for a year but Chelsea had been adamant. An obsessive reader and a voracious re-reader, books had been her comfort all her life. The few memories she had of her mother were of being read to by her and, in those dark days after Dom's death, she'd buried herself in fictional worlds.

Leaving them behind would have felt like a betrayal. Plus Chelsea knew that, if this job was all she hoped it would be, she wouldn't be returning to the UK.

She just hadn't the heart to tell Francesca.

But the truth was there was nothing keeping her back home. Her mother had died in a car accident when Chelsea had been four, and her father had remarried to a woman not much older than Chelsea when she'd gone off to uni in London, and they now lived in Spain. She loved her father, and she was happy for him and had visited him in Spain, but his grief had made him emotionally distant when she'd been growing up and they weren't particularly close.

There were some aunts, uncles and cousins, and of course good friends she'd made over the years, both through work and a couple of friends through Dom, but there were so many ways to correspond these days. Chelsea knew she'd be able to keep in touch. And they could come and visit, just as she would return to the UK in a few years to catch up with everyone.

Including Dom's extended English-Italian family that was big and raucous, with so many cousins and second cousins always in each other's business, Chelsea had lost count. And, of course, Alfie. But by then she'd have had time, distance and perspective, and hopefully seeing Dom's son wouldn't be such a wrench.

Francesca wouldn't like it, she knew, but hopefully over time she'd come to realise that it had been too hard for Chelsea to stay and play the role of dutiful widow when her husband hadn't been the man she'd thought he was.

Or the one his grieving mother tried to paint him as.

She understood Francesca wanting to downplay the inconvenient truth—that her son had not been a faithful husband. He was dead. A war hero. Killed in Afghanistan. But even heroes could be flawed, and Chelsea couldn't keep being a part of the cult of Saint Dom.

Her tummy rumbled. She was hungry but also tired. *Again*. How was that even possible after sleeping for twenty-three hours?

Damn you, jet-lag.

She could eat—that would help. It would give her something active to do and the sugar would perk up her system. Because she was damned if she was going to bed this early after such a long sleep. She'd be awake at three o'clock in the morning.

Of course, she didn't have any food in her fridge, so that was a problem. Charmaine had said the small local supermarket stayed open to nine, so she could go and do some shopping, even though the mere thought made her tired. Nor did leaving the air-con appeal. But it would be something to do. And if she cooked something when she got back it would help to keep her going to a more reasonable hour.

Her phone dinged. A text from Francesca.

Missing us yet?

Chelsea grimaced. She loved her mother-in-law but it was hard to miss her when she texted every five damned minutes. Putting the phone in her pocket, she went to the kitchen to grab the car keys. Her pocket buzzed and she sighed as she removed her phone and read the text.

You must be lonely all by yourself in a strange town where no one knows you.

She almost laughed out loud as she scooped the keys off the white granite top of the island bench. The fact no one knew her in Balanora made it feel as if a boulder had been lifted off her shoulders. The phone buzzed again.

You know you can always come home again if you made a mistake.

'Damn it, Francesca,' Chelsea muttered, scowling at the screen. 'Turn the record over.' Her mother-in-law had been fretting for two months over this move.

Chelsea headed for the sliding door at the end of the kitchen that lead directly into the garage and slid it back just as a knock sounded on her front door.

Who could *that* be?

She didn't know anybody. Not many people, anyway. Maybe it was a neighbour popping by with a welcome casserole, which would save her a trip to the supermarket...

Turning round, she made her way to the front door and opened it, the warmth of the evening instantly invading the screen door that was still shut. Not that she really registered the temperature or the orange streak of the sunset sky behind the head of...*not* a neighbour.

Aaron Vincent.

Looking cool and relaxed in shorts, with a T-shirt stretched across his chest, he smiled his crooked smile and everything south of Chelsea's belly button melted into a puddle.

'I haven't eaten yet, and I took a punt that you haven't either, and thought I'd introduce you to the delights of our very good Chinese restaurant as a formal apology for last night.' He held up a loaded plastic bag.

The outline of takeaway containers confirmed the contents of the bag, as did the aroma of dim sums and honey chicken wafting in through the screen.

'I even brought you a menu for your fridge.' He held up it up in his other hand. 'Because, trust me, you're going to want one.'

Chelsea's stomach growled in response and her mouth watered like a damned sprinkler. 'You really don't have to apologise again.'

'I know but... I am *really* sorry.'

Chelsea had never known a genuinely contrite man—especially one who looked like Aaron Vincent—could be such an aphrodisiac. Bloody hell. She could *feel* her pulse surging through her veins, beating hard at her temple and neck, and throbbing between her legs.

Gah!

A little voice in her head demanded she send him away. Tell him she was too tired. Because him just standing on her doorstep had put her body in a complete tangle. Spending time with him, just the two of them? God alone knew how she might embarrass herself and there'd been enough embarrassment between them already.

And she was hardly dressed for company. She wore frayed denim cuts-off that probably sat a bit too high on her thighs and a snug tank that moulded her chest. Although, he had seen her in just her tank and undies last night.

Her inertia must have clued him in to her indecision. 'If you're not up for company, that's fine. I'll just leave the food with you and catch up with you tomorrow.'

Tell him you're not up to company. Send him away.

'Umm...'

The phone buzzed in her hand and Chelsea was actually grateful for Francesca's timing, for once. It gave her something to do while she thought about how she could politely decline, even though her stomach was now growling loudly enough for the entire neighbourhood to hear it.

Dom would want me to look out for you. You were the love of his life.

It was precisely the worst thing Francesca could have texted in this moment. A spike of rage lanced right through Chelsea's middle as she read the text several times. The love of Dom's life... Francesca kept saying that, but *had she been*? How much had he *really* loved her? Not enough to be faithful. Not enough to honour their marriage vows. Not enough to honour *her*.

Just...not enough.

Goaded by the hypocrisy of the text, Chelsea quashed every impulse to keep Aaron Vincent at a distance and reached for the handle of the screen door. 'Sounds great, thank you. C'mon in.'

Chelsea didn't wait for him to enter, just turned and headed down the hall that led from the front door into the living area. Entering the kitchen, she placed her phone and keys on the counter and opened the cupboard above and to the right of the worktop, grabbing two plates. She wasn't thinking about what she was doing, she was just operating on autopilot, the need to lash out mixing with the irrationality of jet-lag.

When she turned around he was there, on the other side of the island, big and solid, reaching inside the bag, pulling out the containers, busying himself with lining them up next to each other and removing the lids.

'Chopsticks?' he asked, glancing at her as he brandished a pair encased in their paper wrapper, his eyes drifting to the spot where a chunk of hair had just fallen from her up-do.

Chelsea's belly did a funny shimmy and she sincerely hoped it would stop doing that some time soon. They had to work together and feeling this…caught up every time he looked at her…would not be conducive to that. But his eyes were calm and steady, his *presence* was calm and steady, and that felt like the anchor she needed right now when these unexpected feelings had her all at sea.

'I'm afraid I never quite mastered the art.' She quickly scooped the errant slice of hair up, poking it back into the mess on top before opening the draw beside her and reaching for some cutlery. 'Fork?'

'Nah.' He took the sticks out of the wrapper and separated them, drumming them against the counter top. 'I have mad chopstick skills,' he said, then promptly dropped one.

Much to her surprise, Chelsea laughed. These past three years, laughter had felt like some terrible breach of grieving protocols in a house where the laughter had died along with Dom. But, with the constraints of home thousands of miles away, it was actually liberating.

'So I see.'

She blinked, her words taking her even more by surprise. They sounded…*normal*. As if they were just two people having a normal conversation. Normal felt weird after the tension from last night and the awkwardness on the tarmac earlier. It felt weird, too, being alone with a man in her home like this, something of which she was now excruciatingly aware as they faced each other across the island.

She hadn't even known this man twenty-four hours ago.

He grinned, picking up the stick. 'I hope you don't mind, I just picked up my standard order.'

Chelsea blinked at the six containers on the island and the bag holding two dim sums and two spring rolls. 'You eat *all* this?'

'I usually make it do two nights.'

'Does this mean I'm depriving you of dinner tomorrow?'

'I'm sure I'll survive,' he said derisively. 'Now.' He held out his hand for a plate. 'What's your poison?'

Chelsea glanced at the containers, all heavily meat-based—beef and black bean, chicken and cashew, sweet-and-sour pork and crispy duck. 'Is this a bad time to tell you I'm vegan?'

The battered plains of his face took on a startled expression. 'Oh, crap... Are you?'

For the second time tonight, she laughed. The impulse to tease him had come out of nowhere, but God, it felt *so* good to laugh...*really* laugh. 'Sorry, no, just couldn't resist.'

Placing his hand on his chest, he huffed out a laugh. 'Thank God for that! I grew up on a sheep station. I might have had to reassess our friendship.'

Friendship.

Was that why he'd come? Not just to apologise again but to establish their boundaries? Which was probably a very good thing.

There was nothing but appreciative noises and food commentary for a few minutes as they tucked into their meals, sitting on the stools on Aaron's side of the island. He was right, the food was delicious, and Chelsea knew she'd be using the Happy Sun's takeaway menu regularly.

'Want water?' she asked as she slid off her stool. 'I'm sorry I can't offer you anything else until I pick up some groceries.'

'Water is fine, thank you.'

Locating the cupboard with glasses, she grabbed two off the shelf. 'You mentioned a sheep station?' Chelsea flipped on the tap and filled a glass. 'Is that Australian for farm?'

He nodded. 'Very, very big farms, yes. Tens of thousands of square kilometres.'

Chelsea blinked. 'That *is* big.'

'Yup. Curran Downs is small comparatively. Almost four thousand square kilometres.'

Small? That was the size of an entire *county* in the UK. She knew Australia was immense but she couldn't imagine being out in the middle of all that vastness. 'Curran Downs?' Chelsea slid a glass across to him as she took her stool again. 'That's its name?'

'Yep. It's about a hundred K north of here. Dad's still out there and my sister helps him run it.'

'You have a sister?'

'Yeah. Tracey. She's two years older than me and a born farmer. Never wanted to do anything else.'

'But not you?'

'It was expected but…' He shrugged, picking up his glass of water. 'When I was fourteen, there was a bad car accident just outside our property. A tourist had had a heart attack at the wheel and ran into about the only tree within a fifty-kilometre radius. He was trapped inside and needed the Flying Doctors to get him out, and I felt so damned useless.'

He shook his head and there was a distant look in those grey eyes, as though he was back there in that day. 'They landed on the road and managed to get him out. He arrested twice after they extracted him and they had to give him CPR before they could put him in the plane. It was very…dramatic. But they saved his life that day right in front of my eyes and it was…'

His gaze came back into focus, resting on Chelsea, and she could see how much the incident had impacted him. 'Inspiring. I knew that day I wanted to do *that*.'

'And what did your dad say?'

Laughing, he said, 'My father looked at me and said, you'd better knuckle down at school, then.'

Chelsea smiled. 'You weren't a good student?'

'I did okay but I just didn't really see the point in busting my gut studying Shakespeare and advanced algebra when I was going to be running sheep all my life.'

'And what did your mum say?'

'My mother was thrilled. She never could understand why anyone wanted to live out in the middle of nowhere. She left when I was thirteen.'

'Oh… I'm sorry.'

'It's fine.' He shrugged. 'She was a city girl. My father met her when he was on a trip to Canberra in his early twenties. She was a translator working for the French consulate. They had a whirlwind courtship resulting in an unplanned pregnancy, followed by a quickie wedding at Curran Downs. Before she knew it, she had two babies under three and… It's hard out here. Isolating. If you're not born to it, if it isn't in your blood—sometimes even if it is—it can be stifling.'

Chelsea could see that. Flying in, over endless kilometres of earth so barren it could have been another planet, the remoteness had left a stark impression. It would be very lonely, Chelsea imagined, for someone who might be used to a very different kind of life.

'Not a lot of interpreter jobs going around out here,' Aaron continued. 'Particularly in the days before the Internet. She stuck it out for as long as she could before high-tailing it to Sydney but, to be honest, I don't know if she was ever that happy. Even as a kid I could sense that about her. She loved us, of course, but Mum also loves art galleries and restaurants and live theatre. She likes to throw dinner parties. She wasn't cut out for the life out here. It…*we*…weren't *enough*, you know?'

Chelsea nodded, feeling that sentiment right down to her bones. She'd never been enough for her father. Or her husband.

A wave of empathy swamped her chest and for a moment she almost reached out and touched his arm as she'd wanted to do earlier today.

Just as earlier, she didn't. 'Could she not have lived in town?'

'She did, to start with, seeing if they could make that work, but it was in the middle of a drought, and Dad couldn't leave for date nights and conjugal visits when he was hand-feeding the stock. Running a sheep station just isn't a nine-to-five job. And the closest thing to theatre in Balanora is the annual end-of-year school concert.'

Chelsea nodded. 'Was it amicable?'

'Sure, as much as these things can be.'

'Is she still in Sydney?'

He picked up a dim sum before answering, 'Melbourne now.'

'Do you see her often?'

'I saw her quite a bit when I was studying and working in Sydney, but only a couple of times since moving back home three years ago.'

'You and your sister didn't go with her?'

'We could have done, but Tracey was adamant she wasn't going anywhere.'

'And what about you?'

'A part of me wanted to go but it also felt incredibly...disloyal to leave, particularly when things were so dire with the drought. It was all hands on deck all the time.'

Chelsea nodded as she took a mouthful of crispy duck, the skin crunching to perfection. She supressed a moan as the sweetness of plumand the tang of ginger exploded across her tongue. 'But you did leave to go to uni, right?'

'Yes, four years later. To Brisbane. The drought had broken a couple of years prior and the station was in good shape. Plus, Tracey was full-time on the farm by then. I went home and helped out in holidays and, now I'm back, I usually head out there once a week on a day off.' He smiled 'Tracey always has a job for me.'

Although she'd seen him earlier in the doorway of an OA plane with a stethoscope around his neck, it wasn't that hard to imagine him in dusty jeans, a checked shirt and cowboy hat. His face had a weathered, outdoorsy quality about it and his body had a hardness and physicality to it that hinted at manual work.

Same as his hands. Currently wielding chopsticks as if he'd been born out the back of a restaurant in China town, they weren't soft or smooth. There was a toughness to them, a thickness, a couple of tiny scars over the knuckles. Like his face, they were a little banged up. Definitely not soft or smooth.

Rough.

A tiny shiver wormed its way right up Chelsea's centre thinking how those big, capable hands might feel on her belly. On her breasts. On her inner thighs.

Oh, God.

Clearly her body had no plans to stop with whatever this was any time soon. But she could hardly kick him out mid-dinner—which *he* had bought for her—because her libido was on the blink.

That was the problem, she decided—after three years in a deep freeze, her libido had decided to roar back to life. It was probably perfectly natural and normal but right now it was inconvenient. Ignoring it as best she could, she said, 'It was always your plan? To come back home?'

'Yeah, since seeing that accident. Just because I wanted something other than the station didn't mean I wanted to move to the city and forget my roots. I just wanted to serve my community in a different way.'

'I get that.'

'Except to work in any kind of Outback Flying Doctor situation I needed emergency medicine experience, so I was away from home for over a decade, working in both Sydney and Melbourne hospitals, building that experience so I could come back to Balanora.'

She detected a streak of guilt in his voice, something which Chelsea understood acutely right now. Just because something was for the best didn't make it easy to bear.

'I came home and helped when I could, usually during shearing, but it's great to be finally home for good and only a phone call away.'

For good. It sounded very final. 'You're planning on staying with the OA?'

'Absolutely.' He took a drink of water. 'I might need to occasionally go and do a few months here and there in the city to keep my skills up to date or attend a course, that kind of thing. But I *love* this place and I *love* this job. There's such variety, and yet there's a familiarity too that speaks to that fourteen-year-old, you know?'

'Yeah.' Chelsea nodded. 'I know.' She *really* did. She'd left familiarity behind and that had been scary.

But vital.

He drained his glass and set it on the counter top. 'What about you? You're a long way from home. In my experience, people come all the way out here for three reasons. They're from the area, like me.' He held up one finger. 'They're hiding.' He held up a second. 'Or they're running away.' The third finger joined the others. 'Which one are you?'

The frankness in his steady grey gaze was unnerving. This conversation had taken a sudden probing turn. 'What about adventure?' she obfuscated.

'That why you're here?'

'Sure.' She shrugged. 'Why not?' She was *totally* running away but she wasn't going to tell him that.

'A woman after an adventure won't find much in Balanora to satisfy.'

Oh, *Lordy*... Had he chosen *satisfy* deliberately? 'Are you kidding? I'm from cold, rainy England where a lot of people consider an hour's flight and half-board in Lisbon the height of adventurous. Coming to the Antipodes is like the equivalent of climbing Mount Kilimanjaro.'

He laughed. 'Maybe. But you wait until summer reaches its zenith. It'll feel more like a wrong turn than adventure.'

Chelsea paused, a spring roll halfway to her mouth. 'It gets worse than *this*?'

He laughed, and dear God... It was deep and sonorous, settling into her marrow like a sigh. 'It does. Not too late to change your mind.'

She shook her head. 'I have a year's contract which I plan to honour.'

'And after?'

It was obvious that Aaron was trying to ascertain Chelsea's

intentions. She supposed that he'd probably seen a lot of people coming and going in his time when they realised all this isolation and vastness wasn't for them. *Including his mother*. So she understood. But she wasn't about to commit to what happened after her year was up—she'd be stupid to do that when she hadn't started the damn job yet.

'I don't like to plan that far ahead any more.'

'Any more?'

Chelsea shut her eyes. Damn it…that had been a slip. Before Dom had died she'd planned everything, because so much of their lives hadn't been in their control due to his military service so she'd tried to control what she could. From meal planning to holiday itineraries to the cat worming schedule—all had been noted on both her phone calendar and a big paper one on the wall.

Now, she lived from one roster to the next and tried to be more spontaneous. Dom had teased her about how rigid she was, and even three years later she wondered if that was what he'd gone looking for in other woman—spontaneity.

When she didn't answer, Aaron said, 'Charmaine mentioned you were widowed a few years ago. I'm sorry.'

His condolences were gentle and Chelsea opened her eyes to find him watching her carefully, his grey eyes soft, radiating the kind of empathy she'd felt earlier. She looked at her hands in her lap, at the white mark on her bare ring finger, the thumb of her other hand stroking over it lightly. Chelsea had taken off her wedding band on the flight to Australia. She'd thought it would be a wrench—it hadn't been.

It had been freeing.

As freeing as it had been reverting to her maiden name from Rossi. She hadn't realised how much she'd resented them both until they were gone.

'Yes.' She glanced up to find those eyes watching the action of her thumb before they were raised to hers again. 'Thank you.'

Holding her gaze, Aaron asked, 'Do you mind me asking what happened? You don't have to answer if you'd rather not.'

'He was collateral damage,' Chelsea said. 'His unit had been engaging the enemy and one of them had been hit. He—Dom... his name was Dom—was a combat medic. It was on his fifth tour of Afghanistan. He was rendering assistance and got caught in some crossfire when the fighting changed direction. He got hit in the neck...his carotid.'

They were the facts as dispassionately as she could tell them, because thinking about him dying in the dirt of a foreign land, his life ebbing away, was always too much. She might be angry with him, his infidelities might have irrevocably damaged how she felt about him, but it didn't reduce the senseless wrench of his death.

Aaron nodded slowly. 'Nothing anyone could have done about that.'

'No.' Obviously, Aaron was used to dealing with sudden death and the people left behind, but his calm statement of fact was worth a thousand trite inanities.

'I'm truly very sorry.'

A hot spike of stupid tears pricked at the backs of Chelsea's eyes and she blinked them back hard. There was *no way* she was going to cry in front of a guy she barely knew over something she'd already shed a million tears about.

'Thank you.' Clearing her suddenly wobbly voice, she wrenched her gaze from his and stood, picking up his empty glass of water and her half-full one. 'I'll get us some more water.'

He didn't try to stop her, for which she was grateful, and by the time she resumed her seat her emotions had been put firmly back in place. 'So, tell me about sheep,' she said as she picked up her fork to resume eating.

'Sheep?'

'Yeah. I assume you know a bit about them?'

He chuckled. 'You could say that. Yeah.'

They continued eating and he entertained her for the next fifteen minutes about sheep facts and his own personal observations about the animal in question. It didn't require a lot of input from Chelsea, and made her laugh, which helped kick any lingering emotion to the kerb. He moved onto shearing anecdotes. Somehow it wasn't a stretch to believe that Aaron could shear a sheep. He exuded the calm capability of a man who could do anything.

Who could do *everything*. And *that* was sexy.

'I bet you're the only doctor who's actively shearing sheep in the country.'

'I don't reckon I'd be the only one, but there wouldn't be many.' He placed the chopsticks on his empty plate. 'I should also stress that, while I am a dab hand with an electric shear, I am nowhere near as fast or as accurate as the pros.'

'How long does it take them to shear a sheep?'

'About one to two minutes usually.'

Chelsea blinked. 'Holy sheep.'

He laughed. 'Elite shearers can do it in under a minute. It takes me about five minutes.'

'Wow, I'd like to see that.' Realising what she'd said, Chelsea hastened to clarify, 'I mean, the pros. Under a minute. That's gobsmacking.'

'We have a team hitting up our place at the end of the month. There are a couple of elite guys in the crew, if you want to come out and spend some time in the shearing shed?'

'Really?'

'Sure.' He picked up his plate and hers and carried them to the sink.

A tiny trill of excitement put a smile on Chelsea's face as she watched him. 'See?' she crowed. 'I've been here for a day and I'm already lining up my adventures.'

He laughed out loud, his head titled back, exposing the light brush of stubble at this throat. 'I don't know what you think happens in a shearing shed, but it's hot and dusty and full of sweaty, uncouth blokes. Nothing very exciting, and probably a bit too Australian for a genteel English woman with a posh accent.'

It was the first time Aaron had mentioned her accent. Dom had always teased her about her *hoity toity* Reading accent. But then, anything had sounded cultured next to his snappy East End accent. Raising an eyebrow, she said, 'Genteel?' Chelsea would admit to sounding posh but she was hardly a *lady*.

'The guys will think you've just stepped out of Buckingham Palace.'

Chelsea's nose wrinkled. Her accent might sound upper-class but it was far cry from plum-in-the-mouth royalty.

'I'm just saying,' he clarified. 'Look at it as a chance to experience some Aussie farm culture, *not* an adventure.'

'I see what you're doing.' She narrowed her eyes. 'You're lowering my expectations.'

He hooted out a laugh as he re-joined her on the other side of the bench. 'Absolutely. Take your expectations, divide them by two then halve them again.'

'I'm sure it'll be great.'

Shaking his head, Aaron leaned his butt against the edge of the island, not resuming his seat. It gave Chelsea a great view of his profile—the crooked line of his nose, the smooth bulge of his bicep, the flatness of his abs. 'I should get you to sign a waiver in case they damage those cute English ears with their filthy language.'

Chelsea lifted a hand to an ear reflexively, feeling the softness of another wisp of hair that had escaped her up-do. Nobody had ever complimented her *ears* before. 'If you think a nurse who's worked in emergency departments hasn't heard worse on any given Friday or Saturday night shift, then you haven't been paying attention.'

'That's true,' he conceded.

'I've been sworn at, drunkenly propositioned, *lewdly* propositioned, bled, vomited and cried on by the best of British hooligans, and I would pit them against shearers any day.'

He laughed. 'I'm sure my lot would disagree, but I've been on the receiving end of some very colourful insults from a couple of drunk Barmy Army guys a few years back, so I'm prepared to concede.'

Turning his head, he grinned at her, and Chelsea grinned back. As an emergency doctor, he'd have no doubt seen it all too, and a tiny flare of solidarity lit her chest. Their look went on a little too long, however, their smiles slowly fading. His eyes shifted to where strands of her hair kissed the side of her neck. His hands moved and she held her breath for a loaded second or two, her skin tingling beneath the heat and heaviness of his gaze.

Her pulse thudded as time slowed. Oh, God. He was going to touch her. Worse than that, she wanted him to…

CHAPTER THREE

HE DID NOT touch her. He folded his arms instead and looked away, and Chelsea released her breath, 'Not done unpacking yet, I see.' He tipped his chin at the boxes against the far wall.

Chelsea quashed the stupid tingle running up and down the side of her neck. 'Not yet. Just my books to go.'

'Books?' He glanced at her. 'You must be a serious reader if you had to bring your books with you for a year?'

Chelsea wasn't sure if he was fishing again for her future plans, so she steered clear of that pitfall. 'I am. Always have been.'

They'd been an escape from a home life where she'd often felt like an intruder on the silence and intensity of her father's grief. Inside the pages of a book, however, she could be loud, she could be adventurous. She could be free. Free to feel things she hadn't felt able to express to someone who mostly seemed to look straight through her.

He wandered over to the handful of books she'd placed on the shelves above, giving Chelsea an unfettered view of broad shoulders, firm glutes and muscular calves. Picking up her copy of *Animal Farm*, he said, 'You like the classics?'

'I like pretty much everything. Are you a reader?'

'I am. Usually non-fiction, though. Biographies and books about the history of stuff. You know, empires or buildings or political systems. Mostly on audio.'

'That's wise. They're cheaper to lug around the world and don't require bookcases. Speaking of, is there a furniture store in town where I could purchase one?'

'There's Murphy's. In the main street. They're not exactly cheap, though. Might be better to order something online and get it delivered or check out the local buy-swap-sell pages. Lots of bargains and you could get it straight away. I have a ute, if the seller can't deliver, and can give you a hand to put it together if it's a flatpack.'

She didn't know if his offer to help came from ingrained manners, Outback hospitality or something else, but she felt sure inviting Aaron into her house again wouldn't be a good idea. Not until this…jet-lag-induced crush had passed, anyway. 'Thanks. I'll check it out.'

As if to support her jet-lag theory, a feeling of overwhelming weariness hit her out of the blue and she yawned. Aaron turned in time to see it. 'God, I'm sorry. You've had a few big days, you must be exhausted.'

'It's fine,' she dismissed. Then yawned again. He quirked an eyebrow and she gave a half-laugh. 'I'm sorry. I spend the first couple of days not being able to sleep at all and now it appears I can barely stay awake.'

'Jet-lag's like that.'

Yeah. Didn't make it any easier to tolerate, though. 'It doesn't bode well for Friday.' She had a full orientation schedule the day after tomorrow and Chelsea hoped she'd be over the worst of it by then.

'That's still two sleeps away.' Aaron checked his watch. 'It's almost eight, that's not too bad. And you'll be up later tomorrow night because of the welcome dinner at the pub.'

Chelsea's heart sank at the reminder. The thought of going out and socialising, if she felt like this again tomorrow night, made her feel even wearier. But Aaron was right, being forced to stay awake and sync her clock with Aussie time was a good strategy.

He crossed back to the kitchen, the well-developed muscles of his quads far too distracting in her foggy brain. 'I'll go so you can hit the sack. A good night's sleep tonight and you'll wake up a new woman.'

She wanted to tell him she already felt like a new woman. Moving thousands of miles away from the lush green of England to the dusty dry of the Outback, far removed from the things that had defined her since Dom's death, had seen to that. But coherency of thought was getting harder and harder, plus she didn't want to invite closer scrutiny. She'd already told him far too much about herself.

'Let me help you with the leftovers first.'

Chelsea watched dumbly, her head full of cotton wool as he went round the other side of the island, opened the draw and grabbed a fork. Picking up one half-empty rice container, he forked the contents into the other half-empty rice container. 'Oh,' she said automatically. 'You don't have to do that, I can manage.'

'It's no problem.'

Working in tandem, it took a couple of minutes to rationalise the containers to three and fridge them. Aaron flicked on the tap as Chelsea shut the fridge. 'What are you doing?'

'Just going to wash up the empties.'

Chelsea shook her head. 'No need.'

'It's not a bother,' he said dismissively. 'It'll only take me a jiffy.'

'Nope.' Chelsea crossed to the sink and took the washing-up liquid out of his hand. 'Absolutely not.' She shut off the tap. 'You've done far too much already.'

'Okay, okay.' He held up his hands in surrender. 'I know when I'm not wanted.'

Chelsea rolled her eyes even as her breath caught in her throat. If only she *didn't* want him. 'No one told me the Outback Australian male was this domesticated.'

'Sure we are,' he said with a grin. 'I can even darn a sock.'

His grey eyes sparkled and, as their arms brushed together, Chelsea became aware of their closeness. Of his laughing face, the way his fringe swept sideways across his forehead and his lopsided smile. The scar on his chin.

'Where'd you get that?' she asked, turning slightly towards him as she gave in to the impulse to touch.

Her finger pressed lightly against the raised white pucker at the centre before stroking gently, absently noticing the fine prickle of whiskers. Vaguely, Chelsea was aware of the crinkle lines around his eyes receding and the husky change to his breathing as his smile faded.

'Would you believe me if I told you a knife fight?'

Chelsea laughed, glancing into the steady grey intensity of his eyes. The space around them shrunk and her breathing roughened to mimic his, her pulse a slow throb through her temples. 'Is it true?'

'Sadly, no. I tripped over a sheep when I was a kid and conked my chin on the ground.'

'Not quite as dramatic,' she admitted with a smile, her gaze roaming over his features, wondering about every deed and mishap that had resulted in the fascinating mix of imperfections that made up his face.

He smiled too, his mouth curving up, and she itched to run her finger over the crooked line of his top lip. 'Apparently, I was an exceptionally clumsy child.'

She laughed, but it didn't last long, as their gazes locked and the air between them thickened. The heat of his body, the scent of him—honey, ginger and an undernote of something sweeter—infused the air, drawing her closer. Her heart thumped almost painfully behind her rib cage.

What was happening? *How* was this happening?

Becoming aware that her finger was still toying with the scar on his chin, Chelsea let it slide away. What on earth was she doing? She needed to step back.

Step. Back.

But her finger sliding away had parted his mouth slightly and she couldn't look away, she couldn't step back. No more than she could check the impulse to rise on her tip-toes and press her mouth to his.

Aaron's mouth was a strange mix of soft and hard, and she moaned, clutching at the front of his shirt as her pulse swelled in her head. It had been over three years since she'd kissed a man and it felt strange and unfamiliar. Because it wasn't Dom. But it also felt *good* because it wasn't Dom, and she leaned into it, wanting… She didn't know what.

More? Deeper? Closer?

Whatever it was, it was a moot point, as Aaron broke away, taking a half-step backwards. Her brain saturated in a thick fog of lust, her mouth tingling wildly, it took a second for Chelsea to register the sudden loss of sensation. But awareness came back *fast* and, with it, swift recrimination.

'Oh, God.' Her eyes flew to his face, horrified at what she'd just done. At what she'd instigated. 'I am so, *so* sorry.' She shoved a hand in her hair as she took two full steps back, heat flushing up her chest and her neck. 'I…' She shook her head. 'I don't know what came over me. This isn't me. I'm not after… *this*. It must be the jet-lag.'

Why not? People had murdered other people whilst sleep-walking. Surely a random, unsolicited kiss whilst sleep deprived wasn't that much of a stretch?

He didn't say anything, just stood there staring at her, or her mouth anyway, his eyes not quite focused, his lips still parted, a thumb pressed absently against the mid-point of his bottom lip as if he was trying to commit the moment to memory or maybe…savour it? Whatever the reason, his continued silence made it worse.

'Aaron…' she said, her voice low as she twisted her non-existent wedding band. 'Please say something.' God…she was going to have to resign before she'd even started.

Francesca would be delighted.

His hand dropped from his mouth as he snapped out of his trance. 'Its fine,' he assured her with a smile.

Oh, God, *what*? It was so far from fine it was laughable. 'No.' Chelsea shook her head vigorously. 'It is *not* fine. It was…inappropriate and I've gone and buggered up our professional relationship before it's even begun. It'll feel…weird and awkward now.' She folded her arms, feeling nine kinds of idiot. 'I'm so sorry. I can see Charmaine tomorrow about backing out of my contract. I can cover until they get someone else.'

'Whoa.' Aaron gave a half-laugh as he held up both his hands in a stopping motion. 'Hold your horses. There is no need to resign. It won't feel weird or awkward. We're two adults—two professionals. I'm sure we can work together without this being a thing.'

He might not feel weird and awkward, but she sure as hell would, and she wasn't sure she'd get over it in a hurry either. Maybe he had women he'd just met try and kiss him out of the blue every other day but it was not something Chelsea did.

She cringed again, thinking about what she'd done. 'God…' She cradled her hot cheeks in her palms. 'I'm so embarrassed.'

'Have you forgotten I crashed your hotel room last night? Consider us even in the embarrassment stakes.'

The thought cheered Chelsea for about three seconds. Until she realised it wasn't the same at all. *This* hadn't been an accident. It wasn't as if she'd tripped and her mouth had fallen onto his. It had been deliberate, if not very well thought out.

'But it…' Aaron ran a hand along the sink edge. 'Shouldn't happen again.'

Chelsea dropped her hands. Was he mad? *Of course* not. 'Oh, God, *absolutely*. That will *never* happen again. I'm not after anything like this.'

A curious, fleeting expression crossed his face that looked a lot like regret. 'It's just that… I have a—'

'Oh, no,' Chelsea interrupted, a flush of dread hitting her veins. 'You already have a girlfriend, don't you? Or a boyfriend,' she hastened to add, not wanting to presume, because *of course* there was someone out there. The man was seriously good-looking *and* a doctor.

Just then an even worse thought slunk into her brain. 'Dear God…please tell me you're not married.' He didn't wear a wedding ring but then neither had Dom.

He chuckled, and it was deep, warm and low but somehow not reassuring. 'Chelsea, relax.' He reached out a placatory hand. 'I'm single. I just have this rule… Well, not a rule, really, that sounds very formal. More like a preference, I guess, to not get involved with a woman who's not from around here—'

'Right, yes, of course,' Chelsea said, interrupting again as relief flooded her chest. 'You absolutely don't have to say any more. I totally get that.'

She imagined that being with someone—he'd definitely clarified it would be a woman—who knew intimately what it was like to live way out here so far away from anything made relationships easier. He'd lived through the consequences of how badly it could go wrong with his mother leaving.

For a moment it looked as though he *was* going to say more but he didn't. He just nodded and said, 'It really is fine, Chelsea.'

His gaze sought hers but she couldn't quite meet his. 'Okay, thank you.'

'Well.' He lightly bopped his fist on the edge of the sink. 'I'll head off now but I'll see you tomorrow night.'

Tomorrow night. God…her welcome dinner. She was going

to have to sit and socialise with a bunch of new work colleagues *and* Aaron and pretend that she hadn't taken total leave of her senses and impulsively kissed him.

Damn you, jet-lag.

'Yep,' she said, her smile strained. 'I'll be there.'

'Goodnight, Chelsea,' he murmured, then turned and walked away, disappearing round the corner into the hallway.

Chelsea didn't move for a bit, listening to the sounds of his retreating footsteps then the closing of the door. Her hands shaking, she took two steps to the sink, flicking on the tap and splashing cold water on her still hot face. That kiss and the excruciatingly awkward conversation afterwards were nothing compared to the realisation that jet-lag had little to do with what had happened and that she, in actual fact, did have a *crush* on Aaron.

Whom she would be working with and whom had made clear that, even if she decided to ditch all her reasons for coming here—none of which involved hooking up with a guy—and wanted to get into some kind of *something* with him, outsiders were not his preference.

God…how pathetically clichéd was she? Apparently starving-for-affection, widowed nurse sleazing on to sexy doctor. *Ugh.* Chelsea lowered her head, pressing her forehead against the cool edge of the stainless-steel sink.

How was she ever going to look him in the eye again?

Aaron wasn't sure what to expect from Chelsea on Thursday night. He wouldn't have been surprised if she'd made some jet-lag-related excuse and cancelled. But she hadn't. She was here with a dozen OA staff, mostly medical, although Meg, Hattie and Carl, one of the other pilots, along with Brett, had joined them too.

Not only was she here but she was having a great time, chatting away, asking and answering questions as well as laughing at

Brett's terrible dad jokes. She seemed to have slotted in easily, quickly adopting the banter that the team had always enjoyed.

Probably nobody had noticed that she'd barely acknowledged him when he'd arrived and had spoken and looked at him only when necessary. But Aaron had noticed. She was obviously still feeling mortified about the kiss despite his assurances that it was fine.

That he was fine.

The truth was it had been *more* than fine. *He* had been more than fine. He'd been attracted to her from the moment he'd switched on the light in her hotel room and she'd screamed and yelled at him to get out. The gut clench he'd felt in that moment had been *visceral* and it had nothing to do with her being in her underwear. It had been the magnificence of her fire-breathing indignation and how primed she'd been to go on the attack, her eyes spitting chips of brown ice, her messy hair flying around her head with each vigorous shake.

The reaction had been the same when he'd spied her from the door of the plane yesterday, her hair in a slim pony tail flicking from side to side as she talked, fine, escaped wisps blowing around her face.

He'd known plenty of attractive women, had even slept with a few, but none of them had made his abdomen cramp tight or his heart drop a beat the second he'd laid eyes on them.

Unfortunately, the pattern had repeated when she'd opened her door to him last night. It was the closest they'd been physically since she'd arrived and, even through the mesh of the screen, he'd felt the impact of her deep in his belly. He really just should have left there and then. Handed over the food and vamoosed.

But he hadn't.

He'd been too distracted by the way her hair kept falling out of her crazy up-do, sliding against her neck, and then her phone had chimed with an incoming message of some kind and her jaw had clenched and she'd opened the door. By the time he'd noticed her frayed denim shorts and just how well her tank-top outlined her breasts, he'd been committed.

Hell, it had taken all his willpower not to straight-out ogle.

And, when she'd started talking about herself, it had been nigh on impossible to leave because he'd wanted to know all about her, this discombobulating woman from the other side of the planet holding a world of hurt in her eyes. But then of course the kiss had happened and the wheels had fallen off the wagon.

He'd been hoping that by tonight he'd be used to seeing her and the strange pitch of his belly would be no more. Apparently not. His gut had performed its now familiar clench as he'd spotted her sitting between Charmaine and Trent in a strappy green dress, her hair all loose and flowing, dangly earrings sparkling through the strands of sandy-blonde.

It was such a stupid way to feel, given she was patently still in love with her husband. She'd tried, but she hadn't been able to hide the raw emotion when she'd talked about him, her voice turning soft and husky. And then there was that very white line on the ring finger of her left hand. The ring might not be there any more but it had obviously been only a recent removal.

Why she'd kissed him was anyone's guess. Maybe he reminded her of him. *Dom.* Maybe it had been the thought of all the adventures making her reckless. Maybe it had been a long time for her and he'd been there and it'd been a weird moment.

Hell, maybe it *had* been jet-lag.

Whatever had precipitated it, reading anything into it was a dumb idea. Even leaving aside her horrified confirmation that it would *never happen again.* Oh, and the fact *she was still in love with her husband,* and she was here for a year.

One year. If she lasted that long. And then she'd be gone and he was *not* up for that.

Aaron had seen too many mates out here devastated by romances that hadn't worked because a lot of women that came from out of town weren't prepared for the *reality* of living in the Outback. They saw *Farmer Wants A Wife* on the TV and thought it was all picnics around a shady dam and bottle-feeding cute, fluffy lambs.

Thanks to his mother's desertion, Aaron had learned early to guard his heart from women who might not stick around. Especially ones who had signed a one-year contract and had been evasive about what came after. Ones who came from the lush green of a faraway country so different from the red dirt of the Outback, it might as well have been another planet.

Sure, he'd dated local women a couple of times since returning, but it was hard when the eyes of the community were watching and far too invested in the outcome and, frankly, there was zero spark. It had been much easier to indulge in occasional discreet liaisons with women who were just *passing through*. They weren't looking for love, they certainly weren't looking to stay. But a fun night of recreational sex with an Outback flight doctor?

Hell, yes.

And, until somebody came along with spark to burn, he saw no reason to change. Unfortunately, his eyes drifted to Chelsea, his belly going into its usual inconvenient tangle.

No—*not* her. *Absolutely not.*

'Trent, perhaps if you've finished pumping Chelsea for the locations of all the best pubs in London, maybe we could ask some questions too?'

Julie Dawson, another flight doctor, spoke good-naturedly and everyone laughed. She was ten years older than Aaron and had been with the OA in Balanora for six years.

'You can always rely on me to ask the important questions, Ju-Ju,' he said with grin.

Julie shook her head and switched her attention to Chelsea. 'I understand you have a lot of critical care experience.'

Chelsea rattled off her impressive CV that spanned the last twelve years and included midwifery and both neonatal and adult ICU.

'And Charmaine was saying that you did a fair bit of retrieval stuff?' Julie continued.

'Yep. I was on both the NICU and adult ICU teams. Mostly chopper retrievals, due to the shorter distances. But there was a lot of variety, which always kept it interesting.'

'What was the most interesting thing you ever went to?' Trent asked.

'A man who got his arm ripped off by a lion at a small county fair in the wilds of Berkshire.'

There was a round of gasps. 'Was he the lion tamer?' Julie asked.

'No.' Chelsea grinned. 'He was a random local who'd been dared by the lads at the pub over the road to go and pat the lion.'

Winces broke out across faces. 'I bet he was pissed!' Brett said.

'He was roaring drunk,' Chelsea confirmed, deadpan. 'Pardon the pun.'

Everyone laughed and Aaron's lungs got tight. Chelsea was charming them all. Whatever her reasons for coming to Balanora—he was sure she was running away—old Blighty's loss was their gain.

'And what about—?' Julie began.

'Enough, Ju-Ju,' Trent interrupted. 'Enough with the resumé interrogation, it's time to get down to brass tacks.' He turned to Chelsea. 'I just thought you should know that men outnumber women three to one in the district, which means you could have your pick.'

'*Trent!*' Charmaine said sharply.

Aaron had always admired the way Trent clomped his way through awkward moments with his huge size twelve feet. The thing was, it was surprisingly effective with patients, who magically seemed to open up about stuff, *personal* stuff, they often wouldn't disclose to a doctor.

Ignoring the warning note in Charmaine's voice, Trent continued, '*If* you were in the market for some romance. Maybe you're not ready yet, and that's fine, but I volunteer to play Cupid if you want. You just say the word, okay?'

His delivery was matter-of-fact but also gentle, and it seemed everyone at the table held their breath, waiting for her reply. Aaron certainly was as he vacillated between wanting to thump Trent for putting Chelsea on the spot and wanting to hear her reply.

What if she indicated she *was* in the market for romance?

Chelsea smiled. 'Thanks for the offer, Trent, much appreciated. I will definitely keep that in mind.'

It was as non-committal as her response to his questions about her plans after the contract expired, but it seemed to satisfy Trent.

'How are you finding the heat?' Hattie asked, changing the subject.

Chelsea grimaced. 'Brutal.'

There was general laughter and commiseration. 'I imagine,' Hattie said, 'it's a little different to back home right now.'

'Oh, yeah.' Chelsea took another sip of her wine. 'I mean, I've been to Australia before, so I knew it was hot, but this…'

'When were you in Australia?' Renee, another flight nurse, asked.

'About fourteen years ago. I came with a girlfriend during summer break at uni. Went to Melbourne and Sydney, the reef and Uluru before flying home.'

'That's *your* summer, right?' Brett clarified. 'Our winter?'

'That's right.'

He hooted out a laugh. 'Yeah…it's not so hot here then. None of those places would have prepared you for the Outback in summer.'

'You know what's worse than the heat?' Renee said. 'The flies. Sticky, black flies buzz, buzz, buzzing around your face.'

'Shh, don't tell her that,' Charmaine joked. 'She didn't ask me about the flies.'

218   NURSE'S OUTBACK TEMPTATION

'It's fine,' Chelsea assured her with a grin. 'I don't scare that easily.'

Trent pulled a five dollar note out of his wallet and placed it on the table. 'I got five bucks that says new girl here lasts two hours on the ground at her first job before she says *bloody flies.*'

Chelsea laughed good-naturedly as five-dollar notes piled up in the centre of the table and everyone claimed a time. Charmaine wrote them all out on a napkin. 'Nine days,' Aaron said as he threw his money down.

His prediction caused a momentary pause in the hilarity. 'Bold,' Trent murmured.

He shrugged. Aaron knew Chelsea had already been through one of the worst things life could throw at a person and that people put up with a lot when they were running from something. She might wilt in the heat, and for damn sure she'd probably not last the week out without getting sunburned, but the flies would probably take a little longer to get to her.

'Looks like you have a champion,' Trent announced gleefully, snatching up Aaron's money.

Aaron cringed internally. The last thing Chelsea probably wanted after last night was for attention to be drawn to them in that way, but she looked at him properly for the first time tonight with only the tiniest trace of reserve and said, 'Thank you.'

He shrugged. 'You know you *will* say it, right?'

Lifting her chin, she looked defiantly around the table and gave a deliberate little sniff. 'We'll see,' she murmured, a smile playing on her mouth, and everyone laughed.

Which was pretty much how the next couple of hours unfolded as they ate, drank, laughed and chatted through three courses in the cool comfort of the Crown Hotel. They swapped war stories about infamous OA cases over the years, while Chelsea regaled them with her stories, ranging from a ninety-one-year-old man who had fallen down a cliff while mountain-climbing to delivering a thirty-weeker in a cow barn in the middle of a snow storm.

In many ways, the two worlds were as different as night and day. Fire and ice. Feast and famine. Desert and green rolling hills. But it was the job that connected them. The people. Whether they were about as isolated as it was possible to be on the planet, or a fifteen-minute chopper ride to the closest major trauma centre, the work was the same, the mission was the same. *Saving lives.* It was what united them all, no matter where they hailed from, and Aaron felt that link—invisible yet somehow tangible—glowing strong around the table tonight.

He felt it in Chelsea too. Here or there, she was one of *them.* Even if she could barely look at him right now.

Aaron didn't see Chelsea the next day until after lunch—in the store room, of all places. He was whistling as he entered, thinking about the great morning he and Renee had spent out at a remote clinic. The sense of community at these pop-up health sites was palpable, from grandmothers with babies on their hips, to barefoot kids kicking a footy around on a spare patch of dirt while they waited for adults to finish their business, to cups of hot tea poured straight from the billy being shared around under shady trees.

It always reaffirmed why he'd wanted to return to Balanora. Why he'd put in all those years in the city. This was home. He knew he didn't have that ancient, spiritual connection that the Iningai had to their country, but he loved the landscape and the people who lived out here in a deep and abiding way that was hard to articulate.

Seeing Chelsea appear from round the end of the main shelf as the door clicked shut behind him dragged him back to the present. She was in the navy trousers and polo shirt of the OA, *Flight Nurse* stamped in fluorescent block print across her chest. Her hair was pulled back into a pony tail, she held a clipboard in one hand and one of the small wire baskets stashed just inside the door in the other.

'Oh…' Aaron pulled up short. 'Hey.'

She stopped in her tracks too, her eyes widening. 'Hey.'

'Sorry. I didn't realise you were in here.'

'Of course not,' she dismissed, but her throat bobbed and her tone was cautious as if maybe she thought he might have tracked her down here or something. Which was utterly ridiculous. He was *restocking*, for God's sake. He was in and out of this store room most days.

'I was just...' She glanced at the clipboard. 'Searching for these items.'

Aaron nodded. Familiarising themselves with the store room was one of the exercises new employees did as part of the induction day. 'Anything you can't find?'

She blinked, as if her brain had been temporarily elsewhere. 'Oh.' She stared blankly at the clipboard. 'The intra-osseous needles.'

'Around the other side, on the right, about half way, second-bottom shelf.'

'Great.' She nodded. 'Thanks.'

But she didn't move for long moments, apparently rooted to the spot, looking at something just over his shoulder. Possibly the door... 'Something else?' he prompted.

'Um...no.' She shook her head, backing up a few steps. 'Thank you,' she murmured before turning and disappearing around the corner, a pen speared through her hair just above the band of the ponytail.

Man...that had been *awkward*. They were clearly going to need to have a talk because whatever it was they were doing now was bound to be noticed. He'd give her a week and if things were still like this then he'd approach her about discussing the issue.

Turning to his hand-written list, he grabbed a basket and started to fill it with the things he needed. Restocking after using the plane was a shared responsibility and, with Renee doing the clinic paperwork, it was his turn.

It took longer than it would usually, given how excruciatingly conscious he was of every sound Chelsea was making. His body literally *hummed* with awareness.

'Okay,' came her muffled voice from the other side. 'I give in. I can't find them.'

Despite the situation, Aaron smiled to himself. He remembered how long it had taken him to find things in here in the beginning. Placing his basket down, he strode round to the other side to find Chelsea kneeling on the floor in front of the shelf, scowling at the boxes.

Aaron paused for a moment, leaning his shoulder into the edge of the end panel. 'Want me to have a boy look?' he asked, quirking an eyebrow.

She turned her scowl on him and he couldn't help it—he laughed. It was the first time she'd looked at him with no hint of what had happened between them on Wednesday night and it was such a bloody relief.

'They're *not* here.'

Shaking his head, he pushed off the shelf and, as if she realised he was going to be almost on top of her within a few paces, she scrambled to her feet, the wariness back again.

Oh, well…it had been nice while it lasted.

As further proof the unguarded moment was over, she stepped back a couple of paces as Aaron approached. He refused to let it bother him as he stopped in front of the shelf in question, leaned down and reached for where he knew the box was stashed.

After three years, Aaron knew where *everything* lived in this store room. But the box he pulled out was full of ten millilitre syringes. Frowning, he pushed the basket she'd left on the floor aside with his foot and crouched to inspect the other boxes but Chelsea was right. It wasn't there. He checked behind the boxes at the front and the shelf below and above, in case they'd accidentally been put in the wrong place.

'Hmm,' he said, turning to face her.

Clipboard clutched to her chest, she folded her arms. 'I don't like to be the one to say I told you so, but…'

Aaron chuckled. She was looking at him again and, if he wasn't very much mistaken, there was smugness in those big brown eyes. 'I know we recently had some on order but they arrived this week, I thought.'

Intra-osseous needles—special venous-access devices that screwed into the bone, allowing use of the marrow to deliver emergency fluids when no veins could be found—weren't required that often and tended to expire before they were ever used.

'Maybe the box was removed before the replacement came in for some reason,' Aaron mused out loud. Or Tully, who took care of stores, could have been interrupted in the middle of sorting the stock that had arrived on Wednesday and not managed to get back to it yet.

Moving around Chelsea, Aaron headed for a desk area at the end and to the left where the inventory came in and was checked off before being put away. Grabbing the box cutter that lived on the desk top, he sliced several boxes open before he found what he was looking for. 'Found them,' he called, grabbing a smaller box and returning to Chelsea.

She averted her gaze as Aaron strode towards her then crouched to put the box on the shelf where it belonged. Grabbing one, he rose and handed it to Chelsea.

'Thank you,' she murmured, glancing at him briefly as she took it.

Dropping her gaze, she pulled the pen out from her hair and made a tick mark on the form clipped to the board. Rationally, Aaron knew she wasn't doing it as a turn-on but, bloody hell, something about it or about the unselfconscious way she'd done it was super-sexy, and the urge to kiss her throbbed through every cell in his body.

And he really needed to quash that urge right now because, if that was where she always stashed her pen, he was going to see that a lot, and wanting to kiss her every time she did it would be seriously inconvenient.

'Any time,' he said gruffly. 'Anything else?'

She looked at him briefly and opened her mouth, as if she was going to say something then thought better of it, and shook her head, dropping her gaze to the clipboard again.

Aaron sighed. Okay, maybe *the talk* couldn't wait a week. Maybe they should hash it out now. Staring at her downcast head, he said, 'Chelsea… I think we need to talk.'

It took a beat or two, the only sound the low hum of the air-con before there was a definite rough release of breath and her chin lifted, her gaze meeting his. 'Okay.'

'We can't keep doing this…' He waved a finger back and forth between them. 'We have to work together so—'

'I know, God, I know,' she interrupted, her gaze beseeching. 'I'm sorry, I just…can't stop thinking about how much I embarrassed myself on Wednesday night, and you said it wouldn't be weird or awkward, but it is. It really, really is. And that's on me, and I'm just so sorry.'

Aaron shook his head, taking a step towards her because he didn't want her feeling like this, but he didn't know how to convince her. He wanted to grab her arms and squeeze them a little to really get it across but he kept his hands by his sides.

'You *didn't* embarrass yourself. You should try barging into a woman's hotel room in the middle of the night. A woman you don't know and is in nothing but her underwear and you're going to be working with her two days later. *That's* something to be embarrassed about. To be sorry about.'

Her snort was full of derision. '*That* was an accident. *My…* action was deliberate. God.' She shut her eyes briefly and shook her head. When they flashed open again they were full of anguish and she leaned in towards him, as if to implore him. 'You were just being kind and welcoming and I must have come across as the worst kind of sex-starved…' She bugged her eyes at him, leaning in closer. 'Widow. Making a play for the first guy I've been alone with in three years. I totally blew it and I just...' She shook her head. 'I'm so sorry.'

Her impassioned tirade hit Aaron square in the chest, her torment over the incident palpable, and he couldn't take the rawness of it. His heart was beating fast and his breath was as heavy as wet sand in his lungs. She seemed to be under the impression that she'd been the only one feeling something on Wednesday night.

And he just couldn't bear it.

Lifting hands he'd had clenched at his sides, he slid them either side of her face as he swooped in and kissed her—hard—trying to convey that she hadn't been alone in that moment. That her kissing him had not been some kind of unwanted advance.

Her clipboard clattering to the floor broke the spell and Aaron pulled away, his hands dropping to his sides again. For something that hadn't been more than a pressing together of lips, he was breathing rough. So was she.

Bending over, he scooped up the clipboard then handed it back. She took it and they stared at each other for several long beats, not saying anything.

'You and I are going to have to stop apologising to each other all the time,' he said when he found his voice, although it was rough, gravelly. 'I *liked* it...the kiss on Wednesday night.' His eyes burned into hers. 'You weren't the only one who was feeling it, you know?'

Her eyes searched his for what felt like for ever. She swallowed. 'Okay...'

It sounded tentative, but she wasn't rejecting the premise of his statement, which was a relief. 'But, here's the thing,' Aaron continued, his voice a low murmur. 'I think you're still in love with your husband and, as I said on Wednesday night, I don't get involved with out-of-towners, so what say you and I just be friends? Do you think we can do that?'

'Uh-huh.' Her voice was stronger, surer. 'I'd like to.'

Aaron smiled. 'Me too.' Truth was, he'd like a lot more, but there was no way he could see it ending well for him. Why borrow trouble?

Just then the store room door opened and Chelsea's eyes widened as she looked at him. 'Chelsea?' It was Charmaine. 'Are you still in here?'

'Yes…sorry,' she called, her eyes never leaving Aaron's. 'Just finished. I'm coming now.' She started to back away, shoving her pen back through her hair, and Aaron gave her his friendliest smile because, man…that move would be the death of him, he just knew it.

Finally, breaking eye contact, she turned away from him and Aaron's gaze snagged on the swish of her pony tail and the poke of her pen as she turned right at the end and disappeared from sight.

The door closed and Aaron let out a long, slow breath, confident that Chelsea and him were on the same page with the *friends* thing. And it didn't matter how much that kiss—or the one on Wednesday night—had affected him. Had made him want *things*. They were on track to managing the situation between them so he just wasn't going to think about inconvenient truths. Or those kisses.

Yeah… He was never going to think about *them* again.

CHAPTER FOUR

BY THE TIME Chelsea's beeper went off the following Thursday evening, she was mentally ready to go out with Aaron in the plane for the first time on an emergency retrieval to an Outback property. She'd had enough short bouts of exposure to him the past week to feel confident about their interactions, and the idea of accompanying him into the middle of nowhere to an accidental gunshot wound to a femoral artery didn't fill her with panic.

He'd suggested they be friends and, as the excruciating embarrassment of her bungled kiss had ebbed in the face of their growing familiarity, interacting with him had begun to feel more natural. Maybe there'd never be that level of easy banter she already shared with the rest of the team but she'd challenge any outsider to say their exchanges weren't friendly.

Buckling up in the King Air, the stretcher immediately in front of her, a familiar buzz hummed through Chelsea's veins. She'd been in the air three times already this week, flying with Julie and Trent to community clinics in the region. They'd been fun and interesting, and she'd learned so much about how things were done within the organisation and the expectations of the people they served, but this was to her first emergency situation and her pulse kicked up.

That could, of course, have something to do with Aaron buckling up diagonally opposite, his chair facing hers, but she refused to give that thought any air time.

'You guys ready for take-off?' Hattie asked via the cushioned headphone set already snug around Chelsea's ears and doing a very good job of blocking out the propellor noise.

'Roger that,' Aaron confirmed into the mic sitting close to his mouth on the end of the angled arm that protruded from the left cup of his earphones. His voice, deep and confident, sounded simultaneously close yet far away. He smiled at Chelsea and shot her the thumbs-up.

'Roger,' Chelsea also confirmed into her mic as she returned the thumbs-up.

The plane started to taxi to the airstrip and Chelsea turned her head, looking out of the window, watching the OA hangar get smaller in the fading light. She ran through what they knew about their patient, who was situated four hundred kilometres north-west on an isolated property. He was a twenty-two-year-old man who'd been out kangaroo-shooting with his mates. Quite how he'd come to be shot in the leg was vague, the more pertinent fact being that, by the time they arrived in forty-five minutes, the wound would be two hours old.

Of course, it was still way faster than it would have been for the patient to get to a hospital. A lot could go wrong in two hours where blood loss was involved, and the young guy had apparently bled a lot initially until someone had thought to apply a tourniquet using a belt. The bleeding had reportedly slowed dramatically, but if a large vessel had been compromised in his thigh then blood loss could be significant. The guy involved already had an elevated pulse and was clammy to the touch.

Having a tourniquet on for a long period of time was not ideal either. It could be life-saving in the face of catastrophic bleeding, but it could also compromise circulation to the entire limb, and cause a build-up of toxins which could have a detrimental effect when it was eventually released.

His friends had loaded him on the back of a ute and had driven him to the airstrip. Most large properties in the Outback had an airstrip for things like deliveries of supplies and mail, and of course for emergencies, and Hattie had been given the co-ordinates. The strip was dirt, and had apparently been graded last month, but the guys on the ground had been instructed to inspect the surface, make sure it was clear of any debris and check for any kangaroos in the vicinity.

They were also going to place lit kerosene lamps from the shed situated off to the side of the parking apron, ninety metres apart down either side of the strip. Compared to what Chelsea was used to in the UK, it all seemed a bit like the Wild West. Farms didn't have their own airstrips and no one had ever been instructed to check for kangaroos—but it added to the adrenaline.

A few minutes later, they lifted into the dying golden light of evening, the sky streaked with gilded clouds. The ground, the hangar and the lights of Balanora quickly fell away as the King Air climbed towards the first stars just blinking through the veil of night.

'ETA forty minutes,' Hattie's voice informed them as the plane levelled out shortly after.

'Roger,' Aaron murmured into his mic. Glancing over at her, he fiddled with the dial on the right ear cup of the headset, obviously changing channels to a private one for just the two of them. 'You ready for this?' he asked. His words, his voice, flowed directly into her ear, causing a tiny shiver.

She nodded. 'Pumped.'

'Might be a bit of a bumpy landing.'

Chelsea shrugged. She'd been landing on dirt strips all week. 'I think I'm getting used to it.'

'Trust me, this will be worse,' he said with a laugh. 'The strips at the communities where you've been the last few days are well-used and well-maintained. A lot of the remote strips on properties are pretty rough and ready.'

It was odd for him to be so close, his mouth moving, his eyes fixed on hers, and yet for him to sound so far away, as if he were in the middle of a vacuum. She was used to the phenomenon but it always felt a little disjointed.

'Hattie doesn't seem too concerned.'

He chuckled. 'Hattie could land one of these blindfolded in the middle of a dust storm on a dry creek bed with one hand tied behind her back.'

His laughter unfurled delicious tendrils through her body, and the shiver became a trail of goose bumps along the top of her scalp and across her nape. 'Good to know,' she said with a grin, ignoring the goose bumps and the unfurling.

'Don't worry,' he assured her, his gaze earnest. 'She'll get us down safely. And, if she thinks it's not safe, she just won't land. It's always safety first. She won't risk any of our lives or damaging a precious, expensive resource such as this plane.'

Chelsea nodded. She knew that pilots always put the safety of people on board and that of the aircraft first but it was still comforting to have that reiterated. Comforting too that Aaron knew Hattie so well, and there was an obvious bond of trust between them that came from years of flying together. During her time in the UK Chelsea had got to know a few of the chopper pilots she'd flown with, but there were so many of them in a busy twenty-four-hour city medivac hub, it was rare to go up more than two or three times with the same pilot.

It was another thing she was looking forward to—getting to know the team the way Aaron did. Becoming part of this well-oiled machine she'd witnessed all week.

Aaron switched them back to the combined channel and turned his attention to the paperwork he had on his lap. Chelsea gazed out of the window, darkness encroaching on the vast red swathes of earth broken occasionally by narrow veins of green that followed river banks, or the more circular patterns of grass formed around the edges of a dam or billabong.

She watched until the day had completely leached from the landscape and nothing more could be seen apart from an occasional light or small cluster of lights on the ground.

With Aaron still busy, she switched on her overhead light and pulled her current read—a saga set in Sydney—out of her bag. Occasional chatter in her earphones between Hattie and comms broke the cushioned silence created by the noise-cancelling ability of her earphones, but it didn't rouse Chelsea from the story until Hattie announced some time later, 'There she blows.'

Chelsea glanced out the window as Aaron capped his pen. Down below, two straight lines of lights lit up the runway.

'Comms have confirmation from the guys on the ground that the strip is safe to land,' Hattie said.

Aaron, who had pushed the angled mouthpiece up and away from his mouth earlier, pulled it down again. 'Thanks, Hattie. Comms, any update on the patient condition?'

'No worse. Patient's pain level, eight out of ten, GCS fifteen,' a male voice informed them.

'Roger that. Thank you.' The plane banked to the left as Aaron looked across at her. 'You got all that?'

Chelsea nodded. 'Yes.'

'We should be on the ground in a couple of minutes,' he said.

She shot him the thumbs-up as a tiny hit of adrenaline sparked at her middle. Nerves over not being fully familiar with the plane and where things were kept tap danced in her belly, but Aaron had assured her earlier that the job should be a scoop and run, so they shouldn't need anything too complicated. Getting the patient back to Balanora and hospital for surgical intervention ASAP was their priority.

Chelsea's ears popped as the plane descended. 'Okay,' Hattie said, her voice steely, 'Going in to land. Hold tight you two, might be a bit bumpy.'

Keeping her eyes on the window, Chelsea saw the first few

ground lights flash by then the wheels touched down with a jolt and she braced her feet on the floor as she was jostled about. Glancing over at Aaron, she found him braced too, but grinning, and he let out a loud, *'Whoop!'* She laughed.

'You're a legend, Hattie,' he said into his mouthpiece.

'I know,' Hattie replied, and they both laughed.

Within two minutes the plane had taxied into the parking apron and Chelsea unbuckled herself when it pulled to a halt. So did Aaron. The engines cut out and they both took off their headphones simultaneously. 'How was your first Outback property landing?' he asked.

'Amazing!' Because it had been, and she was totally pumped to get out there.

It took another minute for the props to come to a full halt, during which they both donned gloves. As soon as Hattie opened the door, it was action stations. Chelsea exited the plane first into the warmth of the night, a large bag full of supplies slung over her shoulder and Aaron hot on her heels.

The ute was being parked about three metres away towards the rear of the plane as her feet hit the ground. Their patient was on the back tray along with two other guys, and two more sprang from the ute as soon as the engine cut out, pointing torches at Chelsea and Aaron's feet to light the way.

'Hi,' she said as she approached, the fluorescent letters of her shirt reflecting brightly. 'I'm Chelsea.' She smiled at the faces both on and around the ute, harried expressions telling more than words what they'd been through. 'And who do we have here?'

'You hear that, Gazza?' one of the guys joked. 'They sent the bloody Queen of England herself to rescue you.'

Chelsea laughed, as did the patient, albeit it somewhat weak. 'Lucky me.'

'Hey, Brando,' Aaron said. 'I always knew you'd shoot someone with that bloody gun one day.'

'Aaron, man,' the guy called Brando said. 'Sure glad to see

you.' He sounded it too. Every one of the grimy, night-shrouded faces was looking at them as if they were the cavalry.

'All good.' Aaron nodded. 'We'll take over from here.'

And take over they did, two guys helping Chelsea up onto the tray, then moving out of her way while Aaron sprang up unaided like a freaking gazelle, as if he'd been leaping on and jumping off ute trays his entire life.

'Hey, Gazza,' Chelsea said as she got her first look at the patient's face, the torch beams flooding the area. 'How are you feeling?'

He shut his eyes against the light. 'I've had better days.'

It was encouraging to hear him able to joke, but there was a definite pallor to his skin, and his arm was cool to touch despite the heavy coat that had been placed over his torso.

'You kept him warm, that's good,' Chelsea murmured to the guys as she reached for the new oxygen mask she'd hooked up to a cylinder in the emergency bag before they'd taken off. Keeping a shocked patient warm was basic first aid.

'Derek said we should do that,' one of them said.

'Absolutely, you did everything right,' she assured him as she applied the mask to Gazza's face and turned the oxygen up high. All the guys had blood stains on their clothes, so it had obviously been a team effort. 'You put on a tourniquet, you kept him warm, you got help. You did good.'

All the while she talked, Chelsea worked by the torch light, putting on a finger probe to measure oxygen saturation, applying a blood-pressure cuff and slapping electrical dots on Gazza's chest so they could monitor his heart rhythm. The portable monitor bleeped to life with a green squiggle that indicated a normal rhythm but was definitely too fast at a hundred and twenty beats.

Aaron worked too, doing a quick inspection of the wound. The fabric of Gazza's jeans had already been cut away, exposing the location of the injury a few inches above the knee. A cloth soaked in dark red was covering the site and around it another

cloth—a T-shirt, maybe, given one of the guys was shirtless—
had been tied to secure the makeshift dressing. It was blood-
ied too but not soaked, which was encouraging. Chelsea knew
Aaron wouldn't remove it, wouldn't risk disturbing whatever
haemostasis had been achieved.

'Looks like blood loss has been staunched,' Aaron said as he
inspected the belt that sat several inches above the entry wound.
He wouldn't remove it either.

'BP one hundred systolic,' Chelsea said. Not too bad, considering.

'Okay.' Aaron nodded. 'Let's get in two large bore IVs.'

Under the torchlight, and with Chelsea assisting, both were
placed in the large veins in the crook of each elbow within five
minutes. She used Brando and Waz, the other guy in the back
of the ute, as IV poles, tasking them with holding up the bags
of IV fluids.

'Let's run them wide open,' Aaron said.

Chelsea didn't need the instruction, already opening the
clamp all the way on her side as Aaron did the same on his.
Hopefully the replacement fluid would rally Gazza's system
until he could get a transfusion.

'Could someone please take off his right shoe?' Chelsea asked
as she plucked the pen from her ponytail and noted his obs in
a quick scribble on the glove she was wearing.

The boot was off quick-smart and Aaron sprang off the ute
to feel for foot pulses. 'Nothing,' he said when Chelsea raised
an eyebrow at him several beats later.

'Okay.'

She made a note of that and the time on her glove as Aaron
said, 'He's ready to go. I'll grab the stretcher.' And he strode
towards the King Air.

'Is that bad?' the guy who took the boot off asked.

Chelsea smiled at him. 'It means the tourniquet has been
very effective.'

She wasn't about to reel off all the potentially damaging side

effects of applying a tourniquet for long periods of time and how
controversial tourniquets in first aid were, going in and out of
fashion over the years, and the plethora of conflicting advice
about duration. The bottom line was, without it Gazza would
probably be dead. They could do something about any potential
circulation compromise when he got to hospital.

Nothing could be done about death.

'Okay, guys.' Aaron approached with the stretcher. 'We're
going to need your help to get Gazza loaded.'

'Where do you need us?' Brando said.

CHAPTER FIVE

TWO HOURS LATER, they were back in Balanora. Gazza had been taken away by the ambulance and was currently undergoing an emergency operation performed by the visiting flying surgeon to stabilise him enough for aerial transfer to Brisbane for further treatment and management. Hattie had gone home half an hour ago and Chelsea had just finished restocking the plane.

It had been Aaron's turn but Chelsea had wanted to do it so she could keep familiarising herself with where things were, both in the store room and on board. Once she was done, she bade Brett, who was doing checks on the King Air, a goodnight before making her way to the office to find Aaron.

'Hey,' he said, looking up from the keyboard as she opened the door.

The main office was usually brightly lit but at this hour the only light on was the one directly above the desk Aaron occupied.

'Hi.'

It was the first time they'd been alone together at work since the store room and she felt weirdly shy. But it *was* ten o'clock, and kind of dark, with a hush that was the complete opposite of the daytime bustle.

It made her very aware of him, of her attraction to him.

'How do you think it went tonight?' Aaron asked, leaning casually back in his chair.

Chelsea forced her legs to move closer until she was on the other side of his desk. 'I think it went well.' Unless…he didn't think so? 'Why, did I do something wrong?'

'What?' He chuckled. '*No.* You were great. It was just your first emergency call out, so I wanted to check you were okay with how everything went. Ask if you had any questions or observations.'

'Oh.' Chelsea shot him a rueful smile. 'Right. I think it all went smoothly and that Gazza was lucky to have mates who kept their cool. You know them?'

'Not really. Just Brando. I played footy with a couple of his brothers.'

She nodded. 'You think the tourniquet being on for that long will affect the viability of his leg?' His foot had been alarmingly cold and dusky during the flight.

He shrugged. 'It could do. It'll have probably been on for about four hours by the time they take it off. There wasn't another choice, though.'

'Yeah.' Truer words had never been spoken. It had been the ultimate 'rock and a hard place' scenario. 'It'll be interesting to know how he fares.'

'Charmaine will follow up over the coming days and let us know.'

'Excellent.' In her previous jobs there'd been *so* many incidents attended, it had sometimes been hard to keep track. But Chelsea guessed it was different in such a small, tight-knit community.

'Question.' Aaron sat forward in his chair and sifted through some paperwork. Finding what he was looking for, he handed it across to her, pointing with his pen at a numeral. 'Is this a four or a seven? It looks like a seven but that would be odd.'

Chelsea leaned in, taking the patient observation chart from him and inspecting the notation she'd made on the plane. 'It's a four,' she confirmed, passing it back.

His eyebrows drew together as he looked at it again. 'Note to self,' he murmured. 'Chelsea's fours look like sevens.'

She laughed. 'No way. That is clearly a four.'

Letting the piece of paper slide from his fingers, he shook his head. 'And they say doctors have terrible hand writing.'

'They do,' Chelsea said. Except Aaron's, of course, which, despite its bold strokes and slashes, was entirely legible. 'Yours is an exception.'

'What's that you say?' He put a hand to his ear as if he was trying to hear better. 'I'm exceptional?'

He grinned and Chelsea's breath caught in her throat. An outsider might have concluded that he was flirting but, after a week of observing the team and him working together, she knew this was just Aaron being Aaron, bantering as he would with anyone else on the team.

Which was a good thing.

Due to their rocky start, they hadn't got into that groove yet, so maybe this was his attempt to get there. Chelsea was more than willing to pick up what he was putting down because, as soon as their friendship felt more natural, the better for everyone.

'Ha! Good try. Not quite the same thing there, buddy.'

An expression of surprise flickered over his face—whether at her returning his banter or her use of the word 'buddy', she didn't know—but it was gone as quickly as it came as he clutched at his chest. 'Careful, you'll dent my giant doctor ego.'

Her first instinct was to deny he had any such thing. She had worked with some super egos in her past and Aaron's didn't come close. But she went for banter instead. 'Then my work here is done.'

He chuckled and, yes, Chelsea *did* feel the deep resonance of it brushing seductively against her skin. But, hey, Rome wasn't built in a day, right? 'You done with restocking?' he asked.

Grateful for the subject change, Chelsea grabbed it with both hands. 'Yep. All ready for the next take-off.'

'Good-oh.' He nodded. 'You might as well go, then.'

Chelsea shook her head. 'What about you?'

'No, no.' He sighed dramatically. 'I'll be here for hours yet deciphering your writing, but you go on home and get your beauty sleep.'

'Hey,' she protested with a laugh, even though she could see by the twinkle in those grey eyes he was joking. 'Serve yourself right if you are,' she quipped.

Okay, this was *good*. This was feeling really good now. Friends. Banter. *Natural*.

He grinned. 'I'll see you tomorrow.'

'Unless I see you tonight.' An awkward moment passed between them and Chelsea hastened to clarify. 'You know...if we get called out again.'

'Yeah.' He smiled. 'I know.'

'Right, then.' She tapped the desk. 'Goodnight.'

'Night.'

She was halfway to the door when he called her name and she turned to find him looking at her, the spill of light overhead bathing his hair in a golden aura. Something tugged hard down deep and low.

'You did good out there.'

Chelsea didn't need his praise. She knew she'd done a good job because she was confident in her experience and ability, no matter how new and unfamiliar the environment. But she *liked* it nonetheless.

'Thank you,' she said, before turning and continuing on her way.

Sunday afternoon, Chelsea found herself knocking on Trent's door. He'd called that morning to invite her to an impromptu barbecue in her honour—a get-to-know-the-new-girl thing. Stupidly, she'd assumed it was just going to be Trent and his wife, Siobhan, but when she arrived a fashionable fifteen minutes late, with the requested folding chair and a bottle of wine to share, a party was in full swing.

Music met them as Trent ushered her into a back yard playing host to clusters of laughing, chatting people. Some she recognised from work—hell, she'd recognised Aaron immediately, her eyes drawn to him and a pretty blonde in a midriff top— but a lot she didn't know.

'Oh.' She pulled up short. 'You haven't gone to all this trouble for me, I hope?'

'Of course,' he said cheerily, slinging an arm around her shoulder and giving her upper arm a brisk squeeze. 'You're the guest of honour and we're welcoming you, Balanora style. Suck it up, sweetheart.'

'Trent Connor.' A tall, curvy redhead with an Irish accent approached. 'I told you not to spring it on her,' she chastised, but the lilt in her accent softened it dramatically. She shook her head at Chelsea. 'What's he like?' She stuck out her hand. 'I'm Siobhan.'

'It's lovely to meet you, Siobhan,' Chelsea said absently as they shook hands.

'Come on, then.' Siobhan took the chair and the wine off Chelsea and passed them to Trent. 'I'm going to introduce Chelsea around to some people. Be a darling and get her some of that to drink. She looks like she can do with it.'

'Yes, my little Irish clover,' Trent said with an adoring smile.

Chelsea was whisked away then, meeting person after person until her head spun. There were partners and children of OA staff she'd already met and those she hadn't. Also, several more doctors and nursing staff from the Balanora hospital. There were teaching colleagues of Siobhan's from the primary school, as well as about a dozen young local professionals working for places such as the council, the railway, Department of

Parks and Wildlife, estate agents, tourism bodies and various other businesses around town.

It seemed Trent and Siobhan knew everyone and, despite the surprise nature of the party, Chelsea enjoyed herself immensely. Between meeting so many new people and getting to know Siobhan—who was an absolute hoot—the very pleasant afternoon under the shady backyard gums flew into early evening.

She even spoke to Aaron for a while who, unlike every other man at the party, was drinking some kind of fizzy juice instead of something alcoholic because he was on call until seven the next morning. He introduced her to the woman she'd seen him with when she'd first arrived, who turned out to be Gazza's sister, Maddie.

It was great to catch up on his progress, and Chelsea was relieved to find out that the leg hadn't suffered any detrimental effects from the tourniquet, and that the doctors in Brisbane were already talking about a discharge date some time in the next few days.

'Dinner's up!' Trent yelled just after six, rallying everyone to the barbecue area to grab something to eat.

Chelsea's stomach growled as the delicious aromas of cooking food saw her join the mass migration to the undercover patio. She hadn't realised she was so hungry until now. While in the queue for her food, she and Siobhan swapped stories of life back home.

'How'd you end up here?' Chelsea asked.

'The same as most people. Came out on a backpacking holiday a decade ago, met Trent at the Crown and been here ever since.'

Laughing at the matter-of-factness of Siobhan's statement, Chelsea said, 'Have you been back to Ireland at all?'

'Couple of times. Introduced Trent to the family. Showed him around the country. But this land...it owns him.' She shrugged. 'And I don't want to be anywhere he's not.'

'How have you found the heat?'

Siobhan laughed. 'Not my favourite part of the Outback,' she admitted. 'But I acclimatised pretty quickly. And frankly I'd prefer it to the bloody flies.'

Having experienced those flies already, Chelsea was beginning to understand the common refrain. She'd not uttered it yet but she was in no doubt that she would.

'Okay, what'll it be?' Trent asked as they reached the start of the queue. 'I have chicken pieces, rib fillet and kangaroo snags.'

Chelsea blinked. 'Really?' Although curious, Chelsea had no desire to try the meat from such an iconic Australian animal. Where she harked from, kangaroos were considered cute—not a culinary delicacy.

He tossed his head back and laughed. 'No.'

'Ignore him.' Siobhan rolled her eyes affectionately. 'They're beef and pork. Although, kangaroo meat is highly nutritious and less than two percent fat.'

'Noted,' Chelsea said to Siobhan before turning back to Trent. 'I'll have some chicken, please.'

After she'd eaten, an impromptu touch football game between the teachers sprang up. There was much laughter and friendly sledging from the sidelines, and when it came to an end Chelsea was roped into a game, despite insisting, as Trent grabbed her hand, that she'd never played before.

'Come on, medical staff,' Trent called. 'Let's go.'

'Hospital versus the OA,' Charmaine suggested as she joined the people forming up in the middle of the back yard.

Trent shook his head. 'Doctors versus nurses.'

'That gives you three local A-grade footy players on your team,' she pointed out. Apparently two of the nurses from the hospital played in the local competition too.

'You have Aaron,' Trent returned.

The man in question dropped his head to either side to stretch his traps as he gripped a foot behind him and stretched out a quad muscle. His shorts, already mid-thigh, rode up, and Chelsea couldn't help but notice it was a *very nice* quad muscle. 'I can take 'em all, don't worry, Charmaine.'

'Plus,' Trent added, 'We have Chelsea, who's never played before and probably doesn't even know the rules. That's like a handicap.'

'Hey,' Chelsea said with a laugh. 'I thought I was the guest of honour.'

'Sorry, Chels,' Trent said, not sounding remotely sorry. 'Guest time's over! This is footy.'

'Yeah, *Chels*,' Aaron teased, a crooked smile hovering on that crooked mouth. 'Footy's serious business around here.'

She wasn't sure she was a fan of having her name shortened but, given it seemed to be a way to express affection out here, a trill of pleasure bubbled up from her middle. Maybe it was a sign that she was becoming one of the gang.

She nodded good-naturedly but stuck her hands on her hips, her feet firmly apart in a Wonder Woman pose as she shot Aaron a *faux* steely look. 'Looks like I better bring my A-game, huh?'

There were a few 'Ooh's from the crowd as Aaron laughed. 'You better bring your A-plus,' he said, matching her stance and tone, 'Because doctors demolish.'

The half-dozen people behind him cheered, *'Doctors demolish!'*, smashing their fists in the air.

Trent laughed. 'Whatever gets you through the night, big guy. Everyone knows nurses annihilate.'

'Oh, Jaysus,' Siobhan said from the makeshift sideline that had been outlined with white plates. 'You two going to play or should I just get out me ruler so you can measure your dicks?'

Everyone laughed and the game got underway. It took all of a minute for Chelsea to be glad she'd put on shorts and not the strappy sundress she'd almost worn, lest it would have ended up over her head from the physicality of the game. It might only be touch football but there were plenty of spills as members of each team smack-talked back and forth.

Aaron had been right—footy was serious business!

'Hey, ref!' Aaron called, pointing at Trent ten minutes into the second half. 'Offside.'

Siobhan had taken on the role of referee. 'Yeah, yeah.' She rolled her eyes at Chelsea who was standing nearby. 'Anybody'd think they were playing for bloody sheep stations.'

Chelsea grinned and used the back of her forearm to dash at some sweat as Siobhan awarded a penalty to the nurses. The play started again and this time, by some kind of miracle, Chelsea managed to intercept the ball for the first time. She stared at it in her hands for a nanosecond before everyone roared, *'Run!'* and she took off for the try line.

The closest member of the opposition team to her was Aaron—in fact he was suddenly very close indeed, his presence big as he loped just behind and to her left. Chelsea's heartbeat kicked up in a way that didn't have much to do with the exertion and more to do with having Aaron hot on her heels. The anticipation of feeling the tips of his fingers landing in the small of her back, of him *touching* her in front of everyone, no matter how impersonally, caused her to shiver despite how damn hot she was.

She knew there was no way she could outrun him—he was too muscular, too pumped, for that—but she was smaller and nimbler, a fact she proved when he reached for her and said, 'Gotcha, *Chels.*'

Except he hadn't. Her last-second dodge managed to evade his touch. 'Think again, Azza,' she taunted, the cheers of everyone around her filling the night air and her head as she strode for the line which seemed as if it was getting further and further away.

His warm chuckle, so close, followed her and she knew there was no way Aaron would make the same mistake again. So, with the line approaching, she made a dive for it, looking over her shoulder in what felt like slow motion as he too dove, his outstretched fingers coming closer and closer.

She turned back just in time to brace for impact, the ball

touching the ground before his hand touched her back. Laughing at her triumph, she performed a quick roll to twist out of Aaron's path but he countered, his reactions quicker than the processing of the information that the ball had already been grounded, his body landing sprawled on top of her, his torso half-pressing her into the grass, one meaty thigh tangling between hers.

Somewhere Siobhan yelled, *'Try!'* and her team mates hollered as they all ran towards her. But Chelsea was oblivious. She was only slightly winded by the impact but the effects of Aaron—big and strong, pinning her to the ground with his body—were far more cataclysmic.

They were both laughing, but not for long. Hers died pretty quickly as the thrust of the thigh she had admired earlier pressed between her legs. His followed not long after, as if he too was just realising their position. His gaze zeroed in on her mouth as a hot, dark look passed between them.

They might have agreed to be friends, but Chelsea had no doubt that, had they been alone, they'd be doing more than staring at each other right now, wondering who was going to make the first move. One of them would already have made it.

But they weren't alone and suddenly Trent was there, grabbing Aaron by the shoulder. 'C'mon, get off her, you great big lug, we need to congratulate our girl.'

Whether he was dragged off or rolled off, Chelsea wasn't sure. All she knew was she was suddenly being pulled up and enveloped in the centre of a huge team hug, a lump the size of London lodging in her throat. Grief had seen her withdraw from her social life three years ago. The complicated feelings she'd been experiencing since finding out about Dom hadn't loaned themselves to her being particularly social.

She'd missed it, she realised—just hanging out with colleagues. With…*friends.*

The fact that all these people in this tiny town were now in her friend circle made the moment even more bitter sweet.

'Okay, okay,' Trent said after a bit. 'We still got a few minutes of this half! Let's go kick some more arse.'

The huddle broke up and Chelsea realised Aaron was still lying on the ground on his back. She wondered briefly if he'd been hurt until their gazes locked and the same flare of heat she'd felt when she'd been under him only moments ago burned between them again.

Trent broke the connection by bouncing the football off Aaron's forehead, who swore at him. 'Get up, old man.' Trent grinned. 'We're winning.'

Just then the two beepers Siobhan had been holding—one for Aaron, one for Renee—went off. Everyone around paused as Aaron performed a perfect sit-up, and Siobhan handed both beepers over to their respective owners.

'Car accident.' Aaron read off the screen. 'Two hundred clicks south of town.' Rising from the ground in one smooth move that did funny things to Chelsea's insides, he glanced at Trent. 'Rain check, dude.'

'Any time.' They fist-bumped then Trent clapped his hands. 'Okay, who's going to sub in for hotshot here?'

Someone—a cousin of Trent's whom Chelsea thought was a dentist—stepped forward but she only really had eyes for Aaron as their gazes met and lingered one last time before he said to Renee, 'Meet you at the base in twenty?' and they departed together.

Aaron worked hard the following week to act normally around Chelsea after their crash-tackle incident—no easy feat. He knew he hadn't been alone in that heightened moment and that, had no one been around, it would have had a very different outcome. And every time their gazes had met this week he'd seen that same recognition in her eyes too, no matter how fleeting.

Still, despite the counsel of his wiser angels whispering about the friend zone, his attraction hadn't lessened. Unfortunately, his brain and his body were just not on the same page. The fact that he really *liked* her didn't help. These past couple of weeks, she'd fitted in seamlessly with the team—quick with a laugh, a joke or whip-smart comeback and good-natured about all the teasing over her accent, not to mention efficient, methodical and *kind*.

Everyone—without exception, it seemed—had taken to OA's newest member of staff.

In a lot of ways, liking her was worse than lusting after her, because the latter he could dismiss as bodily urges and that kept him vigilant about maintaining distance. The former made him want to draw closer. To really get to know her and deepen the friendship he'd insisted they have. But he was hyper-aware that the line between the two states was razor-thin and deepening one would inevitably ramp up the other.

And it had only been a couple of weeks!

Thankfully, albeit coincidentally, they hadn't worked together this week, which helped. Not on any of the clinic runs or the three emergency retrievals. They hadn't even been on call together. It wouldn't always be that way, he knew, but perhaps until he was used to being around her, used to this crazy kind of tug he felt whenever she was near, just exchanging a few brief words here and there as they passed by was enough.

Except the universe, it seemed, was determined to keep pushing them together. He took a phone call from Meg on Friday, the first day of his rostered three days off, asking him if he could pick up and deliver a book case to Chelsea's. Dan, her partner, had been tasked with doing it but had been called out of town for work for the day.

'I'm sure it could wait till tomorrow,' Meg said, 'But I know you have the day off, and Chels was so excited last night about finally getting her books unpacked.'

Yes, *Chels* had stuck.

Ordinarily, Aaron would have been keen to help out in this kind of situation, particularly for a new member of their team. He had the vehicle and the brawn, after all, and had already previously offered. But she'd gone to Dan for assistance with the bookshelf—not him—which told Aaron all he needed to know about how much she wanted to avoid being alone with him.

Something he utterly endorsed.

But now Meg had asked him to do it and it would seem odd for him to refuse when she not only knew he was free, but that Aaron would have done it for any other staff member without thinking twice. Sure, he was going to Curran Downs today, but hadn't planned to leave until after lunch, which Meg also knew.

And then there was the way Chelsea's voice had softened when she'd spoken about her books, as if they were her friends...

So, here he was, knocking on her door at nine in the morning after picking the flat-packed boxes up from a house in the older part of town. Chelsea had obviously taken his advice about the thriving local buy-sell-swap site and found two brand-new bookcases, still in their boxes.

He propped the first box against the bricks beside the door and didn't wait for an answer before turning back for the remaining box. The door opened just as he was lifting it out of the tray of the ute.

'Oh. You're...not Dan,' Chelsea said, sounding discombobulated by his presence.

She could join the club, because that short dress brushing her legs at mid-thigh and her bare feet were utterly discombobulating him. Her was hair was piled up in that messy up-do again, several silken strands falling around her nape.

'He got called out of town for work this morning,' Aaron explained as he carried the box towards her. 'Meg rang and asked me to do it.'

'Okay, well...thank you.' She smiled. 'I appreciate it.'

'It's what we do around here,' he said dismissively. 'Help each other out.'

Which was the truth, but he realised he probably sounded curt rather than neighbourly, and he ground his teeth at his ineptitude. *What the hell, dude?*

He leaned the second box on top of the first, the sun on his shoulders already carrying a real bite. But that wasn't what was making him feel hot as he stood two feet from Chelsea—far closer than was good for him. It was the silky slide of her hair, that hint of cleavage at the V of her neckline and her bright-purple toenails that matched the tiny purple flowers of her dress. He had no idea why *toes* were turning him on.

It wasn't as though he had a foot fetish. Or he hadn't had, anyway.

'Could I squeeze past?' he asked. Not that he wanted to *squeeze* at all. He'd prefer she give him a very wide berth.

'Oh, right yes…here. I'll hold the door.'

As if the universe had heard his preference for distance, Chelsea pushed on the screen door, stepping outside to hold it open, giving him plenty of room to pick up both boxes and transport them inside to the blissful oasis of cool. Propping them against the inside wall, he took the first one in to the living room as Chelsea shut the screen and wooden door behind her.

They passed each other as he headed back to get the second box and she looked fresh as a freaking daisy with those flowers swinging around her thighs. She shot him a small smile and Aaron's fingers itched to slide up her arms to her neck, push into her hair and tilt her chin so he could kiss the hell out of her mouth.

Instead, he said, 'You know your electricity bill is going to be a shocker?' Because apparently he was determined to be Stick Up His Butt Guy today.

Either oblivious to his mood, or choosing to ignore it, Chelsea laughed as she crossed to where he'd put the first flat-pack on the floor near the boxes of books. 'Yeah. I do.' She crouched to inspect the pictures on the front. 'It makes me cringe thinking about my footprint every time I flick it on but…*ugh*…hopefully I'll be more acclimatised for next summer.'

Aaron's step faltered at her talk of next year, as though she might actually still be around, but he refused to give it, or the flare of hope it caused, any oxygen. A year was a long time in the dust, the heat and the flies for someone not used to any of it.

'Everyone acclimatises at a different rate,' he said noncommittally as he placed the second flat-pack on top of the first.

Some never did at all.

Even twenty years after leaving, his mother still recalled the heat of the Outback with a visible shudder.

Despite the sweat drying rapidly in the cool, a trickle ran from his hair down his temple and he wiped at it with the back of his forearm. 'Oh, God,' Chelsea said as she glanced up, catching the action. 'Sorry, you've been carrying heavy loads for me and it's roasting out there.'

'It's fine.'

'Nuh-uh.' She stood. 'Let me get you a cold drink.' Her arm lightly brushed his as she passed and he swore he heard her breath hitch before she continued on her way to the kitchen. 'I have water. Cold or tap. I also have juice if you'd prefer.'

Every instinct Aaron possessed told him to decline the drink and leave. *Just leave, dude.* But it didn't feel right, going without offering to put the flat pack together, and in the end ingrained good manners won out.

'Cold water, please.' Because he *was* thirsty. And, if nothing else, it'd occupy his hands.

'Coming right up.' She turned to the cupboards on the wall opposite to the island bench.

Aaron tried—and failed—*not* to notice the swing of her skirt and the way the hem rose as she reached up and grabbed two glasses. Deliberately turning his attention to the flat packs, he crouched beside them, pulling out the box-cutter he'd stashed in the back pocket of his shorts. Just in case.

'Have you got an Allen key?' He had a bunch in the tool box in the back of his ute along with sundry other items that would probably be handy.

'Yeah, I bought a set of eight yesterday from the hardware shop, because the seller said she'd lost the key that came with it.' He heard some clinking as her voice drew nearer. 'But it's okay, I'll be fine. You don't have to stay.' She nudged his shoulder. 'Here.'

Looking round, he took the frosty glass from her fingers, a vision of little purple flowers brushing against pale shapely thighs searing into his brain. 'Thanks,' he muttered before turning back immediately to the flat packs.

Aaron's heart bumped in his chest as he gulped down the water in several quick swallows, the icy cold an antidote to the heat licking through his veins and singeing his lungs.

'Thank you for delivering these,' Chelsea continued, clearly oblivious to his inner turmoil as she plonked herself cross-legged on the floor on the other side of the boxes, almost directly in front of him. 'But you're off home today, aren't you?'

Chelsea had come into the staff room yesterday when Aaron had been discussing heading to Curran Downs for his three days off. He didn't think she'd been listening as he and Brett had discussed the pros and cons of dogs versus drones in mustering.

'I can take it from here.' She held up her ring of Allen keys. 'Have tools, will construct.'

She spoke a good game but she was looking at them as though she wasn't sure which end she was supposed to use and Aaron couldn't suppress his chuckle, the tension in his gut and his neck easing a touch. 'I don't mean to call your furniture construction abilities into question but…do you know *how* to put together a flat pack?'

'No, but that's only because I've never tried. It can't be any harder than setting up for ECMO in the ICU, or having to resuscitate a patient who's coded mid-flight, surely?'

Aaron couldn't fault her logic—those were complex and highly specialised medical procedures. 'Not harder, no, just a different kind of skill. Also.' He shrugged. 'Less life and death, so there's that.'

She barked out a laugh, her eyes crinkling and her lips parting, her head falling back a little, the fine escaped tendrils of her hair bushing the bare flesh between her shoulder blades. Aaron's heart went *thunk*. Then he joined her because, really, it *was* just a bloody book case, *not* life and death.

'I'm sure I'll be fine. Plus, I've seen this kind of thing being done loads on DIY shows.'

'You're right,' he conceded. 'It's not that hard once you know what you're doing.'

'There you go then. Plus, I have all day to figure it out. I'll just read the instructions thoroughly and take it one step at a time.'

'Ah, yeah...about that.' Aaron pressed his lips together so he wouldn't smile at her 'what now?' expression. 'The woman who lost the Allen key also couldn't find what she'd done with the instructions.'

She huffed out a sigh, her shoulders slumping as a V formed between her brows. 'No wonder it was so cheap.' But her defeat was only fleeting as she straightened her shoulders. 'Okay, well... I'll just... YouTube it.'

'*Or*, I can do it for you and you can be putting your books into your new bookshelf in an hour.'

Aaron wasn't sure why he was being so damned insistent. He told himself he was just being neighbourly, that he'd do the same for anyone. But he didn't think that was the truth. He just...didn't want to leave. Not yet.

'An hour, huh?'

'*About*. Might take me longer.' He shrugged. 'Might take me shorter.'

'Okay.' Chelsea nodded, looking at him assessingly. 'On one condition.'

'Oh, yeah.' He laughed. 'What's that?'

'I don't want you to do it for me. I want you to show me how to do it for myself.'

Aaron tried not to read between the lines of that statement, but he did wonder if Chelsea was so gung-ho to do it herself as a way to prove her independence. Maybe, he—*Dom*—had been the kind of guy who had done everything for Chelsea. Although, she'd mentioned he'd been deployed *a lot*, so that didn't sound practical. Nor did it sound like the highly competent woman he'd got to know these past couple of weeks.

But maybe carving out her independence was the first step in…*moving on*. Like up-sticking and coming to live on the other side of the planet had been. Because Aaron didn't believe that whole 'adventure' bullshit.

His idiotic heart leapt at the idea before his brain squashed the errant thought harder and faster than a bug on a windscreen. She might be inconveniently attracted to him—something that was entirely mutual—but she *was* holding back and, whether that was because she was still in love with her husband or too afraid to risk her heart again, it didn't end well for him.

It was stupid to feel so envious of a dead man, but Aaron realised he did. Not because he and Chelsea had had a life together but because Dom had known her back before the terrible blow she'd been dealt.

When she hadn't needed to run away.

'If you really want to try and figure this out for yourself, I'm happy to get on my way.' He held up his hands in surrender.

Maybe this stupid book-case assembly *was* just what she needed.

'What?' She cocked a disbelieving eyebrow at him but a smile played on her mouth. 'Are you welching on your offer, Azza? You talked me into it and now you're backing out on the deal? You're sorry now you said an hour, aren't you? Afraid you talked yourself up a bit too much?'

Aaron grinned, assailed by an overwhelming urge to lean across and kiss that smile right off her mouth. He resisted, but only barely.

He laughed. 'Time me, *Chels*.'

CHAPTER SIX

'HOW DO YOU know what goes where?'

Aaron glanced at Chelsea's perplexed face as they stood side by side, looking at all the pieces he'd laid out on the floor so he could see what was what. 'This isn't my first rodeo, you know.'

'It doesn't look enough. Is it enough?'

'Sure.'

'How do you know? All I see are a bunch of differing lengths of plank and a gazillion screws. With no instructions.'

He shrugged. 'I've grown up tinkering with things. All kinds of engines, running repairs on sheds and fences and water troughs and windmills and tanks and dams. It's just…what you do when you're in the middle of nowhere, with not a lot available and not a lot of money for new things or to hire someone to come and fix stuff. You learn to do things for yourself. To improvise and be resourceful—use what you have at hand.'

She nodded, her head turned slightly to look at him. 'So, you're a…jack of all trades?'

Aaron laughed, glancing at her. 'Something like that.'

She smiled at him then and he smiled back, and Aaron was

aware, once again, how close they were. For a second, he even let himself imagine he was free to lift one of those strands of hair off her neck and drop a kiss in its place. Then he gave himself a mental slap upside the head.

'Okay. Let's get this show on the road.'

It took an hour and fifteen minutes to assemble the two three-metre *faux* walnut bookshelves. Chelsea had been a keen apprentice who'd picked up the ropes quickly, even if those purple flowers had been distracting with a capital D. They stood back to admire their handiwork, which took up almost the entire back wall space.

'*That* is freaking awesome.' Chelsea nodded at it, clearly satisfied. 'How's that for team work?'

She held her hand up to him, clearly after a high five, and Aaron slapped his palm against hers. It felt buddy-like and platonic. Something two friends who'd just worked on a project together *would* do on its completion.

But it only made Aaron aware of how far he had to go until it felt *natural*.

'Not bad at all,' he confirmed.

She laughed. 'See? Shearing sheds and flatpacks—I'm totally kicking adventure arse.'

'Lady...' Aaron shook his head. 'Your definition of adventure su—'

'Needs work,' she cut in, folding her arms as she sent him a mock-stern look.

'Okay, sure.' It was Aaron's turn to laugh. 'Let's go with that.'

'Plus,' she said, bugging her eyes at him. 'I'm not a lady.'

True. Chelsea's plummy English accent reeked of class but she was no wilting flower. 'You only sound like one,' he said with a tone that sounded distinctly like banter.

'You think I should throw in a "crikey" or two and say things like—' she cleared her throat '—that's not a knife, this is a knife?'

Aaron really laughed then. 'Absolutely not.' She sounded as if she were Afrikaans, Kiwi and *drunk* all rolled into one.

'Laugh all you want, buddy boy,' she said with a grin. 'That's exactly how you sound.'

He shuddered. 'I bloody hope not.'

Her brown eyes shimmered with mirth. 'You *bloody do*,' she said, flattening her vowels and deepening her voice, clearly attempting to mimic him now.

Aaron groaned but then he laughed, and she joined him, and they did that for several long moments, just staring at each other and laughing, and Aaron couldn't remember when he'd last enjoyed himself this much with a woman.

Which was why he should leave.

'Well, anyway,' he said as their laughter settled and their eyes didn't seem to be able to unlock. 'I'll…get this rubbish out of your way and you can start loading up your books.'

'Thanks.' She dragged her eyes off him. 'That'd be great.'

Aaron gathered up all the detritus from the assembly and took it out to his ute before heading back inside to say goodbye, because it would be weird just to leave, even if it might be wiser not to put himself in the path of temptation again.

'Um…' Chelsea held up something as he entered the living room, frowning at him. 'Should this be left over?'

She was sitting on the floor surrounded by little piles of books, one of the six boxes open beside her. They were spread out on top of the bookcase, stacked around her on the floor and placed haphazardly here and there on the different shelves.

Aaron plucked the object out of her fingers. It was a screw. 'There's always some random screw left over.'

She quirked an eyebrow. 'If there'd been instructions would there be one left over?'

He grinned as he handed it back, deciding not to tell her that he probably wouldn't have paid more than cursory attention to the directions anyway. 'Of course. It's like the law of flatpacks.'

'The law, huh?'

'Sure. The unwritten kind.'

'Okay.' She laughed. 'As long as the bookcases aren't going to collapse like a house of cards one day, because there's going to be quite a lot of weight in them when I'm done.'

'So I see.' Aaron eyes moved over the multiple towers of books five or six high. And she'd only opened one box. 'I can't believe you have this many.'

'These aren't all.' She made a dismissive gesture with her hand. 'I have about twenty more back in Hackney.'

Aaron refused to read too much into the fact she hadn't brought all the books she professed to love so much and tried to wrap his head around just how many books Chelsea *did* own. 'Twenty?'

'Uh huh,' she said, as if it was the most natural thing in the world to own what must be *hundreds* of books.

'How'd these books make the cut to join you on your *adventures*?'

She smiled at his deliberate use of the word, and he had to look away unless he smiled too and then they'd be smiling at each other. *Again.* He picked up the nearest one off the top of its pile, one by Georgette Heyer. In fact, the whole stack was Heyer books.

Beside that stack was another consisting of classics in their iconic orange cover, and surrounding her on the floor were several piles of what appeared to romance novels, if the covers were anything to go by.

'These ones are my absolute favourites. They made the cut when I moved into Dom's parents' not long after he died. The other twenty are still in storage at a lock-up with all my other stuff.'

There was a lot in that sentence to unpack. Not least of which was, her life was still in boxes in the UK. Which was why he shouldn't be here, trying to be friends when he was just beginning to realise that might not be enough. Also...she'd moved in with her parents-in-law? 'You moved in with your...?'

'Mother-in-law.' She laughed. 'And my father-in-law. Yes.'

'That's…' He cast around for a word that wouldn't cause offence. After all, what did he know? He'd never had in-laws.

'Nutso?'

Aaron barked out a laugh at her candour. 'Well, no, but…it's not something you see a lot of, right?'

'No. And a lot of people thought it wasn't a good idea. But…' Chelsea shrugged. 'I love his parents, we were all grieving and it made sense to be a comfort to each other.'

Her voice had taken on a plaintive quality as her gaze fixed on a point just over his shoulder. He wanted to ask about her parents—had they comforted her? But it felt too personal and she seemed too far away right now.

'It just…' Her gaze focused back on him. 'Worked.'

Which led to the next question. Maybe that was too personal as well, but she had at least opened this door. 'Did it stop working? Is that why you ended up here?'

Shaking her head slowly, she contemplated him for long moments, her eyes suddenly unbearably sad. 'No.' Her lips pressed together for a beat. 'It was…time.'

Caught up in the raw emotion in her gaze, Aaron nodded. 'When you know, you know, right?' Like his mother, who had drawn her line in the sand.

'Yeah.'

As if she realised she'd exposed too much of herself, Chelsea dropped her gaze to the book in her hand and Aaron, determined not to pry any further, reach for another too. He glanced at the well-loved illustrated cover of a girl, a pig and a spider weaving a web around the title.

'Charlotte's Web?' He opened the book. 'This yours?' A name had been written in faded pencil on the inside cover— *Deborah Tanner.*

Looking up at him again, Chelsea nodded with a wistful expression. 'It belonged to my mother, yeah.'

'This is her?' Aaron's thumb brushed over the pencil. 'Deborah?'

'Debbie.' Her gaze shifted to the book, to the way his thumb caressed the page. 'Her name was Debbie.'

Was. Aaron knew that look. He knew that tone. The weight of it, the bleakness of it. 'She died?'

'When I was four. Car accident.'

'I'm sorry.'

She roused herself, shaking her head. 'I don't really remember her. But I do remember her reading me this book.' She reached for it and Aaron passed it to her, watching as she opened it in her lap and absently flicked through the pages. 'I re-read it usually once a year. Cry every damn time,' she said, with a tiny self-deprecating laugh.

'It looks well-thumbed.'

'Yeah.' She nodded. 'It was well thumbed when she was reading it to me.'

'She was a reader as well?' Aaron was aware he was prying again and he wasn't sure if she wanted him to or if she was seconds away from shutting him down.

'Oh, yes.' Chelsea nodded but didn't look up from her lap. 'I think that's where I got it from.'

'Did your dad take over? After?'

She stared at the book for a long time before shaking her head. 'No. Dad...' She glanced up at him. 'My father...checked out for a lot of years after she died.'

Aaron tried to read between the lines of her carefully chosen words. 'He...gave you up?'

'No.' The loose tendrils of her hair swished against her neck as she shook her head. 'I mean, he provided for me. He went to work, earned a living. I had all the things I needed for school and hobbies and university. I wasn't...neglected.'

'Physically.' But *emotionally...*?

'Yeah.' She nodded as if in acknowledgement of what he *hadn't* said. 'That was all he was capable of, really. His grief was…all-consuming. It was enough for him to just put one foot in front of the other most days, you know?'

Aaron nodded. 'Yeah. I know.' His mother hadn't died but they had lost her nonetheless, and his father had certainly grieved in the only way men of his generation from land knew how to do—stoically. Ironically, he and his sister had the drought to thank for holding their father back from a much darker state, with the station and the sheep demanding every last skerrick of his attention.

It could have been very different.

'Having me there probably kept him back from the abyss but I was also an…intrusion in a lot of ways. Which was why reading was so good. I could do it quietly and not be too much of a bother.'

God… Aaron's heart broke for her. She'd been a kid who'd lost her mother. *And* her father, by the sound of it. But she had still felt the need to make herself small—to not be a *bother*. He crouched then without giving the action or how much closer it brought him any thought.

'I'm so sorry,' he said, their eyes meeting now they were on the same level.

She shrugged. 'It is was a long time ago.'

'Did he…is he…?'

Brightening, she closed the book. 'He remarried, when I was in uni. They live in Spain now. I've visited a few times. I'm happy for them. She makes him smile and he deserves to find love again.'

'But?' Aaron definitely detected a *but*.

'Our relationship is…stilted.'

Aaron wasn't surprised, with all that emotional distance her father had laid down. His dad had grieved the break-up of his marriage deeply, and it had toughened him even more, but he hadn't shut his children out. In his own way, he'd pulled them closer. 'I imagine it would be,' he murmured, because he didn't know what else to say.

Trite platitudes about it taking time weren't his style or what she needed.

She shot him a sad, grateful smile, her eyes shimmering with emotion that lurked in the still, brown depths, and Aaron wished he could draw her into his arms and just sit with her in that weird solidarity that came when two people understood intimately what it was to experience loss.

'Anyway.' She gave herself a shake, dropping her gaze to her lap. 'Sorry, I'm prattling on.' Lifting her eyes again, it was as if a veil had come down on the simmer of emotions. 'You have to get going.'

Aaron contemplated telling her she didn't have to pretend she was okay with him, but that felt really personal when she'd been here for two and a half weeks and her life was in boxes back in the UK.

So he stood instead. 'Yeah. My sister's probably already smack-talking about me to the jackaroos. Last time I was late, she told them I was getting a pedicure.'

Her laughter broke the strange tension that had sprung between them. 'Thanks,' she said, looking up at him again. 'For everything.'

Aaron nodded, knowing it wasn't just about the bookcases. 'See you next week.'

Before Chelsea knew it, they were in the last days of November and she'd been part of the OA team for a month. And she *loved* it! Something she announced to Aaron as the plane taxied to a halt back at the base at four o'clock on Thursday afternoon after they'd finished up at a remote health clinic a couple of hundred kilometres west of Balanora.

Unlike the first couple of weeks, they'd worked together a lot this past fortnight—about seventy-five percent of the time— and familiarity had bred *content* as their rapport had developed. She'd been worried about how they would go, given her pulse still did a crazy tap dance every time she saw him, but it seemed that enforced proximity had helped to dull her reaction.

Or at least normalise it. Allow her to put it in perspective. She found him attractive. He found her attractive. It didn't mean *anything* unless they acted upon it. Which meant *they* had the power.

'Love, huh?'

'Yes.' She nodded enthusiastically as she hung up her earphones on the hook and unbuckled. 'The remote clinics remind me why I wanted to be a nurse in the first place.'

He laughed, his hands sliding absently to each end of the stethoscope he had looped around his neck. 'Even with the heat and the flies?'

'Yes.' She hadn't uttered *bloody flies* yet but it had almost slipped out many times. 'What we do out here feels so much more important than what I was doing back home. Let's face it, if you're anywhere near a city or even a town, help—good professional, medical help—is usually not that far away. But out here? We're it. And that means something. I actually feel like I make a difference out here, a real difference.'

'You know you're preaching to the choir, darlin',' Hattie said from behind.

'Amen,' Aaron agreed, his eyes twinkling.

'Yeah, yeah.' Chelsea laughed at herself but the glow of satisfaction inside her chest was too big to suppress. 'It was just a really good day out there, wasn't it?'

There'd been nothing particularly complicated medically— immunisations, wound management, suture removal, baby checks and diabetes management—run of the mill stuff. Their bread and butter. But the fact the forty people at the clinic didn't have to drive over three hours into town and three hours back on dirt roads for basic care, and the *appreciation* that had been evident, had given her a real high.

'It was.' He nodded in acknowledgment. 'It was a good day.'

Then they were smiling at each other, which felt good too. The hitch in her pulse be damned.

Chelsea was still buoyed an hour later as she restocked the plane. Being in the cool haven of the store room helped, so did her run of three days off stretching ahead. She—*and* Aaron—were on call tonight but that ended at eight a.m. and her days off officially started. Best of all, in the afternoon, Aaron was going to pick her up and take her out to Curran Downs so she could watch the shearing that had started yesterday.

And she was *really* excited about that.

When she entered the front office after the restocking was done, Charmaine and Aaron were debating something at the comms desk. He gestured her over.

'We can't wait for Ju-Ju,' he said to Charmaine as Chelsea approached. 'They're too far out. I'll be fine.'

She shook her head. 'You know them.'

'I know eighty-five percent of the people we see out here, Charmaine.'

'It's Kath. And Dammo. He's one of your oldest friends. They're not just *people*.' Charmaine turned to Chelsea. 'Kath's membranes ruptured and she's gone into premature labour. It's her third pregnancy, a girl. She's twenty-six weeks.'

Bloody hell. Chelsea had hoped she'd get to deliver an Outback baby but not like this.

'She's had an unremarkable antenatal history,' Charmaine continued, 'And both previous children were born at term.'

Chelsea nodded, her midwifery brain rattling through myriad possibilities of how things could go wrong in the middle of nowhere with a very premature baby. On the other hand, the baby could be delivered with no complications at all, or not be born for hours yet, allowing Kath to be safely ensconced in a primary care hospital.

'Her two previous labours were fast,' Aaron added. 'First was two hours. Second was less than an hour on the side of the highway about ten kilometres from town.'

Okay, so maybe time wasn't on their side. 'How far out are they?' she asked.

'Another hundred kilometres west of where we were today,' Aaron supplied.

'It'll take about half an hour in the jet,' Charmaine added.

'Okay.' The jet was fully equipped with a specialised neonatal transport cot that was practically a mini NICU with multiple monitoring devices, pumps and a transport ventilator set up for every eventuality.

'The neonatal team is being dispatched from Brisbane but they're two hours away.'

'Right.' Chelsea threw her bag under the table. 'So we need to go and get Kath.'

'Yes.' Aaron nodded emphatically. 'ASAP. We can get there quicker than Ju-Ju, and the jet is here, ready to go.'

'I know, Aaron. But…are you prepared for a situation where the baby might die out there? A twenty-six-weeker could go either way, you know that. What if she's born not breathing and needs resus and dies anyway, while Dammo is yelling and begging and pleading with you to do something, *anything*, to save her? Are you ready for that? Can you deal with it?'

Chelsea watched the slight bob of Aaron's throat, the angle of his jaw blanching white. Premature labour was always high stakes but, if the couple involved were good friends, everything became personal. He nodded, a grim kind of determination emphasising the battered plains of his face.

'If the worst happens, Dammo's going to need me more than ever. Even if it's someone to yell at.'

Charmaine glanced at Chelsea. She was obviously torn between looking out for her team and knowing that time was of the essence. She seemed to be asking Chelsea if she was capable not just of dealing with baby delivery but any raw emotional fallout on an airstrip in the middle of nowhere. Chelsea was no stranger to high emotion in critical situations and, despite having known Aaron for only a month, their connection—acknowledged or not—was such that she felt she could give a slight nod.

'Okay.' Charmaine sighed. 'Fine. But keep me up to date.'

Aaron didn't need to be told twice as he turned to Chelsea. 'Let's go.'

'I can see the vehicle headlights,' Aaron said, his nose plastered to the window. He'd been staring out since the plane had taken off, as if he could will it to their destination faster.

Dammo and Kath had been racing to the airstrip while the plane had been en route and had arrived ten minutes ago. The message from the ground via comms was that Kath's contractions were coming very fast now, which probably meant the baby's arrival was imminent.

While Aaron's leg jiggled and his fingers tapped on his knee, Chelsea went over and over the potential scenarios. They'd set everything up before take-off—the warmer was on in the transport cot and all the appropriate medication had been drawn up and labelled—but preparing mentally for all contingencies was just as important.

'Touchdown in two minutes,' Hattie's calm voice announced in her ears.

The plane banked left and a hit of adrenaline surged into Chelsea's system. She changed channels on her headphone and gestured for Aaron to follow suit. 'You going to be okay?'

'Yes.' His response was curt, his expression intense.

'We have everything ready... We're prepared.'

'Yep.' He nodded but he was less curt this time. 'How many prems have you delivered?'

Chelsea smiled. 'More than I can count on my fingers and toes. And I've assisted in heaps more prem intubations.'

'Good.' He let out a slow breath. 'Don't really get many out here, so it's been a while for me.'

'Don't worry,' she said, a light tease in her voice. 'It's just like a riding a bicycle.'

He gave her a grudging smile as the plane made a bumpy touchdown.

They taxied to the siding and within five minutes Chelsea and Aaron were striding into the heat of an Outback afternoon, nothing but scraggly bush, occasional trees and red dirt beyond the strip for miles and miles. The sound of a woman crying out broke the almost eerie hush, followed by a frantic male voice coming from the vehicle, urging them over.

'Hurry, Aaron. *Hurry!*'

Aaron made it to the back seat of the vehicle where all the action was happening, just ahead of Chelsea. 'Jesus, Kath,' she heard him say. 'You always did like to be the centre of attention.'

Chelsea heard a huffed out laugh but she also heard pain and panic. 'It's too soon,' Kath said, her voice wobbling.

'It's fine,' Aaron assured her. 'We have all the bells and whistles and we're going to get you back to Balanora in a jiffy.'

The calm authority in his voice was just what the situation needed as Chelsea manoeuvred in front of Aaron. 'Hi, Kath, I'm Chelsea.' The labouring woman was half-reclined on the bench seat, supported from behind by a man Chelsea assumed was Dammo. He'd obviously come straight from the paddock, his clothes streaked with dirt and all kinds of stains, and he looked as frantic and helpless as he had sounded.

'Chelsea's a midwife, Kath. And she worked in the NICU for years, so you're in very good hands.'

Slipping into a pair of gloves, Chelsea smiled into the anxious eyes of the panting, sweaty-faced woman. Even with every door open, it was stifling inside the car. 'Do you mind if I have a look and see where you're at?'

Too tired to talk, Kath just nodded. Luckily, she was wearing a skirt and top, which made easing her underwear off much easier, but it was immediately apparent that Chelsea wouldn't need to do an internal examination or use the small hand-held Doppler unit she had stashed in her pocket for listening to the heartbeat. The head was on its way and it wouldn't be long before it crowned.

Whatever state the baby was in, it was coming very, very soon.

'Right.' She patted Kath on the leg. 'Baby's almost here. We need to get you in the plane.'

Just then a contraction cramped through Kath's body and she screwed her face up, clutching at the edge of the seat and groaning, forcing herself to exhale against her body's natural urge to bear down.

Aaron looked at his mate when it passed. 'Pick her up, bring her to the jet and I'll take her at the door.'

Once Kath was settled on the stretcher in the plane, it was action stations. Dammo was at her head and Chelsea at the business end. Aaron checked the suction one more time and put a fine catheter next to Chelsea's hand to use as soon as the baby was born, to clear the airway.

'Kath,' Aaron said. 'I'm going to pop in an IV while you do your thing, okay?'

The woman nodded as he inspected her closest hand, a cannular at the ready. He had it in within seconds and, by the time it was secured, the baby was crowning and then it was born. She was tiny—but bigger than Chelsea had expected—and a bit floppy, but perfect.

'Is she okay?' Kath asked as she pushed herself up onto her elbows to inspect what was happening between her legs. 'Is she breathing?'

'One sec.'

Chelsea could vaguely hear Kath starting to sob and Dammo asking Aaron what was going on, but her entire focus was on the tiny new-born as she sucked the airway, clearing mucous from the baby's nose and mouth.

She was about to ask for a towel as Aaron said, 'Here,' passing one of the several that had been warming in the transport cot.

Taking it, Chelsea rubbed the baby vigorously—her face and her back—to stimulate breathing. She knew it might not happen, and that she didn't have long before she'd have to hand the baby to Aaron for more potentially drastic measures, but she'd done this often enough to know to start with the basics.

'C'mon, baby,' she whispered as she rubbed. *'C'mon.'*

When the baby took her first gurgling gasp a few seconds later, blinking up at Chelsea, it was the best damned noise she'd ever heard.

'Was that her?' Kath asked, hopefulness rising like a tide in her voice.

'Sure was.' Aaron grinned.

'She's breathing,' Dammo said, his voice tremulous.

'Like a champ,' Aaron confirmed as he handed another warm towel to Chelsea and a tiny pink knitted hat, which she promptly put on, feeling the fontanelles as she did so.

'Bloody hell, mate.' Dammo huffed out a strangled laugh. 'That was the longest thirty seconds of my life.'

Chelsea knew exactly how he felt—time always slowed the longer it took to hear that first new-born wail.

'Hello there, baby girl,' Chelsea crooned at the tiny baby, face screwed up and fully yelling her displeasure now at her rude early delivery. 'Happy birthday. Let's get you some skin-on-skin with your mummy, hey?'

The practice was routine nowadays, but even more vital for premature babies for warmth, protection against infection and to decrease stress levels on a system thrust into the outside world well before it was ready. It obviously wasn't possible for premature babies requiring immediate invasive therapy but, for this bawling little madam, most definitely.

Ordinarily Chelsea would have asked the father if he wanted to cut the cord, but the space was cramped enough, so she quickly clamped and cut before glancing at Aaron. 'Can you do the honours while I finish here?'

Manoeuvring from behind Chelsea, Aaron gently scooped

the baby up into hands that were slightly bigger than she was. Inching along the side of the stretcher, he said, 'Kath, I've never seen your boobs before, but I have seen you in a bikini, so let's just pretend we're at the river, okay?'

Kath gave a half-laugh. 'Considering you've seen worse than my boobs today, let's just make a pact that what happens in the plane stays in the plane.'

'Deal.' Aaron grimed. 'Dammo, you want to help lift her shirt so I can slide this little one up under?'

Levering up onto her elbows again, Kath made space for Dammo to pull her T-shirt up at the back as she gathered it up at the front with her non-cannular hand. Aaron gently laid the still squalling infant high up on Kath's chest, her tiny, naked front pressed to her mother's décolletage as he pulled the T-shirt down so the baby's body was fully covered, leaving just her head to stick out through the neck hole of the shirt.

Chelsea, waiting for the birth of the placenta, was only vaguely aware of Aaron adding a couple of warm blankets over the top of the shirt and the sudden, rapid *blip-blip-blip* of the monitor as he connected the saturation probe. Subliminally, she registered that the heart rate was where it should be.

By the time the placenta was delivered, the baby had quietened and Aaron was satisfied with all the vitals—Kath's included. Considering the number of ways it *could* have gone wrong out here in the extreme Outback, the outcome had been spectacular.

The baby—Yolanda—would still need to be transported to Brisbane for a whole battery of health checks and observations, and would probably stay until she had reached a good weight, but the signs were looking encouraging. Sometimes, of course, premature babies that did well initially could deteriorate and require varying levels of support in the hours and days that followed, which was another good reason to get her to a tertiary hospital.

Within half an hour of Yolanda's birth, they were taking off again, the newest addition to the Balanora district still snuggled skin-to-skin with her mother, her heart beat pinging reassuringly over the background hum of the cabin. Dammo was in the seat behind the stretcher, leaning forward, his chin tucked in next to Kath's temple as they admired their baby girl.

Chelsea was at the foot of the stretcher facing Kath and the monitor and Aaron was in his usual seat, diagonally opposite and directly across the narrow aisle from his mate. But he wasn't looking out of the window any more, he was looking at Chelsea, grinning at her, clearly thrilled with their accomplishment.

As was she, feeling the solidarity of the moment acutely.

Feeling it, and *other* things, in the hitch of her breath, the loop of her stomach, the kick in her pulse. Feeling it in the ache of her face as she grinned right back.

CHAPTER SEVEN

CHELSEA WAS STILL feeling the high from last night when Aaron picked her up the next day after lunch for their trip to Currans Downs. She definitely felt it when she climbed in the cab of his blessedly cool ute and he said, 'Hey.'

His hair was all tousled around his head, as if he'd just shoved his fingers through it this morning and called it done, and his face creased into a smile of welcome. He was all relaxed and loose, and looked perfectly at home in the ute, his Akubra—almost as battered as his face—stashed on the dashboard.

It wasn't that he didn't look relaxed and loose at work, but it was different, and she wasn't sure she'd get used to the contrast between the laidback flight doctor with the stethoscope slung around his neck and the weekend sheep farmer in work shorts, sturdy boots and a flannel shirt rolled up to his elbows. They were both a sight to behold, but the guy in the ute had an ease about him that was overwhelmingly masculine.

And that connection from last night fizzed anew.

'Hi.'

'You ready for a day of roustabouting?'

Chelsea laughed. She had no clue what it was but she was in. 'Bring it on, buddy.' If only calling him *buddy* would make those acute feelings of connection disappear.

'Dammo rang this morning,' he said as they headed on the highway out of town.

'Yeah?' She'd been wondering how things had gone after they'd transferred all three occupants to the Brisbane jet that had been waiting on the tarmac for them when they'd got to base. She glanced at his profile. 'How's Yolanda doing? And Kath?'

'They're doing well.' He kept his eyes on the road. 'Going like a trooper, apparently. Her condition has remained stable. They inserted a nasogastric tube, because she's not strong enough yet to suck adequately or for very long periods of time, but hopefully she'll stack on some weight quickly and be able to feed properly before too much longer.'

Chelsea nodded. The benefits of breastfeeding increased exponentially with premature babies. 'Did they say what her weight was?'

'Nine hundred and fifty-two grams.'

'Wow.' She laughed out loud. 'Nearly a kilo. I thought she looked a decent size for a twenty-six-weeker. No wonder she coped well with her early outing.'

'Yep, it certainly helped.'

'They were lucky, though.' Chelsea returned her gaze to the windscreen and the haze of heat rising up ahead. The long, arrow-straight road seemed to disappear into the shimmering distance. 'If she'd been smaller, if there'd been something in-herently wrong causing the premature labour, if she'd needed reviving, it could have been really hairy.'

'God, I know. I gave myself nightmares thinking of all the possibilities last night.'

Chelsea smiled as the pocket in the back of her knee-length denim shorts buzzed and she remembered she'd stashed her phone there as she'd left the house. Leaning forward, she reached behind to grab it, conscious suddenly that Aaron's gazed skimmed the dip of her back and the rise of her buttocks before returning his attention to the road.

Her nipples prickled against the fabric of her bra and, befuddled, she had to tap in her code twice. A text alert sat on the bottom of the screen. From Francesca. She almost didn't answer it until Aaron said, 'That was lucky. Won't be long before the signal runs out.'

And then Chelsea *had* to look, just in case it was something important. Francesca's texting had settled after those first few days and she didn't like to let them go unanswered for too long.

Chelsea opened the text and immediately wished she hadn't as a picture of Alfie appeared on the screen. So like Dom. Dom's dark eyes, fringed with Dom's long, dark eyelashes, smiling Dom's irreverent smile into the camera. It kicked her in the chest as per usual.

Alfie says hi.

She couldn't do anything for long moments, just stare at the picture. It had been so good this past month, not having a constant reminder of Alfie around. After the high of last night, it brought her back to earth with a thud.

Aaron's, 'Cute kid,' broke her out of her funk. 'That a nephew? Or a friend's child?'

Chelsea stared so hard at the picture, her eyes almost watered. 'No.' She shook her head. 'It's Dom's son.'

'Oh. I…didn't know he had a child.'

Chelsea could hear the frown in his voice as well as the hesitancy as she looked up from the phone screen and met his soft gaze. 'I didn't either until a year ago.'

Glancing back at the road, he didn't say anything for a beat or two. 'How old is he?'

'Almost four.'

More silence but, studying his profile as she was, Chelsea could practically see his mental arithmetic. A man who'd been dead for three years had a four-year-old son his widow didn't know about. 'Okay, that...'

He halted, as if thinking better of what he was going to say, his lips pressing together. But Chelsea wanted to know. 'What?'

'It's fine.' He shook his head. 'It's not my business. You don't have to talk about it.'

Chelsea had no idea why she'd told him. But Francesca killing her buzz had stirred up feelings that had receded since she'd arrived and she realised she *did* want to talk—finally.

She hadn't talked to anyone about the impact of Alfie, because she knew no one who hadn't also known Dom and hadn't been touched by his death. So she'd just locked it all down. But suddenly it felt too big to ignore.

And Aaron, it seemed, was her confessional. She'd already told him stuff about her mum and dad that she'd never told another living soul. What was one more steaming chunk of emotional baggage from Chelsea's past?

Maybe it was because of how removed Aaron was. Maybe it was because she knew he understood what it was like to not feel *enough*. Maybe there was another reason she didn't want to examine too closely. All Chelsea knew was she *wanted* to tell him.

'I'm okay to talk about it.'

He flicked a glance at her, as if to check she actually meant it. Their eyes met briefly and she saw the nanosecond he understood she *was* okay. Looking back at the road, he said, 'So Dom...'

His voice drifted off and Chelsea could tell he was trying to find a word that was palatable. 'Cheated on me?' Chelsea raised both her eyebrows. 'Yes.'

His knuckles tightened around the steering wheel. 'With Alfie's mother.'

'Amongst others, yes.'

Shooting her a quick alarmed look, he said, *'Others?'*

'Yeah.' She turned her gaze back to the endless road in front of them and the even more endless paddocks of stubbly grass and occasional flocks of scraggly sheep. 'He'd been dead for eight months when I learned about Shari. She was the first one. Via email.'

Aaron winced. 'Bloody hell.'

Yep. 'She'd been going through the AA steps and had got to the making amends part. She decided that she'd wronged me by sleeping with my husband while he was in Afghanistan and she had to confess to move on.'

'That was *nice* of her.'

Chelsea gave a half-laugh at the sarcasm in his voice. 'I confronted Vinnie about it. That's Dom's brother. They served in the same unit so they always deployed together. He denied that Dom had ever been unfaithful. He said that Shari, who worked for the British embassy in Kabul, was known for her dalliances with anything in a uniform, and that Dom had rebuffed her several times, which had left her bitter. He begged me not to tell Francesca, their mother.'

'You believed him?'

'Yes.' She nodded slowly. 'Ninety-five percent. But it niggled, you know?'

'Uh-huh.'

'Then, a year ago, Krystal turned up on our doorstep in Hackney with Alfie. She'd been a nanny for a British official in Kandahar. Dom apparently didn't know she'd had his child.'

'So why did she suddenly decide to turn up out of the blue like that?'

'Her life circumstances had changed and she'd fallen on hard times, and was at her wits' end with nowhere else to go. Vinnie was angry, denying Alfie could be Dom's kid, and Francesca was equally adamant, and they insisted on a DNA test but... I didn't need one.'

'You knew?' He glanced across at her.

'No. Well...' Chelsea huffed out a laugh. 'Yes, I guess I did. That five percent of me did. But Alfie is the *spitting image* of

Dom. I don't know how his family could look at that little boy and possibly deny it. So there was *zero* doubt in my mind.'

'What happened then?'

'The DNA test came back positive—of course—and I confronted Vinnie again, said it was time to stop protecting Dom and that I needed to know the truth. About all his women. Because part of me knew there'd be more. I don't know why I wanted to know. I mean, what good could it possibly do? I'm pretty sure Vinnie felt the same but I *needed* to know.'

'I get that.'

'He blustered around a bit at first. I don't blame him for trying to protect his brother. He was there when Dom died and I know he suffers from terrible survivor guilt. But I was in such a fury at that point that I threatened to tell Francesca about the email from two years ago and he came clean.'

'And there *were* others.'

'Yes. Apparently, the man I loved, and worried about dying over there every single, waking second of the day, was a bit of a man whore when he was deployed.'

'Oh God, Chelsea.' He looked away from the road for a beat or two. 'I am so sorry.'

His gaze was brief before switching back to the road again but it was intense, radiating empathy. The look she'd seen many times these past weeks as Aaron had interacted with patients.

'Vinnie tried to explain the mentality of being deployed in a war zone. How having to confront your own mortality day after day often led to fatalistic behaviour. Living each day like it was your last. Dom loved me, he said, and his liaisons weren't about love, they were about sex.'

'Did it help?'

Chelsea gave a harsh laugh. 'Not really.'

'You must be pretty angry with him.'

She was about to say she was furious but, actually, she wasn't sure she was any more. Not like she had been. She was just... sad. 'I was.'

'I guess it's hard to mourn someone, to love someone, when they hurt you so deeply.'

'I don't love him.'

Chelsea blinked. It was the first time she'd said it out loud. Her instinct to take it back was strong but she pressed her lips together tight. She glanced across at Aaron, who didn't appear to be horrified by her disloyalty to her dead husband, or annoyed that she'd let him think otherwise that day in the store room when she'd not refuted it.

'I mean… I'm not *in* love with him any more. There's part of me that will always love him. Dom was a massive part of my life for many years but…however he justified it to himself, however much I understand how Vinnie justifies it… Dom betrayed me and our vows and the things I held most sacred. And that just…killed off any deep feelings I had for him. Snuffed them right out.'

A slight rise in the road levelled out to reveal three large red kangaroos up ahead, sitting in the middle of the road. They were far enough away for Aaron to slow, which he did, but the sight never failed to thrill Chelsea. If ever she temporarily forgot she was in a vastly different land, the appearance of kangaroos always brought her back to reality. She'd seen a lot out here, both hopping through paddocks as planes landed or stinking everything up as road kill, but she didn't think she'd ever get used to the sight of the strange, quirky creatures.

They hopped away before the ute even got close and Aaron accelerated away again. He hadn't said anything about her declaration and she wondered if she'd shocked him. Sighing, she rolled her head to one side to study his profile.

'I suppose that makes me a terrible person,' she murmured, not wanting to leave their conversation dangling.

'No longer being in love with the man who repeatedly cheated on you?' Aaron shook his head as he glanced across at her. 'I'd say it makes you human.'

If there could possibly have been a right answer to her question, Aaron had nailed it, and the niggling sense of guilt Chelsea too often felt over her conflicted feelings eased back.

'Who sent it to you? The picture. Are you…in contact with Alfie's mother?'

'No.' Chelsea sighed again. 'Francesca sent it.'

'Your *mother-in-law* sent you a picture of the child your *husband* had with *another* woman?'

Chelsea almost laughed at the streak of disbelief in Aaron's voice. It did sound kind of unbelievable when spoken out loud. 'Alfie and Krystal lived with us for four months until she got back on her feet.'

'What?'

She did laugh this time. 'Yeah. I know. It seems bizarre, but Francesca and Roberto had their first grandchild from their dead son, and they weren't about to turn her or him away.'

'Wasn't that hard?'

'Oh, yes.' Chelsea nodded, fixing her gaze on the ever-present heat shimmer ahead. 'Very much so. Dom and I… We had two miscarriages after we'd been married for a few years. The first pregnancy was an accident but the second was planned. When we lost that one too, we decided to give it a rest. Dom was about to be deployed again and we talked about leaving it until after he got out of the military.'

It was hard to keep the emotion of those years out of her voice so Chelsea didn't even try. It had been a long time, but sometimes the searing loss of that period returned with a roaring vengeance.

'So, yeah…' She came out of her reverie, turning her head to focus on Aaron. 'Having to look at a kid that was a replica of Dom, a child that *I* couldn't give him, was hard. Living with the woman who had slept with my husband was hard. Thankfully Krystal got back on her feet and moved out but Francesca and Roberto look after Alfie in the afternoons so she can work, and he usually stays over one night on the weekend.'

'Bloody hell. Do they understand how hard that must be for you?'

'No. They don't see Dom's infidelity when they look at Alfie. They just see… Dom. And they think that I'll love Alfie too because I love Dom—*loved* Dom—and he's Dom's, therefore…' Chelsea shook her head at the convoluted but understandable logic. 'And I do love him. He's a sweet, *sweet* boy, who wormed his way into all our hearts, and none of this is his fault. But… well, let's just say, it's been nice to get away from all that.'

'I bet.' Aaron shook his head. 'Why don't you ask her to stop sending you pictures?'

'Because she's trying to keep me connected and because he's her grandson and she adores him. And she doesn't know that it hurts because I've never told her. She doesn't know the extent of Dom's liaisons. She thinks that Krystal was a one-off. And that I've forgiven him because he's dead. And I'm not going to be the one to tell her that it wasn't, and I haven't, because it'll break her heart and it's already been broken enough.'

Chelsea knew how it felt to lose two babies at a point where neither were much more than a collection of cells. She couldn't begin to image the pain of losing a child who had been a part of your life for over three decades.

'So you just…suck it up. Even though it hurts?'

God, he made her sound like some kind of martyr. It didn't sit comfortably, but it was what it was. 'Yeah.'

Aaron glanced at her incredulously. 'Why?'

'Because sometimes we lie to people we love to protect them, even if it makes us feel bad.'

'Yeah but…' He turned his attention back to the road. 'Isn't it okay to put yourself first at some point?'

'Sure.' And she'd done that. 'It's why I moved here.'

'So…' He slid her another look. 'You *are* running away.'

Chelsea smiled. 'I prefer to think of it as starting over.' She quirked an eyebrow. 'Surely that can be added to your list of reasons people come out here?'

He nodded slowly. 'Yeah. Okay. Consider the list updated.'

She laughed then, and the heaviness that had descended in the cabin lifted. Up ahead, a sign announced a road off to the left, and Aaron slowed the ute and indicated.

'Hold on to your hat,' he said as the car slowed. 'The road gets kinda bumpy from here in out.'

After several hours in the heat of the sheering shed, the stifling air thick with the earthy aromas of lanolin, sheep droppings and sweat, Chelsea's admiration for Aaron and anyone trying to make a living off the land out here grew exponentially. The fact that he was busily striding around in those boots, those shorts, that hat and just a navy singlet now, after discarding his flannel shirt, didn't hurt.

Rock music pumped through rusty old speakers mounted in the corners of the shed as he cajoled sheep and whistled at dogs and flapped away the ever-present flies and lifted fleece, spreading it out on the wool table to class it then toss it in the presser. He was everywhere and Chelsea could barely keep up as he explained and demonstrated and encouraged her to get dirty.

If she hadn't been heavily in lust with him already, she was now.

Although, it was more than just those sun-kissed muscles straining and bending and stretching and contracting and *sweating*. It was the way he laughed and joked with the shearers, as though they'd known him all his life, and the way he teased his sister, who was also bustling around, yet clearly deferred to her, and the respect he showed his father, while bantering with him about getting old and retiring.

He was clearly as at home here, a broom in his hand, as he was in the belly of a King Air, a stethoscope around his neck, and Chelsea's heart skipped so many beats over the course of the afternoon she started to worry she was developing a condition.

Just before knock-off time, the four-shearer team members—who had already sheared over two hundred sheep each—plus

Aaron and his sister had a friendly race to see who could shear the fastest. Mostyn Vincent, sporting the same lived-in kind of face as his son, pulled a stopwatch out of his back pocket as if it was a common occurrence during shearing time and, with all six of them hunched over a sheep, called, *'Go!'*

Chelsea watched as the electrical hum of shears and the hands and legs and instruments all worked in tandem to methodically strip off the fleece in one piece. All four of the pros finished within a few seconds of each other. Aaron and Tracey brought up the rear several minutes later, with Tracey just pipping her brother to the post.

'Now who's the old man?' Mostyn crowed.

Aaron laughed as he finished off the sheep and came up for a high-five from his sister.

'It's those soft hands,' Ed, the team boss, said which earned more laughs all round.

'You want a go?' Aaron asked, his eyes meeting hers.

Chelsea blinked. 'Me?'

'Sure.' He grinned at her as he swiped a muscular forearm over his sweaty brow. 'I'll teach you.'

She glanced at the faces around her to see if this was some kind of set-up. 'Um…'

Before she could get any more out, Ed made *bok-bok-bok* noises and she rolled her eyes at him, which earned her a hoot of laughter. 'What if I…cut the sheep?'

'You won't. I'll be right beside you,' Aaron assured her. 'Where's your sense of adventure?'

Chelsea narrowed her eyes at him but he grinned and she said, 'Okay, fine.'

Before she could blink, she was being ushered to a shearing station as Ed went and got her a sheep. 'Here you are, English, got you a nice docile one.'

The guys on the team had been teasing her all afternoon about her accent and Chelsea laughed as the sheep was positioned between her legs. It felt hot and heavy against her thighs, but there was little time to register that as Aaron turned on the shears and started talking her through the steps.

The shears felt weighty and foreign in her hands and they vibrated like crazy as Chelsea hunched over the sheep and made her first pass on the finer belly fleece as instructed. A little black fly buzzed around the sweat forming on her upper lip and she blew at it, but it was still less distracting then Aaron, who was also hunched over, his body close to hers, his mouth close to her ear so she could hear his pointers.

Even though they were being watched by six other people, it felt as if it were just the two of them. The deep husk of his voice, the warmth of his breath fluffing the flyaway wisps of hair plastered to her neck, the way he occasionally leaned closer, helping her manoeuvre the sheep or showing her how to angle the shears, felt strangely intimate.

Concentrating hard on what she was doing so she didn't nick the poor sheep, she wasn't even aware that she'd muttered, 'Bloody flies,' as she blew another one—or maybe it was the same one—away.

Aaron's warm chuckle drifted down her neck. 'I heard that, *English*, but don't worry, your secret is safe with me.'

Chelsea actually shivered, despite the heat, her concentration officially shot. Standing, she clicked off the shears and stretched out her back. It had been a physically demanding afternoon and she could already feel a niggle in her lumbar area from just a few minutes hunched over.

'Okay, I'm calling it,' she said. 'This is not for the faint of heart.'

Ed grinned. 'Step aside, English, let me show you how it's done.'

Chelsea and Aaron moved over to where Tracey and Mostyn stood and left Ed to it. 'You okay?' he asked.

'Yep.' She nodded. 'I have a feeling I'm going to be sore tomorrow, though.'

'Oh, trust me,' Tracey said. 'You're going to have aches and pains in places you never knew you had muscles.'

'Hey,' Aaron mock-protested. 'Way to kill the adventure buzz.'

Tracey grinned. 'You want to come up to the homestead and take a bath?' she asked Chelsea. 'Get out of those sweaty clothes before dinner?'

'Or,' Aaron suggested, 'She could have an open-air shower at the shearers' digs.'

Chelsea glanced at Tracey who almost imperceptibly shook her head before saying, 'Yeah, tough choice. A long, deep soak for aching bones and muscles with a luxury bath bomb and divine-smelling soap and shampoo... Or a cold shower in a hessian-wrapped cubicle from a bag hanging off a tree branch, a bunch of rowdy blokes nearby belly-aching at you to finish up, and the birdlife dive-bombing you.'

Aaron laughed. 'That only happened to you once.'

What? She might be all about the adventure but bird attack whilst showering did not appeal. Chelsea glanced at Tracey. 'Thanks. A bath sounds lovely.'

'You don't know what you're missing out,' Aaron said.

Chelsea shrugged. 'Maybe next time.'

As soon as it was out she wanted to withdraw it, but Aaron smiled at her reply as if he hoped there *would* be a next time, and she couldn't help but hope the same.

CHAPTER EIGHT

THREE HOURS LATER, Aaron pulled the ute up in the middle of a paddock and killed the headlights, immediately engulfing them in darkness.

'Here?' Chelsea asked after a beat or two, as she peered out of the windscreen and then her window into the inky black of the night.

'Yep.'

She looked around again, as if she'd been expecting stadium seating. 'The best place is near the river, but it's a bit further away, and all we need is to be far enough from the lights of the homestead.'

Unclicking his seat belt, Aaron opened the door, because the temptation to reach for her after their amazing day together was too great. Between how she enthusiastically and uncomplainingly pitched in at the shearing shed, to the way she'd got on with his family, to her easy conversation and witty banter throughout dinner, she'd been building like a drum beat in his blood.

This very English woman just seemed to fit in to this very Aussie setting.

The air was still warm but the sting of the day had dissipated as he strode round to the tray of the ute and grabbed the blanket. Ordinarily, for star-gazing he'd have thrown a mattress in the back, but he didn't want Chelsea to think he'd lured her out here under false pretences.

After today, he was starting to understand his feelings went deeper than how sexy she looked in the strappy dress she was now wearing, or how tempting it was to pull out the band in her hair and let it all fall loose.

Chelsea had been through a lot, and if she really was here not because she was running away but to start over—to *stay*—then they had time to explore whatever *this* was. Because he was sure he wasn't alone in these feelings and he didn't want to screw anything up by going too hard too fast.

She was still sitting in the cab of the car as he came round her side and he smiled to himself as he opened the door. 'Scared of the dark?'

Peering out at him, she blinked. 'I'm not sure I've *been* anywhere this dark.'

He laughed and held out his hand. 'Yeah, moon won't be up for a few more hours. Great? Isn't it?'

The unclicking of her seatbelt sounded loud in the cacophony of silence around them, then her hand slid into his. 'Are we lying on the ground?' she asked as he guided her to the front of the vehicle.

'No.' Aaron threw the blanket on the bonnet of the car. 'We're sitting up here. Best seats in the house.' He shoved his booted foot onto the lower rung of the bull bar and hauled himself up, before turning and offering his hand once again. 'You coming?'

A minute later they were sitting side by side—not touching but still close—their legs stretched out in front of them, the blanket beneath protecting them from the heat of the engine, reclining against the windscreen he'd washed thoroughly when Chelsea had been in the bath.

'Wow,' she whispered as she craned her neck to take in the sky from horizon to horizon.

Aaron smiled at the awe in that one hushed word. 'Yeah.'

Above him a wonderland glimmered and dazzled. Planets and suns and constellations. Far-away galaxies. All blending together to form the rich tapestry of lights making up the great southern night sky.

'Do you know what any of these stars are called?'

'Some.'

He pointed them out then and they whiled away half an hour talking about all things celestial, Chelsea mostly listening, Aaron mostly talking. But Aaron was hyper-aware of *her*. Every breath, every move. Every brush of her arm against his. Every turn of her head as she glanced at his profile. Every adjustment of that one errant strap that kept sliding down her arm. Every shake of her shoulders as she laughed at something he said.

His entire body thrummed with awareness. With the slow, thick beat of his blood and the hot, heavy flow of his breath.

And then she said, 'You know, the first date Dom ever took me on was to the Planetarium at the Royal Observatory.'

It was kind of a mood killer.

Aaron had believed her today when she'd said she wasn't in love with her husband any more. And it had been like a weight off his chest—one he didn't even know he'd been carrying. So the very last name he wanted to hear on her lips tonight was *Dom*.

But it made sense that lying here under the stars would trigger the memory, particularly given how recently they'd spoken about him. And he didn't want to be that guy—a douche about the men in a woman's past.

'How'd you meet?'

She stared into the night sky. 'I was at uni in London and

he and the lads from his unit used to drink at a pub me and my girlfriends used to frequent.'

Keeping his eyes firmly overhead, he said, 'And was it love at first sight?'

She gave a little laugh. 'Good lord, no. He was quite the lothario which, in retrospect, should have been a heads-up.' She laughed again, a shallow echo of the first. 'Sure, I found him attractive, and he kept asking me out, but he was always there with a different girl. He just seemed like a player to me and I wasn't interested in being a notch on anyone's bedpost.'

'But?' There obviously *was* a but—they'd married, after all.

'He was persistent. Not creepily so. Charmingly. And I was so used to being a...ghost at home. Being seen, being wanted, being *pursued*...that was a revelation. Dom gave affection so easily and freely without me having to silently beg for it. I wasn't used to that from a man, so it was hard to trust initially, but when I did, well...it was heady stuff.'

Aaron shut his eyes. Jesus. Poor Chelsea, starved for attention. No wonder she'd fallen for Dom. 'And now?' He glanced across at her, his eyes well and truly adjusted to the night, his gaze following the line of her profile. 'Did Dom's infidelity make you distrustful of men again?'

Surely it had to have had some impact?

She shook her head as she turned her head to look at him. 'It made me mistrust *myself*. But mostly it made me feel...'

The silence grew between them. 'Feel...?' he prompted.

Glancing away, she huffed out a breath. 'It doesn't matter.'

'You can say it, you know,' he murmured, his gaze trained on her profile. 'It's just you and me and the stars.'

Aaron saw the bob of her throat, heard her swallow, heard the rough exhale, and waited. 'It reinforced how I've always felt. Like... I wasn't enough. Not enough for my dad to love me. Not enough for my husband to be faithful to me. Just...' Her voice roughened and her throat bobbed again. 'Not enough.'

The utter dejection in her voice cut Aaron to his core. 'Hey,' he said, rolling onto his side, sliding his hand onto her cheek and into her hair. 'I'm sorry. I'm *so* sorry that happened to you, Chelsea. And that people you loved and trusted made you feel that way.'

Turning on her side, she shot him a sad smile. 'It's okay, you don't have to—'

'Yes,' he interrupted. 'I do.' Someone had to. It was a tragedy that she felt so unworthy, and his chest ached with the unfairness of it because, while his mother leaving had left him feeling similarly, he'd had other people around him—people who loved him—telling him, *showing* him, otherwise.

His hand held firmer in her hair. 'You are enough, Chelsea Tanner. You are *more* than enough. You've been with the OA for a month and there's not one person on the team that wouldn't say the same thing. And any guy who was lucky enough to be in a position to tell you that, and didn't spend every single second of his life doing so, has a lot to answer for. I'm sorry you weren't loved the way you deserve to be loved.'

The way he wanted to love her. Because he *was* falling in love with her—he knew it as surely as he knew the sun would rise over this ancient landscape tomorrow.

Even though she was everything he'd avoided all his life.

She stared at him then as if she didn't know what to say. Aaron didn't know what to say either so he leaned in and kissed her instead.

She tasted sweet, like the golden syrup she'd smothered all over the warm damper they'd had for dessert, and she smelled like whatever the hell had been in that fancy bath bomb Tracey had supplied. Vanilla or orange or passion fruit. Something edible which had driven him crazy throughout dinner. Her lips were soft and pliant, and the small moan that came from somewhere at the back of her throat unleashed a tsunami of lust that Aaron's better angels had been keeping under wraps for what felt like for ever.

His pulse pumped through his chest, his belly and his groin, and he was only vaguely aware of the loud rasp of his breath as he opened his mouth and deepened the kiss, groaning when she did the same.

Then, somehow, she was closer. Or maybe he was. Had she moved, or had he? Had they both moved? Aaron wasn't sure. All he knew was the tips of her breasts were rubbing his chest, her knees were brushing his lower thighs and his hand was dropping from her hair, running down her spine to the dip at the small of her back and palming her butt, urging her closer.

Urging her in all the way.

Until her breasts were flattened and their thighs were smooshed and their hips were aligned and there was no way she could not feel the *full* effect of what kissing her was doing to his body.

It wasn't anything like the two kisses they'd already shared. They'd been rash and brief, halted abruptly out of surprise and a sense of transgression. A sense of being wrong.

This didn't feel wrong. It felt like the culmination of what this day had been leading to. What this past month had been leading to.

Hell, out here under the stars, it felt like their freaking destiny.

But, as her kiss plunged deeper and her knee slid between his legs, her thigh pressing against the almost agonising thickness of his erection, Aaron knew if he didn't stop now it was going to be a lot more than just some first-base action on the bonnet of his ute.

It was going to be a home run.

And that would be the very definition of going too hard, too fast. He was a thirty-five-year-old man, not a horny teenager, and he'd waited for this—for *her*—all his damned life. He didn't want to mess up because he let his libido have the con.

Libidos weren't generally known for their detailed decision-making process. Gathering every skerrick of his willpower,

Aaron pulled out of the kiss. He didn't go far, just pressing his forehead against hers, their rough pants mingling together.

'Aaron?' she asked, her voice small. 'Everything okay?'

God…she sounded as befuddled as he felt. 'Everything is perfect,' he assured her, nuzzling her temple now.

'You…don't want this?'

He shut his eyes. 'Oh, I want it.' He chugged out a laughed as he tipped his head back a little to look at her. 'I'm just trying to be…' God…what? Restrained? Gentlemanly? Respectful? 'I don't want you to think I brought you out here for this.'

She didn't say anything for a moment, then she moved the leg she had jammed between them, causing his breath to hitch and a mini-eruption in his groin. Sliding it over the top of his thigh, she rolled herself up, pressing on his upper shoulder as she went, displacing him onto his back.

By the time she was settled, she was straddling him, the centre of her pressing into the bulge behind his fly. His hands had come to rest on her legs mid-thigh, his palms on warm, bare skin, his fingers on the hem of her dress. Her strap had slipped again but she didn't bother fixing it this time.

'I don't think that.'

'Good.' Aaron was mollified to hear she didn't doubt his motives. His libido, however, didn't care about his motives, it only cared about how good it felt to have her atop him and how easy it would be to push his hands under the fabric of her dress…

'But I'm okay to be going there anyway.'

If she'd applied a cattle prod to his erection, it couldn't have bucked harder than it did and, by the way she shifted, he was pretty sure she'd felt it too. He swallowed. 'Okay.'

She stared down at him for long moments. 'No one had ever said that to me, before…the sorry thing. *Sorry that happened to you, Chelsea*. Not my father. Not Francesca or Vinnie. It means a lot.'

Aaron's pulse thudded thick through his head as an uneasy

feeling took up residence in the pit of the stomach. 'So this is a...thank you?'

'What?' She frowned and shook her head. 'No.'

A very distracting piece of hair slid from her up-do to kiss her nape. Aaron's fingers itched to play with it and he dug them into her thighs to suppress the impulse.

'This is... I didn't know I could feel like this. And...' She paused, as if she was searching for the right words. 'I'm so lucky to have shared this day with you. And... I'm attracted to you, and have been since the room mix up at the hotel, and all this...' She looked up and then back at him. 'Makes me want to do something wild and free, and I haven't wanted to do that with *anyone* for a very long time, but I want to do it with you.'

A well of emotion stormed his chest, each word sliding inside his heart, and Aaron knew that whatever happened with them he'd never forget this night underneath the stars, falling in love with Chelsea.

'Well... I can't fault your logic,' he said with a grin, because this wasn't the moment for such a grand declaration.

She grinned too, momentarily, before reaching for the hem of her dress and pulling it up and off her head, leaving her in nothing but a white pair of panties.

'Holy mother of...' Aaron whispered, his pulse spiking, his gaze fixed on the lush curves of her bare breasts and the pebbled nipples at each centre.

Then she reached up and pulled at the band in her hair and it cascaded down in fine wisps. Christ...she was magnificent. Incandescent against the backdrop of the Milky Way, crowned in a garland of stars.

His hands moved then, sliding up her thighs, glancing over her belly and her ribs to each capture a breast, thumbs stroking across the engorged nipples in unison. Damn if his hands didn't look *good* on her. Big and tanned and a little rough against the pale creaminess of her skin, but *good*.

She moaned and arched her back, and Aaron vaulted up, his

mouth landing on her throat as he kneaded the soft flesh, and she rocked against him.

'God,' she gasped as she tugged at his shirt. 'Please tell me you have a condom.'

It took a moment for Aaron to think through the heavy haze buzzing through his system as Chelsea yanked his shirt free of his head and tossed it. 'Wallet. Back pocket.'

But for damned sure they were going to need more than one.

It had been such a long time since a man had held her in his arms like this and Chelsea realised how much she'd missed it as she groped for the wallet. She hadn't for the longest time. Dom's betrayal had torpedoed the intimacy they'd shared and knocked her libido flat. But, in this small dot on an Outback map, it had suddenly roared to form and life and had a name.

'Aaron,' she whispered as his lips drifted south, and his heat, his earthiness, his closeness overwhelmed her.

He made a low humming noise, his hot, wet mouth replacing the fingers toying with a nipple, and Chelsea cried out, her hand fumbling with the square piece of leather she'd somehow managed to wrangle from his pocket. Her head fell back, the action thrusting her breasts out, and Aaron took ruthless advantage, ravaging them with such skill, Chelsea was lost to everything but the flick of his tongue and the pull of his mouth.

At some point, he lifted his head and panted, 'Condom,' before going right back to his deliberations.

With monumental effort Chelsea got back on task, lifting her head to riffle through his wallet, thanking God for her night vision as her ability to coordinate dissolved under the play of Aaron's tongue and the fine rub of his whiskers that prickled *everywhere.*

Locating the condom, Chelsea almost brandished it up high and called out *Huzzah!* But she chose to conserve her energy for what was to come. Sliding her hands onto the smooth acreage of his shoulders, she pressed more urgently against the bulge in his shorts and started to rub. Sensation flared between her hips and she let out a strangled kind of moan at the same time as Aaron's guttural grunt.

His mouth slipped from her nipple as his hand clamped down hard on the small of her back. 'Chelsea...' He puffed out a strangled kind of laugh into the hollow at the base of her throat. 'That'll end messily if you keep doing that.'

The fact that Aaron seemed to be as out of control, as close to the edge, as she did, quashed any thoughts hovering in the back of her mind about her lack of *practice*. Sliding a hand into the rich layers of his hair, she tilted his head back until they were staring into each other's eyes. It might have been dark but his gaze was utterly transparent. She saw desire—*lust*—but also emotion, something that went beyond this crazy, desperate need thrumming between them.

Something deeper.

Chelsea supposed she should feel exposed, embarrassed even, about sharing her deepest, darkest hurts with this man. But sitting next to him in this deepest, darkest night, knowing he too knew something about loss and inadequacy, felt...right.

She kissed him then, her lips opening over his, her hand sliding to his jaw, the rasp of his whiskers against her palm hardening her nipples. Her belly looped then tightened as her pulse fluttered at her temples, wrists and between her legs. His tongue brushed hers and Chelsea moaned as she returned the favour, tangling with him in a delicious dance. Her head filled with the taste of him, the smell of him. Eucalyptus and leather and petrichor.

Panting, she pulled out of the kiss. Part of her wanted to do nothing but keep her lips locked with his all night, but parts *lower* were demanding more. A fever burned thought her blood and only Aaron—hard and good and deep inside her—could break it.

Chelsea shifted slightly as she handed him the condom. 'Open this,' she requested as she reached for his fly.

The sound of husky breathing, the tearing of foil and the rip of a zipper all seemed amplified in the absolute silence of the landscape. Unlike Aaron's, 'Oh, Jesus,' which hovered rough and low around them as Chelsea finally liberated his erection from his underwear.

He felt good in her hand. Long and thick and solid as Chelsea closed her fingers around him, stroking up and down, familiarising herself with his contours, revelling in the shudder rippling through his body. He groaned again, his forehead pressing into the crook of her neck, his breath hot as he pushed her hand aside, muttering, 'Mercy, woman,' as he rolled the sheath down his length.

Chelsea's pulse accelerated as she pressed closer to Aaron once more, reaching for his hardness with one hand, pushing the gusset of her underwear out the way with the other. Lifting her hips slightly, she looked into his upturned face. The thick, blunt prod of him nudged her entrance as his hands slid to the small of her back. Their slight roughness caused her nipples to bead and Chelsea's entire body pulsed in anticipation.

'When you say you haven't done this for a very long time,' he said, his voice husky, his expression earnest. 'You mean...?'

'Not since Dom,' she confirmed.

He nodded slowly. 'Do you need me to...?'

Chelsea wasn't sure what he was going to say, but she didn't give him a chance to finish. She just sank down—not fast, but not slow either—in a measured, deliberate move that filled her all the way to the hilt, stealing the breath from her lungs and causing Aaron to gasp.

She clutched him to her chest, her arms wrapping around his head and shoulders, his arms wrapping around her waist as she breathed steadily through the thick intrusion stretching her so damned good.

'You okay?' he asked after a beat or two.

'Yeah, just...' Her arms tightened around him as she adjusted to his girth and depth. 'Give me a second.'

A wave of emotion rolled from the pit of her stomach all the way to her throat. She'd felt so broken for so long and in a handful of weeks this man, in a place on the other side of the planet, had put her back together. Or at least, shown her that it was possible to be whole again.

He chuckled. 'Take as long as you want. We could just stay like this all night and I'd be totally down with that.'

Chelsea gave a husky laugh. 'I think you mean...' She undulated internal muscles. 'Up.'

He sucked in a breath, his arms tightening around her waist. 'Christ, yes.'

'Well, I...' She undulated again, exaggerating the move, feeling a delicious tug below her belly button as the raw emotion receded and the thrum of her pulse took its place. 'Would not.' Loosening her arms, she glanced down, searching his gaze. 'I'm going to need to apologise in advance because I don't think this is going to take very long.'

'Are you kidding? If you think I'm going to last more than a second or two longer than you do, then you are seriously underestimating what you do to me.'

Chelsea's heart skipped. Aaron Vincent was *seriously* pushing all her buttons.

She dropped her head then and kissed him, slow at first, then faster and hungrier as his mouth demanded it, his tongue flicking against hers. The fever of her desperation flamed anew and she felt an answering flare in him, *heard* it echoed in the heavy rasp of his breathing. Two large hands slid to her buttocks and squeezed and Chelsea rocked then, setting up a rhythm.

'God...*yes*.' Aaron groaned against her lips as he squeezed harder.

She rocked more but it wasn't enough. Chelsea pushed at Aaron's chest, breaking their kiss. 'Lie back,' she commanded huskily.

Aaron eased back against the windscreen, his hands sliding to her hips, and Chelsea took a moment to admire his big shoulders and his smooth chest and the solid abs that clearly stayed honed from hefting around sheep. She rocked again, her movements freer this time, getting off on the hiss of his breath and the way those abdominals pulled taut.

'God, Chelsea…' He shook his head as his eyes roamed from her face to her breasts to the flare of her hips and to where they were joined, before drifting up again. 'I've never seen anything as beautiful as you with diamonds in your hair riding me into the night.'

Chelsea's heart squeezed hard at the hushed compliment. The awe in his voice humbled her with its intensity and she realised she could fall in love with this man.

And it didn't scare the living daylights out of her.

Sliding a hand onto his stomach, Chelsea felt the ripple of his muscles beneath. Felt every ripple as the other hand joined in and they smoothed their way up to his pecs and then on to his shoulders, her palms grabbing onto their solid roundness. She leaned forward into her extended arms, the position changing the angle of their joining. His hand clutched convulsively at her hip and she shivered as it hit just the right spot.

Staring at each other, he withdrew a little then thrust, and Chelsea moaned and shut her eyes as it felt *so* good. He did it again and it rocked her breasts and her head, and her sex clenched around him. When he went again, she rose to meet his withdrawal and fell to heighten his thrust. He grunted and she gasped, her eyes flying open, their gazes connecting.

They moved together then, just like that, eyes locked, Chelsea leaning into her palms as she rose and fell, Aaron's fingers biting into her hips as he thrust in and out, blood surging and pounding through her belly and buttocks and thighs, every nerve stretching taut, every muscle tightening, ripples of pleasure starting deep inside her sex.

'Oh, God… *Aaron.*'

'I know,' he panted, his eyes boring into hers as he went deeper and deeper with each thrust. 'I know, I know.'

The ripples got bigger and harder and faster until they exploded into an all-consuming deluge. Chelsea cried out, panting and gasping, her eyes wide as a tide of sensation swept her away. 'Oh, God.' Her nails dug into his shoulders as her body trembled with the first pulses of her orgasm. 'Yes, yes, yes.'

As promised, Aaron joined her in the torrent two beats later, shouting his release into the night. *'Chelsea!'*

He vaulted up then, taking her with him, his hands sliding around high on her back, his fingers anchoring from behind on the balls of her shoulders, holding her close as he kissed her, locking her in their starry, starry night together. Stealing her breath and giving her his own, he kissed up the tumult, bucking and shuddering, his climax sustaining hers until the last tremor rocked her core.

Chelsea's mouth left his, her chin coming to rest on top of his head, his lips buzzing her throat as she caught her breath.

'That was…' he said, his breathing still unsteady.

Chelsea waited for him to continue and, when he didn't, she laughed. He sounded satisfied and mystified all at once, as if he couldn't come up with an adequate enough word, and hell if that didn't set up a warm glow in her heart. 'Yeah. I know.'

Chuckling, he eased back, taking her with him, cradling her against his chest, making her excruciatingly aware of how intimately they were still joined. The steady bang of his heart echoed under her ear as his fingers trekked idly up and down the furrow of her spine, and they lay there for several minutes, just breathing in the aftermath.

'You okay?' he asked eventually.

'Mmm,' she said. 'I haven't felt this okay in a long time.'

His arms squeezed around her, and Chelsea snuggled for a beat or two more, but with the night still warm she was conscious of the sweat slicking between them. She roused and pushed up, making to move off him, only to have his hand clamp on her arse.

'Not yet,' he murmured, his gaze settling on hers.

'I'm too heavy,' she protested.

He gave a snort-laugh. 'Half the sheep I moved today weighed more than you.' But he lifted his hand and Chelsea eased away. She shivered and a low kind of hum came from the back of his throat as he slid from her body.

She settled against the windscreen, her knees bent as Aaron sat and ditched the condom before zipping up. Chelsea supposed she should try and find her dress, but then he was beside her again, his hand slipping into hers, and the thought floated away.

Neither of them spoke for a long time. Somehow, the stars seemed even brighter now, and it was lovely lying here with Aaron under that sky with the memory of their joining lingering in the still night air.

'I hear you can see the aurora down here.'

'Aurora Australis. Yes. But not out here... Gotta go further south. You can see them in Victoria sometimes on a good night, but Tassie's the best place.'

'Have you been to Tasmania?'

'When I was a kid.'

'I'd like to see the southern lights in Tasmania some time,' she murmured, her eyes roaming the sky.

'I would, too. Maybe...' He turned his head. 'We could go together?'

Conscious of his gaze on her profile, Chelsea also turned her head. 'I'd like that.'

When he smiled, she smiled back before she returned her gaze to the sky in time to catch a shooting star flaring across the sequined black dome above. She gasped and pointed at it, her finger following its trajectory.

'You get to make a wish now,' he said.

'Nope.' Her lips curved into a smile. 'I think I've been lucky enough for one night.'

'Amen to that,' he murmured.

Chelsea laughed at his deadpan delivery and rolled up onto her elbow, looking down into his smiling face. The starlight fell gently on the crinkles around his eyes, the crooked smile and the slight asymmetry of his eyes.

'How'd you do this?' she asked, her finger tracing the uneven line of his nose.

'Footy,' he said. 'Two broken noses.'

'And this?' Her finger brushed over the asymmetrical bow of his top lip.

'Fractured zygoma. Also footy.' He laughed, as if everyone who played the game ended up with broken noses and cheekbones. 'Didn't quite heal in perfect symmetry so my face has always looked a bit crooked.'

Chelsea drifted her finger over the cheekbone in question before drifting it back to his top lip. 'I like your crooked face,' she murmured.

She liked it a lot.

He smiled and his hand came up to capture hers, their gazes locking as he kissed her fingertips, and Chelsea's lungs felt too big for her chest. How could she have all these feelings for him so soon? It had taken her months to fall in love with Dom.

Before she blurted anything else out, she snuggled down beside him—as much as one could snuggle against glass—her head on his shoulder, her arm across his chest, her fingers absently caressing a nicely pillowed pectoral muscle.

It was so damned quiet out here. Had she been alone, she might have found all this vast black emptiness eerie, but with Aaron it felt...intimate.

'You know,' he said after a while, his fingers drifting up and down her arm, 'I still have my bedroom at the homestead.'

Chelsea's fingers stopped their caress. Stay the night at the homestead? Did he mean sneak in and sneak out again before morning? Or just go on back and not care who saw them?

It was tempting, but part of her shied away from that kind of public declaration. This *thing* was some*thing*. And that was big—for both of them. Except it had just happened, and she couldn't help but feel it would be easier to figure out without the speculation, scrutiny and expectation of family and friends.

'Too soon?'

Chelsea let out a shaky breath. 'Yeah.' Pushing up onto her elbow again, her gaze found his. 'Is that okay?'

'Of course.' Levering himself up, Aaron kissed her lightly, briefly. 'Come on. I'll drop you back to your place.'

'Drop me?' Her index finger traced the crooked line of his top lip. 'I was hoping you might stay.'

He raised an eyebrow, his mouth lifting beneath the pad of her finger into an answering smile. 'I thought it was too early.'

God…this man was just too damned sweet and considerate, but Chelsea didn't want this night to end. 'For your place, sure. Not for mine.'

She grinned at him and he grinned back.

CHAPTER NINE

THREE WEEKS LATER, Chelsea was with Travis and Aaron at a large community health clinic set up under the shade of some towering gums a few hundred kilometres north of Balanora. The morning was hot, as per usual, but there was some cloud cover and a light breeze helping to keep things bearable.

It had been the most blissful three weeks of her life. Bliss hadn't been a state she'd thought she'd ever occupy again, but laughing and talking over takeaway and Netflix, followed by long, steamy nights in bed—thank God for air-conditioning—and sexy lie-ins on shared days off was pretty damn close to nirvana.

The fact they were keeping it to themselves gave it a little extra spice.

Some might call it sneaking around but Chelsea preferred the term 'discretion'. And Aaron was fully on board with keeping things quiet for a while so she just relaxed and enjoyed it. She had thought it might make working together awkward but, compared to their original awkwardness over that hotel barge-in and her snatched kiss, this was nothing and they soon learned to cultivate their at-work personas.

And Chelsea was pretty sure they'd pulled it off. Until today.

Blowing away her third sticky fly in a minute, she administered a vaccine to her patient in one arm while Travis took her blood pressure on the other. Sadie was a well-known indigenous elder and artist in the region, and spritely for her seventy-eight years, given her arthritic knees and partial blindness in her left eye.

'Gotta hand it to you, Chels,' Travis said, his Santa hat sitting rakishly on his head. With Christmas less than a week away, they were all wearing one. Even Hattie, who was currently kicking a ball around with some kids. 'It's been almost seven weeks and you've managed to avoid saying *bloody flies*. Didn't think you had it in you.'

Chelsea slid a glance at Aaron, who was bent over Jasmine, Sadie's great-granddaughter, stethoscope hanging down from his neck as he performed her six-week postnatal check. A smile touched his mouth but he didn't look up from the baby.

Sadie glanced at her, then at Aaron, then at Travis as he ripped off the blood pressure cuff. She cocked her eyebrow at him. 'They're doing it, right?'

Chelsea glanced at Sadie, alarmed, as Travis nodded. 'We're pretty sure. We're taking bets back at the base on when they'll make it official.'

Bets? Her cheeks grew hot as she stuck a plaster over the vaccination site. Sadie hooted out a laugh and slapped her thigh, her snowy-white hair flicking around her face as Chelsea snuck another look at Aaron. He was clearly biting his cheek to stop from smiling.

'They're playing things close to their chest,' Travis said. 'But Siobhan saw Aaron skulking—'

'I don't skulk,' he interrupted, not looking up as he gently pushed on the infant's adducted hips to check for dysplasia.

'Skulking,' Travis continued, 'down Chelsea's front path at

quarter to eight at night two weeks ago with a bag of Chinese takeaway from the Happy Sun in his hand. And when I asked them both at work the next day what they had for dinner, he said beef and black bean and she said...' he paused for dramatic effect '...a cheese toasty.'

Chelsea remembered that incident. As soon as Aaron had said Chinese, she'd known she couldn't say that too in case it roused suspicion. So, she'd panicked and said the other.

'What?' Sadie shook her head dismissively. 'No one has a toasted sanger when you can have Happy Sun.'

Travis leaned in conspiratorially. 'I know, right?'

'Yep.' She glanced at Chelsea then at Aaron. 'They're doing it.'

That was their evidence? 'We're right here, you know!' Chelsea said as she tossed the empty syringe into the nearby sharps container.

'Reckon it'll last?' Sadie continued, ignoring Chelsea's statement.

'We hope so.' Travis grinned at Chelsea. 'We like her.'

Pursing her lips, Sadie inspected them both again, before returning her attention to Travis. 'Yeah. Reckon it will.'

'From your lips to God's ears, Aunty.'

Sadie narrowed her eyes at Aaron. 'About time, boy.' Clearly, Sadie and Aaron had known each other for a long time.

'No comment,' he said, unperturbed.

Chelsea shut her eyes. No comment meant yes—everyone knew that. Another hoot of laughter escaped the old woman's lips. '*Definitely* doing it.'

They were back in the plane three hours later, having done over fifty different vaccinations, a dozen infant health checks, some post-hospital admission follow-up and seen to miscellaneous other things, from a festered splinter to a mild burn to a case of shingles. Chelsea was buckled into her usual seat, diagonally opposite and facing Aaron. They were waiting for Travis.

'No comment?' she murmured into the mouthpiece as she switched over to a private channel.

He just shrugged and smiled. 'It was bound to get out sooner or later. Is that a problem?'

Chelsea expected to feel hesitancy. Doubt. Uncertainty. But there was none forthcoming. She realised she'd been worried about what people—both in Balanora and back in London—would say about how quick it had been. But, maybe that wasn't *her* problem.

Slowly, she shook her head. 'No, actually.'

He smiled his crooked smile and the slight tension she didn't know had been there seemed to melt from around his shoulders before her eyes. 'Why don't we talk about it tonight?' he suggested.

'Yeah,' she said, and smiled too. They'd been avoiding having a conversation about the future. Or maybe *she* had. But her feelings for Aaron weren't going away, and what was she afraid of exactly? That Aaron would turn out to be like Dom? That he'd cheat?

She'd known him for less than two months and already she could tell he was nothing like Dom. Hell, she'd been able to tell that the second she'd rashly kissed him in her house and he'd stepped away. *He'd* called a halt.

Just then Travis made his way down the aisle, adjusting his headphones. Chelsea feigned interest in looking out of the window as she flicked the channel back to a shared one. So did Aaron.

Travis shook his head. 'You two are so damn cute,' he muttered in their ears. 'Don't keep us in suspense for too much longer.'

Hattie's voice said, 'Amen.'

Aaron's mood was buoyant when they landed just before one in the afternoon. He and Chelsea were going to talk and they'd had a great day out at the clinic. He absolutely loved getting to the outer reaches of the district. He might be the doctor but people didn't treat him any differently than they had when he'd been a boy.

Sadie was a classic example. He'd played in the same footy team as a lot of Sadie's grandkids and assorted other relatives, and she'd always been on the side lines, no matter where they'd played, a staunch supporter of the team. She'd always been the first one to clap and say, 'Good tackle,' or 'Great try,' but also the first to tell him to pull his head in if he gave the ref any lip or if she felt he was getting too big for his footy boots.

'Don't need no prima donnas out here, boy,' she'd say.

It didn't surprise him that she'd twigged to what was going on between Chelsea and him. He swore the old people—the women in particular—knew what he was thinking even before he did. It felt a lot like having a mother, and perhaps that was what the women out in these small communities, proudly living on their country were—his mothers. Closing ranks after his mum had split, filling that gap, poking and prodding him to do better, be better.

The fact Sadie seemed to approve of the situation with Chelsea said a lot about the type of woman Chelsea was. Inherently suspicious of newcomers, ingrained into generations of old people who had seen too much sadness and grief in their lives, Sadie didn't just take to anyone. But she'd been joking and teasing, and if that wasn't a stamp of approval then he didn't know what was.

Having Chelsea seem pretty zen about being outed had been the icing on the cake.

So, despite himself, Aaron started to hope. He'd told her in the beginning that he didn't get involved with out-of-towners, and how much more out-of-town could a woman from *London* be? But back then he'd thought she was still in love with Dom, and they hadn't spent weeks together laughing and eating and sharing.

And *talking*. About going to Tasmania, and other places he'd suggested they could go to together. Talking about her being in Balanora next year and the year after.

Aaron knew how he felt. He was in love with her. It was that simple. And that complex. But, these past few weeks, he'd started to think that she felt the same way, or that she might be starting to, anyway. Maybe he was just a giant fool, but her willingness to talk about their relationship—there, *he* was labelling it—only filled him with more hope.

As they were the last two to disembark the plane, Chelsea leered at him cheekily on her way out. Glancing at the swish of her ponytail and the perky little stab of her pen, Aaron made a quick grab for her hand, pulling her back and toppling her onto his lap. She gave a little squeak as she landed.

'Aaron!' she protested on a whisper, laughing as she tried to squirm out of his grasp. 'Trent could come back.'

'I don't care,' he muttered.

It was clear everyone pretty much knew anyway, and that not only made him happy but exceptionally turned on. Keeping his hands to himself around her was difficult at the best of times, but suddenly the possibility of a *them* loomed large, and the urge to kiss the hell out of her beat like a mantra through his blood.

She melted against him the second his mouth touched hers, kissing him back with equal abandon. 'Ever heard of the milehigh club?' he murmured a minute later, coming up for some air.

Laughing, she said, 'We're on the ground.'

A loud knock on the fuselage followed by Trent's stern, 'Don't make me bring a blue light in there,' had them both laughing.

Aaron rubbed his nose against Chelsea's. 'Tonight,' he whispered, and her contented sigh was better than any quickie in an aeroplane loo.

'Can't wait.'

But those plans were dashed about thirty seconds after they deplaned. 'Sorry, Chels,' Charmaine said as she met them at the entrance to the hangar, 'but we've had several phone calls from a Roberto Rossi asking for you.'

She frowned. 'Roberto?'

'He said he'd left you several messages, but I explained that you were in an area with no mobile coverage. He wouldn't say what he wanted but he asked that you ring him urgently and that you knew the number.'

A prickle flared at Aaron's nape as Chelsea delved in her pocket, retrieving her phone and switching it on. Nobody ever had their mobiles on when they went out. They couldn't have it on in the plane, and there was rarely any mobile coverage in the places they went anyway.

Aaron could see what looked like at least a dozen missed-call notifications on her screen as she tapped the first one and put the phone to her ear. He wasn't sure if he should go and give her some privacy, but she hadn't asked him or Charmaine to leave, nor had she walked away, and he didn't want to dessert her in case it was bad news and she needed someone to lean on.

Him, hopefully.

Her brow furrowed further as she listened to what he assumed was one of the messages before she pulled the phone away from her ear and tapped to end the call.

'Is everything okay?' Charmaine asked, getting in before Aaron, who was trying to read her body language, could say a word.

She shook her head as she glanced at Aaron. 'It's Alfie.'

Charmaine frowned this time. 'Is that a niece or a nephew?'

'Yeah.' Chelsea nodded. 'Something like that.'

'What happened?' Aaron asked, moving closer, not touching her but wanting to. Wanting to slip his hand onto her neck or an arm around her waist and hating that he couldn't.

'I don't know, it was pretty garbled. He's in Intensive Care.' She turned to Charmaine. 'Do you mind if I use the phone in your office to ring Roberto back?'

'Of course not.'

Charmaine squeezed her arm and Aaron wished he could do the same. But suddenly he felt very uncertain about where they stood. Her dead husband's child, a child who had *wormed his way into her heart*, was in Intensive Care.

Would she go back? To London. To *home*. The place she knew, where people loved her and most of her stuff was still stored.

And would she return to Balanora?

He felt like all kinds of bastard to be worried about himself in a moment like this, but everything he'd felt less than a minute ago was disintegrating around him, and he wasn't at all sure he'd get it back.

Chelsea placed her hand over top of Charmaine's and returned her squeeze. 'Thanks,' she said before dropping her hand and hurrying across the hangar.

They watched her as she disappeared through the door to the offices. 'You okay?' Charmaine asked, turning to face him.

Aaron gave a snort as he looked at her. 'Am I that transparent?'

Her mouth curved into a gentle smile. 'I've known you a long time.'

'I...love her.'

'That was...' Charmaine paused, as if searching for the right word. 'Fast.'

'Seems like it runs in my family.'

'No.' She shook her head. 'Your mother was a city girl who came here pregnant and always had one eye on the highway.'

'She lives in London, Char.'

'No, Aaron. She lives *here*. She's inordinately qualified. She could have got a job in any of the big capital cities, but she *chose* here. And she's made more effort in the short time she's been here to be part of this community then your mum did in fifteen years. She came to a bloody CWA meeting with me three days ago.'

The Country Women's Association was a service organisation that formed the backbone of any Outback community. His mother had referred to them as the 'blue rinse set'.

'She's going to want to go back.' Aaron wished he didn't know that already, but the sinking feeling in the pit of his stomach said otherwise. Because, as much as Chelsea had wanted out of the situation back home, she was deeply compassionate. He doubted she could turn away from people who had been— *were*—a huge part of her life in their hour of need.

'Okay.' Charmaine nodded. 'We'll work it out.'

'And if she doesn't return?'

She raised her eyebrow. 'Are you that unlovable?'

No, it wasn't that. 'It's new.'

Charmaine gave his arm the same squeeze she'd given to Chelsea. 'Have some faith.' Dropping her hand, she said, 'C'mon, let's go see what she needs.'

By the time they were back in the office, Chelsea was hanging up the phone at Charmaine's desk. Aaron knocked quietly on the door, pushing it gently open. She looked pale and he knew the news wasn't good.

'What happened?'

'He ran out on the road to get his ball. A car knocked him over. He has a fractured skull and a bleed on the brain. It sounds like it's small enough to manage conservatively because they're not talking surgery. Roberto's in shock, so he didn't know a lot of other information. He had a seizure at the scene so he's on a vent and he also has a broken tib-fib.'

'Bloody hell.' That was some major trauma. Aaron moved closer, halting on the other side of the desk. He wanted to hug her but he was conscious of their lack of privacy. 'Is he stable?'

'I think. For now.' She shrugged. 'Roberto was very upset. Francesca was looking after him. She's apparently inconsolable. I...' She paused, placing a hand on her stomach as if she was quelling nausea. 'I have to go.'

Aaron ignored the giant fist ramming straight into his gut

and the slick edge of his own nausea as he accepted that this was probably the end of the road for them.

Damn it, *why* had he left himself hope?

'Of course.' He nodded. 'The afternoon flight leaves at four. You could be on that.'

It cost him to slip into organisational mode but the last thing she needed right now was him being whiny about what Alfie's potentially life-threatening condition meant for them. For *him*. She needed him to be a god damned man and step up.

Her shoulders sagged a little. 'There's usually a few flights to London around nine out of Brisbane.'

Charmaine entered and joined him at the desk. 'Why don't you go home, have a shower, grab what you need and I'll get Meg to book the flights? She has all your passport and preference details.'

'Oh, no.' Chelsea shook her head. 'I can do all that.'

'Nonsense. Meg organises flights all the time—it's a huge part of her job. And she's a bloody whizz at it. She'll find the best value last-minute, most direct flight she can.'

'But I'll need to pay...'

Charmaine waved her hand dismissively. 'We'll worry about that later. You just go to your family.'

'But...' Chelsea glanced at Aaron then back to Charmaine. 'I'm leaving you in the lurch.'

'It's fine.' Another dismissive wave. 'There are nurses at the hospital who can and do cover for us when we have a shortfall.'

Chelsea blinked. 'Thank you.'

Aaron moved to the door. 'I'll drive you home.'

'No.' She shook her head firmly. 'I'm fine. I don't need—' She stopped abruptly and shook her head before dropping her gaze. 'I'm fine.'

He stiffened. He could fill in the blanks just fine. She didn't need him. 'Of course.' He took a steadying breath. 'Safe travels.'

She nodded then glanced at Charmaine. 'Thank you.' And then she was pushing away from the desk, slowing as she neared where Aaron was standing in the doorway. 'I'll be back,' she said, looking at him now.

Aaron nodded, his throat as dry as the red Outback dirt. 'Yep,' he murmured, keeping his voice even and friendly.

Her hand slid over his and squeezed, her brown gaze locking on his. 'I *will* be back.'

And then she was gone leaving Aaron about as wretched as he'd ever felt, clinging to her words but not hopeful, despite the utter certainty of her tone. The thing he'd feared the most had come true—Chelsea was leaving—and there was a giant hole in his chest. He'd let his guard down, broken his own rule and fallen head-over-heels in love, like some damned sappy teenager, and now it was all going to hell.

And that was on him. Not her. Because he'd known better.

Chelsea walked aimlessly around the shops in the forecourt of Brisbane international airport, waiting for check-in to open. She'd arrived at the international terminal from the domestic one not long after she'd got off her flight from Balanora. She was a few hours early, but there was no point leaving the terminal complex when the flight left at nine-thirty.

She had managed to get through to Great Ormond Street hospital and talk to the neurosurgeon in charge of Alfie's care, whom she'd worked with several years ago at another hospital. The news had improved, it seemed. Alfie's vitals were stable, he had woken and recognised his mother and they'd removed the ventilation. He was sleepy but there hadn't been any more seizures.

All encouraging signs.

The surgeon had stressed that the bleed was tiny and the skull fracture only hairline, and had been cautiously optimistic. She knew, of course, things could turn on a dime, but it had settled the knot of nerves sitting like an oily lump in her stomach and freed up some headspace to think about Aaron.

About his neutral expression and the forced friendliness in

his voice and the way his walls had come up before her eyes. The ones that had been there when he'd stepped back from her clumsy kiss at her house that first night, and in the store room when he'd said they were just going to be friends.

Before that magical night at Curran Downs. And all the ones since.

She'd tried to assure him she was coming back, but she could tell he hadn't believed her, and she hated that maybe she'd made him feel *not enough* by leaving. It wasn't a nice way to feel. But she hadn't been able to face him coming home with her, either. She didn't want him there with those walls in his eyes, watching her pack, taking her to the airport, wishing her a stiff goodbye.

Not to mention she wouldn't *want* to go. They'd have closed her door behind them, shut the world out and she'd have broken down and clung to him. She'd have cried at the unfairness of life and how this pocket of joy she'd found here in Balanora was being ripped out from under her...and what kind of a person did that make her when Alfie was in ICU?

Selfish. Callous. Heartless.

No, she had to do this by herself. Francesca and Roberto, who had already been through so much, needed her. And she'd figure out the rest as the next few days unfolded.

With thirty minutes to go until check-in opened, Chelsea found a quiet corner in a café and ordered a coffee. It had just arrived when her mobile rang—Roberto.

Answering it immediately, she said, '*Ciao*, Roberto.'

'No, Chelsea, it's me,' Francesca said. 'I'm using Roberto's phone.'

'Francesca, how are you?'

She broke down in tears and Chelsea spent the next five minutes soothing and calming her, assuring her she hadn't done anything wrong, that accidents happened, and encouraging her to see the positives in Alfie's condition.

'Thank you so much for coming, Chelsea. Dom would want you to be with us.'

Chelsea gritted her teeth. Not that long ago the mention of Dom's name would have tugged on all her emotional strings, served up with a hefty dose of guilt because she couldn't keep loving him the way his parents clearly wanted her to.

Not so any more.

She wanted to say, *You didn't know Dom. I didn't know Dom.* But Francesca was distressed enough, so Chelsea cut her some slack.

'This is what I was afraid of. Something bad happening after you left, and it's come true.'

Grinding her teeth now, Chelsea took a steadying breath. Francesca was stressed and feeling guilty about Alfie's accident. She *would* cut her slack, damn it. 'It's just coincidence,' Chelsea soothed, well used to this role with her mother-in-law who, despite being born and raised in a third-generation English household, could lean heavily into her Italian *mamma* roots.

'At least you'll be home for Christmas. That's good.'

Christmas. Chelsea's stomach sank.

'Roberto tells me you changed your name back to Tanner but...why, Chelsea? How could you do that to us?' she chided. 'To Dom. Reject his name. Betray him like that just three years after he was put in the ground.'

Chelsea blinked. Okay. *No.* A red mist blurred her vision. She was officially out of slack. Francesca had to be freaking kidding.

'Betray *him*?' Chelsea didn't even recognise her own voice as she gripped the phone.

'Chelsea. Come on now.'

'Betray *him*?' she repeated.

'We don't speak ill of the dead.'

She didn't have to be there to know that Francesca was probably crossing herself. 'He betrayed *me*, Francesca.' Her hand shook and she wrapped it around her coffee cup. 'He *betrayed* me. He slept with another woman and got her pregnant.'

It was on the tip of Chelsea's tongue to unload about the other women too, but she couldn't let the rage storming through her system destroy everything in its path. She would only regret it later.

'Chelsea, *bella*, women always threw themselves at him. You know that. He was such a good-looking boy.'

Chelsea barely bit back her gasp. 'Francesca!' Several people nearby turned to look at her as her voice whipped from her throat. 'Your son *cheated* on me.' She lowered her voice but there was no mistaking the edge of fury. 'He took our vow of fidelity and he stomped all over it and there is no excuse for that. *None*. He can hide from the responsibility of that in death, but I won't let you hide from the truth of it or pretend he was some kind of saint any more. I had to spend the last year in Hackney seeing the woman he betrayed me with and their child almost every day. Do you understand how much that *hurt*? Do you have *any* idea?'

She drew a shaky breath. Every part of her trembled. She'd never spoken to her mother-in-law like this but this was her line in the sand.

No more Saint Dom.

'Dom was my husband and, yes, I loved him. But he *hurt* me and that changed everything. Sure, he was human and he was flawed, and neither of us can go back and change what he did. But *I* can change how *I* feel. And I don't love him any more, Francesca.'

She loved Aaron. Yes—*she loved Aaron*.

A rush of emotion swamped Chelsea's chest as quiet sobbing sounded in her ear, and she sat with the truth of her feelings, growing and glowing, giving her courage not to take back every word in the face of Francesca's tears. It felt as if a yoke had been ripped from her neck and Chelsea wouldn't pick it up and put it back on again.

Dom was her past. Aaron was her future.

'I'm sorry, Chelsea,' Francesca said eventually as her weeping subsided. 'I didn't understand. You were always so good and kind about it, I underestimated how much having Krystal and Alfie around hurt you. How much *Dom* hurt you. I'm so, so sorry.'

Breathing out slowly, Chelsea's chest filled with a different kind of emotion. For the first time since Alfie had arrived on the scene, she actually felt as though Francesca *really* understood how difficult the last year had been for her, and the shackles that had kept them joined together in a cycle of grief and guilt fell away. Which made her next decision even easier.

'I'm not coming, Francesca.'

'Chelsea…please, *bella*.'

She was so used to being the one that Francesca and Roberto relied on since Dom's death, it was strange to realise that they'd be okay without her. They had plenty of family—they'd always had plenty of family. And now it was time to lean on them.

She was drawing a line in the sand.

Charmaine had told her to go to her family, and for a long time Hackney and the Rossis had been her family. More so than the house she'd grown up in. But things happened, feelings altered, directions changed. And, even though she'd been in Balanora for such a short period of time, when she thought of family she thought of that hangar baking under the Outback sun in the middle of nowhere.

She thought of Charmaine and Hattie and Travis. She thought of *Aaron*.

'It's time, Francesca. Krystal and Alfie need you, and Roberto and the rest of the family. They don't need me.' Francesca had been trying hard to hang on with both hands but it was time to let go. 'You've got to let me live my life now.'

There were more quiet tears, but when Francesca next spoke she said, 'You will keep in touch, won't you?'

'Of course. I'm not cutting you out of my life, and I want to keep across Alfie's progress. We're just…turning a new page.'

'You like it there?'

Chelsea smiled. 'I *love* it here.'

Five minutes later, with her carry-on bag rolling behind her—her only piece of luggage—Chelsea strode out into the Brisbane sunshine.

The next morning, just after eleven, and almost seven weeks to the day she'd first landed in Balanora, Chelsea was back. It was still scorching hot as she walked off the plane and onto the Tarmac but she barely noticed. She only had one thing on her mind as she got into the nearest taxi—go to Aaron.

He had a couple of days off now and she knew he'd planned to go to Curran Downs because she'd been going with him. A quick phone call to the house phone confirmed that he'd arrived there last night and had gone straight to the river to camp for a couple of days.

So, the river it was.

Chelsea was home for five minutes—just long enough to divest herself of her suitcase and get into that green strappy dress he liked so much. Then she was in her car and heading to Curran Downs. She'd been there three times now, so she knew the way, but the trip felt ten times longer, her anxiety growing more acute as her car ate up the miles.

What if she'd blown it? What if she'd permanently damaged things between them by her abrupt departure?

When she reached the homestead, Tracey was waiting for her with a four-wheel-drive vehicle. Even though Aaron had taken her to the river last time she'd been to Curran Downs, it was a slightly more complicated path, and Tracey had suggested on the phone that she drop Chelsea there and she and Aaron could come back in Aaron's vehicle when they were ready.

'Is everything okay with Alfie?' Tracey asked as she gave Chelsea a quick hug.

'Yep. Off life-support. Talking. Not quite his usual chatty self but apparently doing well.' She'd checked in with Great Ormond Street and Francesca this morning before her flight to Balanora.

'A good outcome.'

Chelsea nodded. 'Yes.'

'Get in,' Tracey said in her typical no-nonsense way, which suited Chelsea just fine.

She had no desire to swap pleasantries—she just needed to find Aaron. They needed to talk. And she needed to feel his arms around her.

Any other time, Chelsea would have enjoyed the drive. The vast canvas of the Outback topped off by a bright-blue sky was magnificent in that grand sweeping way of all landscape vistas. But today she was too preoccupied to be appreciative of the scenery.

'Is Aaron okay?' she asked, staring out of the window at nothing, conscious only of her own heartbeat as they jostled along through the scrub.

'He's fine.'

She turned sharply. 'Really?'

Tracey glanced over. 'Aaron's not much of a talker,' she clarified as she returned her attention to the bush track.

'I screwed up.' Unfortunately, admitting it out loud didn't help any.

'But you're here to fix it, right?'

'Yes.' A thousand times yes.

'Well, then…'

'What if it's too late?'

Tracey laughed. It wasn't cruel or unkind, merely amused. 'You've been gone one day.'

'That's long enough for regret to set in.'

'Nah.' Tracey shook his head. 'Aaron's not built like that. Our mother leaving taught him to guard his heart, sure. But, unlike me, it also taught him how to forgive, and how to understand that this place isn't for everyone, and that's actually not some horrible kind of flaw.'

Tracey's mouth tilted upwards and Chelsea smiled at his sister's self-deprecation, despite the niggle of anxiety pecking at her brain. 'It's for me,' Chelsea said.

This vast expanse of red dirt and blue sky, so different from where she had come from, had worked its way under her skin. Just as Aaron had.

'Good.' She nodded. 'Tell him that.'

Twenty minutes later, Aaron's ute came into view, parked under the shade of some river gums. Chelsea spotted him sitting on the back tray, a frosty bottle in his hand, the same time he heard the engine, craning his neck in its direction. She could see his brows knit together as he tried to figure out why his sister was here, and who was in the passenger seat, and she clocked the second he realised it was her, his expression briefly surprised before turning guarded.

He leapt off the back of the ute as Tracey pulled her vehicle up alongside his. She put the window down but kept the engine running. 'Brought you a visitor,' she said with a smile.

Chelsea swallowed as Aaron looked at her as if she was some kind of mirage. His eyes ate her up as hers did him. It had been less than twenty-four hours but she'd *missed* him. Missed his crooked face and his carelessly messy hair swooping across his forehead. Missed the way he filled out a T-shirt and shorts.

Missed the way he looked at her as though she was special. As though she was *enough*.

A trill of anticipation caused her hand to tremble as she placed it on the door handle and pushed. Chelsea's pulse fluttered at her temple and she wondered if she'd ever stop feeling as though she'd been plugged into an electrical socket when he was near.

She hoped not.

'Thanks, Tracey,' she said as she slid out of the four-wheel drive, the heat hitting hard after the frigid air-con in the cab.

'No worries,' Tracey replied cheerfully, then winked at her brother as Chelsea shut the door and stood clear. 'You kiddies behave now, you hear.'

She drove off then, but neither of them really noticed as they stood staring at each other for long moments. 'Chelsea?' There was so much hope in his voice as he took a step forward, then his brow furrowed and he halted. 'Is Alfie…? Did he…? He didn't…?'

'No.' She shook her head. 'He's fine, doing well. Off the vent, stable GCS, in a stepdown ward. The fracture was hairline and the bleed quite small. They're confident it should resolve reasonably quickly and he should make a full recovery in time.'

He breathed on a rush. 'That's so good. Everyone must be very relieved.'

'Yeah. They'll feel better when he's home but they're counting their blessings.'

'So, you…' He eyed her speculatively and she swore she saw hope in his eyes. 'Didn't get on the plane?'

She smiled as she shook her head slowly. 'I did not.'

'Because Alfie's condition had improved?'

'Not because of that, no.'

'Okay.' He looked as though he wanted to come closer but shoved his hands on his hips instead. 'Because?'

Chelsea took a step towards him instead. 'I had an epiphany at the airport.'

'Oh.' He swallowed. 'You did, huh?'

'I did.'

'Care to share?'

Taking another step, Chelsea halted about three metres from him, aware suddenly of the volume of silence all around them. 'I realised that I wasn't responsible for Dom's family. And that it wasn't fair of them to expect me to keep playing the part of grieving widow. That I needed to move on. That we all needed to move on.'

A beat or two passed between them then Aaron took a tentative step in her direction. 'That sounds…healthy.'

Chelsea nodded. The husky edge to his voice sounded strained. 'I also realised that I'd fallen in love with you.'

He blinked. 'You…did?'

'I know it's crazy, Aaron.' Her pulse was jumping all over the place as she inched closer to him. She was pretty sure he felt the same but he didn't seem to be leaping for joy at her admission. 'I know it's not been very long but...'

Within two strides he was grabbing her up and hauling her close, her breasts flattened against his chest, his hands cradling either side of her face as he kissed her—hard. Her pulse thrummed madly, the scent of the bush and the taste of beer filling her senses, making her dizzy.

'God,' he muttered, breaking away to kiss her eyes and her nose and nuzzle her temple, his fast, raspy breath ruffling her hair. 'I didn't think you'd come back.'

Chelsea's breathing was equally as erratic. 'I'm sorry, I'm so sorry I left so quickly, I just panicked and reacted without thinking things through properly.' She shut her eyes as his lips caused all kinds of havoc. 'But I always planned on coming back. Always.'

'I thought the pull of home would be too much when you got there.' His lips trekked down the side of her face. 'With everything familiar that you knew and loved at your fingertips again. And I've been sitting here, kicking myself one moment for being such an idiot to fall for you, and planning on moving to the UK the next.'

Chelsea blinked. '*What?* Moving to the UK?'

'Of course. If it means being with you? Absolutely.'

She drew back, needing to make eye contact. Needing him to know. 'There's no need for that. *This* is my home now.' Her gaze captured his and locked. 'Balanora. And you. *You're* my home. I love you, Aaron, and I swear I'll never leave you like that again. *Never.* I think we've both spent a lot of our lives feeling like we weren't enough for people, but now we get to be each other's enough, and that's all I want. Just you and me for ever.'

'That's what I want too.' He kissed her again quickly, as if to assure her. 'I love you, Chelsea Tanner...and I know I've said this before, but you are *more* than enough. You are my everything. I am yours, and *only* yours, for ever and always.'

And that was all she needed. This man loving her in the same way she loved him—as big and as vast and as fathomless as the landscape around them.

For ever and always.

EPILOGUE

One year later, Christmas morning

CHELSEA STARED OUT of the window of the King Air as it made its descent to the graded red earth of the community airstrip below. Just beyond the strip, behind a low, tinsel-emblazoned partition, stood a gaggle of cheering kids, their eyes squinting expectantly at the approaching plane.

She was excited to be part of the annual Christmas Express run by the OA, which involved hopping from community to community on Christmas day, distributing gifts to kids in isolated areas and giving every child a chance to have a photo with Santa. It was one of the highlights of the OA calendar and Chelsea had been looking forward to it. Last year she'd been on call, and therefore unable to take part, but not this year!

She glanced across at Aaron as Hattie landed the plane with her usual light touch. He was dressed in a red Santa suit, complete with snowy beard and a pillow for his belly, and Chelsea laughed as the plane taxied. 'Have I told you how hot you look in that suit?' she said into the headphone mic.

Santa might not usually be considered a sex symbol but it sure worked on Aaron.

'You look pretty hot too, elf girl.'

Chelsea blew him a kiss. She'd bought the elf suit online a few months ago when Charmaine had asked her what she wanted to dress up as for the Express. Seeing Aaron's face in the office this morning when she'd changed into it just prior to boarding, she was very pleased she had. The skirt was short-ish and flirty, and the top, with the addition of a push-up bra, showed off a hint of cleavage.

It wasn't overtly sexy but he'd obviously liked what he saw and had whispered to her, 'You better wear that to bed tonight,' as he'd passed her by.

Thinking about it now, her heart overflowed anew with the depth of her feelings for this man who had filled her life this past year with so much love and joy. She couldn't remember ever being this happy. Their relationship had gone from strength to strength, and they'd moved in together six months ago. Three months ago, they'd spent two fantastic weeks in Tasmania, in-cluding one glorious night witnessing the spectacle and maj-esty of the aurora.

And now this. Christmas day playing Santa in the Outback. Pinch her!

Alfie, who had made a full recovery, had been impressed when she'd told him she was flying with Santa today, and she'd promised him a picture of her with the man himself.

The plane came to a halt and Chelsea removed her head-phones, unbuckling and springing up from her seat, eager to get outside, the bell on the end of her jaunty elf hat tinkling as she scooped up the Polaroid camera.

It was Aaron's turn to laugh. 'Having fun?' he teased as he pulled his headphones off and reached for the sack in front of him, neatly labelled by Meg as being for this stop.

She grinned, her heart full of love and Christmas spirit. 'Santa baby, this is the best time I've ever had.'

He shook his head slowly, his gaze capturing hers. '*You're* the best time I've ever had, Chelsea Tanner.'

Chelsea's insides melted to goo. The man said the sweetest damned things. *All the time.* 'Merry Christmas,' she murmured.

'Merry Christmas,' he replied. 'Here's to many more.'

Then, from a pocket, he produced some plastic mistletoe, held it up high with one hand and snagged her closer with the other, kissing her in a very un-Santa-like way.

Yes, Chelsea thought on a sigh. *Here's to many, many more.*

* * * * *

Outback Surgeon
Leah Martyn

For Hilary, who knows the journey.

CHAPTER ONE

'THANKS, GUYS. That was terrific!'

Off camera, the television producer favoured his guests with a satisfied grin, his gaze lingering with obvious approval on the female of the pair, Dr Abbey Jones.

Abbey dredged up a dry smile. 'I'm always happy to comment on rural health matters, Rob. You know that. But next time, warn me if I'm here for a debate, will you?' Lifting her chin, she sent a cool, tawny look at her opponent in the debate, Dr Nicholas Tonnelli.

Tonnelli's mouth quirked in a smile that just missed being patronising and she practically had to force herself to accept the hand he extended to formally end their debate.

'You presented an irresistible challenge, Dr Jones.'

Abbey took a shallow breath as her hand vanished inside his. His touch was warm and dry and his green eyes gleamed down at her. 'I enjoyed our encounter,' he added softly.

Disconcerted, she reclaimed her hand as though she feared being burned by the impact, turning away to gather up her hastily scribbled notes. Her lungs heaved in a controlling breath. Her hands, with a mind of their own, began shoving the A4 pages awkwardly into her briefcase.

Chewing her bottom lip, Abbey reluctantly admitted that Tonnelli had been a formidable opponent, his skilled ad lib presentation spurring her on to try to salvage something even halfway credible for her side of the argument.

And it had hardly been fair of Rob, she remonstrated silently, pitting her, a rural GP, against one of Sydney's up and coming spinal surgeons.

Physically, he hadn't been what she'd expected either. But, then, what had she expected? Occasionally, when she'd flipped through the Sydney newspapers, she'd glimpsed pictures of him in the social pages. But now, having met him in the flesh, she had to admit that the black and white images hadn't done him justice. They'd certainly given no indication of the man's almost tangible charisma.

She caught back a huff of irritation. Perhaps he'd won the debate, perhaps he hadn't. But whatever the TV ratings showed, she'd just bet his high-voltage sexy smile had sizzled all the way to the female viewers' little hearts.

But not to hers. Heavens, she wasn't that easily taken in!

A glance at her watch told her she'd have to forego the coffee and cake Rob usually offered and make a quick exit from the studio.

'I'm just off, Rob.' Her professional smile in place, Abbey looked to where the two males were seemingly in close private conversation beside the now-darkened set.

'Already?' Rob Stanton turned, taking several quick strides towards her. 'Thanks again, Abbey, for making yourself available at such short notice. You saved my bacon.'

A chink of wry humour lit her smile. 'A nice fat donation to our hospital funds should be in order, then.'

'Hey, you've got it!' Rob was enthusiastic, as though he'd thought of the idea himself. 'I'll OK it right away.'

'Thanks,' Abbey murmured and shot a level look at Tonnelli.

'Goodbye, Doctor.' She began to turn away and then took a quick breath, her senses clanging when the surgeon moved fast enough to block her way as she made to go past him.

'Do you have to rush off, Dr Jones?'

Abbey glared at him, realising belatedly that now they were not seated, she had to raise her gaze a good six inches to meet his eyes. 'Yes, I do.'

'Let me buy you lunch.'

'No, thank you.'

'What've I done?' The charismatic, mocking face was close to hers and she felt every nerve in her body contract. His mouth, wearing its sexy smile, was getting close to hers, so close she could feel the warm whisper of his breath, take in the clean smell of sandalwood soap on his skin.

Get out of my space, she wanted to tell him calmly and coolly. Instead, she felt her insides grind painfully, as she took an uncertain step backwards, rocking a little on her high heels. 'If you don't mind, Dr Tonnelli, I have a tight schedule today. I just want to get on with my own business.'

'Oh, come on, Doctor… We're off camera now. Can't we bury the hatchet?' he asked, his tone almost an amused drawl.

Abbey tried to fix him with a steely glare and failed miserably. 'I don't have time to sit around having long lunches, Dr Tonnelli.'

He lifted a shoulder dismissively. 'It needn't necessarily be a long lunch. I know a place where the service is fast and the food actually pretty good.'

'McDonald's?' Abbey parried innocently.

His mouth gave the merest twist of a smile. 'A little more upmarket. Margo's. Heard of it?'

'No.'

When she still hesitated, he added persuasively, 'Surely you usually eat something before you head off on that long drive back to Wingara?'

'I *usually* just grab a sandwich or some fruit to eat in the car.'

Abbey began to feel pushed into a corner, almost mesmerised by the subtle challenge in his eyes. And they couldn't stand here much longer. The TV crew packing up their gear were beginning to latch onto the possibility of some gossip. 'Oh, all right, then,' she said, uncomfortably aware her acceptance sounded ungracious, explaining, 'I've a dozen things still to do and a patient to see at Sunningdale rehab centre before I head back west, so I'll need to keep it short, OK?'

'Deal.' He looked pleased. Or rewarded, Abbey thought waspishly, watching him. 'Did you come by cab?' he asked.

Oh, for heaven's sake! Who could afford cabs any more? 'I drove my own vehicle. I'm parked outside.'

'Me too.' Moving smoothly away from her, he opened the heavy glass door to the foyer.

This is crazy, Abbey fretted, her heart fluttering like the wings of a trapped bird as they made their way past the flowering shrubs to the car park. And why did it have to be *him* she'd had to cross swords with and ruin her day? There were any number of registrars at the district hospital Rob could have approached to fill the gap. But, then, they wouldn't have had the impact of Tonnelli.

She sighed and brought her head up, her fair silky bob sliding back from her cheekbones, her thoughts still on the surgeon. It was rumoured in medical circles that he was a genius at just about anything he turned his mind to. A man firmly at the centre of his own universe.

Not to mention his reputation with women...

Well, I don't want him propositioning *me,* she decided through gritted teeth, coming to a stop beside the door of her maroon Range Rover. 'This is me.' Her shoulder brushed against his upper arm, and she found herself staring into his eyes. And taking a sharp little breath. His eyes had the luminosity of an early-morning ocean, she thought fancifully. A kind of wintergreen...

'I'm over there.'

She blinked, following the backward flex of his thumb to the metallic grey Jaguar. It suits him, she decided, having no trouble at all personifying the car's sleek elegance and controlled power and making the comparison with its owner.

'It's probably best if you follow me.' He looked at her from under slightly lowered lids. 'Margo's is rather tucked away, an old house that's been refurbished into a restaurant. But I'm afraid the parking's non-existent—just stop along the street, wherever you can.' He raised the briefest smile. 'See you there in a bit.'

Abbey nodded assent, climbing into her vehicle, tapping her fingers impatiently on the steering-wheel, her gaze following his tall, lithe figure as he strode towards his vehicle on the periphery of the car park.

Her wide, sensitive mouth with its gloss of soft coral firmed into a moue of conjecture. Just what was Nicholas Tonnelli doing here in Hopeton anyway? As far as she knew he didn't operate anywhere outside his own hospital, St Thomas's in Sydney's rather affluent North Shore area. So what had brought him here to a small provincial city in the Central West of New South Wales in the middle of a working week?

He'd almost blown it.

Nick Tonnelli wondered why he'd pushed her so hard. 'Male ego at its worst,' he muttered, grimacing with self-derision, groping in the glove box for his sunglasses. But she *had* accepted his invitation, hadn't she? Yeah, right! Reluctantly, mate. Get real.

A tight little smile drifted around his mouth. Who'd have thought spending a couple of days R and R in his home town and doing a favour for his mate, Rob Stanton, would have led to his meeting someone like the feisty, quite delectable Dr Abbey Jones?

The lady was like a breath of sweet, clean air. And he'd become so bored with the Sydney social scene lately. So utterly, utterly bored.

* * *

Abbey glanced across the car park once more. At last! Tonnelli was in motion. In a kind of sick anticipation, she lowered her hand to the ignition switch, her mind simultaneously agonising over what on earth they'd find to talk about over lunch.

Alternatively, she supposed she could save herself the grief and lose him deliberately on the way to the restaurant... A jagged laugh caught in her throat at the very idea.

The journey to Margo's was completed quite quickly, with Abbey keeping Tonnelli's distinctive vehicle in sight as she followed him in and out of several back streets, until he indicated he was about to stop and she glanced sideways and saw the restaurant's sign.

She looked in vain for a parking spot and ended up having to drive further along the narrow street, scattering tiny bits of gravel, when she finally ground her four-wheel-drive to a halt.

Tonnelli gave her an apologetic half-smile when she joined him outside the restaurant. 'The food will more than compensate for the parking hassles,' he promised, guiding her along the flagstone path to the entrance.

Although it was just on midday, the place was already filled with the hushed sounds of patrons dining—a muted hum of conversation, the soft clink of cutlery on china—and an absolutely delicious aroma wafting from the kitchen.

'Oh, it's lovely!' Abbey's comment was spontaneous. Entranced, she looked around her at the walls, papered with a country-style pattern of meadowsweet flowers, and at the framed prints, each one essentially outback Australian, depicting the lifestyles of its drovers, ringers and stockmen.

Told you so, Tonnelli's little nod of satisfaction seemed to imply. 'It's a blackboard menu.' His dark head was turned attentively towards her. 'We'll order first and then with a bit of luck we'll find a table.' His green gaze swept over the precincts. 'It's crowded today. The livestock sales must be on in town.'

He considered the blackboard. 'Ah, it's Italian today. Fancy some pasta?'

Abbey's teeth caught on her lower lip. 'I think I'll just have the house salad, thanks.'

'OK.' Nick Tonnelli tapped his fingers on the polished countertop, considering his own choice. 'But you must try one of their stuffed potatoes,' he insisted. 'And the home-made bread.'

Abbey spread her hands helplessly. 'You must think I need fattening up.'

'Hardly.' His eyes softened for a moment. 'I'd say the packaging is perfect as it is.' He added a slow, very sweet smile then, and it was as though his fingers played over her skin.

For a split second Abbey registered a riveting awareness between them. Raw and immediate. Like an electric current and just as tangible. She swallowed thickly. 'I'll, um, freshen up while you order, then.'

'Will you have something to drink?' He detained her with the lightest touch to her forearm. 'White wine, perhaps?'

Abbey considered her options swiftly. 'A mineral water, I think. I've a long drive ahead of me.'

'We'll meet at the bar, then.' Two little lines appeared between his dark brows. 'Don't do a runner on me, will you?'

Abbey felt the heat warm her cheeks as she spun away. How had he guessed she'd actually considered it? Perhaps he read minds along with his other talents, she thought cynically.

In the restroom, she did a quick make-up repair. Taking out her small cosmetic bag, she freshened her lipstick, swiped a comb through her hair and added a squirt of her favourite cologne.

In the mirror with its lovely old-fashioned gilded frame, she looked critically at her reflection, unnerved to see a flush in her cheeks she hadn't seen there in ages.

She was suddenly conscious of her stomach churning. She must have been crazy to have agreed to this lunch, she berated herself for the umpteenth time. She and Tonnelli had nothing in common. For starters, their lifestyles had to be poles apart.

As a senior surgeon in a state-of-the-art hospital, he could have no concept of her world, she reflected thinly. Her little hospital at Wingara was reasonably well equipped, mostly due to the tireless money-raising efforts of the locals. But even so it had to be light years away from what she imagined as Tonnelli's clinical environment.

She hitched up her shoulder-bag, her mind throwing up yet again the question of what on earth would they find to talk about. Heart thrumming, she left the restroom and began making her way back to the bar. She saw him at once, his distinctive dark head with its short cut turning automatically, almost as if he'd sensed her approach. 'Thanks.' Abbey took the drink he handed to her.

'I believe there's a table for us in the garden room.' He began leading the way towards the rear of the restaurant to a cleverly conceived extension like a conservatory, complete with glass walls and ceiling.

He saw her comfortably seated and Abbey took a moment to look around her. Their table was set with crisp, palest cream linen, gleaming silver and glassware, and decorating the centre was a trailing arrangement of multicoloured garden flowers. She felt her spirits lift and decided to make a huge effort. 'I'm actually looking forward to our lunch.'

'Much better than a sandwich from the deli,' he agreed. 'Cheers.' Lifting his glass of ice-cold lager, he took a mouthful. 'I asked for our peasant bread to be brought first. I don't know about you, but I'm starving.'

Even as he finished speaking, a smiling waitress placed the still-warm loaf on the table with the accompanying little pats of butter.

Abbey eyed the crusty, flour-dusted high round loaf hungrily, feeling her digestive juices begin to react.

'This looks good, hmm?' Without hesitation, Nick Tonnelli

took up the breadknife, wielding it with surgical precision, separating the loaf quickly and efficiently into easily manageable portions.

Watching him, Abbey said faintly, 'You must be a whiz with the Sunday roast, Dr Tonnelli.'

'Each to his own talent, Abbey,' he responded blandly. 'And for crying out loud, call me Nick.'

'Tell me about your patient in the rehab centre.' Nick Tonnelli's tone was suddenly professional and brisk.

Startled, Abbey looked up from her plate. Was he just being the polite host? she wondered. Pretending an interest? Making conversation for the sake of it? Whatever he was doing, she could hardly ignore such a pointed demand.

'His name is Todd Jensen. He's a twenty-five-year-old professional rodeo rider.' She looked bleak for a moment. 'Although I probably should be using the past tense here. It's almost certain we won't see him back on the rodeo circuit again.'

Nick's dark brows rose. 'What was it, a workplace accident of some kind?'

'Todd was participating in a buckjumping event. His mount threw him and in its panic struck him on the lower back with its hind hooves.'

The consultant winced and murmured a commiseration.

'It was a dreadful afternoon,' Abbey said quietly. 'Everyone was so shocked. Fortunately, the CareFlight chopper was on standby. Todd was flown straight here to Hopeton.'

Nick's mouth compressed. 'What did the MRI show? That's assuming he had one?'

'Of course he did.' Abbey resented his inference that Todd had somehow received second-class medical attention.

'The new scanning devices for magnetic resonance imaging are ruinously expensive,' Nick clarified. 'I merely wondered whether the district hospital here had managed to install one.'

'They have,' Abbey conceded guardedly. 'Mostly due to the efforts of Jack O'Neal and his committee.'

Nick rubbed a hand around his jaw. 'He's the SR on Kids', isn't he?'

Abbey nodded. 'Jack and his wife, Geena, are tireless fundraisers for the hospital.'

'Commendable.'

'Essential, seeing the shortfall in funding for rural hospitals.'

Nick acknowledged her comment politely. 'To get back to your patient. What did the MRI show?'

'Irreversible nerve damage.'

Nick frowned. 'So, what's his prognosis?'

Biting her lower lip, not sure where they were going with this, Abbey elaborated, 'A wheelchair existence. His accident placed a cloud over our whole community. Todd was well liked, a kind of icon to the young kids. And very good at what he did. The really sad part is he'd had an invitation from one of the rodeo associations in the States. He was about to take off and try his luck in the big time.'

She ran the pad of her thumb across the raised pattern of her glass. 'He's still so angry. Just recently, he told his wife to go and make a new life for herself—that he was only half a man...'

'So he's dropped the ball. That's a fairly normal reaction, Abbey,' Nick pointed out reasonably. 'At the moment his feelings have to be loaded with issues of masculinity and virility so, of course, he's told his wife to get lost. What's more to the point is what's being done presently for your patient? For starters, is his medication up to scratch? How intense is his physio programme? Has there been input from a psychologist? An occupational therapist?'

Abbey lifted her head and regarded him warily. He seemed in his element, rapping out questions. While she, on the other hand, felt as though she were under the microscope, almost an intern again being put through a consultant's wringer.

The silence stretched for a tense moment, until Abbey responded steadily, 'Todd's programme is as good as Sunningdale can provide. And distance-wise, it suits his family to have him there. At least they can make the three-hour drive once a week to see him. But realistically, I'd guess, he's gone about as far as he can go there. Sunningdale will want to discharge him soon.'

'And then what?'

Abbey frowned. 'Well, at this stage his parents are proposing to have him back home with them.'

'In the bush?'

She tilted her chin defensively. 'That's where they live.'

Nick made an impatient sound. 'What's he going to do there, cut wood for the fire from his wheelchair?' The surgeon shook his head. 'Surely we can do better than that, Abbey? Have you heard of the Dennison Foundation in Sydney?'

Abbey frowned. 'It's a fairly recent concept, isn't it?'

'State of the art in every way. Structured specifically for spinal rehab, with patients being taught how to accustom themselves to the physical realities of being disabled in an able-bodied world. I'm sure you'd see a great improvement in your Todd's ability to cope after a stay there. I'd refer him urgently, if I were you.'

A flush of annoyance rose in Abbey's cheeks. 'Ever heard of waiting lists, Doctor? Besides, his family couldn't afford those kinds of fees. And I can't imagine the management would be prepared to cut a special deal on a rural GP's referral.'

'What if I referred him?'

Something like resentment stirred in Abbey and she couldn't let go of it. 'Why should you bother? Todd's nothing to you.'

Nick Tonnelli's expression closed abruptly. 'As professionals, isn't it up to all of us who go under the guise of medical practitioners to assist all humankind where we can? So, Doctor, I suggest you pocket your false pride and face the facts as we have them.

'I'm willing to carry out a reassessment on your patient.

Like Todd, I'm good at what I do. Maybe I can help him further. Maybe I can't. But I'm willing to try and if you think my name will help, I'll refer him to the Dennison, if I deem it appropriate. It's up to you.'

Abbey clenched her hands on her lap and stared at them fiercely. He'd given her a terrible dressing-down. All done so quietly and lethally. Dear God! How she would hate to have to work with the man! Thoughts, none of them pleasant, crowded in on her. She should *never* have agreed to this lunch. She should have quit while she was ahead and left him standing in the car park, watching her dust.

She took a deep breath and tried to leave personal issues out of it. Todd's youthful face, stark with hope one minute and dark with despair the next, impinged on her vision. Much as she hated to admit it, Tonnelli was right. Pride had no place here. She would swallow hers, no matter how galling it might be, and ask for his help.

'When could you see Todd?' she asked hesitantly. 'I mean… I don't know your movements… If you have other commitments here…' She broke off helplessly.

He bit into his bread, his even white teeth leaving a neat half-circle. 'We could start the ball rolling after our lunch, if that suits you.'

'Fine.' Abbey teased at her lip. She should have known that once the decision was made, he'd want to sweep ahead.

'I would prefer to keep my involvement quite informal, if you don't mind,' he said easily. 'I'll need some time to study Todd's case details and speak with the staff, his physio and OT in particular.

'If I decide the programme at the Dennison will benefit Todd, I'll speak personally with the director, Anna Charles.' At once his expression lightened. 'We trained together. She's done extensive post-grad work at Harvard. A brilliant practitioner. Todd couldn't be in better hands.'

Abbey blinked uncertainly. 'And would she take him—just like that?'

'As a favour to me? Yes, she would.' He smiled, a mere sensual curving of his lips.

Abbey felt her cheeks burn as the possible meaning behind his remark occurred to her. She pulled in a shattered breath. Forget Tonnelli and his women and think of Todd, she told herself with quiet desperation. 'What about the fees?'

Nick lifted a dismissive shoulder. 'I'll arrange something. Nothing in this life is set in concrete, Abbey. Nothing at all.'

CHAPTER TWO

THE MAIN PART of their meal was served just after Abbey's capitulation. She looked down at the appetising char-grilled strips
of chicken, the crisp salad and accompanying stuffed potato,
and despaired.

After the last few minutes, the tense trading of words with
Nick Tonnelli, her throat seemed closed, her stomach knotted.

He, on the other hand, she noticed with faint irony, seemed
not be suffering any repercussions at all. And after the first
few uncomfortable minutes, after which he obviously set out to
charm the socks off her, she felt a lessening of tension.

'So, Abbey, what do you do for relaxation at Wingara?' he
asked, as they sat over their coffee later. 'No chance of snow
sports, I expect?' he added with a touch of humour.

'Hardly.' She laughed, activating the tiny dimple in her cheek.
'I play tennis when I can and we have a sports centre with a
pool and quite an active Little Theatre. And I have friends there
now, good friends. One couple in particular, Stuart and Andrea
Fraser, have quite a large property so I'm able to spend the odd
weekend there, picnicking and so on.'

'So, no regrets about opting out of city mainstream medicine, then?' he teased gently, fixing her with his keen, gemstone gaze.

'Often,' Abbey rebuffed him sharply.

He blinked, appearing a little surprised by her answer. 'In what way?'

She lifted a shoulder. 'Broadly speaking, I could give you a dozen examples. But the bottom line is all I can do in a major medical emergency is to stabilise my patient and have them airlifted to the nearest major hospital. And just hope they survive the journey.'

'So what are you saying?' Nick's eyes took on a steely glint.

'Nothing I didn't say in the debate,' Abbey responded bluntly. 'That if a specialist surgeon could be on call to come to us, it would halve the trauma for both patient and family. And would, I dare say, be more cost-effective.'

'Bunkum!' Nick's hand cut the air dismissively. 'Logistics for one thing. Our rural population is so scattered, our distances so vast. All things considered, I believe we, as specialists, do a reasonable job.'

Abbey tossed her head up, throwing into sharp relief the long silky lashes framing the haunting beauty of her tawny eyes. 'When was the last time you conducted a clinic outside St Thomas's, then?'

With a reflex reaction Nick's head shot up, his green gaze striking an arc across the space between them. 'I've considered it but so far the consensus seems to be that it's more appropriate for the patients to come to me than vice versa.' In an abrupt movement, he dipped his head and pulled back the sleeve of his pale blue shirt. His mouth compressed briefly. 'If you've quite finished your coffee, we should be moving, I think.'

So, end of discussion. Abbey curled her mouth into a cynical little moue, bending to retrieve her shoulder-bag from the carpeted floor near her feet. Had she really expected the conversation to go any other way?

While Nick settled the bill, she made her way slowly outside, annoyance with herself shifting and compressing against her ribcage. It wouldn't do to get the man offside. Not now, when it seemed they were about to become involved professionally with Todd's care.

Beside her, a butterfly scooped the air, darting in and out of a border of cornflowers, its pale yellow wings a gauzy haze against the deep blue petals. Her shoulders lifted as she took a calming breath, belatedly registering the near-perfection of the afternoon—the crisp air, the softly falling leaves, the sky an unbroken bowl of china blue...

'Wonderful day.' From behind, Nick softly echoed her thoughts.

Startled, Abbey jerked back. How long had he been standing there? 'I love autumn.' She rushed into speech, embarrassed to be caught mooning like a teenager. 'Especially in this part of the state where the seasons are so clearly defined.'

'Perhaps.' Nick looked unconvinced but he was smiling. 'I still think I prefer the coast. I can well do without all this.' He scuffed a gathering pile of fallen leaves with his shoe.

'Didn't you have fun running through them when you were a kid, though?'

His head went back on a laugh. 'You know, I'd forgotten all that.'

Abbey listened to the small talk threading between them like a line of careful stitches, but at the same time acknowledging she'd have to upset the pattern and get things rather more settled in her own mind. 'Dr Tonnelli—Nick...' she began awkwardly, 'I hope you didn't feel obligated to get involved with my patient...'

Nick's gut tightened. She looked so uncertain, so vulnerable, he wanted to just to hold her, reassure her. Instead, he shoved his hands into the pockets of his trousers out of temptation's way. 'Abbey, I want to do it, OK?'

Her lips parted on a shaky breath. 'Are you sure?'

'I'm sure.' He permitted himself the ghost of a wry smile.

'Actually, it occurs to me I might have seemed to have taken over in there, come on a bit strong about your management of Todd. If I did, I apologise.'

Abbey's senses tightened and she felt confused at the odd mix of reactions chasing around inside her. 'Honestly, you don't need to.'

'Oh, I think I do.' He gave a taut smile. 'I stormed all over you. But, then, I have been accused of being arrogant once or twice. And what's the expression? If you have to eat crow, it's better to do it while it's still warm.'

Abbey smothered a laugh. 'Consider the crow eaten, then.'

She was thoughtful as they made their way down the path to the street. She guessed it had cost him something to have placed a question mark over his earlier behaviour.

But on the other hand, to have put her on the defensive the way he had had probably been nothing more than a normal re-action from him. Everything about the man indicated a natural authority, an obvious ability to give orders and have them car-ried out without question. There was no doubt about it, Nick Tonnelli was a man of substance and of power.

She stifled a sigh, seeing the stream of professional differ-ences between them widen to a river.

'My time is my own but does it suit you to go across to Sun-ningdale now?' he was asking.

She nodded, grateful for his courtesy. 'I'll introduce you and stay for a quick visit with Todd. Then I'm afraid I'll have to leave. I've to go and plead for some lab reports I'm waiting on to be rushed through and collect a package of drugs from the pharmacy—What's that noise?' Suddenly, she turned her head up, listening.

Nick frowned. 'I don't—Ah! Motorbike by the sound of it.' Instinctively, he stiffened, stepping in front of Abbey as if to shield her. 'And going way too fast for a built-up area. Hell's bells!' he gasped as the high-pitched roar cut the still of the afternoon and a big black machine shot into view at the top of the street.

'Oh, lord!' Abbey watched in stark disbelief. 'The intersection's too narrow—he'll never take the corner! Nick...' Horrified, she grabbed the surgeon's arm as the bike became airborne.

Nick reacted like quicksilver. 'My car's closer—get my bag!' Wresting his keys from his side pocket, he slapped them into Abbey's hand. 'In the boot—go!' He'd already taken off, running in the direction of the crash, his arms pumping hard into the rhythm of his long strides, even before the final sickening thump of metal could be heard.

Abbey bit back a little sob of distress, her heart hammering, as she pelted along the tree-lined street to Nick's car. Hand shaking, she touched the remote locking button on the keyring and whipped the boot open. She hauled his case out, slammed the boot shut and relocked the car, turning to run back to the accident scene as fast as she could in her high heels.

Hearing the crunching sound of metal, two men had rushed from nearby houses to help.

'Right—let's do it, lads!' Nick took charge and, with muscles straining, they partially raised the heavy bike, bracing it against their legs.

'We need traffic lights or a roundabout there.' One of the men was breathing heavily with the effort.

His companion snorted. 'That won't slow 'em down. 'Struth,' he gasped and they strained again. 'One last heave should do it. You beauty...' he grunted as the motorbike was finally righted.

'Has someone called an ambulance?' Nick rapped, hunkering down beside the prostrate form of the injured rider.

'The wife will have done that.' One of the rescuers flipped his hand towards his house across the street. 'You got first-aid training or something, mate?' he tacked on, watching Nick's hands move with deft swiftness over the accident victim.

'Doctor.' Nick was curt.

'How bad is it?' Panting to a stop, Abbey dropped to Nick's

side. She felt her throat dry. Dear God, the youth wasn't even wearing proper leathers.

'Severed femoral artery by the look of it.' Nick looked grim. 'See if you can find a tourniquet, please, Abbey. Step on it! We've got a major problem here.'

Abbey's hands moved like lightning through his medical supplies. In seconds she'd handed over the belt-like elastic band.

'How's his pulse?' Nick rapped, expertly securing the tourniquet around the youth's upper thigh.

'Rapid and thready. He's not responding to stimuli. I'll get an IV in.' Moments later, she was saying tensely, 'This is a nightmare, Nick—I can't find a vein.'

'Keep trying.'

'OK, I've got it.' Abbey's words came out in a rush of relief. 'IV's in and holding.'

Nick swore, his brow furrowing in concentration. 'BP's dropping like a stone. Come on!' he gritted to the youth's unconscious form. 'Don't shut down on me, sunshine—don't you dare!'

At last the ambulance siren could be heard. The vehicle screamed to a halt beside them, two officers swinging out.

Nick quickly introduced himself and Abbey, adding authoritatively, 'The patient's in shock. We need to run Haemaccel fast. And alert the hospital, please. We'll need a blood specimen and cross-match immediately on arrival.'

Within seconds the officer had passed the flask of blood product across to Nick.

'I found some ID in the kid's saddlebag, Doc.' One of the men who had helped lift the bike flipped open a wallet. 'Bryan Weaver.'

'Give it to the police when they get here,' Nick said grimly. 'It'll be up to them to get hold of the family. But at least we'll be able to give the hospital a name. Thanks, mate.'

'Think he'll make it?' the man asked soberly, as the youth was stretchered into the ambulance.

'Let's be positive.' Nick's response was terse.

'Are you coming with us, Doc?' The ambulance officer was hovering expectantly by the rear doors of the ambulance.

'Yes.' Nick slammed his medical case shut and hitched it up. 'Keys.' He put out a hand and touched Abbey's wrist.

'Oh—sorry.' She fumbled them out of the pocket of her linen blazer. 'He's lost a lot of blood, hasn't he?'

They stared at each other for a brief, painful moment.

Nick lifted a shoulder, the lines of strain etching deeper into his mouth. 'Let's pin our hopes on the Haemaccel keeping him stable until he gets some blood.'

'What about your car?' Abbey blinked uncertainly. 'It's locked but—'

'I'll get a cab back and collect it later.' He looked at her broodingly. 'And I haven't forgotten about Todd. I'll make my own way over to Sunningdale as soon as I can.'

'Yes—OK—thanks.' With an odd feeling of finality, Abbey watched as he swung into the waiting ambulance with all the grace of a superbly fit athlete.

'I'll be in touch,' he called to her before the doors closed and the ambulance was on its way, the chilling sound of the siren pitching into the quiet of the afternoon.

Abbey's thoughts were still scattered as she turned in through the wide gates at Sunningdale. Finding a vacant space in the staff car park, she took it thankfully.

Already she'd decided not to undertake the long drive back to Wingara. It would be quite late by the time she was ready to get on her way and she had no desire to travel the lonely highway on her own at night. Instead, she'd leave at first light tomorrow.

The rehabilitation centre was a pleasant structure with wide verandahs overlooking the well-tended gardens. There was much good work being done here, Abbey thought earnestly, but in Todd's case was it enough?

Her insides twisted. The force of Nick Tonnelli's argument had raised more questions than answers for her patient.

She was relieved to find the nurse manager, Lauren Huxley, still on duty in the Macquarie wing where Todd was a resident. In Abbey's opinion, the bright, vivacious, forty-something nursing sister had great empathy with the patients.

In the first few weeks after Todd's admission Lauren had kept Abbey in close touch with his state of mind, and now the two women had formed an easy friendship.

'We expected you much earlier,' Lauren said warmly, ushering Abbey into her office.

Briefly, Abbey explained about the biker's accident and her involvement.

'Tea, then,' Lauren said firmly. 'You do have time?' Her fine brow rose in query. She was well aware of Abbey's gruelling schedule on the occasions the young GP was able to get into Hopeton.

Abbey huffed a wry laugh. 'I've lost so much time today another few minutes won't matter. Tea would be lovely, thanks.'

'Good.' Lauren flicked on the electric kettle.

'You've had a face-lift in here since I was in last.' Abbey looked around interestedly, admiring the bright curtains and crisp paintwork. 'It's lovely, Lauren. So cheerful now and comfortable.'

'That was the idea.' Lauren placed the tea-tray on the table between them. 'The new committee's been pretty generous with funding.'

'So they gave you carte blanche?'

'Within reason. But I stuck out for the oval table and upholstered chairs instead of that huge monstrosity of a desk. It's so much less daunting for the families who have to be briefed. I mean, they're down in the pits already in lots of cases. Surely they don't need to be spoken to across a desk like less than bright schoolchildren?'

Abbey smiled, easing off her shoes and wriggling her toes

in relief. 'Mmm, the tea's wonderful, Lauren, thanks.' They sat in companionable silence for a moment, until Abbey asked gently, 'How's Todd doing?'

Lauren chuckled. 'Actually, he's had rather a good day. I could even say a riotous day.' She paused for effect. 'He's learning to paint.'

Abbey looked stunned for a moment and then her face lit up with a wide smile. 'But that's wonderful! Who's teaching him? One of the OTs?'

'Mmm, Amanda Steele. She reckons our Todd has real potential.'

Abbey bit the inside of her cheek. 'This may not be the right time to tell you my news, then.'

'About Todd?'

'By a remarkable coincidence I was, uh, introduced to Nicholas Tonnelli today.'

'The *surgeon*, Tonnelli?' Lauren's eyebrows shot up into her long fringe.

'Sounds a bit incredible, doesn't it? I arrived at the TV studios this morning to take part in their usual *Countrywide* programme.'

'And?' Lauren leaned forward, her expression expectant.

Abbey gave a huff of uneasy laughter. 'When I arrived, the producer was hovering. Asked me if I'd mind a slightly different format. In short, what he called an impromptu debate.'

'What?' Lauren squawked. 'And he threw you in against Tonnelli? How did you fare, for heaven's sake?'

Abbey grimaced. 'Actually, I think I did better off camera. But I made sure he got the message on the state of rural health.' She coloured faintly. 'He asked me to lunch. And I found myself telling him about Todd...'

'I get the picture Abbey,' Lauren said with some perception. 'Is Dr Tonnelli suggesting a transfer to Dennison by any chance?'

'He suggested the possibility.' Abbey was cautious. 'And

there seems no doubt he could get Todd admitted.' She hesitated, suddenly feeling her relative inexperience in this field of medicine. 'But if Todd's formed a special rapport with his new occupational therapist and is doing better, maybe it's not the right time to move him...'

Lauren shrugged philosophically. 'I think the decision is out of our hands, Abbey. We're all aware Todd is special but we can't go around with our collective noses out of joint if someone of the calibre of Tonnelli suggests he can be better rehabilitated elsewhere.'

'You all do amazingly dedicated work here, Lauren,' Abbey jumped in supportively. 'But I guess I have to agree with you.'

'I presume Dr Tonnelli will want to see the case notes and talk to us first, before he sees Todd?'

'Oh, yes,' Abbey hastened to clarify. 'He's already mentioned that's the way he likes to work. He wants to be as unobtrusive as possible.'

'Yeah, right.' Lauren snickered. 'Like a tiger going unnoticed amongst the deer.' She got to her feet. 'You'll find Todd on the verandah, I think. I'm off duty in two minutes. Oh—any idea when we can expect the dashing surgeon?'

'Not really.' Abbey explained about Nick's involvement with the biker. 'I have no idea of his movements while he's here in Hopeton. In fact, apart from a courtesy phone call to tell me what he proposes for Todd, I don't expect I'll be seeing him again.'

'I see...' Lauren's eyebrows lifted in mild conjecture. Surely that wasn't a blush on the face of the usually so cool Dr Abbey Jones, was it?

Back in her motel room at the end of the day, Abbey took a shower and then planned what she'd do with the rest of the evening.

Not much, she thought wryly, pulling on a pair of plain denims and a peasant top. Taking up her brush, she scraped her hair back into a casual knot, leaving several strands to feather out in the current fashion. Her motel was only half a block from the hospital so she'd walk over and hopefully find out the condition of the young biker, Bryan Weaver. After that, she'd pick up a take-away meal of some kind.

The hospital was well lit and Abbey drifted inside with a group of early-evening visitors and began making her way towards Reception.

'Hello again, Dr Jones.'

Abbey stopped as if she'd been struck. 'Nick...' Soft colour licked along her cheekbones and she did her best to ignore the swift jolt of pleasure at seeing him. 'What are you doing here?'

'I could ask you the same question.' Slipping a hand under her elbow, he gently drew her aside. 'I imagined you'd have been well on your way to Wingara by now.'

Abbey feigned lightness. 'Oh, it got too late so I decided to stay overnight. I'm really here just to enquire about our biker.'

'Snap.' Nick's eyes seemed to track over her features one by one before he went on. 'I've had a chat with the surgeon. The boy's stable and they're pretty hopeful there'll be no residual damage to his leg.'

'That's good news.' Abbey felt relief sweep through her. 'Did you happen to find out why he was travelling like that, so out of control? I mean there are wheelies and *wheelies*.'

Dark humour spilled into his eyes and pulled a corner of his mouth. 'As a matter of fact, I found his girlfriend waiting like a wilted flower outside Recovery. She told me they'd had a fight and our Bryan had stormed out minus his leathers. Young idiot. He could have killed himself.'

'Yes.' Abbey's look was sober for a moment, before she began to cast a restive look towards the entrance. 'Well, now I know he'll be OK, I won't bother the staff...'

'Have you eaten?' Nick asked sharply.

'Ah...no.' Abbey felt her throat dry. 'I thought I'd just grab a burger or something and take it back to my motel room.'

'That sounds like a crummy way to spend your evening.' His eyes narrowed on her face and suddenly the intensity of his regard hardened, as though he'd made up his mind about something. 'Why don't we link up, then? Have dinner together?'

In a quick protective movement, Abbey put her hand to her heart. 'I…wasn't counting on a late night.' She heard the slightly desperate note in her voice and winced. 'And you don't have to keep offering to feed me, Nick.'

His made a dismissive gesture with his hand. 'It's no big deal, Abbey. Do you have a problem with two colleagues having a meal together?'

Oh, about a thousand, she thought, with the kind of uncertainty she was feeling around him. 'Put like that, I—guess it would be all right, then.' She shrugged her capitulation. 'But I'm not dressed for anywhere grand.'

'No more am I.' He tipped her a lopsided smile and Abbey blinked, taking in his appearance. He was wearing comfortable cargo pants and a cream lightweight sweater, the sleeves pushed back over his tanned forearms.

'I walked over,' Abbey explained, as they made their way outside to the hospital car park.

'Makes things simple, then.' Nick slowed his strides abruptly. Then, as if it was the most natural thing in the world, he stretched out his hand towards her. 'I'm round the corner in the doctors' car park.'

Feeling somehow as though she was taking a giant leap into the unknown, Abbey slipped her hand into his.

They agreed on a small pub a few kilometres out of town, mainly because Nick said they did a decent steak.

'I have an appointment first thing in the morning at Sunningdale,' he told her as they drove.

Well, he hadn't wasted any time. Abbey turned her head on the car's cushioned leather headrest and addressed his darkened profile. 'I had a chat with the nurse manager, Lauren Huxley, this afternoon. They'll be expecting you.'

He grunted a non-committal reply.

There were only a smattering of patrons at the pub.

'Mid-week,' Nick surmised gruffly, placing a guiding hand on her back as they descended the shallow steps into a sunken lounge-cum-restaurant.

'It's nice,' Abbey said perfunctorily, gazing around her at the exposed timber beams and the rich oaken sheen of the furniture.

Seated, they studied the wine list. 'They serve a nice local red here,' Nick said. 'Like to try it?'

'Fine.' Abbey managed a faint smile.

With their wine served and their steaks ordered, Nick leaned back in his chair, his green gaze travelling musingly over her face and dropping to the soft curve of her throat. 'Life plays strange tricks on us from time to time, doesn't it?'

Abbey swallowed. 'In what way?'

He seemed to think for a moment, before reaching out and taking her left hand. 'Well, when we woke this morning, we hadn't met.' Turning her hand palm up, he stroked the inside of her wrist with his thumb. 'We seemed to have packed quite a bit of getting to know each other in the past eight hours, wouldn't you agree?'

Abbey's heart rate had begun rocketing at the intimacy. 'I suppose,' she conceded, every nerve in her stomach tightening. She wanted to reclaim her hand without appearing like a frightened adolescent. Which was how she felt, she fretted, more than a little unnerved by the arousing effect his stroking was having on her senses.

She took in a fractured little breath, hoping frantically their steaks would arrive so that at least his hands would be occupied with his cutlery.

As if he'd sensed her unease, Nick released her hand abruptly, changing position to fold his arms across his chest. 'What time will you start back in the morning?' he asked, one dark eyebrow arched, the trace of a provocative smile touching his mouth.

'I'll be long gone before you even open your eyes.' Abbey

touched the small medallion at her throat. 'I have to be back for surgery at ten.'

'Do you take any special precautions for the journey?'

'I make sure my vehicle is always in good running order. And I let the police sergeant at Wingara know when I'm about to leave. From that, barring mishaps, he's able to gauge my ETA. And why the sudden interest in my lifestyle?' she challenged, lifting her glass and taking a careful mouthful of the deliciously smooth merlot. 'I'm just a rural GP, Nick. I work my tail off with incredibly long hours.'

'Are you suggesting I don't?'

Oh, for heaven's sake! She didn't want to keep getting into these kinds of endless comparisons with him. She looked down at her fingers locked painfully tight around the base of her glass. She wasn't naïve. And she was not about to deny the wild kind of physical chemistry lurking between them—but other than that, they had nothing in common at all.

They each belonged in vastly different areas of medicine. Nick Tonnelli would be like a fish out of water in her world—just as she would in his.

THEIR STEAKS ARRIVED, grilled to perfection and accompanied by a huge pile of mixed salad on the side. Abbey's mouth watered at the lushness of three kinds of lettuce, fresh tomatoes, chopped black olives and bits of avocado and red pepper thrown in for good measure. 'This is fantastic, Nick. How come you know all these places?'

His mouth tipped at the corner. 'Hopeton is my home town. I'm here for a few days R and R visiting my *nonna*.'

'Your grandmother?'

'I can see you're surprised.' He grinned and Abbey caught the pulse of deep laughter in his voice. 'Did you imagine I just leapt into life from somewhere? As a matter of fact, I have quite an extended family. Parents, two sisters, brothers-in-law, a niece and two nephews. They all live in Sydney now but my *nonna*, Claudia—' he made it sound like *Cloudia* '—still lives here in the old family home. She's almost eighty-five,' he said proudly.

Abbey thought painfully of her own diminished family and asked quietly, 'Is she in good health?'

'For the most part.' His face softened into reflective lines.

'She's still feisty, demanding when I'm going to find a wife and continue the Tonnelli line.'

Abbey huffed a laugh. 'That's a bit archaic.'

'Hey, she's our matriarch! She's allowed to.'

'Have you ever been in love?' she asked suddenly, prompting raised eyebrows from the surgeon.

'I'm thirty-eight, Abbey. Of course I've been in love. Have you?'

The question hung in the air between them.

'I was engaged once.' Abbey's downcast lashes fanned darkly across her cheekbones. 'He was my trainer. Such an honest, generous man. But when it came down to it, I couldn't set a wedding date. And I realised I didn't feel about him the way I wanted to feel about the man I intended to marry.'

'And how is that?' Nick asked softly. Gaze lowered, he began to swirl the ruby-red wine in his glass.

Suddenly Abbey felt vulnerable. She blamed the wine and Nick Tonnelli's clever probing questions. She came back lightly with, 'Well, if I knew that, life would be a doddle, wouldn't it?'

They went quietly on with their meal.

Nick chewed thoughtfully on his mouthful of prime rump steak. He could hardly believe his luck in running into her again. OK, so maybe they had little in common except their medical training, but he knew enough about himself to realise he had to get to know Abbey Jones better. Though at the moment, how and where seemed insoluble questions.

But he hadn't got to where he was without overcoming a few stumbling blocks. He'd think of something. And it would all be worth it. He had a distinct gut feeling Abbey was as disturbed by his nearness as he was by hers. His gaze lifted, straying momentarily to the enticingly sweet curve of her mouth...

'We'd better exchange phone numbers, hadn't we?' Nick kept his tone deliberately brisk. 'I imagine we'll need to consult about Todd over the next little while.'

'Oh—OK.'

Nick thought she sounded cautious and hastened to reassure her. 'You have my word I won't steamroller anyone, Abbey.' He placed his knife and fork neatly together on his plate and casually swiped his mouth with his serviette. 'I'll study Todd's case notes and take into account all you've told me before I make an assessment about whether the Dennison can benefit him.'

'But you're reasonably certain it can, aren't you?'

He shrugged a shoulder. 'I truly believe what they can teach Todd there will give him a new lease on life. Granted, not the kind of life he's been used to but, even as a differently abled person, there have to be possibilities for the sports-fit young man he once was.'

The thought of Todd's world being shaken on its axis all over again gnawed at Abbey. He was at such a vulnerable point in his young life. But at least she had Nick's promise that he would act with sensitivity. She could only hope Todd would speak up if felt he was being pressured.

'Time to go?' Nick had seen her quick reference to her watch.

'If you don't mind.' It was only when they walked outside into the foyer that Abbey realised his guiding hand at her back had shifted and now she was warmly pressed to his side. Her nerve ends pinched alarmingly. She didn't want this—an involvement with a big-time surgeon like Nick Tonnelli was crazy thinking. It could go nowhere, lead to nothing.

Yet she couldn't pull away.

'Oh—it's raining!' She held out a hand to the light sprinkle.

'Let's move it, then.' Nick grabbed her hand and they sprinted across the car park and threw themselves into the Jaguar. 'OK?' He arched a questioning eyebrow.

'Hardly damp.' Releasing the scrunchie holding back her ponytail, Abbey finger-combed her hair into a semblance of order and then bent to fasten her seat belt. 'How much longer will you be in Hopeton?'

'Only another day or so.' The engine came to life with an expensive purr and within a few moments he was nosing the car out through the exit and onto the road. 'Basically, I had a few days to call my own and I decided to spend them with Nonna. I like to keep an eye on her.'

Abbey could understand he would. He seemed to care a great deal about people in general. How much more would he care about his own family? His wife? If he had one—

'I have to be back in Sydney on Friday anyway to attend a charity do at the Opera House.'

Probably with one of those women he was always being photographed with on his arm. Abbey's fingers interlinked tightly and she wondered why the mental picture caused her so much anguish.

'It just occurs to me...' He sent her a brooding look. 'What do you do about a locum when you have to be out of the place?'

'Were you thinking of offering?' Abbey shot back with the faintest hint of derision. Run-of-the-mill rural medicine wouldn't interest him at all. He'd really consider himself slumming.

'Think I couldn't handle it?'

Abbey flicked him a puzzled glance, not sure where he was heading. She answered levelly, 'My predecessor, Wolf Ganzer, fills in for me. He retired in the district. And he keeps himself fit and in touch so it suits us both.'

Nick nodded and after a minute enquired softly, 'How about some music to carry us home?'

It seemed to Abbey that the journey back to her motel took very little time. One part of her was thankful, wanting it over. The other part, the silly, romantic part of her, wanted to prolong the evening, the contact with Nicholas Tonnelli.

When he nosed his car in behind her Range Rover in the parking bay outside her unit, she released her seat belt and looked at him. 'Thanks for this evening, Nick. And for agreeing to see Todd.'

'I don't want thanks, Abbey.' His eyes were broodingly intent and he lifted his hand to knuckle it across the soft curve of her cheek. 'But I wouldn't mind a coffee, if you have the makings?'

Abbey stiffened, the faint elusive scent of his aftershave catching her nostrils. She swallowed heavily. 'Um…it'll have to be instant out of those sachet things.'

'Instant's fine.' He sent her a slow, teasing grin. 'I love instant.'

'And my room's a mess.'

'Do I look like I care?'

Abbey could hardly breathe. This was the last thing she'd expected—or wanted, she told herself. She'd thought he'd just drop her off and—

'Come on, the rain's stopped.' Nick broke into her thoughts, releasing the locks. 'Got your key handy?'

She fished the tagged piece of metal out of the side pocket of her jeans and handed it to him.

'Nick…perhaps this isn't such a good idea,' she backtracked huskily. 'I mean, we should probably just say goodnight and…' She stopped and swallowed, his gravity making her frown. 'Why are you doing this?'

'I don't want the evening to end,' he said simply. 'Do you, Abbey?'

A beat of silence.

Abbey felt she was trying to walk through sand knee-deep. But she couldn't lie. 'No…'

Out of the car, she waited while he unlocked the door of her motel room. Nick ushered her inside and then followed her in.

Abbey had left the standard lamp burning and now its soft glow was drawing the small space into an intimate cosiness. She sent a disquieted glance at the double bed littered with her clothes, and pointedly crossed to the tiny kitchenette on the far side of the unit. 'Coffee won't be long.' Feeling as though her hands belonged to someone else, she filled the small electric jug, and set it to boil.

'I promise I won't keep you up, Abbey.' Nick fetched up one of the high-backed stools and parked himself.

She gave a weak smile. 'The coffee will probably do that anyway.'

'Do you have times when you can't sleep, however you try?' he asked, his voice low.

'Most people do, don't they?' Abbey tore open the sachets and shook the coffee grains into the two waiting cups. 'Especially people in our line of work. Sometimes, when I find it impossible to relax enough to coax sleep, I go outside and look at the stars.'

'I imagine they'd be something special out west.'

'With the sky so clear, absolutely. The stars appear like so many diamonds. Their sparkle is…well, I imagine it's like being in fairyland.' Vaguely embarrassed by her flowery speech, Abbey hastily made the coffee. She passed Nick's black brew across to him, watching as he sugared and stirred it.

'You make it sound wonderful.' His long fingers spanned his cup as he lifted it to his mouth. 'I'll come out and experience it for myself someday.'

Abbey refrained from comment. Instead, her shoulders lifted in a barely perceptible shrug. She poured milk into her own coffee and, beset by a strange unease, took the seat next to him at the counter.

'Don't believe me, do you, Abbey?'

She brought her head up, seeing the crease in his cheek as he smiled, the action activating the laughter lines around his eyes. And quickly lowered her gaze to blot out the all-male physical imprint.

But it took a while for her heart to stop beating so quickly.

Nick couldn't take his eyes off her. He felt his fingers flexing, his arms aching to draw her to him, to touch her hair, feel its silkiness glide through his fingers. The thought of something else far more urgent was enough to set his body on fire.

He raised his cup and took another mouthful of his coffee.

Anything to stop the hollow, self-derisive laugh erupting from his throat, he thought ruefully. He cast about for a safer topic. 'Tell me about yourself, Abbey.'

'Oh. There's not much to tell—I'm fairly ordinary.'

'I don't believe that for a second,' he countered, hoping he'd managed to give the wry words the right touch of lightness. 'What about family? Siblings?'

She lifted one shoulder uncertainly. 'One brother, Steven. He's a GP, currently working at a health post in New Guinea.'

Nick's mouth compressed momentarily. 'So not much chance for weekend visits, then?'

'No.' Abbey shook her head. 'But we did manage to catch up last Christmas. I took a flight north and Steve flew south and we met in Darwin. It was good,' she tacked on, an odd little glitch in her voice. 'Really good. More so, because these days we only have each other...'

Nick was startled by the sudden change in her voice. She looked almost...haunted. 'Tell me,' he said quietly.

After a tense moment, she responded, 'Our parents were killed two years ago. One of those tragic road accidents. They were fulfilling their retirement dream of a motoring trip around Australia. They were somewhere west of Adelaide when a petrol tanker ran out of control in front of them and then exploded. They had no chance.'

Nick saw the heart-breaking emotion that froze her face for an instant and recalled how he'd rabbited on about his extended family. What a smug, self-satisfied clod he must have sounded.

He clenched his fists as if he wanted to pound at an unkind fate on her behalf. 'I'm so sorry, Abbey.' He shook his head. 'So sorry you had to go through that...' On an impulse he couldn't explain, he held out his hand, using the action to draw her up from her stool and into his arms.

There was a long moment when they were still. When anything was possible. Abbey took a shaken breath, tilting her face up to his, thinking she should stop this now. But the urge to touch him and to be touched in return was too great. Suddenly all her senses began to stir, unfold, waken. Her heart did a back flip in her chest. And she was waiting, expectant when Nick leaned forward to claim her mouth.

Nicholas. She said his name in her head, closing her eyes, revelling in the subtle warmth of his body as he held her closer. He made her feel wildly sensual, as if she wanted to go on tiptoe, take him to her, absorb the very essence of his maleness.

She made a little sound in her throat, waves of heat sweeping over her as she opened fully to the demanding pressure of his lips.

It was much too soon when Nick broke away from her. He turned his head a little, smudging kisses across her temple, her eyelids and into the soft curve of her throat, sending erotic visions to her mind, searing heat along each vein.

Abbey clung to him, clung and clung, her cheek hard against the warmth of his chest, while his arms cradled her as though she was infinitely precious.

She had no clear idea how long they stood there.

Finally Nick's chest rose and fell in a long sigh and he slowly untwined the hands she'd looped around his neck and pulled back from her. 'Abbey...this is a hard call but I have to go—while I still can.'

She lifted weighted eyelids to look at him, realising he was right. If he didn't leave now, there was only one way they could go from here and she wasn't about to let that happen. She shivered when his thumb touched her full lower lip.

'Don't forget me, will you?' His voice sounded raw.

She swallowed jerkily, wondering how her legs were still holding her up.

'I...don't know where any of this is leading, Abbey.' He sent her a strained look. 'But let's not shut the door on the possibilities...please.' Then, as if he couldn't bear to leave her, he kissed her again. Just briefly but hard. 'I'm going...'

'Take care,' Abbey whispered, her eyes wide and dazed-looking.

'I'll see you.' He placed the softest kiss at the side of her mouth. 'Somehow.'

Abbey waited until she heard the throb of his car engine fade away before she trusted her legs to move. Was he saying he wanted a serious chance at some kind of relationship?

She lifted her shoulders in a shaken sigh, crossing to the bed. The idea was impractical. And totally impossible.

It took only a few minutes to pack her small suitcase for her return to Wingara in the morning.

Her head was spinning, and already there was a giant gnawing emptiness in the region of her heart.

On the other side of town, Nick sat sprawled on the old swing-seat on his grandmother's back porch, his lean fingers cradling a glass of neat bourbon. He felt dazed, as though he'd gone a round or two with a heavyweight boxer.

Hell's bells.

The ice cubes rattled as he rolled the whisky glass between the palms of his hands. Abbey Jones. A grunt of self-derision left his throat. 'Turned on like a randy adolescent, Tonnelli,' he muttered, downing the rest of his drink, feeling the spirit scorch his insides like a ridge of fire.

Impatiently, he put the glass aside and then shot out of the seat, leaving the swing rocking. Leaning against the railing, he lifted his hands, tunnelling them through his hair and linking them at the base of his neck.

His gaze narrowed on the old pear tree, his body attuned, hearing the stillness, and he faced the fact that emotionally he'd fallen headlong into the deepest water of his life.

But what to do about it?

Abbey's alarm work her at five a.m. Blinking her eyes wide open, she stared at the ceiling. 'Oh, no,' she groaned, as the events of last night enveloped her.

She felt the sudden heat in her cheeks, waiting to feel shocked at how she'd opened herself to Nick Tonnelli. But it didn't happen. Instead, she remembered the way he'd held her, the tenderness of his kisses before he'd left...

But how could they share any kind of future? she fretted, throwing herself out of bed and under the shower.

How?

Ten minutes later, dressed in the jeans she'd worn last night and a plain white shirt, Abbey swallowed a hastily made cup of tea. She'd get breakfast along the road somewhere, she decided. After she'd put some distance behind her.

Hitching up her bits and pieces, she left the motel quietly and only seconds later she'd reversed into the forecourt and nosed her four-wheel-drive out onto the road.

After almost an hour into her journey, Abbey suddenly realised she'd completely forgotten to call Geoff Rogers, Wingara's police sergeant. Well, there was a first time for everything, she thought dryly. Slamming the Range Rover into second gear to cut back on her speed, she pulled to a stop at the edge of the road.

Picking up her mobile phone, she activated the logged-in number, her gaze thoughtfully assessing the dun-gold grass of the paddocks on each side of the road. There was still something so untouched about Australia's wide open spaces, she thought philosophically. Something fearless.

It had had the hottest kind of sun blasting down on it for thousands of years, had seen drought, bushfires and floods but, despite all that, the country still came up smilingly defiant. It didn't surprise her that its stark beauty created a kind of spiritual awakening for many of the tourists who frequented the region...

'Wingara Police.' Geoff's voice came through loud and clear.

Abbey blinked a couple of times as though she'd been in a trance. 'Geoff, it's Abbey Jones. I'm just through Jareel township.'

'Abbey! You OK?'

'Fine. Sorry, I forgot to call earlier.'

Geoff chuckled. 'You're forgiven. Wild night out, was it?'

More like a wild night *in*. Abbey pursed her lips and scrubbed a pattern on the steering wheel with her thumb. 'I should be home by eight, Geoff.'

'OK, Doc. It'll be good to have you back. Ah…how's young Todd? Did you manage to see him?'

'Yes, I did.' Abbey hesitated. Literally everyone in Wingara was going to ask about Todd. 'There may be some better news about his progress in the not-too-distant future, Geoff. I can't say any more just now.'

'Understood. You always give us your best shot, Abbey. And it's not just me reckons that.'

Abbey closed off her mobile, Geoff's remarks warming her through and through.

It was a few minutes to eight when she coasted down a slight incline and glided into the township. But this time the familiar skip in her heart as the quaint wooden shopfronts with their old-fashioned awnings came into view was missing.

Why did she feel she'd left a part of herself back in Hopeton? The question buzzed around in her head and she bit off a huff of impatience at her crazy thinking.

Deciding she'd get herself sorted out before she went into the surgery, she took a side street to the rambling old house she called home. The place was far too big for her needs and she used only a tenth of its space, but it came with the job so the matter of where she lived had been largely taken out of her hands.

Almost absent-mindedly, she hauled her luggage out of the boot and made her way inside. For some reason, today the house seemed almost eerily quiet. How odd, she thought, catching the edge of her lip uncertainly. It had never seemed that way before.

A curious, unsettled feeling swamped her as she pulled stuff from her suitcase and piled her used clothing into the hamper in the laundry. 'For heaven's sake!' she muttered. You'd better get your mind back on your practice, Abbey, she told herself silently. Nick Tonnelli and his kisses are history!

But her body still tingled in memory.

Half an hour later, she'd freshened up and changed into a longish dark green skirt and pinstriped shirt. Stifling a sigh, she left the house quickly. Her surgery list was probably a kilometre long and she'd never felt less like work.

'You're back nice and early.' Meri Landsdowne, the practice manager-cum-everything greeted Abbey warmly. 'Good trip home?'

That word again. Abbey sent the other a wry smile. 'No dramas.' She took the few steps and joined Meri behind Reception. 'How have things been here?' Abbey pulled the desk diary towards her.

'Fairly quiet, actually. Wolf even managed to get his midweek game of bowls in.' Meri made a small grimace. 'Frankly, I think everyone's been holding off until you were back. Ed Carmichael for starters.'

'Again!'

'First cab off the rank,' Meri commiserated. She gave a snip of laughter. 'Perhaps we could get a moat built around the surgery to keep him out.'

'He can probably swim like a fish,' Abbey surmised dryly. 'But he's a lonely man, Meri. He misses his days as a shearers' cook. We shouldn't be too hard on him.'

'Oh, Abbey, we both know half the time he only comes in for a yarn. And there are plenty of things he could be involved in. For heaven's sake, he's barely sixty!'

'I've had lengthy chats with him about what he could do to fill in his time.' Abbey flicked through the list of appointments. 'But nothing seemed to appeal to him. He reckons he's read every book in the library.'

'Oh, please!' Meri turned away to activate the answering-machine. 'Come on, let's have a cuppa before the hordes arrive. Did you get breakfast somewhere?'

Abbey gave a rueful grin. 'I meant to...'

'So, what distracted you, Doctor?' Meri sent her a laughing look as they made their way along the corridor to the kitchen. 'Or, should I say, who?' The practice manager cocked her auburn head at a questioning angle. 'You look...different, somehow.'

'New shirt,' Abbey dismissed, feeling her cheeks warm. Meri's green eyes were filled with curiosity.

A few minutes later, they were settled companionably over a pot of tea and the still-warm banana bread Meri had brought in. 'Heaven,' Abbey sighed, as she took a slice and bit into it with obvious enjoyment. 'Much nicer than anything I could've eaten at some greasy-spoon café along the highway.'

Meri raised an eyebrow. 'You never skip breakfast, Abbey. How come?'

Abbey felt goose-bumps break out all over her. 'Just preoccupied, I guess. Um...there may be some changes with Todd Jensen's rehab coming up,' she deflected quickly, and then stopped. There was no getting away from it. She'd have to fill Meri in to some degree about Nick Tonnelli's involvement. Meri was the first point of contact at the surgery and would need to be put in the picture when Nick began liaising about Todd. But her manager would be discreet. And in a small-town medical practice, that was always a great bonus.

'That's fantastic,' Meri responded softly, after she'd heard what Abbey had to say about the surgeon and the Dennison clinic. 'Audrey and Keith will need careful handling though,' she added thoughtfully, referring to Todd's rather fearful parents. 'They won't want him moved to Sydney.'

Abbey lifted a shoulder. 'That'll be up to Dr Tonnelli. And I don't imagine he'll have much trouble convincing them if he decides the Dennison is the place for Todd.'

'Charmer, is he?'

Abbey felt the flush creep up her throat. 'Not bad…' She hiccuped a laugh, her embarrassed gaze going to the floor. 'For a surgeon.'

CHAPTER FOUR

AS MERI HAD INDICATED, Abbey's first patient for the day was Ed Carmichael.

'What can I do for you today, Ed?' Abbey looked up expectantly as her patient made himself comfortable, stretching out his legs and folding his arms across his chest. Abbey noticed that as usual he was dressed very neatly in a bush shirt and jeans and the inevitable riding boots.

'It's my right eye, Doc. Just noticed it getting dry and a bit uncomfortable, like.'

Abbey nodded. 'How long since you've had your eyes properly checked?'

'Earlier this year. I got new specs, bifocals this time.'

'No problems with them?'

Ed shook his head and then asked gruffly, 'Could it be a cataract?'

'That would have been picked up when you had your eyes examined. And cataracts don't just happen, Ed. You'd be noticing a clouding of your vision over many months or even years.'

'So I'm not likely to be going blind, then?'

'No, Ed. I think that's very unlikely.' Abbey blocked a smile, but really it wasn't a smiling matter. She sobered. Her patient's real problem was having so much time on his hands that he'd begun to imagine that every twinge signalled a medical crisis of some kind. She got to her feet. 'Pop over here to the couch now, and I'll have a look under some light. Just to make sure there's no infection that could be causing the dryness.'

Ed Carmichael obliged and, with as little fuss as possible, Abbey settled him under the examination light. 'Your eye looks fine,' she said, scanning the eyeball for anything untoward. 'Some dryness is fairly common as we age, though, but drops can help with that.

'Now, these will just help to make tears.' Back at her desk, Abbey scribbled the brand names of several appropriate eye-drops. 'Any one of these will be suitable and they don't contain an antibiotic so you can get them over the counter without a prescription. Use the drops several times a day if you need to.'

'And that'll help, will it, Doc?' Ed's pale blue eyes regarded her seriously. 'Not that I'm doubting you,' he added hastily, taking the folded piece of paper and shoving it into his shirt pocket.

Abbey smiled. 'It should. And as I said, this kind of thing is usually age-related. But as well as the drops, you could try holding a warm flannel briefly against your eye, say, three times a day. The gentle heat will give all those little nerves and blood vessels a wake-up call and a reminder to make some moisture.'

'Thanks, Doc.' Ed pulled himself up from the chair. 'I'll give it a go.'

Abbey worked conscientiously through her patient list, but felt somewhat relieved when Meri popped her head in to announce, 'Last one. Natalie Wilson, new patient with a bub.'

'Which one is the patient?' Abbey threw her pen down and stretched, rotating her head to ease the muscles at the back of her neck.

Meri placed the new file on the desk. 'Mrs Wilson didn't make that clear, actually. Just said she's recently moved to the district and wondered whether she could have a word with the doctor.'

'Better trot her along, then.' Abbey flashed a faintly weary smile at the practice manager.

'After that, I'll lock the door and put the kettle on,' Meri announced firmly.

'Come in, Natalie, and have a seat,' Abbey invited warmly, as the young mother stood uncertainly in the doorway.

'Thanks.' Natalie Wilson dipped her fair head and took the chair beside Abbey's desk. 'This is Chloe,' she said proudly, her arms tightening around the pink-clad chubby infant on her lap.

'She's gorgeous.' Abbey's look was soft. 'How old is she?'

'Four months.' Natalie swallowed unevenly. 'We're...um, new in town. Ryan, my husband, has just been appointed manager for the organic growers co-operative.'

Abbey nodded. 'So, how can I help you?'

'I—That is, we wanted some advice, really.' She hesitated. 'About immunisation for Chloe. Are there any natural alternatives?'

Abbey took her time answering. Whether or not to immunise their children was every parent's choice, of course. But in her paediatric rotation Abbey had seen the needless pain and suffering little ones had been put through as a result of not being properly immunised against what amounted to killer diseases.

'Natalie, I have to say, the short answer is no.' Abbey looked levelly at her patient. 'Is there a reason why you don't want your baby immunised?'

The young mother nibbled on her bottom lip. 'It's just you hear of such terrible things happening afterwards—like brain damage...'

'Those cases are extremely rare,' Abbey discounted. 'In fact, I've never seen one in all the years I've been practising medicine.'

A smile nipped Natalie's mouth. 'That can't have been so long. You don't look very old.'

'Sometimes I feel about a hundred.' Abbey gave a low, husky laugh, warming to the other's light humour. 'But there's no problem with Chloe, is there? She's in good health?'

'Oh, yes,' Natalie was quick to answer. 'And I'm breastfeeding her.'

Abbey's gaze grew wistful. The little one did seem utterly content. 'You know, Natalie, on the whole, most vaccines cause minimum side effects. And it's a sad fact that some of the crippling diseases that were around in our grandparents' time are making a comeback.'

'And that's because parents are not having their children immunised, isn't it?' Nevertheless, the young mother still looked doubtful.

'Look...' Abbey swung to her feet and went across to her filing cabinet. 'Why don't I give you some relevant stuff to read, the latest statistics and so on, and you and your husband can make up your minds? I certainly wouldn't want to pressure you. In the end the decision has to be yours. If you decide you want Chloe done, pop her back in and we'll take care of it, OK?'

'Thanks so much, Dr Jones.' Natalie took the printed matter and tucked it into her big shoulder-bag. She stood to her feet, carefully cradling her daughter in the crook of her arm. 'You've been really laid-back about all this.'

'You sound surprised.' Abbey held the door open for her.

Natalie's mouth turned down comically. 'I really thought I'd be in for a lecture,' she admitted wryly.

'No lectures here,' Abbey said with a smile. 'I can guarantee it.' She touched a finger to Chloe's plump little cheek. 'Take care, now.'

Abbey's afternoon surgery kept her busy with a trail of small emergencies, one of which was the situation of two lads from the high school who needed stitches after clashing heads during a game of rugby.

'How on earth can they call it a *game*?' Meri shook her head in bewilderment, watching the two walking wounded leave the surgery in the care of their teacher.

'Rugby depends on skill,' Abbey said knowledgeably, recalling her own brother's brilliance at the game when he'd been at university. 'The more skill you have, the better you can keep out of trouble on the field.'

Meri sniffed. 'I'm just glad I have daughters. At least they can't get into too much strife with their ballet.'

Abbey pulled across a couple of letters that were waiting for her signature. 'Except ballet dancers quite often suffer horrendous problems with their feet,' she pointed out evenly.

'Do they?' Meri looked appalled.

'Well, some of the professional ones appear to. It's all that stuff on points they have to do.'

Meri lifted a shoulder. 'Oh, well, Cassie and Georgia haven't advanced to that stage yet. And by then perhaps they'll be into something sensible like tennis,' she said hopefully.

Abbey chuckled. 'Or kick-boxing?'

'Don't!' Meri pretended to shudder and then smiled a bit grimly. 'When you have kids, there's such a minefield of decision-making involved, isn't there?'

Thinking of her earlier discussion with Natalie Wilson, Abbey could only silently agree. But as yet I don't have to concern myself with that kind of responsibility, she thought broodingly. And until the right man came along, the subject of having children was hardly up for discussion...

'Oh—Wolf phoned earlier.' Meri deftly creased the letters into neat folds and slipped them into the waiting envelopes. 'Did you want him to do a late ward round? If not, he's off gallivanting somewhere.'

'I'll give him a call and let him off the hook.' Abbey blocked a yawn, edging off the tall stool behind Reception and standing to her feet. She glanced at her watch. Almost five o'clock. 'It won't take me long to pop over to the hospital and do a round. Then, barring further emergencies, I'm off home.'

'You must be out on your feet after that long drive,' Meri commiserated. 'And you haven't stopped all day. Who'd be a rural GP, eh?' She turned aside to answer the ringing telephone. Several seconds later she was holding out the receiver towards Abbey. 'For you. It's Dr Tonnelli.'

Abbey felt her heart slam against her ribs. 'I'll take it in my room, thanks, Meri,' she instructed quickly. 'And you pop off home to the girls now. I'll lock up and set the alarm.'

'If you're sure?'

'Go.'

''Night, then.' Meri waggled her fingers, her look faintly curious as she watched Abbey almost skip towards her consulting room.

Abbey entered her office, her heart pounding sickeningly. Then, blowing out a long, calming breath, she reached out and picked up the cordless receiver.

'Nick, hello!'

Tonnelli curled a low laugh. 'Hello, yourself, Dr Jones. How are things?'

Personally—crazy, mixed up, scary. Take your pick. 'Fine. And with you?'

'Oh, can't complain.' A heavy beat of silence. 'I thought of you the moment I woke this morning, Abbey. Did you think of me?'

He'd spoken quietly, his voice so deep it made her shiver. Not only had she thought of him, she'd still had the smell of him on her clothes, the taste of him on her mouth. 'Nick…'

'I'm here.'

Another silence.

'Do you want me as much as I want you, Abbey?'

Her eyes closed. 'Nick—this is all a bit unreal.'

'What part of it? Our kisses seemed pretty real to me,' he said with a wicked chuckle.

'That's not what I meant.' Sounding strangled, she tried to block out the memory, the sweet shock when their mouths had met for the first time. When he'd leaned forward and teased her lips apart—and had kissed her as she had never been kissed in all of her thirty-one years.

'Not very experienced, are you, Abbey?' he asked gently.

Not with men of his calibre, certainly. With the phone still clamped to her ear, she swung up from her chair and went to the window, as if fighting against the sensual cocoon he'd begun weaving around her. 'Where are you?' she asked, desperate to normalise the conversation.

'Not where I want to be, that's for sure.'

Abbey's heart raced, thudded, missed a beat. 'Please, could we not talk about this?'

'We have to talk about this—*us*,' he went on doggedly. 'Surely it was more than just a momentary…*attraction*?'

'Perhaps it was,' she agreed tightly. 'But, Nick, we're hundreds of miles apart. Our *lives* are hundreds of miles apart!'

'So you're baling out without even giving us a shot? Turning your feelings off like a tap? You disappoint me, Abbey. I took you to be a far more gutsy lady than that.'

Abbey's fingers tightened on the phone. She wouldn't let him get to her. 'This kind of conversation is pointless, Nick, and if that's all you called for—'

'It isn't,' he emphasised almost roughly. 'I've seen Todd.'

Immediately, Abbey felt on safer ground. She swallowed. 'And?'

'I think the Dennison can help him. I've already begun liaising with Anna Charles and lined up an ambulance. Todd should be installed by next Monday. I'll have my secretary fax my findings to you.'

'Oh, Nick, that's brilliant.' Hardly aware of what she was doing, Abbey turned from the window and began to pace her room. 'And what about Todd's parents? It could be a bit sticky.'

'I've already spoken to them. They'll be in Sydney on Monday to help him settle in.'

So he had everyone eating out of his hand. Abbey felt the

ground sliding out from under her. She gave a brittle laugh. 'When you decide to move, you really move, don't you?'

'There's no point in procrastinating, Abbey—about anything.'

Abbey's throat tightened. 'Don't go on as though we have some kind of future together, Nick. Tell me more about Todd's situation,' she sidetracked quickly. If she could keep him to medical matters, maybe she could cope—just. 'What about the fees?'

'It's sorted.' He sounded irritated. 'And to make Todd feel really at home, his OT is going to continue working with him.'

'Amanda? She's going to Sydney with him?' Abbey could hardly contain her disbelief. 'Just like that?'

'No, Abbey, not just like that.'

'What did you do,' she cut in harshly, 'bribe her?'

'Don't be extreme. At Anna's request, of course, I offered her an increase in salary. It's rather more expensive to live in Sydney than in Hopeton.'

It sounded like they were all closing ranks around her patient and leaving her out. Big-time specialists pulling professional strings, as though they were controlling puppets. 'Well, isn't that just typical?' she snapped, fighting against a sick kind of resentment.

'What?'

'Do you enjoy stripping expertise from rural health, Dr Tonnelli? Amanda Steele is one of the best occupational therapists Sunningdale has had in years. Her methods are nothing short of inspirational to the residents—'

'Abbey, you're putting the wrong spin on this.'

'The hell I am...' Abbey felt her throat close. 'I was right about you from the beginning, Nick. You just steamroller over everything to get your own way. Well, you've shot all your ducks now, so I hope you're happy!'

'Abbey, listen—'

'No, Nick, you listen. You said you were disappointed in *me*,' she went on, her words echoing with hurt and disillusionment.

'Well, I'm disappointed in you—more than I can say. I'll expect your fax!' She ended the call abruptly and promptly burst into tears. Her heart was shattering, destroyed just like the trust she'd foolishly built around him.

Nick felt as though his insides were tied in a thousand knots. And it wasn't a condition he was used to, he admitted uncomfortably. For the most part he had always been in control of his life. Now his thoughts were jumbled, too incoherent to organise rationally.

Thanks to Abbey Jones.

In an abrupt movement, he threw himself out of his armchair and prowled across the room to stare through the big picture window, his gaze reaching beyond the canopy of trees. Early evening mist hung across the mountains and already the sharpness of winter was in the air.

He stifled a sigh, turning and retracing his steps to the fireplace. Hunkering down, he carefully placed a new log on the fire and then eased the fireguard back into place.

'You have problems, Nikkolo?'

Claudia Tonnelli's snow-white head was lowered intently over her needlework but Nick knew his grandmother in her wisdom had missed nothing of his agitation. For an instant he was tempted to blurt everything out, as he'd done when he'd been much younger, and wait for her advice. Because she'd be bound to offer it, he thought dryly, uncurling to his feet.

'Nothing you need worry about, Nonna.'

'Come.' The elderly lady patted the space beside her on the sofa. 'Talk to me.'

Nick pushed his hands roughly through his hair. 'Not just now, Nonna. In fact, I think I'll go for a long run.'

During the days following her phone conversation with Nick, Abbey pushed all thoughts of him to the back of her mind. It was the only way she could cope.

His fax had arrived, together with a penned footnote from Nick himself telling her that Todd had been persuaded to let his wife visit and at least they'd begun to talk. Which is more than *we* are doing, Abbey thought bitterly, adding the faxed information to Todd's already thick file.

Nevertheless, every time the phone rang, she'd foolishly hope it would be Nick but, of course, it never was. Well, who could blame him? The pain in her heart welled up again, and again she beat it back. Why would he bother to call, when she'd told him off in no uncertain manner?

Had she been too hasty in judging his actions over Todd? Abbey shook her head. I just would have liked to have been consulted, she rationalised for the umpteenth time. Surely that hadn't been too much to ask?

Heavens, she'd have to stop this!

Resolutely, she made a notation on the file in front of her and placed it aside. Spinning off her chair, she moved to the window, absorbing the stillness, her gaze going to the distant low hills and then drawing back to the tangle of vivid bougainvillea that wound itself in glorious abandon across the roof of the pergola in the surgery's back garden.

'With such a beautiful view from my window, why on earth am I wishing I was somewhere else?' she whispered to the late afternoon air, almost absently glancing at her watch and realising it was Friday again.

And remembering it was two weeks and two days since Nick had kissed her. And held her as though he'd never wanted to let her go. She sighed, her thoughts becoming so bleak it seemed almost a relief to let the anguish engulf her momentarily.

Closing her eyes, she began to relive it all, losing herself in hopeless longing.

Reality came back with a snap when her door opened and was softly closed again.

Abbey spun round, coming to a shocked halt, her eyes snapping wide in disbelief. 'Nick…' His name came hoarsely from her throat.

'Your secretary said it was all right to come in.' He raised an eyebrow in query and waited.

Abbey's wits deserted her. She didn't know what to do. But all her instincts were screaming at her to bolt. To pretend he wasn't there. But that wouldn't work, he was blocking her exit. And not looking entirely friendly.

In fact he looked…*intense*, for want of a better word. Almost as if she'd never seen him before, she stared at the imposingly broad-shouldered physique, delineated by the close-fitting black ribbed jumper, his jaw jutting almost arrogantly over its poloneck. Blinking, she met the brunt of his gaze with its sea-green luminosity…

Her heart skittered. 'What—what are you doing here?'

'I've taken a month's leave.' He stood very still, the fingers of his left hand hooked into the collar of a leather jacket he'd slung over one shoulder. 'Do you think we can pick up where we left off, Abbey?'

Nick watched her eyes cloud and cursed himself for the ambiguity of his question. He allowed himself a small smile. 'Not from where you put the phone down on me, obviously,' he clarified.

Abbey winced at the memory, crossing her arms over her chest, her fingers kneading her upper arms. 'I don't believe any of this—that you've come all this way…' Breaking off, she stilled and gave a little frown. 'What am I going to do with you for a month?'

Green eyes regarded her levelly. 'Put me to work.' With a smile Abbey wasn't sure she trusted, he continued smoothly, 'You could do with some help, couldn't you?'

Well, of course she could. Abbey felt almost sick with vulnerability, and tried telling herself she wasn't feeling what she thought she was feeling, that her insides hadn't turned to mush, that his closeness wasn't making her nerves zing like the strings of a violin gone mad. She shook her head, asking throatily, 'Why, Nick?'

'You must know why, Abbey.' There was a slight edge to his voice and suddenly he seemed to come to a decision. Moving purposefully towards her desk, he unfurled the leather jacket from his shoulder and hooked it over the back of a chair.

As though he was staking some kind of claim. Abbey bristled. 'Being an MO here is light years away from your brand of high-tech medicine,' she pointed out, fighting to regain her poise.

'I'll adapt.'

Her heart skipped a beat. It could never work. Could it…? She looked at him warily.

'What, no comeback, Dr Jones?' Nick's mouth tightened fractionally. He moved a few paces to park himself on the edge of her desk and gazed at her broodingly. 'I scare the daylights out of you, don't I?'

Snapping her chin up, she huffed forcefully, 'Of course not!'

His mouth folded in on a smile. 'Then that has to be a start.' In one easy movement, he straightened from his perch, taking the two steps necessary to gather her into his arms.

'Nick…' Her voice sounded breathy. 'You're taking a lot for granted.'

'Really, Abbey?' He brought her a few centimetres closer. 'Then let's make it worthwhile…'

His lips ravished her, seduced her then teased her lightly, exquisitely until she shivered and arched against him.

She sighed against his mouth, her hands seeking out the solidness of him, her fingers digging into his shoulders, moving to shape the muscles at the base of his neck, going higher to run through the silky tufts of hair at his nape.

And then slowly he lifted his head.

Breathing hard, he tilted her face, one hand sliding among the strands of her hair. Scooping them up gently, he let them fall away in a cascade of gold and light. 'I could eat you, Abbey.'

Her insides heaved crazily. Locking her hands around his neck, she mustered a shaky smile. 'How would you explain that to my patients?'

His chuckle was warm, as rich as cream on apple pie. 'You're lovely,' he murmured deeply, his hand gliding to her breast and cupping it through her silk shirt.

'Nick...' She melted back into his arms.

And then abruptly pulled away.

'What is it?' A frown touched his forehead.

'Meri could walk in at any minute.' Quickly, Abbey finger-combed her hair into place. 'And speaking of Meri, if you're going to be working here, you'd better come out to Reception and meet her properly. And who knows? She'll probably find you the occasional chocolate biscuit if you bat that sexy smile at her now and again.'

'Really?' Grinning, he placed his hands on Abbey's shoulders, his thumbs stroking the soft hollow at the base of her throat. 'Do I have a sexy smile, then?'

'Stop fishing for compliments, Doctor.' She gave a strangled laugh, unfastening his hands and stepping back. After a moment she asked carefully, 'Was it difficult, getting time off?' She still felt amazed and slightly panicked at the lengths he'd gone to to be with her.

'The hospital needed a bit of persuasion,' he admitted. 'But they owed me the time anyway. They've appointed an excellent locum to cover my caseload, so in the end everyone's needs were met.'

Abbey felt riddled with guilt. 'I hope you won't be bored rigid here.'

'How could I be?' He sent her a dry look. 'I expect you to keep me very busy, Dr Jones.'

Abbey flushed. 'I...can't pay you much,' she deflected quickly. 'There is some extra funding to cover a locum but nothing like your normal salary.'

He shook his head. 'Abbey, the money isn't important. I

wanted—*needed*—to spend this time with you. End of story. Now, where should I stay? I noticed several pubs on the way here.'

Abbey made a face. 'The Sapphire's the best but you don't need to shell out money to stay in a pub. I'm rattling around in a huge house that comes with the job. You can live with me.'

His mouth kicked up in a crooked smile. 'Live as in *live*?' he inquired softly.

Abbey felt the heat rising, warming her throat, flowering over her cheeks. She knew he was teasing her—well, she hoped he was. But she couldn't help wondering just what he expected from this month he was proposing to spend here.

And whether or not she was going to be able to meet those expectations.

'I meant to say, you can share my home—if that suits, of course...'

Nick's heart somersaulted. She looked even more lovely than he remembered and he suddenly knew without a shadow of a doubt he wanted to test the strength of this relationship as far as it would go. And despite the frustration ripping through him, he knew he'd have to tread very softly around Abbey Jones. Very softly indeed.

'Thanks.' He rubbed the back of his neck. 'That will suit me very well.'

CHAPTER FIVE

'I'LL GIVE YOU the tour,' Abbey said, as they went out, closing the door on her consulting room. 'Then I'll take you home to my place and you can get settled in while I do a hospital round.'

'Why can't I come to the hospital with you?'

Well, no reason, Abbey supposed, nibbling at the corner of her bottom lip. 'It's all pretty basic medicine,' she warned.

Nick's eyes clouded slightly. 'Abbey, I'm on your patch now. I'm keen to learn about rural medicine.'

She opened the door of the second consulting room. 'I was just pointing out that there'll be none of the drama associated with Theatres.'

'I'm quite looking forward to the change of pace.' His voice was carefully neutral. 'But who knows?' He raised an eyebrow just slightly and grinned. 'You kind of lose the feel of general medicine when you detour into a speciality. I might turn out to be a real dud at your brand of medicine.'

As if! Abbey angled her gaze quickly away from the lively intelligence of those amazing eyes. 'This will be yours.' She led him into the reasonably sized surgery. 'Wolf uses it when he covers for me. Feel free to move things around if they don't suit.'

'I'll bear that in mind. But on first glance it seems fine.'

'Treatment room through here. It's quite large,' she said, pulling back a screen to reveal an identical set of equipment. 'Once upon a time there were several doctors working here.' Her mouth moved in a rueful little moue. 'But not for some years now.'

They moved on to the staff kitchen and walked onto the outdoor deck leading off it.

'Oh, boy,' Nick breathed in obvious approval, placing his hands on the timber railings. 'This is really something...' His gaze went towards the hills and the magic of a vividly pink and gold sunset. 'The last time I saw something like this was in Bali.'

'Have you travelled a lot?' Abbey came up to stand beside him.

'Some.' He lifted a shoulder. 'Dad took us over to Italy when we were youngsters and I've been back a couple of times. Done most of Europe. I worked in the States for a year, Canada for six months.'

She sent him a strained little smile, feeling like a real country bumpkin. Sadly, she realised she'd hardly travelled at all outside her own country. But there'd scarcely been time—or money, she reflected ruefully, considering the whopping great study loan she'd had to repay.

'Is your family very wealthy, Nick?'

A smile nipped his mouth. 'We never wanted for anything, I suppose. My grandparents established a vineyard outside Hopeton when they migrated from Italy. They never looked back. It just went from strength to strength.'

And brought in lots of money obviously. 'Is it still in your family?'

'Oh, yes. But they put in a manager some years ago, when we moved to Sydney. My parents run the sales and promotional side of things from there. Anything else you'd like to know?' he drawled with his slow smile.

'Sorry.' Embarrassed, Abbey looked away. 'I didn't mean to sound as though I was interrogating you.'

'You weren't,' he denied blandly. And then he frowned slightly, his eyes on her face with the intensity of a camera lens. 'Abbey, stop looking for the differences between us. This will work,' he said with conviction. 'We'll be good together.'

'Well, let's hope the patients think so,' Abbey waffled, feeling the warmth of his regard all over her. 'End of tour.' She turned abruptly from the railings. 'Let's put Meri in the picture and then we'll be on our way.'

'I'll follow you,' Nick said, as they left the surgery and made their way to their respective vehicles. 'How far is it to the hospital?'

'About five minutes.' Abbey waggled her bunch of keys until she found the one for the ignition. 'Seven if it's a foggy morning.'

Nick grinned. 'Perhaps I should invest in a pushbike? Save on petrol.'

'Or a sulky,' Abbey shot back impishly. 'That would go quite well with your new rural image. And there happens to be a beauty on display at the heritage village. Maybe they'd let you borrow that. I'm sure we could round up a nice fat pony to pull it.'

'And perhaps you could rustle up an old-fashioned Gladstone bag and a jar of leeches while you're at it?' Nick's eyes were full of laughter.

He'd never felt so light-hearted. And he was still wearing a smile as he tailed Abbey's Range Rover through the town proper and across the disused railway line. As she had predicted, they were at the hospital within a few minutes.

Nick got out of his car and looked around him. The hospital was a low-set building of weathered brick with several annexes at various points. There was a strip of lawn, faded to winter-brown, around the perimeter. And further over again, a windsock flapped gently in the breeze at the end of a large unfenced paddock.

'We do have the odd emergency,' Abbey explained, coming to stand beside him. 'The strip's regularly maintained for the CareFlight chopper to land.'

He shook his head. 'It's so quiet.'

'Mmm.' Abbey's gaze stretched to the shimmering water of a lagoon in a farmer's adjoining paddock and the wild ducks resembling tiny specks swimming serenely on its surface. 'It kind of folds in on you, especially at night.'

'You're not lonely?'

'For a while at first. Not now. But living here is vastly different from living in the city. In every way.'

'Yes.' Nick's reply was muted.

After a minute, they turned and began making their way across to the hospital entrance. 'Like me to fill you in about the staff?' Abbey flicked him a brief smile.

'Please.'

'We've a husband-and-wife team, Rhys and Diane Macklin, as joint nurse managers. They're terrific. Keep the place ticking over. Usually one of them is on duty. And we have a regular staff of RNs. They're rostered parttime as necessary. And there are two youngish aides, Zoe and Tristan. They're really just getting the feel of working within a hospital to see if they'd like to go ahead and train as registered nurses.'

Nick nodded. 'That sounds remarkably innovative.'

'Well, in a small place like Wingara, it can work quite well. And Rhys and Diane have the necessary accreditation to be their preceptors.'

'Who's the cook?' His grin was youthfully hopeful.

'I wondered when we'd get to that.' Abbey lifted her gaze briefly to the sky. 'Bella Sykes provides the meals at the hospital and also does for me.'

'Does?' Nick lifted an eyebrow.

Abbey chuckled. 'She looks after the doctor's residence which means she comes in a couple of times a week to clean and keep the place looking reasonable. She's an absolute gem.'

Nick looked thoughtful. 'The local community obviously values your presence enormously, Abbey. How will they respond to me being here, do you suppose?'

'Thinking of backing out, Doctor?'

Nick's jaw jutted. 'With you to hold my hand? No way.'

Diane Macklin was just coming out of her office as they approached the nurses' station. 'Abbey!' The nurse manager's dark head with its smooth bob tilted enquiringly. 'Three times in one day. Are you concerned about a patient?'

'With you in charge?' Abbey laughed. 'Not a chance. Um, Diane, this is Dr Nick Tonnelli.' Abbey turned to the man beside her. 'He'll be giving me a hand for the next few weeks.'

'Welcome aboard, Doctor.' Diane extended a hand across the counter. Her gaze skittered curiously from Nick to Abbey. 'I'll just bet you're old friends from medical school. Am I right?'

Nick tipped a sly wink at Abbey. 'I was a few years ahead of Abbey,' he deflected smoothly. 'Wasn't I?'

Abbey almost choked. 'Ah...yes.' Well, she supposed he would have been. He was several years older than her after all. 'And Nick's here for a holiday as well,' she added boldly.

'My first trip so far west,' he admitted, keeping the patter going but flicking Abbey a dry look.

'Oh, you'll love it,' Diane enthused. 'And I'm sure we'll keep you busy.'

Abbey stole a glance at her watch. 'Diane, we'd best get on. I'll just give Nick a quick tour of the hospital so he can find things.'

'Good idea. But do yell if you need anything, Dr Tonnelli.'

'It's Nick, Diane.'

The RN beamed. 'OK, then—Nick. Oh, Abbey, before you go...' Diane gave an apologetic half-smile. 'There was something. I wonder if you'd mind just having a word with young Brent.'

A frown touched Abbey's forehead. 'I've signed his release. He's going home tomorrow. What seems to be the problem?'

'Oh, nothing about his physical care,' Diane hastily reassured her. 'But he's seemed terribly quiet for most of the afternoon and he's asked me twice if I thought he was ready to go home.'

'That's odd.' Nick stroked his chin in conjecture. 'Most patients can't wait to get shut of us.' He raised a brow at Abbey. 'What was he admitted for?'

'Snakebite.'

'Oh—excuse me, folks.' Diane spun round as a patient's buzzer sounded. 'That's old Mrs Delaney.' She made a small face. 'Poor old love probably needs turning again.'

'You go, Diane.' Abbey made a shooing motion with her hand. 'I'll certainly pop in on Brent. See if there's something needs sorting out.'

'Thanks.' Diane flapped a hand in farewell, looking smart and efficient in her navy trousers and crisp white shirt, as she hurried away to the ward.

'You know, he may just need to talk.' Nick backed himself against the counter and folded his arms. 'And, just for the record, I've never seen a case of snakebite.'

'That's not so surprising,' Abbey said, moving round beside him so that their arms were almost touching. 'Although these days, more and more snakes are being found in city environs and most of them are now being placed on the potentially lethal list.'

'Charming.' Nick's response was touched with dry humour. 'So, is it still the same treatment we were taught in med school? Compression, head for the nearest hospital and combat the poison with an antivenom?'

'Mmm.' A smile nipped Abbey's mouth. 'Much more civilised than in the old days. They used to pack the bite puncture with gunpowder and light the fuse.' Seeing the horror on

Nick's face, she elaborated ghoulishly, 'You can imagine what it did to the affected part of the body.'

'You're kidding me!'

'Go look it up in the local history section at the library. It's all there. And there was another method—'

'Stop, please!' Nick raised his hands in mock surrender.

Abbey chuckled. 'Put you off your dinner, did I? Better get used to it, Doctor. You're in the bush now. Um, what did you mean about Brent?' She changed the tenor of the conversation quietly. 'That he might need to talk...'

'Just a thought. Give me the background.'

'Brent is sixteen,' Abbey began carefully. 'He's left school, works on the family property about seventy kilometres out. He was bitten on Monday last.'

'So he's been hospitalised all this week.'

'It seemed the best and safest option. To make sure there were no residual effects. And don't forget, if I'd released him too early, it would have been a round trip of a hundred and forty K's if his parents had needed to get him back in.'

'So you erred on the side of caution,' Nick said. 'I'd have done the same. Was it a severe bite?'

'It was a blue-bellied black snake.' Abbey identified the species with a shudder. 'And it got a really good go at Brent's calf muscle. Fortunately, he was near enough to the homestead to be found fairly quickly and he didn't panic.

'Out here kids are indoctrinated about what to do in case of snakebite. I remember when I'd been here only a few weeks, the principal of the school rang and asked when I'd be available to do "the snake talk".' She gave a low, throaty laugh, lifting her hands to make the quotation marks in the air.

Nick tore his gaze away from her smiling mouth. 'You said Brent didn't panic?'

'Ripped up his T-shirt, used it as a tourniquet and stayed put. He was visible from the track to the homestead and it was late afternoon. He knew his dad would be along within a reasonable time and he could hail him. It worked out that way and Tony and Karen brought their son straight in.'

'So, given all that, how calmly he appeared to handle things, is it just possible young Brent is now suffering from PTS?'

Abbey looked taken aback. 'Post-traumatic stress?'

Nick shrugged, palms out. 'It happens as a result of dogbites and shark attacks.'

Was it possible? Her hand closed around the small medallion at her throat.

'How's he been sleeping?'

'Not all that well, actually. But I put it down to the strangeness of being in hospital for the first time.' Abbey felt the nerves in her stomach tighten. Had she been less perceptive than she should have been where her young patient was concerned? She shook her head. 'He hasn't seemed to want to talk especially. In fact, I've been flat out getting two words out of him.'

'Well, there could be a reason for that.' Nick sent her a dry smile. 'He's sixteen, Abbey. His testosterone is probably working overtime and you're a beautiful lady doctor. The kid was probably struck dumb.'

Abbey felt the flush creep up her throat but then her chin rose. 'That's crazy!'

'Is it?'

'So I should try and talk to him, then?' Her hand clutched at her cloud of fair hair in agitation. 'Is that what you're saying?'

'Why don't you let me?'

'You?'

'I'm on staff now,' he reminded her. 'And your Brent may just open up to another male. This is how we'll handle it.'

Brent Davis was the only patient in the three-bed unit. Clad in sleep shorts and T-shirt, he was obviously bored, his gaze intermittently on the small television screen in front of him.

Abbey braced herself, going forward, her greeting low-key and cheerful. 'Hi, there, Brent. Just doing a final round.'

Colour stained the boy's face and he kept his gaze determinedly on the TV screen.

'This is Dr Tonnelli.' Abbey whipped the blood-pressure cuff around the youth's left arm and began to pump. 'He's from Sydney. Going to spend some time with us here in Wingara.'

'Hi, Brent.' Nick extended his hand. 'Dr Jones tells me you crash-tackled a death adder recently.'

Brent looked up sharply. 'Don't get adders this far west.' He sent Abbey an exasperated look. 'I told you it was a black snake.'

'So you did.' Abbey smiled, releasing the cuff.

'How did it actually happen, mate?' Casually, Nick parked himself on the youngster's bed and raised a quizzical dark brow.

Almost holding her breath, Abbey watched Brent's throat tighten with heartbreaking vulnerability, before he made faltering eye contact with the male doctor.

'I...was just walking through the grass. This time of year it's pretty long and it's dry, tufty kind of stuff. I must have disturbed the snake—maybe it was sleeping.'

'Don't they usually sleep on logs?' Head bent, Abbey was making notes on Brent's chart.

'Not always.'

'So, you disturbed it...' Nick folded his arms, and gave the boy an encouraging nod to continue.

'Bastard gave me one hell of a fright.' Brent made a sound somewhere between a snort and a laugh. 'It went straight into a strike pattern—like an S.' The boy flexed his hand and forearm to illustrate.

'Hell's teeth...' Nick grimaced. 'And then it struck and bit you?'

'Yeah. Quick as a flash.' Brent's demeanour had suddenly lightened with the enthusiasm of recounting his tale. 'I almost wet myself.'

'Hmm, lucky you didn't do that.' Nick's grin was slow. 'And Dr Jones tells me you kept your head and did all the right things until you were able to get here to the hospital. I don't know whether I'd have been so cool.'

Brent lifted a shoulder dismissively. 'Out here, you have to learn to take care of yourself from when you're a kid. Otherwise you're dead meat.'

Over their young patient's head, Nick exchanged a guarded smile with Abbey. This response was just what they'd hoped for. And, it seemed, once started, Brent couldn't stop. Aided by Nick's subtle prompting, he relaxed like a coiled spring unwinding as he continued to regale them with what had happened.

Finally, Nick flicked a glance at his watch. 'So, it's home tomorrow?'

'Yeah.' Brent's smile flashed briefly.

'What time are your parents coming, Brent?' Abbey clipped the medical chart back on to the end of the bed.

'About ten. Uh—thanks for looking after me.' He rushed the words out, his gaze catching Abbey's for the briefest second before he dipped his head shyly.

'You're welcome, Brent.' Abbey sent him a warm smile. 'And better wear long trousers out in the paddocks from now on, eh?'

'And watch where you put those big feet,' Nick joked, pulling himself unhurriedly upright. 'Stay cool, champ.' He touched a hand to the boy's fair head.

'No worries, Doc. See you.'

'You bet.' Nick raised a one-fingered salute.

Out in the corridor, he turned to Abbey. 'Told you we'd be a good team.'

Abbey's smile was a little strained. '*You* were good, Nick. Thanks.'

'Hey, you.' As they turned the corner, he tugged her to a halt. 'You look as though you've just hocked your best silver.'

She smiled weakly. 'I don't have any silver.'

'You know what I mean.'

Her mouth tightened momentarily. 'Why didn't I see Brent

needed to unload all that stuff? He was relaxed as cooked spaghetti when we left.'

'And he'll probably sleep like a baby tonight. It's what's called getting a second opinion, Abbey, and I imagine they're a bit thin on the ground out here. Am I right?' he tacked on softly.

She nodded feeling the pressures of being a sole practitioner close in on her. 'But I would have sent him home still all screwed up—'

'Stop it!' Nick's command was razor sharp. 'You can't second-guess everything you do in medicine, Abbey. Imagine, as a surgeon, if I did that. I'd be residing at the funny farm by now. You do the best you can. None of us can do more than that.'

'But—'

He gave an irritated 'tsk'. 'Abbey, physically, your patient is well again. He's young and resilient. He'd have sorted himself out—probably talked to his parents about it, or a mate.'

'I suppose so…'

'I know so.' Nick's eyes glinted briefly. 'Now, come on, Dr Jones.' He took her arm again. 'You promised to show me through the rest of this place.'

Wingara hospital was old but beautifully maintained. Nick looked around with growing interest, deciding the wide corridors and carved wooden panelling over the doorways could have easily graced a fine old homestead. 'It's got a long history, obviously,' he remarked.

'Oh, yes.' Abbey nodded, regaining her equilibrium. 'Built in the days when Wingara was a thriving centre. In those days there was a permanent senior reg on staff and always a couple of residents, plus several GPs in private practice as well.'

'So, what happened?'

'The usual things.' Abbey's mouth turned down. 'The sapphire mine gave out, the rail line closed, the sawmill went into liquidation and people had to relocate to get work. Suddenly, it was the domino effect at its worst. Money leaves the town so shops lose business or fold. The pupil numbers at the school diminish so a teacher is lost, and so it goes on. But there's talk of the mine reopening and the local council has embraced tourism, so there's a bit of a revival happening.' She smiled. 'Things are looking up again.'

'What's the bed capacity?' They'd stopped and looked into one of the spacious private rooms.

'Only ten now. And, thank heavens, we've never had a full house since I've been here.'

'Do you have an OR?' Nick began striding ahead, his interest clearly raised.

'We have a *theatre*,' Abbey emphasised. 'You're not in the States now, you know.'

Nick laughed ruefully. 'Force of habit. Makes more sense to say OR when you think about it, though.'

Abbey looked unimpressed. 'Here we are.' She turned into an annexe and opened the door to the pristine operating theatre. Her mouth had a sad little droop. 'It's hardly used any more but Rhys insists the instruments are kept sterilised.'

Nick shook his head slowly. 'It's brilliant—for a rural hospital, that is...' His mouth compressed. He could comprehend more clearly now Abbey's underlying anger and frustration at the bureaucracy's continued neglect of rural medicine. Although he'd assumed things were improving...

He strode into the theatre then, as if to better acquaint himself with its layout, his movements sure and purposeful as he gauged the angle of a light here, stroked the tips of his fingers over a stainless-steel surface there.

'Do you want me to leave you here to play while I go home and start dinner?' Abbey queried dryly from the doorway.

Nick's head came up and he grinned a bit sheepishly. 'Be right with you.'

CHAPTER SIX

THE DOCTOR'S RESIDENCE was next door to the hospital with a vacant block between. Again, like the hospital, it was of brick, a sprawling old building with a bay window at the front and with a large veranda on the eastern side, positioned to catch the morning sun in the winter and to offer shade during the hot summer afternoons.

As Abbey led the way inside, she had the strangest feeling a whole new chapter of her life was about to begin.

'Ah—sure there's enough room?'

Abbey wrinkled her nose at Nick's mocking look, her heels tapping as they walked along the polished hallway. 'There are four bedrooms, all quite large. You can take the one with the bay window, if you like. Bella keeps them all aired—don't ask me why.' She opened the door on the freshness of a lemon-scented furniture polish. 'What do you think?'

There was something very homely and intimate about it, Nick thought. His gaze swept the room, taking in the fitted wardrobes, the dark oak dresser and bedside tables with their old-fashioned glass lamps. 'It looks very comfortable,' he said, his mouth drying as he looked across at the double bed with its plump navy blue duvet and lighter blue pillowcases.

He took a breath that expanded the whole of his diaphragm. 'Thank you, Abbey.'

Abbey's heart did a tumble turn. She swallowed. 'For what?'

'For inviting me to share your home.'

Suddenly the atmosphere changed, the light-hearted harmony disappearing, replaced with tension as tight as a trip wire.

Her startled eyes met his and widened, and her lips parted to take in a soft little breath.

It was too much for Nick. With a muted sound of need, he drew her into his arms. Raising his hands, he cupped her face, his thumbs following the contours of her cheekbones. She looked so beautiful, he thought, looking down at the little flecks like gold dust in her eyes.

Lowering his head, he tasted the fluttering pulse at her throat, before catching her lips, threading his fingers through her hair to lock her head more closely to his.

On a little moan of pleasure Abbey welcomed his deepening kiss, shivering at the intensity of her feelings the like of which she'd never experienced with any other man. Winding her arms around his waist, she urged him closer, closing the last remaining gap between them, tasting heaven.

But surely this shouldn't be happening.

With a tiny whimper, she dragged her mouth from his, her breathing shallow. 'Nick...' Her hand flew up to cover her mouth.

'Abbey?' He stared down into her wide, troubled eyes.

She held his gaze for a searing moment and then looked away, taking a step back as if to separate herself from the physical boundary of his arms.

In a show of mild desperation, Nick brought his hands up, locking them at the back of his neck. Did she expect him to apologise? Well, he was damned if he was going to. She'd kissed him back, hadn't she?

'I…think we need some ground rules.' Abbey wound her arms around her midriff to stop herself trembling. She licked her lips, tasting him all over again.

His jaw tightened. 'Are you trying to tell me you don't like me touching you?'

She flushed. 'That's not the point. This is a small community. We both have a professional standard to uphold.'

'You're having second thoughts about having me here?'

'No.' Abbey took a shallow breath. 'I'm just saying we need to be aware of how things look.'

A grim little smile twisted his mouth. 'In other words, to use the vernacular, you don't want it to appear as though I've come here merely to shack up with you.' And then he looked at her wary, troubled expression and his gut clenched. 'Look.' He pressed his palms against his eyes and pushed out a gust of breath. 'I'll get a room at the pub.'

'You don't have to do that!' Abbey shook her head and wondered why she was trying so hard to keep him under her roof. 'Just…as I said. We need to talk a few things through.' Seeing how his expression darkened at that, she added hurriedly, 'But we could do that later, perhaps—over a glass of wine or something…'

'Fine,' he agreed heavily. 'Is it OK if I take a few minutes to unpack? It's been a long day. I'd like to get squared away.'

'Of course,' she said quickly, almost breathlessly in her haste to try and normalise things between them. In a brief aside, she wondered if Nick was obsessively neat about the house. Oh, lord. She wasn't a particularly messy person but she did like to kick her shoes off the minute she walked in the door and she'd been known to leave empty coffee-mugs in odd places.

But I won't keep looking for the negatives between us.

She rallied, even dredging up a passable smile. 'I'll, um, grab a shower and see you in a bit, then. My bedroom has an *en suite* bathroom so feel free to use the main one.' She heard herself babbling and stopped. 'See you in a bit,' she repeated and hurriedly left the bedroom.

Barely forty-five minutes later, Nick joined Abbey in the kitchen, showered, his suitcase unpacked and his gear more or less sorted.

'That was quick.' She gave a stilted smile. 'I've just been checking the fridge. There's nothing very interesting for dinner and I wouldn't insult your ancestral palate by offering you a supermarket-brand lasagne.'

'I've eaten worse things.' His mouth folded in on a smile and he hooked out a chair to sit back to front on it, his arms folded along the top. 'Honestly, Abbey, I'm not pedantic about food. But I do like to choose what I eat, if that makes sense.'

It did. 'I usually do a shop on Saturday after I've finished surgery.' Abbey met his mild look neutrally, before her eyes darted away again. 'I guess we could make a list of the kinds of things we like...' She paused, as if waiting for his approval.

'Sure. That's fine with me.' He rolled back his shoulders and stretched.

Her expression lightened. Perhaps sharing living arrangements would work out after all. 'The Sapphire does a nice roast on a Friday,' she offered tentatively.

'The pub it is, then.' Nick kept his tone deliberately brisk. 'But I might make it an early night, if you don't mind.'

She suppressed a tight smile. 'And there I was imagining you'd want to hang about for the karaoke.'

'Maybe next Friday.' As if he was trying hard to regain his good humour, Nick's return smile was wry and crooked. Spinning off his chair, he placed it neatly back at the table. 'Let's go then, if you're quite ready.'

They took Abbey's four-wheel-drive. 'And while you're here, Nick, we split living expenses down the middle. OK?' They'd crossed the old railway line and were re-entering the town proper.

'Whatever you say, Abbey.'

She sent him a quick enquiring look. His remark had sounded as though he was humouring her. She frowned slightly. Suddenly the outcome of this month he proposed spending here with her seemed very blurred and uncertain.

'Be prepared to be well looked over,' she warned him. She'd parked neatly opposite the hotel and now they were making their way across the street to the beer garden.

'So, I shouldn't try holding your hand, then,' he interpreted dryly.

Abbey's heart thumped painfully. If he didn't lighten up, she'd jolly well send him home to eat that awful lasagne.

The beer garden was not overly crowded for a Friday evening and Abbey breathed a sigh of relief, scattering a smile here and there to several of the townsfolk who were obviously enjoying a meal out.

Seeing her action, a flash of humour lit Nick's eyes and he mimicked her greeting.

'Cheeky,' Abbey murmured, hiding a smile and taking the chair he held out for her.

'I always say, start as you mean to go on and at least now the locals will know I'm a friendly soul. I must say this all looks very civilised,' he sidetracked, looking around the precincts. And suddenly, he felt a lift in his spirits. Already he was sensing something special here in Abbey's world, not least the slower pace. His expression closed thoughtfully and he sat back in his chair, the better to take in his surroundings.

Fat candles on the wooden tables were giving out an atmosphere of light and shadow. And there was a sheen on the leaves of the outdoor plants dotting the perimeter of the raised timber platform, the fairy lights strung between them twinkling like so many diamonds. Or stars, he substituted, slightly embarrassed at his attempt at poetic language.

Tipping his head back, he looked up, his gaze widening in awe. The slender winter moon looked almost like an intruder amongst the canopy of stars, some of which looked close enough to touch, bright, like welcoming windows of light in a vast darkened abyss, while the myriad of others were scattered far and wide like so much fairy dust in the swept enormous heavens.

'Stunning.' Nick's voice was hushed.

Wordlessly, Abbey followed his gaze and felt her heart contract. 'Yes,' she agreed in a small voice, and didn't object when his fingers sought hers and tightened.

'You...haven't mentioned Todd.' The words slipped a bit disjointedly from Abbey. They were halfway through their roast dinners, their glasses of smooth merlot almost untouched beside their plates.

Nick gave her a brief, narrowed look and then dropped his gaze. 'I wasn't sure if the subject was taboo. But to answer the question you're probably burning to ask, he's going great guns. Even talking of getting involved in the sporting wheelies. In fact, I believe Ben Bristow, one of our champions from the Sydney paralympics, has been to see him.'

'Oh, that's fabulous. Sunningdale couldn't have managed anything like that for him,' Abbey said with quiet honesty. 'I imagine Todd would take to any kind of sporting challenge like a duck to water.'

'And Ben's influence will be invaluable.' Nick picked up his glass unhurriedly and took a mouthful of wine. 'His own story is not dissimilar to Todd's. Ben was a brilliant athlete, training for a triathlon event, when his spinal column was damaged after a road accident. It happened about five years ago. But he picked himself up, and now his list of sporting achievements would put an able-bodied athlete to shame. Consequently, he's become a bit of a hero, especially to disabled kids. He and Todd would seem to have that in common as well.'

Nick put his glass down and went quietly on with his meal, leaving Abbey feeling less than proud of how she'd berated him about his handling of Todd's care. 'I should apologise,' she said, and Nick arched an eyebrow.

'About how I reacted, when you told me what had been decided about Todd.' Her downcast lashes fanned darkly across her cheekbones. 'I—I know it's no excuse, but I felt, as his GP, I'd been left entirely out of the consultative process.'

His mouth compressed. 'I never in a million years would have wanted you to feel I'd put you down in some way. So that's why you let loose on me.' He smiled a bit crookedly, as if recalling the conversation. 'I must admit I was confused about your reaction.'

Abbey picked absently at her food. 'Perhaps I was feeling a bit...*intense* about things when you called.'

'Perhaps we both were,' he concurred quietly.

An awkward silence descended over them, until Nick rescued the situation smoothly. 'You know you were way off the track about Amanda Steele, Abbey. I didn't hijack her to the detriment of Sunningdale. Her moving to the Dennison was a reciprocal arrangement with one of the OTs there. And it's only a temporary arrangement until Todd gains enough confidence in his ability to cope.'

'Now I feel doubly foolish,' Abbey wailed. 'And on the phone, I must have sounded so...'

'Insecure?' Nick prompted with a smile.

'All right—insecure,' Abbey echoed in a small voice but nearly smiling.

'So...' He put his hand out towards her. 'Have we sorted that out now? Put an end to your...insecurities?'

She held her breath, looking straight into his eyes, feeling the sensual charge of his thumb tracing the top of her hand. Every nerve in her body was singing with sensation. Her heart thumped against her ribs and she wondered starkly whether, instead, her insecurities around this man were just beginning...

When she woke next morning, Abbey couldn't shake off the feeling of unreality.

But within seconds the soft closing of Nick's bedroom door

and his muffled footsteps along the hall put paid to any fanciful idea that she may have dreamed his presence under her roof.

But where on earth was he going at this ungodly hour? She frowned at the clock-radio on her bedside table and stifled a groan. The man's mad, she decided, turning over and pulling the duvet up to her chin.

She was in the kitchen and dressed for work when she discovered the reason for him disappearing so early.

'Morning, Abbey.' He surged into the kitchen via the back door.

Her eyebrows lifted. 'You've been out running!'

Nick gave a warm, rich chuckle. 'Give the lady a prize for observation.' He'd obviously discarded his trainers in the adjoining laundry. He padded across the tiled floor in his thick sports socks. Looking thoroughly at home, he helped himself from the jug of orange juice Abbey had squeezed earlier and left on the counter. 'May I?' The glass was already halfway to his lips.

She nodded, suddenly utterly aware of the very essence of him. Heavens, he stripped well. She swallowed against the sudden dryness in her throat. He was wearing black shorts and a black and white striped football jersey that had obviously seen better days, but that only served to make him look deliciously rumpled and as sexy as—

'Where did you go?' She held tightly on to her tea-mug, trying not to notice the ripple of his thigh muscles and the faint sheen of healthy male sweat in the shallow dip of his collarbone where the neck of his jersey had fallen open.

'Someone's paddock, I think.' He drained his glass and refilled it halfway. 'I did a couple of laps of the helipad and then I climbed through the fence near the lagoon.'

'That would be the Dwyers' place.' Abbey slid off the tall stool and rinsed her mug at the sink.

He turned to her with a grin. 'They wouldn't have mistaken me for a wallaby and taken a shot at me, would they?'

Abbey made a click of exasperation. 'The farmers don't

go round shooting randomly at anything that moves! Besides, you're way too tall for a wallaby,' she reproved, and he grinned, propping himself against the counter and crossing his ankles.

'Do you run every day?' she asked.

'When I can. And when I can't manage it, I use the air walker at home.' He raised his glass and swallowed the rest of his juice. 'I work long hours in Theatre. I need to be fitter than most.'

Abbey blinked. She'd never thought of it quite like that, but she guessed he was right. He certainly would need excellent physical stamina to stay alert and on top of his very demanding speciality. 'There's a sports track at the showgrounds,' she told him. 'I believe the early-morning joggers use that. I'll show you where it is later, if you like.'

'Thanks, but I think I'll stick to the paddocks. I like the sense of freedom running alone gives me.'

In a nervous gesture Abbey ran her hands down the sides of her tailored trousers. She couldn't help thinking Nick Tonnelli was one dangerous, potent mix and with no surgical list to keep him occupied for the next month, all that latent masculinity and coiled physical energy was going to need an outlet.

Just the thought that it all could be directed at her made her say, jerkily, 'Um, if you want breakfast, there's muesli in the pantry. And low-fat milk in the fridge.'

'I can't stand that stuff!' He shot her a rueful grin. 'Better add whole milk to the shopping list, hmm?'

Abbey gave him a pained look. 'I take it wholemeal bread is acceptable?'

'Very.'

'And canola spread? Or do you indulge in lashings of butter for your toast?'

He tapped her on the end of her nose with the tip of one finger. 'Canola's fine. Are you going across to the surgery now?'

'Shortly.'

'Like me to do a hospital round, then?'

Her mouth kicked up in a smile. 'Dressed like that? Hardly,

Doctor. Even in Wingara, we like to observe some semblance of respectability for visiting medical officers.' With a quick twist of her slim body, she dodged the teatowel he threw at her.

Giving release to a wry chuckle, Nick turned to the sink to rinse his glass and then put the jug of juice in the fridge. 'I'll shower and make myself respectable first. That do?'

'Nicely. And when you've finished your hospital round, you may like to come over to the surgery. I'm sure Meri will be more than happy to clue you in about our style of paperwork and anything else you'll need to know about how the place runs. And don't forget I'll need your help with the grocery shopping this afternoon.'

'So bossy,' he grumbled, turning to refill the kettle at the sink, but Abbey could see the smile hovering around the corners of his mouth.

'I like to be organised,' she defended herself lightly, quite unable to stop her own smile. And five minutes later, as she made her way out to the carport, she was conscious of an absurd sense of light-heartedness.

Flipping open the door of her four-wheel-drive and settling in behind the wheel, she was suddenly overwhelmed with a rush of feeling. Oh, heck! Leaving aside the undoubted physical attraction Nick's body presented, was it just possible she was beginning to actually *like* the man?

Abbey's last consultation was over by eleven o'clock and Nick had joined her in the staff kitchen for a coffee-break.

'Do you normally finish about this time?' He took another slice of the apple cake he'd bought from the local bakery. 'This isn't half-bad.' He grinned, tucking in unabashedly.

'The way your eyes lit up when Meri mentioned chocolate biscuits and now this.' She pointed to the crumbly mess on his plate. 'I'm beginning to wonder if you've a shocking sweet tooth,' Abbey said laughingly.

'No worries, Doc.' Nick sprawled back in his chair, looking

smug. 'This baby will run it off easily. Now, what about your Saturday surgery?'

Abbey became serious. 'I usually start at eight, earlier if it's necessary. Some of the rural workers have special needs, like a limited timeframe when they get into town. So I do my best to accommodate them. But normally I'm through by noon.' She twitched a wry smile. 'Meri books only what's essential, otherwise I'd never be out of the place.' She tilted her head in query. 'So, what about your morning, then? How was your ward round?'

'Different.' They exchanged smiles of understanding. 'Rhys was on duty so I made his acquaintance, and Brent's parents turned up early so I had a word with them as well.'

'And Brent seemed eager to go home?'

'Oh, yes.' Nick grinned. 'Quite an air of self-importance about him.'

'Mainly thanks to you,' Abbey said softly.

'Abbey, don't labour this. We're…' The rest of Nick's words were lost when Meri popped her head in the door.

'We have an emergency, folks.' She darted a quick worried look from one to the other. 'Rhys Macklin's on the line. They've had a call from a mobile at Jumbuck Ridge. One of a party of climbers is in strife.'

'I'll speak,' Abbey said briskly. 'Could you put the call through to my room, please, Meri?'

Nick shot her a sharp look, as they simultaneously sprang to their feet. 'How far is it to this place?'

'About twenty K's out.' Abbey pushed open the door of her consulting room, sensing his presence close behind. 'But we've no ambulance available today. We've only the one and it left this morning to transport a patient to Hopeton for kidney dialysis.'

'So we're it?'

'Looks like it.' Abbey picked up the phone.

Arms folded, Nick took up his stance against the window-ledge, listening with scarcely concealed impatience as Abbey fired questions into the mouthpiece. He could hardly comprehend the implications of having no ambulance available.

But surely to heaven they had an alternative procedure they followed in emergencies like this—or was it in the end all down to Abbey? He shook his head, the realisation of the terrifying uncertainties she probably faced on a regular basis shocking his equilibrium like the chill of an icy-cold shower on a winter's morning.

'Fine. Thanks, Rhys.' Abbey replaced the receiver and snapped her gaze to Nick. 'Right, we have a clearer picture now. Apparently, it's an abseiling group from the high school—seven students, one PE teacher, one parent.'

'And?' Instinctively, Nick had moved closer.

'The last one of the student team to descend pushed out too far. He came back in at an angle instead of front-on to the cliff and appears to have come up against some kind of projecting rock and knocked himself out. Fortunately, his locking device has activated and that's saved him from further injury.'

Nick's breath hissed through his teeth. 'So, we can assume he's still unconscious.'

'Would seem so.'

'Then we'd better get cracking.'

'We'll take my vehicle.' Abbey began locking drawers and cabinets. 'And we'll need to stop off at home and change into tracksuits and some non-slip footwear and then swing by the hospital. Rhys will have a trauma kit ready for us.'

'I've been on to Geoff Rogers.' Meri was just putting the phone down as they sped through Reception. 'The police sergeant,' she elaborated for Nick's benefit. 'He'll do his best to round up an SES crew. But it's Saturday—the guys could be anywhere.' She bit her lip. 'Want me to stay here at the surgery in case…?' Meri drew to a halt and shrugged helplessly.

'Lock up and go home, Meri.' Abbey was firm. 'There's

nothing further you can do here. We'll co-ordinate everything through the hospital.'

Meri nodded. 'OK. Mind how you both go.'

'So, apart from the injured student, do we know what kind of scenario we're facing when we get to this Jumbuck Ridge?' Nick asked. They'd left the town proper behind and were now travelling as fast as Abbey dared on the strip of country road.

'The rest of the youngsters plus the parent have already made their descent and are at the base of the cliff. The teacher, Andrew Parrish, is at the top. But he's more or less helpless until help arrives.'

'In the form of you and me.' Nick scraped a hand around his jaw, considering their options.

'Yes.' Abbey's eyes clouded with faint uncertainty. 'Can you abseil?'

'I've done a bit. But not for a while,' he qualified. 'You can, I take it?'

'Steve urged me to get the gist of it when I'd signed the contract to come out here. I learned the basics at one of those artificial walls at the gym first and then Andrew kindly gave me a few practical lessons after I'd taken up residence.' She sent him a tight little smile. 'I didn't want to appear like a wimp and have to stand on the sidelines every time something like this happened.'

'As if abseiling would come under your job description,' Nick growled, his eyes on the brush of flowering red and yellow lantana that flanked the roadside. 'And how many times have you had to *throw* yourself into your work like this?' he asked pithily, clamping down on his fear-driven thoughts for her safety.

'A few, but it doesn't get any easier.' Abbey gunned the motor to take a steep incline. 'This is the first time we've been without an ambulance, though.'

'Then let's hope the State Emergency lads will get there before too long. I take it they'll make their way to the base of the cliff and wait for us?'

'Yes.' Abbey felt the nerves of her stomach screw down tight at the thought of the logistics involved in the retrieval of the injured youth, let alone without the back-up of an ambulance at the end of it. 'It's a pretty rough track but they have a kind of troop-carrier vehicle. And they'll be able to improvise so we'll end up with an ambulance of sorts.'

They were quiet then, each occupied with their own very different thoughts.

Physical education teacher Andrew Parrish was waiting for them at the clifftop. 'This is a real stuff-up,' he said grimly, after Abbey had skimmed over the introductions.

'So, do we have a name and how far down is the boy?' Nick demanded, already beginning some warm-up arm and shoulder stretches for the physical demands of the descent ahead.

'The lad's name is Grant Halligan,' Andrew said. 'Aged sixteen. By my estimation, he's about twenty metres down.' He looked at Nick as if sizing up his capabilities. 'Uh... I don't know how savvy you are with any of this, Doc...'

'I've abseiled enough to know what I'm doing.'

'OK, then.' Andrew looked at him keenly. 'Grant obviously needs medical attention so one of you will have to drop down to him—'

'We'll both go,' Abbey cut in, her raised chin warning Nick not to argue.

'I'll organise a harness for each of you, then.' The teacher looked relieved to be getting on with things. 'Doc, you're obviously physically stronger than Abbey so, as well as your normal sit-harness, I'd like you to wear the special retrieval harness.'

Nick's dark brows flexed in query.

'It's a full-body harness.' Andrew pointed out the sturdy shoulder straps and leg loops. 'If Grant's out of it, and it looks as though he is, you're going to have to attach his harness to yours to get him down safely.'

Abbey bit her lip. 'That doesn't sound like it's going to be terribly easy, Andrew.'

'We'll cope,' Nick snapped. 'Now, could we move it, please?'

Silently and quickly, they climbed into the borrowed abseiling gear. Automatically tightening the waist belt above his hips, Nick felt the unmistakable dip in his stomach. Suddenly the smooth order of his operating room seemed light years away. And much, much safer.

'Now take these clip-gates,' Andrew instructed, handing Nick the metal locking devices. 'They're the best and easiest to operate in case you happen to have only one hand free. And when you've secured Grant to your harness, you can cut his line away.'

'With this?' Nick looked dubiously at the instrument Andrew pressed into his hand, no more than a small piece of sheathed metal.

'Don't worry. It's sharp enough to skin a rabbit,' Andrew said knowledgeably. 'So watch how you handle it.'

Nick grunted and slid the knife into an accessible pocket.

'Abbey, you set?' Andrew touched her shoulder.

'Yes.' She swallowed the dryness in her throat, checking the trauma kit's bulk which she'd anchored at the rear just below her bottom. 'If we're ready, then?' Her eyes met Nick's and clung.

'Ready.'

'Don't forget, now, Nick, you'll have Grant's extra weight on your line.' Andrew issued last-minute urgent instructions. 'So be aware of the sudden impact when you cut the line away. But I'll have you firmly anchored and it'll be fairly smooth sailing from where he's stuck right down to the base. Just steady as she goes, OK?'

'Fine.' Nick's teeth were clamped. Adrenalin was pumping out of him and already the tacky feel of sweat was annoyingly obvious down the ridge of his backbone.

Minute by minute his respect for Abbey's dedication to her responsibilities as a doctor in this isolated place had grown.

Along with his fears for her.

How the hell did she cope, living with this insidious kind of pressure? How? She was one gutsy lady—that went without saying. But surely enough was enough!

Whatever means he had to use and however he had to use them, he resolved he'd take her away from it all.

And sooner rather than later.

CHAPTER SEVEN

BOUNCING DOWN THE granite face of the cliff, Nick felt his skill returning. Cautiously, he cast a look downwards, just able to glimpse their patient in his bright yellow sweatshirt. 'We're nearly there,' he called to Abbey, who was slightly above him and to his left. 'Slacken off.'

'I hear you.' Abbey paid out her rope little by little, moving on down the rockface until she was alongside him.

'Right—this'll do us.' Nick signalled and together they swung in as closely as they could to the boy. 'And the gods are surely with us…' Nick's voice lightened as they landed on a ledge of rock and he began testing its viability. Finally, he managed to position his feet so that he was more or less evenly balanced. 'This should hold both of us, Abbey. Close up now.'

'I'm with you…' She edged in beside him.

Nick's gaze swung to her. She looked pale. A swell of protectiveness surged into his gut. 'You OK?'

'Piece of cake.' Her brittle laugh jagged eerily into the stillness.

Grant Halligan was hanging in space, quite still. But the top part of his inert body had drooped so far forward he was almost bent double into a U-shape.

Nick swore under his breath. 'Another couple of centimetres of gravity and he'd have turned completely upside down. OK, Abbey, let's reel him in.'

'Can you reach him from there?'

'Just about…'

With sickening dread, she watched as Nick edged perilously along the ledge, making the most of his long reach to grip the boy's waist harness and guide him in close to the cliff face. Lord, were they already too late?

Grant's colour was glassily blue. If they didn't act fast, he would be in danger of going into full cardiac arrest. And how they would begin to deal with that, suspended as they were on the side of a cliff, was something Abbey didn't want to contemplate.

Gingerly she positioned herself to receive Grant's torso and support his head. 'Right, I've got him!' Immediately she began to equalise the position of his head and neck, which would automatically clear his airway. 'How's his pulse?'

Nick's forehead creased in a frown. 'It's there but it's faint. And no breath sounds. Damn.' He dragged in a huge breath and in one swift movement bent to deliver five quick mouth-to-mouth breaths into their patient.

'Bingo…' Abbey let her own breath go in relief as the boy began to splutter and then cough.

'Best sound in the world.' Nick's voice roughened. 'But he's still well out of it. Grab me the torch, Abbey!' Automatically, he took Grant's weight so Abbey could access the trauma kit.

Tight-lipped, she leant into her sit-in harness and almost in slow motion slid her hand down, feeling around for the pocket containing the pencil torch. Convulsively, her fingers wrapped around it but then she fumbled getting it out, almost dropping it.

'Oh—help!' Her stomach heaved and she could feel the sudden perspiration patch wetly across her scalp under her safety hat. 'Here...' She swallowed jerkily and handed the torch to Nick.

Nick's face was set in concentration as he flicked the light into the boy's eyes. 'Equal and reacting,' he relayed, feeling the tightness in his temples ease fractionally. But they still had a mountain of uncharted territory to traverse before anyone could begin to relax.

So, no bleed into the brain, Abbey interpreted Nick's findings silently. She gnawed at her lip. 'His knee seems to be at an odd angle.'

'I had noticed.' Nick began feeling around for the clip-gates attached to a runner looped over his shoulder. The injured knee was an added complication. The sooner they got the kid down and treated, the better. He lowered his gaze to where Grant's injury was just visible below the coloured leg-band of his shorts. The scraped skin was of little importance but his instincts were telling him that the puffy state of the student's knee and the blood seeping from the wound the rock had inflicted were matters for concern.

'He's obviously hit the rock with some force,' Nick surmised. 'Possibly after he banged his head and lost control. I can't do much from here. I'll look at him properly when we get him down.'

Watching Nick clench his fingers across the special clips that would anchor Grant to his harness, Abbey felt a swirl of nervous tension in her stomach. 'Are we about to try and hitch him to you now?'

'We can't hang about—sorry, joke,' he said heavily. 'But this could be tricky. I'm going to have to try to align Grant's body to mine, chest to chest. That's the only way I can anchor him to my harness.'

Abbey's nerves tightened. 'In practical terms, how do you want to work it, then?'

Nick gave an irritated snort. 'Like I do this for a living!'

In other words, your guess is as good as mine. Charming!

She knew he was uptight but there was no need to snap her head off. Swallowing a sharp retort, she beat back a sudden wave of nausea, the result of inadvertently looking down.

'Abbey?' For a moment they looked at each other and Nick's mouth twisted with faint mockery. 'Sorry for my lapse just then.' His hand tightened on her shoulder, his gaze winging back to their patient. He took an obviously deep controlling breath. 'We'll manoeuvre Grant upright now. I'll help as much as I can, but I'll have to concentrate on getting him adjacent to my own body so I can secure the clip-gates to both our harnesses. OK, let's do it. But keep it slow and steady…'

It was useless. Abbey shook her head in despair. It was like trying to steady a ton-weight balloon with a piece of string. Grant was a well-built young man, his unconscious state only adding to their difficulties. And in their precarious position, it was well nigh impossible to co-ordinate the lift so the two harness belts were close enough to link.

'This isn't going to work.' Nick's lean, handsome face was stretched tautly. His shoulders slumped and he shook his head.

Abbey sensed his anguish. But they couldn't give up now. Grant's life could well depend on their teamwork. She pushed down her fears. 'Give me the clip-gates, Nick.'

His head went back as though she'd struck him. 'Are you mad? Grant's way too heavy and you're not wearing the right harness—'

'Stop trying to be a hero,' she snapped. 'And anyway, I didn't mean I'd try to take him. But we have to get a resolution here, Nick. It's not working—when you're steady, he's either too high or too low.'

'Well, I'd gathered that, Abbey,' he spat sarcastically.

She squeezed her eyes shut for a second and counted to ten. 'Could you link your hands under his behind and try to lift him to your waist? Then I could make a grab for his harness and snap you together.'

Nick's jaw tightened. 'Hell!' he spat the word between

clenched teeth. 'I hate not being in control of this situation. I hate it!' But nevertheless he did what Abbey had suggested, gripping Grant, lifting him as high as he could, his muscles straining with the effort.

Abbey was pale and tight-lipped, knowing she had only the barest window of opportunity to hitch the two harnesses before Nick's hold on the boy would of necessity have to slacken. She steadied her breathing, conscious of almost choreographing her movements.

'I…can't hold him much longer.' Nick gasped, pulling his torso back so Abbey could use what little access there was between him and the injured youth. 'Now!' he yelled. 'Quick— or I've lost him!'

In a flash and remembering everything she'd been taught, Abbey used her feet in a technique called 'smearing', where most of the climber's weight was positioned over one foot to reduce the overall load on the arms. Twisting slightly, she turned her upper body so that her arm closest to the rockface could counter-balance her movement and give her other arm maximum extension…

'Now! Abbey…' What the hell was taking her so long? The muscles of Nick's throat and around his mouth were locked in a grimace and sweat pooled wetly in his lower back. His mind was so concentrated he hardly felt the nudge of Abbey's fingers as she secured one then quickly two more clip-gates to link the two men.

'Done…' Her voice was barely above a whisper.

Abbey hardly remembered how they'd got down. She only remembered the relief she'd felt when Nick had cut Grant's rope and they could begin their descent.

And there were plenty of hands to help them once they were safely on the ground. A subdued cheer had even gone up. Grant was released from his harness and placed on the stretcher provided by the State Emergency Service personnel.

Abbey divested herself of her own harness, dimly aware her legs felt as unsteady as a puppet's.

'I'll take that, Abbey.' Terry French, the leader of the SES team, hurried to her side to unclip the trauma kit and heft it across his shoulder. 'You did a great job.'

'Thanks, Terry, but I couldn't have made it without Dr Tonnelli.'

'He did well.'

Abbey gave in to a tight little smile. That, from the usually laconic SES leader, was high praise. She must remember to tell Nick—that's if they were still speaking...

'But it's the last time young Parrish pulls something like today's effort,' Terry said forcefully.

'Oh?' Abbey's eyes widened in query.

'He should've checked the ambulance was available, and when it wasn't he should've cancelled the abseiling. *And* he had no business taking that many kids without another trained adult. I'll have something to say at the next P and C meeting, I can tell you.'

Well, the Parents and Citizens committee could sort all that out later, Abbey thought wearily. All that mattered now was Grant's welfare.

Quickly, she pulled her thoughts together. She removed her safety hat, shook out her hair and began making her way across to where Nick was already leaning over the stretcher to attend to their patient.

Abbey could see Grant had begun to come round but he seemed confused and emotional. 'It's OK, Grant.' She bent to reassure him. 'You'll be fine,' she murmured over and over, rubbing warmth into his hands.

'Could we have the portable oxygen unit over here, please?' Nick began issuing orders, a deep cleft between his dark brows. 'And a space blanket.'

'Anything presenting yet?' Abbey watched as he palpated the boy's stomach.

'Feels soft enough so no spleen damage. Check his breath sounds, please, Abbey.'

'Bit raspy.' Abbey folded the stethoscope away. 'Could be a lower rib fracture. What about his knee?'

Nick was gently manipulating the swollen joint, his look intense. 'Fractured kneecap,' he said shortly. 'No doubt about it. But I can fix that.'

Abbey's gaze widened in alarm. 'You'll operate here at Wingara?'

'I thought that's what you wanted, Abbey.' His voice was suddenly hard. 'A specialist to come to the patient.'

Abbey bit her lips together. Nick's arbitrary decision had literally taken control right out of her hands.

Again.

Her mind flew ahead. Was their little operating theatre up to it at short notice? Given that it could be, this was still her practice and her patient. So, didn't that make her the MO in charge? But surely it would be petty in the extreme to start pulling rank when Nick's suggestion made perfect sense?

She had only a few seconds to decide on a course of action. Terry was already liaising with the CareFlight base. The sharp prongs of indecision tore at her and wouldn't let go.

'We'll run normal saline.' Nick was inserting the cannula in Grant's arm as he spoke. 'We don't want him shocking on us. And would you draw up twenty-five milligrams of pethidine, please? That'll hold him until we can get him to the OR.'

Abbey hesitated.

'What?' Nick's brow darkened ominously. 'Don't we have emergency drugs with us?'

Abbey took a thin breath. Grant's eyes had fluttered open again, dulled with pain, expressing all the heart-breaking youthful uncertainty of his situation.

'Abbey!'

She seemed to come back from somewhere.

'Do you need my instructions written on a whiteboard?'

Nick shot the words at her with the lethal softness of bullets from a silenced gun.

Stung by his air of arrogance, Abbey jerked, 'Just who made *you* the boss here, Dr Tonnelli?' As soon as the words were out, she regretted them, for his expression darkened and his mouth tightened into a grim line.

She shook her head, biting the soft inside edge of her bottom lip. This was totally unprofessional behaviour. Why on earth did Nicholas Tonnelli bring out the worst in her?

And the best, another saner, kinder voice insisted.

Smothering her resentment, she drew up the required dose and shot the painkiller home.

'That's more like it.'

His growled patronising response infuriated Abbey all over again. She drew a deep breath, almost grateful for the diversion of Terry calling her name.

'Hey, Abbey!' Terry's tone was urgent. He jogged across, his face set in concern. 'The CareFlight chopper can't get here for a couple of hours. Three-car pile-up just south of Jareel. What do you want to do?'

Click! In an instant, Abbey knew the decision regarding Grant's surgery had been made for her. She took a steadying breath before she spoke, keeping her voiced instructions low. 'Cancel our request for a chopper, please, Terry. Dr Tonnelli's a surgeon. He's offered to operate on Grant's knee here.'

The SES leader beamed. 'Well, that's a turn-up. I'll get onto CareFlight and let them know we don't need 'em this time.'

Meanwhile, *she'd* better get on to Wingara hospital. Her mouth drying with apprehension, Abbey pulled out her mobile phone. Co-ordinating everything was going to be the ultimate test of their staff's abilities to deal with an emergency. And she could only pray that Rhys would be co-operative and back the decision to open the theatre for Grant's procedure.

'It'll be fantastic to have the theatre in use again!' Rhys's enthusiastic response shot Abbey's doubts to pieces. 'What will Nick want to do?'

'He's going to be wiring Grant's patella. He can't be sure of the degree of complexity until he goes in, of course.'

'OK. I'd like to be involved and I'll do a ring-around for a couple of extra hands. Carmen and Renee should be available. They'll be glad of the chance to hone their theatre skills, I'm sure,' Rhys said confidently.

Abbey brushed a fingertip between her brows, thinking quickly. 'We'll need to cross-match blood on arrival and X-ray as necessary. Especially, we'll need some pictures of his chest. There's evidence of a fractured lower rib. And could Diane come in and hold the fort while we're in Theatre?'

'Absolutely,' Rhys confirmed. 'No worries. What's your ETA, Abbey?'

Abbey ran through the logistics in her head, casting a quick look to where Nick was supervising the stretcher lift into the emergency vehicle. The improvised ambulance would have several kilometres of slow travel over rough terrain out to the road but then they should be able to pick up speed... 'Forty-five minutes maximum, Rhys.'

'Fine. That'll give me enough time to get prepped. See you in a bit, then.'

'Oh, Rhys.' Abbey spoke urgently. 'Andrew Parrish will have contacted Grant's parents. They'll probably turn up at the hospital to wait for the chopper.'

'I'll have someone look out for them,' Rhys said calmly, 'and explain the change of plan. Tea and sympathy until either you or Nick can speak to them?'

'Thanks, Rhys.' Abbey felt a sliver of responsibility slide from her. 'That would be brilliant. See you soon.' Switching off her mobile, she moved swiftly to Nick's side.

'Ah, Abbey.' He inclined his head, his eyes gleaming with determination. 'We're about to go. I'll travel with Grant, if that's OK with you?'

'You mean you're actually asking me?' she acknowledged thinly.

His hand flew out, clamping her wrist, his dark brows snapping together. 'Don't turn territorial on me again, Abbey. This isn't the time.'

Abbey's heart thumped. Had she gone too far? 'I'll grab a lift back up to the top and collect my car,' she said throatily, feeling relief when his hand returned to his side.

'See you back at the hospital, then.' Nick's expression gentled. 'Uh...' He snapped his fingers. 'About anaesthetising Grant for the op—I forgot to ask. Can you help out? I can guide you if—'

'That won't be necessary,' she cut in. 'I did my elective in anaesthesiology at John Bosco's in Melbourne.'

'You wanted to specialise?'

Abbey stiffened. 'Is that so strange?' She turned away before he could answer.

Abbey could scarcely believe how smoothly the hospital was coping. She was still basking in a sense of real pride as she finished scrubbing.

The sound of the door swinging open sent her spinning away from the basin, and by the time Nick had begun scrubbing beside her, she was drying her hands and asking sharply, 'What size gloves do you need?'

He sent her an abrupt look from under his brows. 'Eight and a half, if the stocks can manage it. But I can get by with nine.'

'Rhys will have everything under control.' Abbey forced lightness into her tone. 'Even glove sizes, I imagine. Since the alert went out that you were going to operate, he's apparently been beavering away like you wouldn't believe.'

'I'm extremely grateful for his flexibility over this.' The tightening of Nick's mouth suggested her own compliance had been hardly won.

Abbey opened her mouth and closed it. This wasn't the time

to start sniping at one another. They had a job to do on a vulnerable young patient and for that they needed calm and total professionalism.

Abruptly, she turned and left the little annexe and crossed to the theatre. Rhys had prepared the anaesthetic trolley perfectly and Abbey felt a rush of adrenalin she hadn't experienced for the longest time.

She'd do a brilliant job for Grant. And perhaps at the end of it, she might have actually appeased Nick as well. At the thought, warm colour swept up from her chest to her face, but there was no time now to consider why it mattered so much to have the wretched man's approval. But somehow it did.

An hour and a half later, the procedure was all done.

'Thanks, team. Fantastic effort.' Nick inserted the last suture in Grant's knee and signalled for Abbey to reverse the anaesthetic.

'Are this lad's climbing days over, do you think?' Rhys handed the surgeon the non-stick dressing to seal the site, and then waited with the bulky padding that would be placed over Grant's repaired kneecap.

'Not at all.' Deftly, Nick secured the wide crêpe bandage that would hold the padding in place. 'Does Wingara boast the services of a physiotherapist?'

Rhys nodded. 'Fran Rogers, the sergeant's wife, runs a practice from the sports centre.'

'She's good,' Carmen, one of the nurses assisting, chimed in. 'Sorted out the crick in my neck in a couple of sessions.'

'Sounds like we'll be in business, then.' Above his mask, Nick's eyes lit with good humour. 'OK, guys, that's it.' He stepped back from the operating table, working his shoulders briefly. 'I'd like Grant's leg elevated on pillows for the next twenty-four hours, please. And I'll write him up for some antibiotics and pain relief to be going on with.' His green gaze shifted from the nurses to Abbey. 'Would you mind finishing up in here? I don't want to keep Grant's parents waiting any longer than necessary for news.'

'I don't mind at all.' Abbey paused and then added huskily, 'That was a fine piece of work, Nick.'

Nick's eyes met hers and held. 'You made it easy, Dr Jones. We make a good team.' With that, he turned on his heel and left the theatre.

There seemed nothing more she could do at the hospital, so Abbey made her way home. Letting herself in, she acknowledged a feeling of vagueness, as if her body and mind were operating on autopilot.

It had been the oddest kind of day.

Walking into the kitchen, she looked around, registering her and Nick's breakfast dishes neatly stacked in the drainer.

A soft breath gusted from her mouth and she shook her head. Had it been only this morning they'd stood here fooling about like teenagers, exchanging light-hearted banter?

Absently, she turned on the tap and got herself a glass of water. Peering through the kitchen window as she drank it, she noticed that already the afternoon was rapidly drawing to a close, the sunset throwing huge splashes of dark pink and gold into the sky.

She lingered, watching several wood doves flutter in and out of the shrubbery before settling for the night. What was it about this time of the day that made her feel so introspective, so lonely, so strangely vulnerable?

'Mind sharing the view?'

Nick's soft footfall and equally softly spoken question had Abbey spinning round, a hand to her heart. She swallowed jerkily. 'I didn't realise you were home.'

'Have been for some time.'

His smile left a lingering warmth in his eyes and Abbey felt her heart lurch.

'I reassured Grant's parents and left a few post-op instructions with Diane. There didn't seem much else you needed me for. There wasn't, was there?'

She faltered, 'No—not really.' She desperately needed a hug but she couldn't tell him *that*. Her eyes flew over him. He'd obviously showered and changed into comfortable cargo pants and a navy long-sleeved sweatshirt.

Nick tilted his head, his eyes narrowing. 'You look shattered.'

'Thanks!' She lifted her chin, spinning back to the window, putting her glass down with a little thump in the sink. Was he saying she wasn't up to it? That she couldn't cope with one medical emergency? 'That's real music to my ears, I don't think!'

Nick clicked his tongue. 'Don't go all huffy on me, Abbey. I'm trying to help, dammit. Why don't you let me? For starters, are you hungry? I know I am.'

Abbey half turned to him. She supposed she was. They'd had nothing since his apple cake at morning tea. Perhaps it was hunger that was making her feel so hollowed out, so on edge around him. She nibbled the edge of her lower lip. 'We—we didn't get round to doing our grocery shopping, did we? And the supermarket will be closed by now.'

'I'm sure the pantry will yield up something edible.' His eyes captured hers. 'If not, I'll improvise.'

'You'll cook?'

'I don't just wield a knife in the OR, you know.' He flashed her a heart-thudding grin. 'I'll knock up some kind of pasta to delight your palate, OK?'

'Very OK.' Abbey felt her gastric juices react in expectation. 'There's bound to be a can of tomatoes in the pantry,' she said, warming to the idea. 'And I'm almost certain there's pasta of some description in a glass jar—'

'I'll find everything.' Nick's hands dropped to her shoulders to give her an insistent little nudge towards the door. 'Go and have a relaxing bath or whatever.'

Abbey made it to the doorway and turned back. 'There are a few herbs in pots at the bottom of the back steps—'

'Out, Dr Jones!' Nick waved an arm to get rid of her. 'I'm doing this. Go and have your bath.'

She sent him a wide-eyed innocent look. 'I prefer showers.'

He sighed audibly. 'Then have a nice relaxing shower, for Pete's sake. Now, scoot, before I lose all control and join you there.'

That did it. 'Consider me gone.'

Nick waited until he heard the soft click of her bedroom door, then lowered his head, bracing his arms against the bench. Hell, it was taking all his will-power not to follow her. But that was not the way. Every instinct was telling him that.

Ruefully, he looked down at his white-knuckled grip on the edge of the benchtop. It would be the death knell to his hopes if he rushed her. But holding back was hard—harder than anything he'd ever had to do.

CHAPTER EIGHT

ABBEY GOT OUT of the shower knowing she was in a state of wild anticipation of the evening ahead.

Oh, for heaven's sake, get a grip! Giving herself the silent admonishment, she padded through to the bedroom. It was merely going to be a quiet evening at home with a colleague, accompanied by an impromptu meal. And perhaps said colleague was a dud cook anyway and the food would be awful…

Who was she kidding? She gave a jagged laugh, throwing her softest, sleekest pair of jeans across the bed, then collected lacy underclothes from the bureau drawer.

The evening wasn't about colleagues or food, good or bad. It was about a man and a woman. And they both knew it!

With an effort, she managed to get her thoughts under control, dressing quickly in her jeans and a close-fitting red V-necked pullover. The colour gave her a sense of power, she decided. Besides, it went well with her complexion.

She took in a calming breath and then picked up her brush, stroking it almost roughly through her hair. In a final dash of bravado, she coloured her mouth expertly with a rose lipstick and fluffed on a light spray of perfume. After one last glimpse in the mirror, she left her bedroom and made her way along the hallway to the kitchen.

Nick was bent over the cook top. The pasta was boiling merrily and he was stirring something in a saucepan on another hotplate. 'Something smells good,' she said, sniffing the appetising aroma as she peered over his shoulder.

'It's getting there.' Grinning, he turned his head and kissed her, a sweet undemanding little smooch that took her by surprise. 'What about setting the table?'

'So, does this concoction have a name?' Abbey got down some large bowls for their pasta.

Nick gave the pot a final stir. 'Officially, Tortiglioni alla zingara. But this version has sweet potato instead of aubergine, otherwise it's pretty much authentic.' He drained the pasta with a flourish and gave it a shake. 'I've left the Parmesan separate—not everyone cares for it.'

Her mouth watering, Abbey watched as he swirled the pasta into a large bowl and then folded the rich red sauce through it. 'It's hardly Italian fare without it, though, is it?'

'Probably not.' Lifting a hand, he playfully ran the tip of his finger down her nose and across the top of her cheek. 'I found some oregano as well in one of your pots. I haven't managed to prepare it yet.'

'I'll do that.' Her heart gave a sideways skip and she gave an off-key little laugh, stepping away from him to the worktop. She took up the rather scraggy-looking bunch of leaves. 'Should I chop it or tear it?'

'Roughly chop, please.' Nick was precise. 'And then chuck it over the pasta.'

They ate with obvious enjoyment. 'How did I do, then?' Nick gave her a look so warm that Abbey caught her breath.

She coloured faintly. 'You did so well I might just keep you.' She laughed. 'Honestly, Nick, this is wonderful.'

He lifted a shoulder modestly. 'But, then, we were both starving, weren't we? Probably bread and cheese would've seemed like a feast.' Something flickered in his gaze, something Abbey couldn't immediately define, and then he looked away.

'It's still very early, isn't it?' They'd come to the end of the meal and Abbey cast around for something to say, and in the process sent a distracted look at the quaint little cuckoo clock on the wall.

'Meaning what, exactly?' Nick's gaze shimmered over her face and then roamed to register the gleam of lamplight in her hair and on the ridge of her collar-bone. Hell's bells, he could almost taste her...

Abbey felt panic-stricken. What on earth were they to do with the long evening ahead? What did Nick expect to do? Her teeth caught on her lower lip as she drummed up an awkward smile. 'Meaning, do you play Scrabble—or Trivial Pursuit?'

His gaze went briefly to the ceiling. 'I've a much better idea. Let's make some coffee and take it through to the lounge. Is it cool enough for a fire, do you suppose?'

'Oh, yes, I should think so.' Glad of something to do, Abbey shot to her feet. 'The kindling's all there. If you'd do that, I'll make the coffee.'

She took as long as she dared. Finally, when it was obvious she couldn't delay any longer, she picked up the tray of coffee and walked through the arched doorway to the lounge room.

Nick had the fire going and he'd lit one table lamp at the end of the comfortable old sofa. He was sitting under the light, leafing through one of her *Town and Country* magazines, and when she walked in he looked directly at her, his face still in shadow. 'I thought you must have gone to Brazil for the coffee beans,' he said blandly.

Abbey felt herself beginning to flush. 'Sorry if I was a bit long. I stacked the dishwasher as well.'

He raised a dark eyebrow. 'I didn't know we had one.'

'It's in the laundry for the moment.' She placed the tray on the mahogany chest in front of the fire. 'We're still waiting for the plumber to do the necessary adjustment so it can go in the kitchen,' she lamented. 'It certainly would make things a lot easier.'

'Well, don't look at me!' Nick raised his hands in mock horror. 'My mechanical skills stop a long way short of anything to do with plumbing.'

'Surely you can replace a tap washer?' she teased.

He looked baffled. 'Taps have washers? That's news to me.'

Abbey's mouth tucked in on a grin as she sent down the plunger on the coffee. They were shadow dancing again—fooling about, as if it was obvious to both of them that if their conversation became too serious, too personal, it would all be too confronting.

And because anything else would have seemed ridiculous, she took her place beside him on the sofa, feeling his gaze on her as she leant over and poured his coffee.

'Thanks.' Nick's fingers brushed hers as she handed him the steaming brew. 'That smells wonderful.' His mouth quirked in the faintest smile. 'Well worth the trip to Brazil.'

Abbey hiccuped a laugh and their gazes met and clung. His look was warm and heavy and on reflex she moistened parched lips. His gaze dropped to her mouth, almost burning her with intent.

With fingers that shook, Abbey poured her own coffee, taking several deep breaths to steady herself.

'How long does your contract have to run?' he asked.

She swallowed the sudden dryness in her throat. Where on earth had that sprung from? 'Six months or thereabouts. Why?'

'Just wondered.' He took a careful mouthful of his coffee. 'Any plans to come back to the coast?'

At his question, their gazes swivelled and caught and Nick's eyes held hers for a long moment, before he looked down broodingly into his coffee-cup.

'I...hadn't actually thought about it.' Leaving her coffee untouched on the tray, Abbey wrapped her arms around her midriff, as if warding off his question. 'It would be very difficult to find a replacement. The people had been waiting for over a year for a full-time medical officer when I came.'

'So, what are you saying?' Nick's jaw hardened. 'That you're bound here by some kind of emotional and ethical blackmail?'

Abbey's sound of disgust indicated what she thought of that. 'Does it occur to you I might like it here?'

'It sure looked like you were having a barrel of laughs coming down that cliff today,' he growled. 'I hate the thought of you taking those kinds of risks, Abbey.'

She bristled. 'For heaven's sake, Nick! It's not like Wingara has a team of paramedics on call. Attending the scene of an accident is my job!'

The silence fell thickly between them.

Jerkily, Abbey picked up her coffee, taking several quick mouthfuls. 'You can't tell me what to do, Nick,' she said quietly. 'It's none of your business anyway.'

'What if I were to make it my business?'

'And how would you do that?' More composed now, although her heart was rattling against her ribcage, she turned her head towards him, leaning back into the softness of the sofa, her coffee balanced high against her chest.

'Convince you to come back to Sydney with me.' His eyes locked with hers, dark in shadow, caressing, powerful.

'You're asking me to dump my patients?' She barely controlled the accusation in her voice. 'I'd have to find your offer pretty damned irresistible to make me even consider that.' Their eyes skittered away from each other and then reconnected and all of a sudden, once again, it was dangerous territory.

'Perhaps you will.'

Abbey opened her mouth and closed it and then opened it again. 'So, the chase is on, then?' she blurted, almost unable to believe they were having this conversation.

He sent her a dry smile. 'If you want to put it like that, yes, Abbey Jones, the chase is on.'

His meaning was quite clear and her response was instinctive. 'This is insane, Nick. But much more fun than Scrabble, I have to say.' She finished her coffee slowly and placed her cup back on the tray. 'So, what would you like to do now?' She tilted a slightly challenging look at him, letting her shoes drop to the floor and curling her legs beneath her.

Nick's sudden action made her jump.

'What are you doing?' she gasped, as he swung her feet around and then lifted them onto his lap.

'Just this…' With strong, supple hands, he began to massage the soles of her feet.

Abbey felt like purring. No one had ever massaged her feet before. She'd had no idea anything could be so seductive and, in a way, so liberating… 'I shouldn't be letting you do this.'

'Indulge me, hmm?' His dark head came up, his mouth curling slightly, as his hands moved up and down her feet and ankles, first her left and then right. 'Good?'

Abbey took a shaken breath then smiled, false brightness covering a multitude of mixed emotions. 'It's fantastic.'

As he'd known it would be.

'I could go to sleep,' she murmured a bit later. Her head had dropped back on the cushions and her whole body felt like liquid silk.

'I'll help you to bed,' Nick promised softly.

'No, you won't.' His words had her shooting determinedly upright, bracing her hand against the back of the sofa and preparing to lever herself off.

But Nick was quicker. Before she could properly make her move, his arms had cradled her and scooped her up. 'Bed for you, Dr Jones,' he murmured into her hair. 'It's been a very long, very full day.'

'It's not that late.'

'Maybe it's later than you think.'

'Nick, put me down!' But her outrage was muted and only half-hearted.

'Don't argue, Abbey.' He carried her easily as if she weighed no more than an armful of roses.

She made a tiny sound in her throat. It felt so good in his arms... So safe. Safe? Now, that was odd... She was aware of him opening the door to her bedroom and carrying her inside.

The moon was out in earnest now, striping the walls and the white bed cover with soft light.

'Nick...?' Abbey reached up to stroke his face, and felt him stiffen. 'Will you start the dishwasher?'

His mouth twitched. 'You're a real romantic.'

'You're trying to seduce me...'

'Of course I am.' She felt his smile on her temple as he pressed a kiss there. 'But not tonight.' He lowered her to the bed. 'Sleep well.'

'Mmm.' Her eyes were already closed.

Abbey rose earlier than usual next morning but it was obvious Nick had risen earlier still. She found him in the kitchen, his hands wrapped round a mug of tea.

'Oh...' Her gaze ran over his attire. 'You've already done your run.' Her tone showed her disappointment. She'd been hoping some exercise would have helped chase away the inner turmoil she'd felt from the moment she'd woken. 'I was going to come with you.'

'You have to be up early to catch me.' The sides of his mouth pleated in a dry smile. 'Sleep well?'

'Yes, thank you,' she murmured, her throat suddenly dry. Jerkily, she turned her back on him, helping herself to a cup of tea from the pot he'd made.

'You had a phone call last night.'

'Was it the hospital?' Abbey spun round, cup in hand.

Nick shook his head. 'Your friend, Andrea Fraser. I introduced myself, said you'd turned in early. She's invited us out to their place today. I accepted. I hope that's all right?'

'It's fine.' Abbey swallowed some of her tea. 'And it'll be nice. I haven't seen the Frasers in a while,' she remarked with a tiny frown. 'You'll like their property, Risden. There's a lovely expanse of river and places to picnic. What time do they want us?'

Nick lifted a shoulder. 'As soon as we'd like. I said we'd need to do a hospital round and so on first.'

'I'll do that.'

'I prefer to check my own post-op patients,' he said evenly.

So, thanks but, no, thanks. Abbey could have let it go but didn't. 'Don't you trust me to know what to look for?'

He made an impatient click with his tongue. 'It's not like we're swamped, Abbey. Lighten up.' He swung to his feet, brushing her arm as he emptied the dregs of his mug into the sink.

She moved away as if she'd been stung, his scathing tone negating any closeness she'd felt towards him last night. She brought her chin up. 'We should arrange an on-call roster, then. I certainly don't want to be treading on your precious toes every time I open my mouth.'

'Now you're being childish,' he said mildly. Dumping his mug in the sink, he walked out.

'I know who's childish!' she flung after him. 'Nick...' She went after him, catching up with him in the hallway opposite his bedroom. 'Why are you being like this?'

He folded his arms, leaning back against the wall and looking big and determined. 'Like what?'

She raised a shoulder uncertainly. 'So... cross.'

'Cross?' The word seemed to amuse him.

Abbey sucked in her breath. 'You know what I mean.' Her gaze steadied on him. The faint shadows under his eyes were obviously a residue of a restless night. Could that mean...? She felt weak suddenly, too near him. 'Didn't you sleep well?'

His shoulders lifted in a long-suffering sigh. 'I slept fine, thanks.' He rubbed a hand through his hair, his mouth compressing on a wry smile. 'I promise I'll be more reasonable after a shower and some breakfast.'

Abbey's thoughts were churning. 'I'll, um, make something, then. I'm quite good at scrambled eggs…'

Several expressions chased through his eyes. 'I know for a fact you're good at any number of things, Dr Jones,' he said, his voice not quite even. 'See you in a bit.'

They left for the Frasers' property just after ten.

'We'll take my car,' Nick said. 'Roads OK?'

'Fine.' Abbey's felt her nerves tighten. Dipping her head, she slid into the passenger seat as he held the door open for her. 'It's about fifty K's out and we'll be travelling in the opposite direction to Jumbuck Ridge,' she told him. 'The country is much more pleasant, softer.'

'So, fill me in about your friends.' Nick was obviously enjoying himself, gunning the Jag along a straight stretch of country road.

'Stuart's a born and bred local. Risden's been in his family for ever. But he's the new-breed grazier. Been away to university and all that stuff. He's a lovely guy. And Andrea and he are just so well suited. Where he's rather considered in what he does, she's all bubbly and spontaneous.'

'Do they have children?' Nick asked interestedly.

'Two. Michael who's eleven and Jazlyn who's nine, I think. They do school at home. Andi was a teacher so she's able to see to all that.'

Nick raised a dark eyebrow. 'How did they meet?'

'Andi was transferred to Wingara Primary. They met at a fundraiser for the hospital.'

For a while then there was silence, until Nick said quietly, 'It really is something special out here, isn't it?' He silenced a self-deprecating laugh, a little amazed at how some inner part of him had begun to respond almost unconsciously to the rich, bold colours of this huge landscape. The true deep blues and rusty reds were stuff from an artist's palette. And the stillness was so intense, he could almost hear his own heartbeat.

'It all kind of takes you over.' Abbey's eyes glowed. 'The landscape seems so pure and clean. And everything seems so incredibly *still*.'

He swung his head towards her and lifted an eyebrow. 'How did you know that's what I was thinking?'

'Just did,' she answered on a half-laugh, and saw a frown notch his forehead. Now what? Was it all right for him to guess her thoughts but not the reverse? Turning her head, she stared out through the side window, her eyes following the distant line of trees that marked the river.

Her thoughts began spinning this way and that. He'd set out deliberately to spend this time with her. Was he now in a way being hoist with his own petard—being made vulnerable by the same physical closeness he'd orchestrated?

The breathtaking thought sent a wild ripple through her veins that powered to a waterfall when his hand reached out, found her fingers and carried them all the way to his lips.

'Well, aren't you the dark horse?' Andrea's blue eyes were alight with conjecture.

'Who, me?' Abbey pretended innocence. She was helping her friend stack the dishwasher after a delicious barbecue lunch of best Risden-produced steaks, potatoes cooked in their jackets in the coals and heaped helpings of salads.

'Yes, you.' A muted 'tsk' left Andrea's mouth. With brisk precision, she slotted the dinner plates into their racks in the dishwasher. 'How long has this been going on?'

Abbey felt warm colour flood her cheeks. 'Nick and I met a few weeks ago in Hopeton—at the TV station of all places. Over a medical debate scheduled for the *Countrywide* programme.'

'Oh, my gosh!' Andrea's hand went to her heart. 'That's brilliant!'

'You wouldn't have thought so if you'd been me,' Abbey said with feeling. 'Anyhow...' she lifted a shoulder expressively '... Nick kind of followed it up.'

'Followed *you* up, you mean!' Andrea was blunt. 'It's obvious something's clicked between you. He can't take his eyes off you. Are you just as keen?'

Abbey groaned. 'Andi, it's early days and it's complicated.'

'He's not married, is he?'

'Of course not!'

'Divorced with dependent children?'

'No!'

'Then, ducky, if you've fallen for him, go for it!' Andrea gave an odd little laugh. 'Not that *I'm* an expert on matters of the heart…'

Abbey looked closely at her friend. All through lunch she'd seemed unlike herself, a bit brittle—especially around her husband. Which was peculiar to say the least. Abbey frowned. Andi and Stuart had always appeared so happy together, their marriage strong…

'OK, that's all done.' Andrea set the cycle, bringing her head up and agitatedly pushing a strand of dark hair away from her face. 'Now, while Stu and the kids are giving Nick the short guided tour of Risden, let's open another bottle of wine and take ourselves out onto the veranda for a while.'

'Um, I'll just have some of your homemade lemonade, thanks, Andi.' Abbey felt a small twinge of unease. Andi was a very moderate drinker at the best of times. But today she'd had several glasses of wine with lunch, and now she was proposing to start on another bottle. But it wasn't Abbey's place to say anything…

'You're giving me your doctor's look.' Andrea's mouth tipped in a crooked smile. 'And you're probably right to stay with the soft stuff. So I'll be good and join you in a lemonade. I've the beginnings of a rotten headache anyway.'

Abbey put her hand on the other's shoulder. 'Can I get you something for it? I brought my bag.'

'I'll take a couple of paracetamol.' Andrea pressed a hand across her eyes. 'And perhaps a cup of tea might be helpful.'

'I'll make it.' Abbey turned to fill the kettle. 'Go and dose yourself and put your feet up. I'll bring the tea out in a jiffy.'

Something was definitely out of kilter here. Two little lines pleated Abbey's forehead as she filled the china teapot and placed two pretty cups and saucers on the tray. Somehow she'd have to get Andrea to open up, because Abbey's trained eye was telling her that her friend was under stress of some kind. She could only hope Andi would let her help.

They sat on the veranda in comfortable old wicker chairs and looked down over the home paddock.

'It's so peaceful here,' Abbey sighed, leaning back in the plump butter-yellow cushions.

'On the surface, yes.' Andrea's throat convulsed as she swallowed. 'I think Stuart's having an affair,' she said in an abrupt way, as if this was what had been simmering in her mind all day.

Abbey's mouth opened and closed. She shook her head. 'That's ridiculous!'

'Is it?' Andrea looked directly at Abbey and her chin lifted defensively. 'We haven't made love in weeks. All he wants to do at night is to sit in front of that bloody computer screen.'

'And that constitutes an affair?' Abbey was in total disbelief. 'Have you asked him what's going on?'

Andrea looked bleak. 'He says he's checking out the market price of beef on the internet.'

'Well, that's feasible, isn't it? It's your livelihood after all.'

'How come he logs off the second I go into his office, then? As though...' Andrea paused and bit her bottom lip. 'As though he's got something to hide?'

Oh, lord. Abbey swung off her chair and went to stand at the railings. She needed to think. Something didn't add up here. Being devious was just not in Stuart's character. Something deeper was happening. She turned her head, her eyes running over her friend's taut face. 'So, are you saying he's *met* someone on the net and it's developed into an on-line affair?'

Andrea put her cup down carefully on its saucer. 'I know it

sounds a bit off the wall for Stuart—but what else could it be?'
She palmed the sudden wetness away from her eyes and gave
a choked laugh. 'He's certainly gone off me...'

'Honey, that's crazy talk.' Abbey stepped back quickly from
the railings, pulling her chair close to the other woman's. She
took Andrea's hands and held them firmly. 'It's obvious something is going on with Stu, something he can't talk about. But I'd
bet my last dollar he's not been unfaithful—even in cyberspace.'

Andrea's shoulder lifted in a long sigh. 'I'm at my wit's end.
That's really why I asked you to come today—I had to talk to
someone and I couldn't get into Wingara. It's all been hectic
here and the kids have had exams to prepare for—'

'Shh.' Abbey tightened her grip and squeezed. 'I'm glad you
called. You and Stu are my friends. And, for whatever reason,
I'm always happy to come to this beautiful place, you know
that.'

Think. Abbey's troubled gaze left her friend's for a minute
and she looked out across the dun-gold grass of the paddocks
to the blue-green of the eucalyptuses that lined the stretch of
river away in the distance. Suddenly, her fair head came up in
query. 'Could Stuart be ill?'

Andrea looked shocked. 'Surely I would've known? I mean,
he's still working all the hours God sends...'

'Well, that's what he would do,' Abbey reinforced softly.
'Keep on keeping on, pushing his fears into the background.
Pretending everything was normal.'

'Oh, my God...' Andrea's hands came up to press against her
cheeks. 'But why wouldn't he have gone to see you? Surely—'

'Andi, listen,' Abbey came in forcefully. 'In the first place,
I'm female. Not all men are comfortable with women doctors,
especially if it's something highly personal. And in the second,
Stu is like every other male in rural Australia. Their health is
the last thing they concern themselves with. They're indestruc-
tible, as they see it.'

'Could that be it?' Andrea pushed her hair back from her

face, pleating a strand as if it helped her think. 'But if he's ill...' Her eyes widened in sudden panic. 'What should I do? Confront him or—Oh, heavens, look! They're back!'

Abbey's gaze swivelled to where the battered Land Rover was coming up the track towards the house. 'Leave it with me,' she counselled quietly. 'Nick's here for a while and he'll be in the surgery each day. Somehow, between us, we'll get Stuart in to see him for a check-up.'

CHAPTER NINE

AS IT TURNED OUT, Abbey found the delicate matter of persuading Stuart to see a doctor was taken right out of her hands.

On their way back to Wingara township, she chatted to Nick about their day. 'Did you enjoy your tour of the place with Stuart?' she asked.

'Immensely. The whole experience has given me a new perspective. Oh, by the way, remind me to have Meri clear a longer than usual appointment time for Wednesday next. Stuart wants a word about a few symptoms he's experiencing.'

Abbey's heart skittered. So her guess had been right. 'Then I hope to heaven he's going to tell Andrea about his appointment with you.'

Nick frowned and then said slowly, 'I didn't realise he'd been keeping things to himself. That's not good.'

'No.' Abbey sighed, letting her head go back on the seat rest. 'She's up the wall with worry—Stuart's begun distancing himself from her emotionally. Andi thinks he's having an affair.'

'Good grief...' Nick muttered, and shook his head.

After a while, Abbey asked, 'Should I say anything to Andi,

Nick? I mean, I did point out the possibility that Stuart could be ill—'

'Don't start playing go-between, Abbey.' Nick was firm. 'If you've planted the seed, Andrea can approach her husband. After that it's up to Stuart as to whether or not he wants to open up and express his fears. With the best will in the world, no one, not even his wife, can force him.'

'But that's so infantile!' Abbey exclaimed. 'And so unfair to Andi.'

'Abbey...' Nick warned. 'It'll sort itself out in time.'

Next morning, Abbey went to the surgery early, leaving Nick to do the ward round at the hospital. As she began putting things to rights on her desk, she realised she was on tenterhooks. She'd been hoping with all her heart she would have heard from her friend by now. But Andrea had not been in touch.

Abbey shook her head. Obviously, Stuart hadn't confided in his wife. Instead, he'd probably given her some lame excuse for his trip to town on Wednesday—like having to buy feed for the cattle or go the bank!

Sighing, she moved across to the window of her consulting room and looked out, not registering the beautiful crispness of the morning.

Anxiety for the Frasers' well-being was eating her alive.

She stayed at the window another minute longer and then, determinedly pushing aside her misgivings, returned to her desk, buzzing Meri for her first patient, Rachel Petersen.

'Good morning, Rachel. Are you playing hookey?' Abbey smiled. Rachel was the deputy principal at the primary school.

'I am, actually. But someone's covering for me—at least I hope so.'

Abbey could see at a glance that Rachel was not her usual calm self. She waited until her patient was comfortably seated and then asked, 'So, what can I do for you this morning, Rachel?'

'My hair's falling out.'

Abbey frowned briefly. 'In handfuls or have you just noticed it coming away when you've brushed it?'

The teacher lifted a shoulder. 'It's been a general loss, I suppose—but enough to make me panic. What could be wrong, Abbey?'

'Any number of things.' Abbey was cautious. 'Are you feeling unusually stressed at the moment?'

The woman's shoulders lifted in a heavy sigh. 'Well, as a working single parent, I'm used to keeping all the balls in the air, but just at the moment it's a real effort catching them.

'And teaching is hardly a doddle these days,' she went on ruefully. 'When I first began, it was so much more creative. Now...' She shook her head. 'There are so many rules and regulations. And the calibre of families has changed. For instance, I heard the other day that several of my pupils had been seen foraging from the rubbish bins at the back of the pub. They were hungry, poor little mites, and that's terrible, Abbey! Sorry.' She chewed her lip and gave a wry smile. 'I'm going on and I don't mean to waste your time.'

'You're not.' Abbey was firm. 'But there are two separate issues here, Rachel. First, we'll deal with your health and then I want to hear more about these children. Perhaps if we liaise, something can be done for them. But for the moment, your health is my concern.'

'Well?' Rachel asked a few minutes later, as she pulled herself up from the examination couch and slid her feet to the floor.

'You do appear a little tense.' Abbey said cautiously, washing her hands at the basin. 'And it may be just a case of everything catching up with you and depleting your energy stores, both physically and mentally. But in view of your hair loss, we'll run a check to rule out any thyroid imbalance.'

'How will you do that?' Rachel slipped her shoes back on and took her place back at Abbey's desk.

'A blood test is the most accurate. If your thyroid is underactive, it can certainly cause premature hair loss. Fortunately, simple replacement medication can soon put things right.'

Rachel's hands interlocked on the desktop. 'And if it's not that causing the hair loss?'

Abbey heard the thread of anxiety in her patient's voice and sought to reassure her. 'There are several options we can try. A multimineral tablet containing zinc can be helpful and there've been good results from a new lotion that can be rubbed into your scalp to help hair growth. Of course, don't neglect the obvious.' Abbey smiled. 'Regular shampooing and massage.'

'Massage...' Rachel managed a wry smile. 'That sounds like a recipe for relaxation.'

'We'll start with the lotion while we're waiting for the result of your blood test to come back.' Abbey pulled her pad towards her. 'And you'd probably benefit from some actual relaxation therapy.' She looked up, her eyebrows raised in query. 'Isn't something happening at the sports centre along those lines?'

'We received some flyers at the school about it.' Rachel looked uncertain. 'I could perhaps try that, couldn't I?'

'Absolutely.' Abbey smiled. She handed the prescription across. 'Now, I'll take some blood and while I'm doing that, you can tell me about these children.'

When her last patient for the morning had gone, Abbey sat on at her desk, her head lowered, her fingers gently massaging her temples.

It had been one of those mornings when she'd been expected to be all things to all people. She sighed, considering her own emotional state.

Everything always came back to Nick Tonnelli—large as life, a man waiting for some kind of sign from her that they could move forward. But to where? And to what? Abbey made a little sound of frustration, suddenly at odds with the emotional games people were forced to play.

She looked up as a rap sounded on her door.

'Come in.' Abbey hurriedly schooled her expression.

'Got a minute?' Nick's dark head came through the opening.

'If you've come bearing coffee, I've probably got several.' Abbey forced a wry smile and brought her gaze up to meet his.

'Ah...' Nick looked rueful. 'I've already had some. Could I—?'

'No, it's OK.' Abbey waved him in. 'I'm just feeling the aftermath of a heavy morning. I'll buzz Meri to bring some. Could you manage another?'

Nick shrugged. 'If Meri doesn't mind.'

'Of course not,' Abbey said dismissively. 'We look after each other here.' Reaching out, she pressed a button on the intercom.

'Tough list?' Nick parked himself in the chair opposite her.

'I'm not complaining.' In a nervous gesture, Abbey caught up her hair from her collar and let it go, for the first time noticing he was carrying a patient file.

'Stuart Fraser doesn't seem to have much of a medical history with us.' Nick tossed the notes to one side and sent her a quizzical look.

'He probably doesn't.' Abbey shrugged. 'I think I've only seen him once, when he needed a tetanus jab. In the past he may have seen Wolf.'

'Obviously just for routine stuff,' Nick said. 'Minor farm accidents and so on.'

'Here we are!' Meri announced cheerfully, as she arrived with a pot of coffee and a plate of chocolate biscuits. 'Energy hit for you. And I'd guess much needed. Patients coming out of the woodwork this morning,' she lamented. 'But probably half of them only came to get a look at Nick.'

'They don't still do that, do they?'

'With bells on.' Abbey felt a bubble of laughter rise in her chest at his look of disbelief. 'Thanks, Meri.' She sent the receptionist a warm smile. 'This will really hit the spot.'

'You're welcome,' Meri responded cheerfully, and turned to leave. 'Oh, Nick...' She paused at the door. 'Some emails have come through for you.'

'Excellent. I wasn't expecting to hear back so promptly.'

'I'll print them out and leave them on your desk,' Meri offered obligingly, fluttering a wave as she left.

'I shot off a couple this morning to colleagues in Sydney,' Nick explained, spinning his hands up behind his neck. 'I want to cover all the bases before I see Stuart.'

Abbey felt her stomach twist at the implication. 'What do you suspect?'

'Prostate.'

'He's only forty-two.'

Nick looked tensely back behind her to the startling brilliance of blue sky. 'And his father died of prostate cancer at sixty-eight.'

'Oh, lord.' Abbey closed her eyes for a second and then opened them, staring down at her hands clasped on her lap. She looked up, her eyes meeting Nick's with a plea. 'If Stuart has prostate cancer, what are his options? From my knowledge, they're few and fairly radical.'

'Abbey, don't go there, all right?' Nick's eyebrows jumped together in sudden irritation. 'At least, not yet. We'll know more on Wednesday after Stuart's been in.' His mouth tightened. 'I urged him to come and see me this morning, practically pleaded with him. But apparently he had to do something with his bloody cows!'

'Stu's a farmer, Nick,' Abbey explained patiently. 'His cows will always come first. And you beating yourself up for not persuading him to come in immediately won't change his mindset. By the way, he's booked for eleven o'clock.'

At fifteen minutes to eleven on Wednesday, Meri rang through from Reception. 'You've no one else booked for today, Abbey, but Andrea Fraser's here with her husband. He's just gone in to see Nick and she wondered if you'd have time for a word.'

'Of course.' Abbey's mind flew into overdrive. 'I'll be right out, Meri.' Her hand shaking, she put the receiver down, a new foreboding shadowing her thoughts.

She found Andrea standing stiffly beside the reception counter, her face pinched-looking, her hair uncombed and sticking out at odd angles, as though her appearance had been the last thing on her mind when she'd left home. Abbey looped a comforting arm around her friend's shoulders. 'Let's go out onto the back deck where we can talk,' she said quietly.

'He told me this morning,' Andrea said without preamble, shredding the tissue she was winding in and out of her fingers. 'It's his prostate for sure. He hasn't been able to pee properly.' Tears suddenly welled in her eyes. 'The awful part is his dad died from prostate cancer.' She stopped and took a shuddering breath. 'Stuart's been sick with worry and that's what he's been doing on the net, trying to find out about the symptoms and treatment. Oh, Abbey... I don't know what I'd do if anything happened to Stu...'

'Andi, you're getting way ahead of yourself,' Abbey cautioned firmly. 'Self-diagnosis is a dangerous thing. We have to wait for Nick. But in view of his family history, Stuart is right to seek medical help. Difficulty in passing urine is the first symptom something is amiss.'

Andrea's eyes widened momentarily in apprehension. 'What will Nick do first, then? And what will he be looking for?'

'He'll do a physical examination, which will tell him if the prostate gland is enlarged.'

Andrea shook her head. 'It's all such gobbledegook. I mean, I don't even know exactly where the prostate *is,* for heaven's sake!'

'The prostate gland is about the size of a walnut and it's situated at the base of the bladder,' Abbey explained gently. 'So, of course, when it begins to enlarge, as it seems to have done in Stu's case, it puts pressure on the urethra. That's the clinical name for the urine-carrying tube.'

'It's very much a male thing, isn't it?'

'Yes.'

'Oh, lord, Abbey.' Andrea laughed, a strange little tragic sound. 'What if he—if we can't ever—'

'Stop it, Andi.' Abbey homed in exactly on her friend's scrambled thoughts. 'Your mind's running too far ahead.'

Andrea dabbed at her eyes. 'C-can you blame me?'

'No, of course not. Stuart has always been well and strong. It comes as a great shock to any of us when illness suddenly makes us vulnerable. But come on, now,' she said bracingly. 'Let's cheer up. I have a feeling Nick will want to speak to you and Stuart together after he's done Stu's medical.'

'I should fix myself up a bit, then.' Andrea gave a shaky smile. 'I don't remember whether I even washed my face this morning. And my hair must look like it's been shoved in the microwave.'

'Well, Doc, what do you reckon?' Stuart began zipping up his trousers.

'First things first, Stuart.' Nick stripped off his gloves and went to wash his hands. 'As a matter of urgency, we need to get your urine moving again.'

'Tell me about it.' Stuart sank wearily into his chair. 'What do I have to do?'

Nick's mouth clamped as he took his place back at the desk. 'It's more what I have to do, mate. But I think you'd be more comfortable over at the hospital for the procedure.'

'You mean you have to cut me?' Stuart looked alarmed.

'No surgery.' Nick shook his head. 'Not at the moment anyway. But for starters I'll have to do some fancy stuff with a flexible tube to drain your bladder.' His dark head bent, Nick scribbled something on Stuart's card. 'How would you be placed to make an immediate trip to Sydney?'

Stuart's eyes clouded. 'How immediate?'

'Tomorrow?'

'I'd have to think about it, Doc.'

'Stuart, we can't wait on this.' Nick was frank. 'You need to be under the care of a urologist. I'd willingly stay as your doctor but it's not my field.'

Stuart chewed on his bottom lip. 'Could I maybe see someone in Hopeton?'

Nick lifted a shoulder. 'You could, but the regular guy isn't due to take a clinic until next month.'

'And that's not soon enough?'

'Not from my information, no.' There was moment of intense silence and a creak of leather as Nick leaned back in his chair and steepled his fingers under his chin. 'To begin with, the specialist will want to do an ultrasound of your prostate or a biopsy or both. He'll follow this up with a PSA—a diagnostic prostate-specific antigen blood test.'

"Struth!' Stuart's large hand clenched on the desktop. 'Now you're sounding like the vet around one of my cows.' He gave Nick a very straight look. 'Does all this stuff have to be done because of my dad's history?'

'It would be remiss of me not to refer you.' Nick was guarded. 'Do you have brothers?'

'One. He lives in Hopeton.'

'Then he should get himself along to his doctor and have this test done as well.'

Stuart looked shell-shocked, as if the seriousness of his situation had just begun to sink in. 'I've a wife and two young kids, Nick.' His throat jerked as he swallowed. 'If I've got it—the big C, I mean—what are my chances?'

Nick's mouth pursed thoughtfully. 'No one's going to rush you into anything, Stuart. And if you're comparing your situation with your father's, don't. You told me he was in his late sixties when he was diagnosed and the cancer spread swiftly. You're a much younger man and you'll have options your dad didn't have. But look…' Nick spread his hands across the desktop '…don't let's jump the gun. Let's just get you over to the hospital and made more comfortable for a start.' He glanced at his watch. 'But first we'd better get Andi in here and tell her briefly what's going on. Then I suggest we schedule a proper talk for a bit later on today. Suit you?'

'Guess so.' Stuart rubbed a knuckled hand along his jaw, sending Nick a beseeching blue look. 'Does she have to know everything?'

Nick swung out of his chair and crossed to his patient's side, propping himself on the edge of the desk. 'I understand you want to protect your wife, Stu, but for both your sakes, Andrea needs to know what's going on. Besides…' Nick's mouth crimped at the corners in a dry grin '… Abbey would skin me alive if I let you off.'

Later that afternoon arrangements for the Frasers were discussed and clarified. And then things began moving swiftly.

As it was the larger of the two, they'd all gathered in Abbey's consulting room.

'OK.' Nick opened Stuart's file and began to refer to it. 'I've got you in to see James Ferguson on Friday morning, nine o'clock, Stuart. Is that going to give you enough time to get to Sydney and settle in?'

Stuart looked at his wife. 'Should do, shouldn't it?'

'We fly out on the noon plane from Hopeton tomorrow and it's only an hour's flight so, yes, that sounds good, Nick.'

'What about the children?' Abbey asked.

'Oh, we'll take them with us.' Andrea was unequivocal. 'We need to stay together as a family through this.' She sent a brave little smile around the assembled company. 'Don't we, Stu?'

For answer, Stuart reached across and took his wife's hand, bringing it across to rest on his thigh. 'This Ferguson chap, Nick…' Stuart looked uncertain. 'He won't be all stiff and starchy, will he?'

'Not at all.' Nick's pose was relaxed as he leaned back in his chair and folded his arms. 'I play squash with him. He's about your age, wife and kids. Laid-back kind of guy. You'll find him easy to talk to.'

'How did you get us in so quickly?' Andrea still looked a little bemused at the speed with which everything had been arranged. 'I mean, sometimes it takes months to see a specialist.'

Nick's hand moved dismissively. 'We exchange favours from time to time. It's no big deal.'

Andrea dropped her gaze. 'I thought perhaps Stu's case was desperately urgent or something…'

'It is in a way,' Abbey came in guardedly. 'For your peace of mind, you both need to know what's going on, rather than waiting in limbo until Stuart can be seen some time in the future. Wouldn't you agree?'

The Frasers' nods of agreement synchronised and they clasped their hands more tightly. 'Thanks, both of you.' Andrea's voice came out huskily and she bit her lips. 'And thank God you were here for my man, Nick—that's all I can say.'

'Fair go, love,' Stuart protested mildly. 'I would've got my act together eventually and consulted Abbey. I was just…'

'Chicken?' supplied his wife with a grin.

Everyone laughed, breaking the tense nature of the consultation.

'Well, if that's all you need us for, I think we'll get home.' Andrea looked expectantly at her husband who nodded and looked relieved that the taxing day was almost over.

'Right. Here's your letter of referral.' Nick handed the long white envelope over to his patient. 'I'll email Jim anyway so he'll have your history in advance. And we'll be in touch, Stu, when you get back.'

'You betcha.' Stuart held out his hand. 'Thanks, Nick. I don't know what else to say. And, Abbey…' His face worked for a minute. 'Thanks for the support. You don't know how much it means to us…'

* * *

When they'd seen the Frasers out, Nick closed the door and stood against it. He lifted his gaze and looked straight at Abbey.

Her mouth opened on a little breath of sound, glimpsing something in the sea-green depths of his eyes that alarmed her. 'You're worried, aren't you?'

Nick's mouth tightened. 'It shows, huh?' He shovelled both hands through his hair, moving across to stand with his back against the window-ledge.

'What did you find?' Abbey felt a curl of unease.

'Enough to wish Stuart had got himself checked out long before this.'

'Oh, no…' She sank down on the edge of the desk. Everything Nick was saying indicated that Stuart and Andrea could be facing some agonising decisions. 'Traditionally, we were taught that prostate cancer was a tortoise,' she said bleakly. 'So slow-growing that something else was likely to kill a man off first. Now…' She stopped and shook her head.

'Now we find it's a whole new ball game,' Nick picked up flatly. 'Traditional thinking is out the window. Heart attacks and strokes have lost some of their first-strike capacity and prostate cancer is right up there as a possible killer.'

Abbey's throat lumped. 'If it's bad news, how are the Frasers going to cope?'

Nick returned her stricken look without flinching. 'They'll cope, Abbey. They'll have to. And we'll do everything we can to support them.'

'We shouldn't pre-empt the outcome of the tests, though,' she pointed out logically, clinging to the thread of hope.

Nick's mouth compressed into a straight line. 'We could be more optimistic if the father's medical history wasn't staring us in the face.'

Sweet heaven. Abbey tamped down the sudden dread in her heart. 'Poor Andi and Stu,' she said faintly. 'It makes you realise just how tenuous life is. How precious.'

'Hell, yes.' Nick sent her a searching look and felt a fullness in his heart he couldn't deny. Almost defensively, as if he needed to hide his emotions, he turned away and looked out of the window. A beat of silence. 'Did you have anything planned for the rest of the day?' he threw back over his shoulder.

Abbey looked blank for a moment and then rallied. 'I have a meeting over at the school. It seems we have a batch of "new poor" in Wingara—families who through no fault of their own are finding life very difficult.'

'Surely that's a matter for the social security people?'

'More often than not, it's the long way round a problem,' she pointed out with a sigh. 'Where possible, we prefer to handle things like this on a community level. And with that in mind, the deputy principal is liaising with several relevant organisations and yours truly to try to see if we can get a breakfast group going at the school, feed any child who's hungry for one reason or another.' Abbey stopped, her teeth biting into the softness of her lower lip reflectively. 'Although getting someone to run it might be a problem. Everyone's so busy with their own lives these days.'

'Mmm...'

Abbey looked at him sharply. Had he heard anything she'd said? His attention seemed to have dissipated like leaves in the wind. She straightened off the edge of the desk and stood upright. 'What about you?' she asked, taking the few paces to join him at the window.

He drew in a deep breath that came out as a ragged sigh. 'If you don't need me for anything, I think I'll go for a long run, slough off some of this gloom. After sending Stuart off to face who knows what, I feel carved up inside.'

'Oh, Nick...' She shook her head in slight disbelief. Nicholas Tonnelli feeling vulnerable? How wrong could you be about people? She'd had no idea the Frasers' situation would have got to him like this. With his kind of professional experience, she would have thought he'd have had objectivity down to a fine art—be, at the very least, case-hardened.

He gave a huff of raw laughter. 'Pathetic, isn't it?'

'No, it's not,' she came back softly. 'It's just being human.' She took a tentative step towards him. 'How can I help?'

'Just let me hold you.'

Her heart gave an extra thud. 'A medicinal hug?'

'Yes, please, Doctor.' Wearing a faintly twisted smile, Nick drew her unresisting body against his.

Pressed against the hardness of him, Abbey made a little sound in her throat, the clean familiarity of his scent surrounding her. After a long time, she pulled back and said shakily, 'I... should get to my meeting.'

'Should you?' His dark head swooped towards her, his mouth teasingly urgent against her lips, the corner of her mouth. 'Off you go, then,' he said, regret in his gruffness. 'I'll come out and see you off.'

They walked out to Reception together. 'Mind how you go.' Opening the outer door, he ushered her through.

Abbey sent him an old-fashioned look. 'I'll be sure to watch out for the teeming masses at the intersection. Enjoy your run.'

Nick's eyes glinted with dry humour. Propping himself against the doorframe, he watched her drive off with a fluttered wave in his direction. He huffed a frustrated sigh as he turned back inside. Hell, he was missing her already.

Wandering through to his room, he collected his bag and set the alarm. Was it possible to fast-track love? It must be. He certainly had a king-sized dose of it!

'Abbey...' He said her name softly. Already she'd stirred such powerful feelings in him, imbued him with a zest for the ordinary things of life, the precious, simple things that he'd all but forgotten.

CHAPTER TEN

AT THE MEETING, Abbey tried to pay attention. But every now and again she was conscious of her thoughts wandering, becoming way too fanciful for comfort.

Was she in love with Nicholas Tonnelli? Colour whipped along her cheekbones at the mere thought. Was this how it felt—wild for the sight of him, the touch of him? Merely thinking about the possibility made her remember the night he'd massaged her feet. The night he'd carried her to bed...

Dreamily, she propped her chin on her hand. Just recalling the way they'd batted the loaded suggestions back and forth was doing crazy things to her insides, fuelling the slow crawl of nerves in her stomach—

'What do you think, Abbey? Feasible?'

'Uh...' Abbey snapped back to reality, surveying the expectant faces of the newly formed committee around her. She'd heard Rachel Petersen's voice but her question had become lost in the fog of Abbey's introspection. Hastily, she picked up her pen and twirled it, gaining time. 'Just run that past me again.'

Rachel raised a finely etched eyebrow. 'Are you OK, Abbey?

You look a bit hot.' She gave a 'tsk' of irritation. 'It's probably this blessed air-conditioning again. It's never been adjusted properly.'

'I'm fine.' Abbey took a mouthful from the glass of water in front of her. 'Just a bit of a headache starting.' She drummed up a quick smile. 'You were saying?'

'I suggested we use the facilities at the school tuck shop for this breakfast club. It's just had a major revamp and, as it's on school property, we could keep an eye on things.'

'It sounds ideal.' Abbey linked the assembled group with a questioning look. 'If everyone is happy about that?'

Sounds of agreement echoed around the table. 'What kind of tucker would you suggest we serve the kiddies?' Geoff Rogers asked practically. 'It's winter now. Poor little blighters need something to warm their insides.'

'Porridge?' Fran, Geoff's wife, suggested.

'Not all kids like porridge,' Abbey said thoughtfully. 'But, of course, we could still offer it. Perhaps cereal and warm milk? Toast with a nourishing spread?'

'I'm sure we could manage fruit when so much is grown locally.' Rachel's voice bubbled with enthusiasm. 'We could even run to grilled tomatoes or scrambled eggs.'

'And what about a nice thick vegetable soup at lunchtime?' Fran suggested. 'Then, if the parents can't provide much for supper, at least the little ones will have something in their tummies.'

'It's not just the poorer families of the town who need the facility,' Rachel said earnestly. 'Some of the children who come on buses from the outlying districts have to leave home very early. I'm sure half of them aren't up to eating much breakfast, even if it's put in front of them. But by the time they get here to school, they're ravenous.'

'How are we going to judge numbers, then?' One of the members of the P and C committee came in for the first time.

'I do have some knowledge of this kind of venture from an inner-city practice where I worked once,' Abbey said, and realised everyone was looking speculatively at her. 'We may err on the side of ordering too much at first but things usually even out after a while. And basically...' she rocked a hand expressively '...if the leftovers are stored properly, there won't be much loss.'

'There's just one tiny thing.' Rachel sent a hopeful look around the table. 'Who's going to run it? We need someone who's used to catering for numbers but who can order economically at the same time. Funding is available but we certainly can't waste it.'

There was a beat of silence while everyone thought, and then the obvious solution hit Abbey like a bolt of lightning. Looking pleased, she snapped her diary shut. 'What about Ed Carmichael?'

There was a momentary hush. And then a babble of excited voices. 'I must say, I'd always thought in terms of a woman running the scheme.' Geoff stroked his chin thoughtfully. 'But crikey! Ed's a natural when you think about it. He's been a camp cook for the shearers. And there's no doubt we could rely on him to do the right thing by the kids.'

'I often see him around the town.' Someone else sought to have their say. 'He always looks very neat and clean.'

'And I know Ed would do a wonderful job.' Abbey's eyes were lit with warmth. 'Plus I'm almost sure he'd want to give this service to the children on a voluntary basis.'

There were smiles of satisfaction and little nods of approval. 'I'll approach Mr Carmichael officially, then.' Rachel positively beamed. 'We could have our children eating properly within a matter of hours. Thank you, everyone, for coming. A most gratifying result.'

Abbey drove home slowly. It was almost dusk and she wondered whether Nick was back from his run. Her stomach tightened. She *needed* him to be back, she realised with a little jolt. Switching off the engine, she climbed out of her vehicle and went into the house by the back door.

A wonderful aroma drifted out from the kitchen. 'Nick?' She walked quickly through the laundry, not believing the joy she felt. He was planted firmly at the stove, cooking.

'Hi.' He turned his head as she came through and they shared a tentative smile. 'Good meeting?'

Abbey nodded. 'Very productive. Looks like you've been productive as well. What are you making?'

'Vegetable curry.' He went back to his stirring. 'I'll do the rice now you're home.'

Home. Abbey's heart slammed against her ribs. If only she and Nick were sharing a real home together. As a couple. In love…

'Oh—OK. I'll just, um, get a shower, then.' Heart pounding, she slipped past him, her thoughts whirling. So what am I going to do about you, Nick? she fretted, stripping off her work clothes and stepping under the jets of warm water.

'Oh, lord,' she whispered, feelings of apprehension rushing at her. How could this have happened? In so short a time and with her hardly realising it, she'd come to depend on him so much. In all the ways that counted. But he had a life in Sydney. A life in the fast lane.

A life she could never be a part of.

The week dragged to a close.

On Friday at four o'clock, Nick poked his head into Abbey's consulting room. 'I'm off to do a ward round.'

'Fine,' she responded dispiritedly. She'd been hoping against hope there would have been some word from Andrea by now. But apart from James Ferguson's brief advice to Nick that Stuart had been seen and that the specialist had put a rush on the test results, there'd been nothing.

'It's too soon to have heard anything definite, Abbey.' Nick homed in on her worries accurately. He came in and closed the door.

'I know.' She lifted a shoulder. 'Are you releasing Grant today?'

'I thought so, yes. He's made a very quick recovery.' Nick parked himself on the corner of her desk. 'I've begun liaising with Fran Rogers about some physio for him. I gather she's already been in for a chat and told Grant what he can expect by way of rehab.' He arched an eyebrow. 'What's the status of the flu jabs for Wingara's senior population?'

'Down on last year.' Abbey looked taken aback at his abrupt change of conversation. 'Why do you ask?'

'There's been a procession of elderly folk going down with flu right throughout the district, according to Rhys and Diane. Some are being cared for at home by their relatives, but the hospital's receiving its fair share of patients as well.'

Abbey dropped her gaze. Nick had placed himself on ward rounds for the entire week so she hadn't been near the hospital.

'Ideally, they should all have had their flu vaccinations way back.' Nick spun off the desk and paced to the window. Turning, he folded his arms and frowned. 'What kind of preventative campaign did you run?'

Abbey's chin came up. What did he think she was running here, the World Health Organisation? And surely he wasn't blaming her for people's failure to take responsibility for their own health? 'We had the usual reminders around the surgery and I put a piece in the local paper advising folk that the vaccine was here and it was time to get their shots,' she snapped defensively. 'It's up to individuals, Nick. It's not as though they can be corralled like cows and given a jab.'

His dark brows drew together. 'I'm not so far removed from grassroots medicine that I'm unaware of that, Abbey. But perhaps it's time to think ahead and see what we could do for next year.'

Next year? Abbey felt as if all her muscle supports had suddenly let go. Where was Nick Tonnelli coming from? He wouldn't be here next *month*—let alone next year!

'What did you have in mind?' she asked in a tone of controlled patience.

He took a few steps to spin out a chair and drop into it, leaning forward earnestly. 'I thought I'd have a word with Rob Stanton, get a couple of his documentary team out here.'

'In what capacity?'

'We could film a segment for the *Countrywide* programme.' Nick's gaze lit up with the enthusiasm of his plan. 'Feature several of the locals who have come down with flu, speak to them now, when they're recovering, and have them recount how debilitated they've felt and how they'll be sure to have their flu shots in future. We could get Rob to put it to air—say, March, April next year. What do you think?'

Abbey had to admit the idea had merit but nevertheless voiced her reservations. 'People may not want cameras and microphones in their faces, though.'

'Naturally, we'd need their permission.' Nick remained undaunted. 'But I'm sure Rob would do a sensitive, folksy piece that would have the right amount of impact. And he certainly owes you big time for that business over the debate,' he ended darkly.

Abbey avoided his eyes, her mouth trembling infinitesimally at the mention of that particular day. The day her life had been altered for ever. 'All right.' She picked up the phone as it rang beside her. 'But I want to see the film clip before it goes to air. I don't want any of my patients being made to look like yokels. If Rob can work with that...'

Nick shrugged. 'I'll run the idea past him and get back to you.'

They did the grocery shopping on Saturday afternoon, bickering lightly over the menu for the coming week. 'We could have a cooking session tomorrow,' Abbey suggested, stopping by the meat cabinet. 'Cook enough food for the week and store it in the freezer.'

'Not on your life!' Nick's mouth turned down. 'I've got more to do with my Sunday that spend it in the kitchen, thank you.' Gently, he prised her fingers off the large tray of beef cuts.

'Nick!' She grabbed his hand to stop him and was startled by the wild shiver of electricity that ran between them. Flustered, she met his eyes and saw an answering flare before he doused it.

'Let's have a picnic tomorrow instead,' he suggested, his voice slightly uneven. 'I'll grab a couple of these T-bone steaks. We could find a spot by the river and barbecue them. How does that sound?'

Abbey's heart wrenched. It sounded wonderful.

By mid-week, Abbey was beginning to feel that as far as the Frasers were concerned, no news was definitely not good news. And when Nick took a phone call during their lunch-break and didn't return, her nerves began gathering and clenching like fine wires.

She glanced at her watch. Heavens, he'd been gone for ages. Hastily, she rinsed the crockery they'd used for their simple snack and then, as if compelled by forces outside herself, went along to his consulting room and knocked.

'Come in and close the door, Abbey.' Nick looked back from his stance at the window and beckoned her inside. He pulled a couple of chairs together and they sat facing one another. Silently, he reached out and took her hands, rubbing his thumbs almost absently over her knuckles. 'I'm afraid it's not good news about Stuart.'

Her mouth dried. 'Was that Dr Ferguson on the phone?'

'Yes. Stuart's been advised to undergo a radical prostatectomy.'

Abbey paled and whispered. 'Oh, no...'

'Jim called in a second opinion, Magnus Nahrung from the Prince Alfred. He agreed with Jim's findings.'

'When will they do the surgery?'

'He's down for tomorrow morning.' At Abbey's little gasp,

Nick continued flatly, 'Apparently, Stu didn't want to hang about.'

Abbey was aghast. 'He could be left impotent, Nick!'

'Or dead within ten years if the cancer gets into his bones and he doesn't have the surgery.' Nick's response was brutally frank. 'Optimistic inaction certainly isn't an option. And whatever it takes, Stuart wants to stay with his family, Abbey. He told me that much.'

Abbey took a shaken breath. 'Have they had counselling? Of course they have…' She grimaced, answering her own question. She swallowed the tears clogging her throat. 'Did Dr Ferguson say how Stuart and Andi are handling things?'

Nick allowed himself a lopsided smile. 'With amazing calm and stoicism, he said. Whatever their own misgivings, they're putting a positive spin on things for the kids' sakes.'

Abbey bit her lip. 'That sounds like them, doesn't it?' She spun up off the chair, wrapping her arms around her midriff. 'I wonder why Andi hasn't called?'

'She'll have all her thoughts focused on her husband at the moment, Abbey. Frankly, outside the hospital staff, I doubt she'd have the energy to talk to anyone right now. But she'll know our thoughts are with her and Stuart.'

'Yes.' Abbey swallowed hard and nodded. 'Yes, she will…'

That night, Abbey woke from a dream with her heart pounding and a scream in her throat.

In seconds Nick was in the doorway. 'Abbey—what's up? Are you ill?'

She sat upright and snapped the bedside lamp on. 'I must've had a bad dream.'

'More like a nightmare.' Nick's voice was gruff and he came further into the room.

Abbey pushed a strand of hair away from her face. 'It was about Andi and Stuart…'

'You're trembling.' The mattress gave under his weight, and

then his arms were around her, cradling her against his chest. 'You can't let it get to you like this,' he murmured throatily. 'What happened to objectivity?'

'Pie in the sky.' Abbey gave a shuddery little breath, snuggling into the hollow of his shoulder. 'You haven't been to bed,' she said, feeling the soft stuff of the track top he'd put on earlier, after his shower.

He gave a hard laugh. 'I'm too wired to sleep. Stuart's been on my mind, too.'

'What happened to objectivity?' She brought a hand up and stroked his face, loving the smooth sweep of his skin against her palm.

'Out with the bath water.'

'We're a fine pair, aren't we?' She smoothed back his eyebrow with the side of her thumb. 'What've you been doing?'

'I tried to read. Ended up watching a late movie on TV.' His arms tightened. 'Try to get back to sleep now, OK?'

'I don't think I can,' she sighed. Beside which, his scent was too disturbing. So was the warmth of his body against hers.

'What should we do, then?' His voice was low, deeper than deep. It sought out hidden nerve ends, whispered along blood vessels and right into her heart.

'We could make some cocoa,' she said throatily.

'I hate cocoa.'

Abbey could hardly breathe, arching against him as strong fingers touched where she so longed to be touched. 'Bedtime story?'

'Mmm. About a man and a woman...' he said huskily, drawing her to her feet.

Safe in his arms, Abbey closed her eyes, feeling every sense spring alive, the drugging drift of the sandalwood soap on his skin swirling around her like so many strands of silk.

Her hands, with a mind of their own, smoothed over him, from the hardness of his shoulder muscles to curve lower, then round by the hollow of his hip, then on, dragging a primitive groan from his throat.

'Abbey—enough!'

'I'm sorry...' Stung by the reprimand, she pulled back, inflamed by the response of her own body.

'God, no! That's not what I meant.' Nick spoke as if the air was being pushed out of his body. Tipping her face up, he stared down into her eyes. 'I want you,' he said deeply. 'I think you're wonderful. And beautiful. And perfect...'

'I'm not perfect,' she countered softly, her hair glinting silver in the lamplight as she shook her head.

'Perfect for me...' With a long shudder, he dragged air into his lungs. 'Do you want me as much as I want you?'

Drawn by something in his voice, her gaze came up slowly, meeting such a naked look of longing it took her breath away. Desire, fierce and unrelenting, tore through her, annihilating at a stroke any doubts she might have had.

'Don't you have too many clothes on?' Her huff of laughter was fractured, nerves gripping her insides like tentacles.

With fingers that were not quite steady, he slid the lacy strap of her nightie off her shoulder. 'I wondered when you'd notice.'

Abbey took a shaken breath, held captive by the look in his eyes. The first touch of his mouth on hers shattered the last slender threads of her control as he gathered her in.

Their clothes seemed to fall away.

He's beautiful. Abbey's breath lodged in her throat. Strong, lean, powerful, the sprinkle of dark hair tangling across the centre of his chest, arrowing down...

In the warm glow of the lamplight, she touched him, her fingertips sensitised as they travelled over his body, his gasp of pleasure fuelling her own desire.

And then it was Nick's turn. Using his hands like a maestro, he raised her awareness to fever pitch, his lips following with a devastating intimacy that left her reeling, a jangle of senses, of touch and taste and feeling.

When they arrived at the moment when all was trust, she looked right into his eyes, the moment so tender, so precious. 'Sweet Abbey,' she heard him whisper, before they closed their eyes and the pleasure of giving and receiving claimed them, the intensity whirling them under and then as they reached flashpoint, rolling in long, flowing waves to envelop them.

Afterwards, they lay for a long time just holding each other. Abbey could hardly believe it. She'd become Nick Tonnelli's lover. Oh, lord, she thought.

She must have spoken the exclamation aloud for Nick frowned suddenly. 'Not regretting anything, are you, Abbey?' Lifting his head slightly, he smudged a kiss over her temple. 'It was beautiful—wasn't it?'

'Beautiful,' she echoed. There was no point in saying otherwise. It would have been a lie. But what in real terms did being lovers mean? And where did they go from here? Abbey closed her eyes, her face warm against his naked chest. 'Nick...' Her voice was hesitant. 'We, um, didn't use anything.'

He went still. 'I assumed—expected you to say something if it wasn't all right.'

She placed a finger across his lips. It probably was all right. She was as regular as clockwork. 'It should be OK. I'm in a safe time.'

Not two minutes later the phone rang. Nick swore. 'Stay there—I'll get it.' He reached for his track pants and dragged them on. He wasn't away long.

'Well?' Struggling upright, Abbey pulled the sheet up to her chin.

'MVA, sole occupant. ETA ten minutes. Doesn't sound too serious. I'll handle it. Curl up now and try to get some sleep, OK?'

She took an uncertain breath. 'Yes...all right. Mind how you go.'

He leaned over and knuckled her cheek. 'Always do.'

Not always, Nick. The sobering little thought stayed with Abbey until she finally fell into a dreamless sleep.

Next morning she was up and dressed and in the surgery before Nick had even surfaced. Her excuse was that she had paperwork to get up to date, scripts to write…

She worked for nearly an hour and then put her pen down. She'd have to see Nick the moment he got in. At the thought of what she had to ask him, her stomach somersaulted. And when, shortly after, she heard his steady footfall outside in the corridor, the soft closing of his surgery door, her heartbeat quickened alarmingly, almost choking her.

The walk to his consulting room seemed endless. She paused for a moment outside his door then, taking a deep breath, she knocked and went in.

'Abbey…' Nick wanted to spring from his chair and gather her in but something in her expression held him back. 'Meri said you'd left a note not to be disturbed.'

'Reams of paperwork to catch up on.' She gave the semblance of a smile. 'How was your MVA?'

Nick made a dismissive movement with his hand. 'Suspected drunk driver. Silly young kid still on his provisional licence. Geoff Rogers wanted a blood alcohol reading.'

'Much damage?' Immediately Abbey's caring instincts were aroused.

'Whiplash, gash to his head. I've just been over to check on him. He's a bit sick and sorry for himself. It's to be hoped he's learned his lesson about drinking and driving.' Abruptly, Nick stood to his feet, his eyes raking her face. 'Are you OK?'

'Fine,' she lied. 'I just need you to—that is, I wondered if you'd mind signing this.' She slid her hand into the side pocket of her skirt and withdrew a slip of paper. 'It's a script,' she elaborated, handing it across to him.

'Yes, I can see that.' He frowned down at the computer printout. 'It's made out to you.'

She gave a strangled laugh. 'It's not ethical to sign one's own prescription, Nick. You must know that.'

'It's for the morning-after pill.' His voice had risen and tightened. He looked up, his eyes unguarded. 'Why, Abbey?'

Thoughts, all of them confused, clawed at her. 'Because I don't want to take any chances,' she said wretchedly.

'You said you were safe.' He dropped back into his chair, as if his strings had been cut.

'I'm as sure as I can be that I'm safe, but who can ever be that sure? I mean, we're both fit and healthy. There's every reason to think we could...' She stopped and faced him with uncertainty and wariness clouding her eyes.

Nick felt something cold run down his backbone. He flicked at the piece of paper in his hand. 'Are you sure you want to go this road, Abbey? I mean, if we've made a baby together—'

She interrupted him with a humourless little laugh. 'Nick, you're a free spirit. You don't want a baby. You like the unencumbered lifestyle you've chosen, otherwise you'd have changed it long ago.'

His dark brows shot together. 'Don't presume to know how I want to live *my* life, Abbey,' he countered with dangerous calm. 'Are you sure this isn't about you and your own misgivings about parenthood?'

Abbey was appalled. 'I love children,' she defended herself hotly. 'But I'd prefer to have them when the time is right and with a man I love and who l-loves me. A man I can *rely* on!'

Nick recoiled as if she'd slapped him. For several moments he just sat there. Then with a savage yank he hauled his pen from his top pocket and added a bold signature to the prescription. 'There you are, Dr Jones.' He stood abruptly, as if to physically distance himself from what she'd asked him to do. Moving to the window, he reached out like a blind man towards the sill, gripping it with both hands, staring out.

Shakily, Abbey picked up the slip of paper. Her composure

was shattering. 'I'm just trying to be responsible, Nick.' She fluttered the words accusingly at his back and left quietly.

Oh, God, why was his throat tightening like this? 'How could she *think* I wouldn't want a child?' he rasped under his breath. '*Our* child.' He pressed his fingers across his eyes, as if staving off pain. What the hell was last night about then? His gut wrenched. How dumb can you be, Tonnelli? Obviously their love-making hadn't stopped her world the way it had stopped his!

Abbey sat frozenly at her desk, her head buried in her hands. She felt sick to her stomach. Nothing she'd said to Nick had come out right. Remembering, she felt her heart lurch painfully. It had taken her under five minutes to completely destroy everything precious between them. *Everything.*

When her phone rang, she reached out groggily and picked it up. 'Yes, Meri.' Her voice came out cracked and she swallowed thickly.

'The Wilsons are here.' Meri kept her tone pitched confidentially low.

'Who?' Abbey tried to concentrate.

'Ryan and Natalie. They want their baby immunised.'

'Oh, I remember now.' Abbey massaged a hand across her forehead, as if to clear her thinking process. 'We could probably fit them some time today, couldn't we?'

'Actually, they wondered if you'd see them now. They're a bit edgy. I gather it's been quite a big decision for them.'

'Oh, OK...' Abbey's brow furrowed. 'Give me two minutes and then show them in.' She replaced the receiver slowly.

She'd have to pull herself together somehow. She had a full list of patients and the world could not be shut out indefinitely. As Meri knocked and showed the Wilson family in, she whipped her prescription off the desk and into her top drawer. Before the day got much older, she'd have to find a minute to nip out to the chemist.

About eleven o'clock, Nick called through on her intercom. 'I thought you'd like to know, Jim Ferguson just called,' he said crisply. 'Stuart's surgery went well. He's in Recovery.'

Abbey felt relief rush through her. 'That's wonderful news. Thanks,' she added after a second, but he'd already hung up.

Somehow they managed to avoid each other for most of the day. Only once did she encounter Nick, when she'd gone out to Reception and he'd been seeing off a young couple with their toddler. A cute little boy with a thatch of dark curls.

The young mother was smiling disarmingly at Nick. 'Keiran was so good today. You must have a way with kids, Dr Tonnelli. Could we book to see you for his next shot?'

His mouth a tight line, Nick shook his head. 'Dr Jones will look after you, Mrs O'Connor.' He looked up and stared mockingly at Abbey. 'I won't be here.'

Abbey turned on her heel and almost ran back to her room, the drum-heavy thud in her chest almost suffocating her. Damn! Sick with hurt and disillusionment, she stabbed the computer off and shaded her eyes.

All day long, she'd allowed herself to nurture the faintest hope that somehow she and Nick could put things back together. But he couldn't have made it more clear that it was over. *Over.* She blinked through a blur of tears. Oh, Nick, what have I done?

CHAPTER ELEVEN

HOW ON EARTH were they to go on from here? How?

Abbey stretched her time in the surgery for as long as she could and then went across to the hospital. Pinning a bright smile on her face, she went through the motions, doing a ward round slowly and methodically.

Anything to delay going home. Except how could she think of it as home any longer? She and Nick would be stepping round each other like strangers. She bit her lips tightly together, smothering a bitter smile. The only time she'd fallen headlong in love in the whole of her life—and it had ended in disaster and heartbreak.

There was no feeling of warmth in the house when she opened the back door. No comforting aroma of a meal being lovingly prepared. But the lights were on so Nick must be home. Perhaps there was still hope…

Her breath caught and shuddered in her throat and her lips parted softly as she called, 'Nick?'

'In here.'

Abbey took a breath so deep it hurt, then on rubbery legs she made her way through the archway into the lounge. Nick was there, standing by the fireplace, his bags packed and set neatly against the wall beside him. Staring at him, the tight set to his mouth and jaw, Abbey felt her heart was splitting in two. She closed her eyes briefly and then forced herself to look at him. 'You're leaving.'

'There's no point in me staying.'

'But you came for a month!'

He made a rough sound of scorn. 'Just gives weight to your perception of my unreliability, then, doesn't it?'

'That wasn't what I meant to say!' She defended herself raggedly. 'It just came out that way...'

'The hell it did.' Pretending not to see the raw look of hurt on her face, he hardened his gaze even further. 'I wish I could say it's been worth it, Abbey, but we both know I'd be lying. I was an arrogant fool to have come here at all.' Their gazes locked for a long time, before he stooped and picked up his bags. 'I won't ask you to think of me sometimes,' he stated bitterly, and then he was gone, leaving her alone.

Except she wasn't alone.

The house was full of reminders of him. From the stoneware he'd bought to make his special lasagne to the bottles of wine he'd chosen so carefully and which they'd never opened.

Dull depression settled on her like a cloud, but resolutely she went through to her bedroom, stripping off the sheets and pillowcases and stuffing them into the washing machine.

And she'd be darned if she'd use this particular bed linen ever again—not with the scent of him still clinging to it and swathing her in a heartbreaking mist of remembering...

'Nick not coming in today?' It was the next morning and Meri had just put a mug of coffee on Abbey's desk.

'No...' Abbey sighed, daunted by the need for explanation. 'Actually, Meri...he's left Wingara.'

The two women stared awkwardly at each other, and then Meri took the initiative. 'I'm really sorry to hear that, Abbey.

But I've been around the traps long enough to know neither of you would have made the decision lightly.'

Except the decision for him to leave hadn't been hers at all. 'Thanks, Meri.' Abbey's voice shook fractionally. 'We'll just have to soldier on, won't we?'

Meri looked wry. 'Women have been doing it since time began.'

The next month brought no relief to Abbey's pain and deep sense of loss. On the lighter side, the Frasers were home and quietly optimistic that Stuart would have no residual effects from his surgery.

'I'm just so happy to have him beside me at night,' Andrea confessed during a flying visit to Abbey for a pap smear. 'Just to hold each other. And if that's all we can have...' Her eyes misted over.

'Andi, it's early days yet.' Abbey swabbed the specimen onto a slide. 'And you said the specialist's last report was very encouraging. Let's just concentrate on things working out wonderfully for you and Stuart.'

'Amen to that.' Andrea settled herself back in the chair. 'Do you want to talk about what happened between you and Nick?' she asked with the easy frankness of friendship. 'You were so right for each other, Abbey.'

'Oh, please...' Abbey went to wash her hands. 'It didn't work out, Andi,' she said wearily. 'Can we leave it at that?'

Andrea bit her lip. 'You look awful, Abbey—so strained. Couldn't you...?' Andi waved her hands about helplessly.

'No.' Abbey's answer was unequivocal. 'I should have the results of your test back in a week,' she sidetracked professionally. 'I'll ring if there's anything untoward.'

Another month went by.

'Meri, I have to go to Hopeton next week.' Abbey pushed the desk diary aside and pocketed her ballpoint. 'Could you call Wolf and see if he's available to provide cover? I'll need Wednesday and Thursday.'

'Sure.' Meri made a note on her pad. 'Regional meetings again?'

'Mmm.' Amongst other things, Abbey thought sombrely.

'You have a visitor.' Meri was all smiles when Abbey arrived back during the late afternoon from her trip to Hopeton.

Abbey came to a halt, her lungs fighting for air. Was it Nick? Had he come back?

'Go on,' Meri insisted in her best managing voice. 'He's waiting in your office.' She reached out a hand and swept up the post. 'I'm just off. See you both in the morning.'

Afterwards, Abbey had no clear idea how her legs had carried her along the corridor to her office. Heart trampolining, she turned the knob and pushed the door slowly open. And gave a tiny gasp, as the tall male figure turned from the window.

'Steve!' She dropped her bag and ran into her brother's outstretched arms. And promptly burst into tears.

'Have you missed me that much, little sis?' Steve seemed amused.

'Must have, mustn't I?' With a watery smile, Abbey eased herself away.

He gave her an astute brotherly glance. 'Don't think so, Abbey. You look like you've just come from Heartbreak Hotel.'

Abbey sniffed and gave a funny little grimace. 'Very droll. Are you writing an agony column these days?'

'Not me.' He shook his fair head. 'But I know the signs, kiddo, and my doctoring instincts tell me my little sister is in need of some TLC. Come on.' He looped an arm around her shoulders. 'Let's get you home and fed.'

It was lovely to be cosseted. Tucked up on the sofa in the lounge room, Abbey sipped gratefully at the big mug of scalding tea, replete from the helping of fluffy scrambled eggs Steve had magically produced in record time.

Watching her fork up the meal hungrily, he'd demanded, 'Why aren't you eating properly?'

'I am.'

'Not from what I saw in the fridge.'

Abbey had shrugged uninterestedly. 'There's stuff in the freezer.'

She looked up now as he sauntered back into the room and asked, 'All squared away?'

'Yep.' He looked at her narrowly. 'More tea?'

'No, thanks. But that was lovely, Steve.' She leaned over to place her empty mug on the side table.

Steve seemed to hesitate and then, as if coming to a decision, bounded across to the sofa. 'Shove up a bit, hmm?' Obediently, Abbey drew her knees up and he plonked down beside her, his head resting on the cushioned back, his legs outstretched and crossed at the ankles. He glanced across at her. 'OK, let's have it, Abbey.'

Abbey sighed and closed her eyes. 'Do you have all night?'

'If necessary. Come on.' His hand covered hers, hard and strong. 'Roll it out. It's probably not half as bad as you think.'

Abbey swallowed and swallowed again and made a tentative beginning. 'There's a man…'

'Does this man have a name?'

'Nicholas Tonnelli.'

'Hell. How did you get hooked up with him?'

So she told her brother the whole sad story.

When she'd finished, Steve rolled his head across the cushioned back to look at her. 'So you're going to contact him, right?'

'How can I?' she said bleakly. 'He hates me.'

'Rats! How could he hate you? You've both got your wires crossed, that's all.'

If only it was that simple.

'You have to see Nick and talk to him, Abbey,' Steve repeated. 'Or I will.'

She snatched her hand back. 'Don't you dare! Keep out of it, Steve.'

'No, I won't. These are lives we're talking about here, Abbey, yours and—'

She let out a wail and he stopped and hugged her close. 'Come on, kid. You can do it. Remember the courage you found when Mum and Dad died? Through all the stuff we had to do?'

She met his eyes, her own troubled. 'It's not the same.'

'Yes, it is. Trust me, I'm a doctor.'

That old cliché brought a wobbly smile to her mouth. 'Will you come with me?'

'Uh-uh. But I'll hold the fort while you're gone.'

'How long are you down for?'

He lifted a shoulder. 'As long as I need. My contract's finished.'

Abbey perked up. 'So you're going to settle back in Australia?'

'Eventually. Actually...' He looked at the floor, faintly embarrassed. 'I've met a girl, Catherine. She's a surgeon.'

'And?' Abbey prodded him with her toe.

He looked sheepish. 'We, uh, got married.'

'Oh, my God! That's fantastic!' She took both his hands in hers, for the first time noticing his gold wedding band. 'So, what are you doing here? Why aren't you with your wife?'

'I came down to see you. To tell you about the marriage and take you back for a holiday with us. But I guess there's no chance of that now, is there?'

Abbey shook her head slowly, pushing a strand of hair back from her face. 'How long had you and Catherine known each other?'

'Couple of months. But we just knew it was right between us, Abbey. As right as it will be for you and Nick.'

If only she could believe that.

Steve insisted she take a few days off work and rest. 'I'll muddle along with Meri's help. And I promise I won't kill off any of your patients. Well, not intentionally.' He grinned.

She gave him a shaky smile. 'Thanks, Steve. I owe you one.'

He reached out and cuffed her chin. 'Just be nice to Catherine when you meet her.'

'Of course I'll be nice to Catherine. When is she coming down?'

Steve made a face. 'As soon as she can. Her contract still has another few weeks to run. Hopefully, there'll be a suitable practice somewhere we can invest in. We've managed to save a bit. But back to you,' he said softly. 'When are you going to see Nick?'

Abbey's stomach heaved alarmingly. 'You're not going to give up, are you?'

'Nope.'

'Day after tomorrow, then. I'll drive to Hopeton and get a flight to Sydney from there.' And pray to heaven Nick would see her.

Abbey had travelled barely thirty minutes from Wingara when her mobile phone rang. She rolled her eyes. It was probably Steve again, checking on her. He'd already rung once. Automatically, she reduced her speed and pulled her car to a stop. Activating the speak button, she put the phone to her ear. 'Hello.'

'Abbey, don't hang up!'

Abbey felt as though her heart had flown into her mouth. Her lungs, starved for air, felt crushed. For a second she feared she was about to pass out. 'Nick?'

'Yes. I'm on my way to Wingara to see you.'

'But I'm on my way to see *you*!' She heard his swift intake of breath. 'I've only just left town.'

'All right...' He seemed to be thinking. 'I'm about an hour away. Turn round and head back, Abbey. I'll meet you at home.'

Home. Abbey swallowed. Had she heard right?

'Abbey, did you get that?'

'Yes.' Silly tears clumped on her lashes and she swiped them away. 'I'll be waiting for you...'

Abbey leaned back on the headrest until she felt calm enough to restart the Range Rover. But first she should call Steve, she supposed, and tell him what had happened.

'So, I'll steer clear for the next day and a half, then, shall I?'

'Idiot brother.' But she was smiling.

Abbey had steeled herself for a great deal of awkwardness when they met, running over little speeches in her head. But the reality turned out to be very different from what she'd imagined.

Nick drove in slowly and parked around the back of the house. His heart was clamouring. Switching off the engine, he sat for a moment looking into space. Suddenly his hand clenched on the wheel, the sharp edge of need ripping through him. He swallowed against the sudden constriction in his throat. Just don't mess this up, Tonnelli, he cautioned himself silently. Or you'll lose her for ever.

And why was he still hanging about here? He threw open the door of the Jag and swung out.

And Abbey was standing there. Waiting.

'Hello,' she croaked.

'Hello, yourself.' Nick's gaze snapped over her. 'You've lost weight.'

'And you need a shave,' she told him candidly.

He smiled slightly, lifting a hand and scrubbing it over his jaw. 'I've been on the road since four o'clock this morning.'

'You've driven all the way from Sydney?'

'Yes, Abbey.' His eyes burned like emeralds. 'To ask you to marry me.'

'Oh.' Abbey thought she might have fallen in a heap if his arms had not gone around her, holding her as if he'd never let her go.

After a long time he pulled back, lifting his hands to bracket her face, his entire heart in his gaze. 'This feels so right, doesn't it? You and me?'

Abbey nodded, tears welling up and overflowing.

'Don't cry, sweetheart!' Nick took her hands and curled them over his heart. 'I love you!'

'Now he tells me...' Abbey hiccuped a laugh. 'After I've spent the loneliest weeks of my life.'

'It's been hell for me, too.' His voice shook. 'You should never have allowed me to walk out the way I did, Abbey.'

'How was I supposed to stop you?' flashed Abbey, dazed by the brush of his lips against hers. 'Let the air out of your tyres?'

'Might have worked.' Smiling, Nick felt the knot in his chest begin to unravel. It was going to be all right. His arms went around her again, wrapping her against him, his mouth claiming hers as if he was dying of thirst.

A whimper rose in her throat and, breaking the kiss, Nick scooped her into his arms and carried her inside to the lounge room, making a beeline for the sofa. He sat down, settling her on his knee. 'So, what's your answer, Abbey?' he asked softly, his throat working. 'Will you marry me?'

'Of course I'll marry you.' Shakily, she stretched out a hand, touching his hair, the outside edge of his ear, the soft hollow in his throat. 'But I don't want to put any pressure on you.'

He lifted his head and looked at her in puzzlement. 'How could you possibly do that?'

She looked into his eyes, reading the sincerity and, unmistakably, the love. Joy, clear and pure, streamed through her. She dropped her gaze shyly. 'I have to tell you something, Nick.'

'That you love me?' His voice was gentle.

'Of course that.' She burrowed closer. 'I—That is—we...' She hesitated and blinked rapidly.

'You've got me worried now, Abbey.' Nick gave her a little shake. 'Just tell me.'

'I'm pregnant.'

A beat of absolute silence.

'Pregnant!' Nick sat back hard in the sofa. 'You mean you didn't take the—?'

'No.' Abbey shook her head. 'It was such a terrible day and

the patient list was endless.' She stopped and took a long shuddering breath. 'And by the time I realised I hadn't had the script filled, it was late and we'd had that awful fight. Well, I just wanted to die and—'

'Oh, Abbey. My poor sweet darling.' His arms went around her and he was rocking her. 'You should've thumped me. I behaved so selfishly, so ego-driven. But a baby?' His gaze clouded and he turned her head and looked into her eyes. 'Are you sure?'

'Yes.' She choked on a laugh. 'I've had it confirmed.'

'Whew!' Nick let the air out of his lungs in a long hiss. 'We're having a baby.'

'Are you pleased?' Abbey's voice was suddenly thin with unshed tears.

'Oh, God, yes!' His hand smoothed over her tummy, as though already he hoped to find there might be changes. 'Oh, this is something, isn't it? But how have you managed on your own?' A frown touched his eyes. 'Have you been sick?'

'A bit queasy,' she confessed with a grimace. 'But something wonderful happened.' Excitedly, she told him about her brother's unexpected arrival and the support he'd offered.

'Then thank heaven for Steve.' Nick held her more closely. 'I'd better buy him a beer.'

Abbey chuckled. 'He'll want several, I should think. And he's recently married.' She filled Nick in about Catherine.

'Good grief,' he grumbled. 'I leave the place for five minutes and all this happens.'

'Then you'd better stick close to me in future, hadn't you?' Abbey pressed her forehead against his.

'Depend on that.' Nick caught her hand and began kissing her fingers one by one. 'Will you mind living in Sydney?' His mouth twisted with faint irony. 'I don't think it would be practical for me to relocate here.'

Abbey wriggled closer. 'As long as we're together, I don't mind where we live.'

'But knowing you and how much you care about your patients, I imagine you'll want to find a replacement before we can make any firm wedding plans?'

'Actually...' She made a little moue of conjecture. 'It's just occurred to me Wingara might be the ideal set-up for Steve and Catherine.'

They smiled like a pair of conspirators and Nick raised a dark eyebrow. 'So we could get married soon, then?'

'Soonish. I'd like to wait for Catherine to be here.' Thoughtfully, Abbey ran her finger down the front of his shirt. 'I don't have much family...'

'Silly girl—of course you do,' he murmured unsteadily. 'You have me—and our baby.'

A slow, radiant smile lit her face. 'I do, don't I? I love you, Nicholas.'

His eyes closed and when he opened them, the message shone clear. 'And I love you, Abbey Jones.'

And the way he kissed her then convinced Abbey, as no words ever could, that he certainly did.

* * * * *

Subscribe and fall in love with a Mills & Boon series today!

You'll be among the first to read stories delivered to your door monthly and enjoy great savings.

WE SIMPLY LOVE ROMANCE

MILLS & BOON

JOIN US

Sign up to our newsletter to stay up to date with...

- Exclusive member discount codes
- Competitions
- New release book information
- All the latest news on your favourite authors

Plus...

get $10 off your first order.

What's not to love?

Sign up at **millsandboon.com.au/newsletter**